Royal Com. on Historical Manuscripts, Great Britain Privy Council

# The Manuscripts of the Right Honourable F.J. Savile Foljambe, of Osberton

Royal Com. on Historical Manuscripts, Great Britain Privy Council

**The Manuscripts of the Right Honourable F.J. Savile Foljambe, of Osberton**

ISBN/EAN: 9783337242206

Printed in Europe, USA, Canada, Australia, Japan

Cover: Foto ©Andreas Hilbeck / pixelio.de

More available books at **www.hansebooks.com**

# HISTORICAL MANUSCRIPTS COMMISSION.

## FIFTEENTH REPORT, APPENDIX, PART V.

THE

# MANUSCRIPTS

OF

THE RIGHT HONOURABLE

# F. J. SAVILE FOLJAMBE,

OF

# OSBERTON.

Presented to both Houses of Parliament by Command of Her Majesty.

LONDON:
PRINTED FOR HER MAJESTY'S STATIONERY OFFICE,
BY EYRE AND SPOTTISWOODE,
PRINTERS TO THE QUEEN'S MOST EXCELLENT MAJESTY.

And to be purchased, either directly or through any Bookseller, from
EYRE AND SPOTTISWOODE, EAST HARDING STREET, FLEET STREET, E.C., and
32, ABINGDON STREET, WESTMINSTER, S.W.; or
JOHN MENZIES & Co., 12, HANOVER STREET, EDINBURGH, and
90, WEST NILE STREET, GLASGOW; or
HODGES, FIGGIS & Co., LIMITED, 104, GRAFTON STREET, DUBLIN.

1897.

[C.—8550.]     *Price* 10*d.*

# INTRODUCTION.

These manuscripts consist of (1.) A manuscript entitled " Book " of Musters, 1588 ;" (2.) A collection of letters from James, Duke of York, to William, Prince of Orange, in 1678 and 1679 ; and (3.) A number of miscellaneous letters and papers between 1636 and 1789.

(1.) The general contents of the so-called " Book of Musters " are fully described at the commencement of the Report. It will be seen that while it comprises much that may be found in other collections, on the other hand it furnishes a quantity of important materials which do not appear to exist in the public archives. It is proposed here to call attention to the fresh information now made available for the first time.

The designs of the French on Calais and. the neighbouring territory were well known to Philip and Mary, and the final loss of the English possessions in France was not due to any want of foresight and preparation. This is evident from their commission to William Herbert, Earl of Pembroke, dated 3rd July 1557, in which they announce the declaration of war with France, and their intention to levy " an army or power " of their subjects, which should be sufficient not only to defend Calais against the anticipated invasion, but even to carry the war into the French King's dominions. Of this army the Earl was appointed their Lieutenant and Captain-General, with ample powers both for defence and offence, and for the administration of martial law.

In another commission to William Wightman, as Treasurer of the Army, dated 2nd July 1557, King Philip announces his intention to " pass the seas " and invade France in person, saying nothing about the preservation of Calais, the latter object being no doubt considered to be included in the former. A number of warrants and schedules relate to the payment of the Captain-General and the officers under him. Some of these warrants are dated at " the English camp before Hawne," 15th September 1557. But the English troops were employed in assisting Philip in Flanders instead of being employed to garrison Calais, and consequently the town and territory fell an easy prey to the French.

In 1571 an army was sent "into Scotland" under the Earl of Sussex, and a paper copied in this manuscript gives the names of the gentlemen serving under him, and the amounts of their "entertainments."

A comparative table of the numbers of foot and horse attending "the general musters" in 1574 and 1577, shows that the forces of the realm in the former year were a little under 300,000, and in the latter year considerably exceeded that number. The Isle of Wight and the coast of Hampshire were then supposed to be most liable to invasion, and an elaborate scheme was prepared for the concentration of the forces of that county wherever an attack might be made.

Between 1583 and 1587 there are copies of numerous Council letters, and a few of Queen Elizabeth, with instructions, certificates, and other papers relating to musters, training, ordnance, and ammunition. Many of these are also to be found among the State Papers. Some attention was paid to the defence of the Channel Islands and the Isle of Sheppey. Schedules on p. 107 show the total numbers of ships, masters, and mariners throughout England in 1583. Other schedules give many details of the composition of the Royal Navy, apparently in 1587.

The preparations of the King of Spain for the invasion of this country were known to the Council early in 1587, and orders were given for putting both the inland and the maritime counties in a posture of defence. The instructions sent to Devon, Cornwall, and Wales for opposing the landing of the enemy are to be found here, but not among the State Papers. A special warrant was issued to the Master of the Ordnance to supply certain counties with various kinds of guns and ammunition out of the Queen's "Store" in the Tower of London. In August, the barons of the Cinque Ports were reprimanded for their remissness in not defending the coast of Kent against the spoil of the Dunkirkers, and in not making reprisals.

From this point the manuscript is professedly devoted to recording the measures taken by the English Government to encounter the Spanish invasion. Directions were from time o time sent to the Lords Lieutenants in every county; and though in some cases there were several counties under one Lord Lieutenant, every county on the south coast had a separate head. The Earl of Leicester was "Lieutenant-General" in Essex and Hertford, and Sir Walter Raleigh was "the "Lieutenant" in Cornwall, while he was also one of the Deputies in Devon. The instructions given by the Queen and Council to the Lords Lieutenants are minute, and vary according to the needs of each district. No detail was considered too small for the attention of the central authorities. The actual mustering and training of the troops, however, devolved chiefly upon the Deputy-Lieutenants in each county.

As early as 5th October 1587, the Council announced to the Vice-Admirals that the Queen had "ordered that her own "Navy should be forthwith made ready to pass the seas," and that it should be reinforced by the ships and mariners of her subjects. The Vice-Admirals were therefore to lay an embargo on such ships, and to charge the owners not to quit their respective ports till they should receive directions from the Council or the Lord Admiral. As, however, it is stated that the Vice-Admirals made no return to this order, it was probably countermanded.

The official date of Lord Howard of Effingham's commission as "Lord High Admiral, being appointed to go to the seas," is 21st December 1587, but his instructions are here dated the 15th (p. 109). The Queen states therein that she had been "sundry ways most credibly given to understand of the "great and extraordinary preparations made by sea, as well "in Spain by the King there, as in the Low Countries by the "Duke of Parma, and that it is also meant that the said forces "shall be employed in some enterprise to be attempted either "in our dominions of England and Ireland, or in the realm of "Scotland." To "impeach any descent" on Ireland or on the south-west parts of the realm, Sir Francis Drake was to be instructed by Lord Howard to "ply up and down" between the Irish coast and the Scilly Isles or Ushant; and if any forces were sent by the enemy in that direction against Scotland, Drake was to "intercept and distress" them. To withstand any attempt which might be made from the Low Countries, Lord Howard himself was to "ply up and down, sometimes

" towards the north, and sometimes towards the south;" and he likewise was to be on the watch for any forces that might be sent to Scotland by way of the East coast.

If Drake's ships should prove to be inadequate to face the navy expected from Spain, Howard was directed either to recall him and "join both their forces together," or to send him as many ships as could be spared for his reinforcement. No similar direction was given for Drake to join or to aid Howard, because the forces of the Duke of Parma were not considered likely to give much trouble. From this it is evident that Drake's squadron was to bear the brunt of the invasion. His commission does not appear to have been issued till 15th March 1588, but in this volume he is said to have been sent to the seas in December 1587 (p. 109).

The names of the ships under the commands of Howard and Drake, with the tonnage of each, are given on pp. 114, 115. Drake had the larger number of ships, but Howard the greater tonnage.

Howard's instructions direct that all foreign ships bound from the East for Spain were to be stopped "in some courteous and favourable manner," and sent to England, there to be searched for any victuals or munition that might be intended for the enemy. Howard was further to take under his command the Dutch ships which were to be furnished by the States, and to see to the defence of Brill, Flushing, Ostend, and Bergen-op-Zoom, which were garrisoned by the Queen's subjects.

It might be thought that these arrangements were much too premature, considering that the winter was then close at hand, but this was not the opinion of the Queen and her councillors. Equal forwardness is observable in the military preparations on land. General musters and training by muster-masters, and instruction in camp-duties by expert "martial men," were ordered in the same month of December, to which month, and not to "September," the Queen's letter to the Earl of Pembroke is, no doubt, referable (p. 28). Some time "before November" an engineer was sent to Portsmouth to plan new works for its protection.

It may, therefore, be assumed that these defensive measures were being carried out as far as possible during the winter, and although the invasion did not occur till the following summer, there can be no doubt that the Government was able to bring them to greater perfection than if they had been left to the last moment. It was even anticipated that they would be sufficient to deter King Philip from the invasion of England by alarming him for the safety of Portugal and the Indies.

In March 1588, the Queen announced to the Corporation of London that the whole of the realm had been fully provided for, with the exception of the City, which she commanded to furnish ten thousand able men, with suitable armour and weapons.

On 1st April the Council, including Howard, required "the Ports" to supplement the Queen's "navies" by sending serviceable ships and "handsome" pinnaces, furnished with mariners and with victuals and munition for two months from the 25th of April. Some were to be sent to Drake, others to Howard. As some justification for this demand, the merchants of the ports are alleged to have "received no small gain and benefit" from reprisals effected by their ships of war.

On 12th April, special instructions were given to Sir John Norris and "other martial men" to confer with the Lords Lieutenants of the maritime counties for the prevention of the enemy's landing, and, in case a descent should be effected, to choose places where the best stand might be made against him, and his advance impeded. Great secrecy was to be observed with regard to the dangerous and weak points on the coast; and in each county some naturally strong situation was to be rendered still stronger with the aid of "the pioneer" for the reception of a defending force, able to occupy the invader's attention till the neighbouring counties should come to the rescue, according to the scheme of mutual aid which had already been prescribed. The pioneers and their implements were to be provided and kept in readiness by the Lord Lieutenants, who were also to employ the "horsemen" (cavalry) of their respective counties in the open country for offence as well as for defence. Cattle and victuals were to be removed inland, where any landing might be effected.

Returns were sent up to the Council from all parts of the numbers of "able men," trained and untrained, "furnished"

and unfurnished, some of the men being distinguished **under
the** heads of "shots, corslets, bows, and bills," and the "shot"
being further subdivided into "calivers and muskets." The
cavalry consisted of **"lances, light** horsemen, and petronels."
In London **the total number of able men between** the ages of
seventeen **and sixty was** returned at 17,083. Out of these were
selected four **regiments, each** of 1,500 trained men. The names
of the **captains in** every ward of the City are stated. In the
country **the** principal noblemen and certain gentlemen were
summoned **"to** attend upon her Majesty's person," and offered to
**bring** 3,058 horse and foot, while the clergy contributed 4,444.

On 13th May the Queen sent fresh instructions to Lord
Howard, cancelling the former orders for his remaining in the
Narrow Seas. She now commands him to repair to "the West
" parts**" of the** realm, and to dispose of the navy under him
between those parts and the coast of Spain, so as to protect not
only England and Ireland, but "also the realm of Scotland."
An undated **note on p. 28 probably refers to** this countermand,
**and** states that Howard was to "join with the forces under Sir
Francis Drake's leading;" but a royal letter to Lord Henry
Seymour shows that the former was in command of the whole,
and explains that some ships **were** still **to be left for defence of**
the Narrow Seas.

Of these ships, as well as of the 36 ships furnished **by the**
States according to "the contract," Seymour **was to have**
charge, under the direction of the Lord Admiral. Howard's
instructions to Seymour are also contained in this volume, and
make special provision against any invasion of Scotland by the
Duke of Parma in that direction. Some "enterprise" upon
the City of London was also suspected, and two ships had been
stationed at the mouth of the Thames to guard against this,
but were to be under Seymour's orders. Howard recommended
Seymour to maintain a supply of six weeks' victuals on board
his ships, or at least sufficient for a month; and if he required
more, her Majesty was to be urged to grant it.

All things were thus in readiness when, on 15th June, the
Council announced to the Lords Lieutenants that the Spanish
**navy** was "abroad upon the seas, and gone to the coast of
Biscay," and that an invasion was to be feared, though no

certain information of the King of Spain's intentions had been obtained. All gentlemen in each county who were "captains " and leaders of men " were required "in no wise to be absent " out of the shire," and to see that the trained bands were complete and ready to serve at an hour's warning. The beacons were to be constantly watched, and provosts-marshal appointed to arrest all vagrant and idle persons who refused to work, lest they should do mischief during the absence of the trained men.

Later in the same month, the Queen herself wrote letters to the respective Lords Lieutenants, thanking them for what they had done, and informing them that she had discovered an " intention not only of invading, but of making a conquest also of this our Realm," which had been " fully resolved on, an army being already put to the seas for that purpose." " The best sort of gentlemen " were therefore to be convened, and informed of this " purposed conquest, wherein every man's particular estate is in the highest degree to be touched ;" and that the Queen expected them to provide a still " larger proportion of furniture both for horsemen and footmen, but especially horsemen."

On 27th June, the Council ordered each Lord Lieutenant to hold 2,000 men in readiness, either to attend on her Majesty's person, or to repair to the army about to be assembled, but " the General " of which had not yet been appointed. Two armies were, in fact, to be formed, one for attendance on the Queen, and the other to meet the enemy on his landing; the number of foot, lances, light horse, and pioneers required for them being stated. Each was to consist of more than 30,000 men. The former had been projected as early as the preceding March.

Circumstances compelled the Spanish Armada to return to port for a time, and it was not till 23rd July that the Council was able to inform the Lords Lieutenants of its expected arrival, and of the probable intention of the Spaniards to land in Essex, where the Earl of Leicester was Lord Lieutenant, and had the command of the army appointed to meet them there. A copy of his commission, of about the same date, shows that he was Lieutenant-General not only of the army in Essex, but

" over all men of our (the Queen's) armies " in the South parts.
This commission does not appear to be enrolled at the Public
Record Office. It is of considerable length, and confers very ample
powers, including that of repressing any rebellion or insurrection
which might happen, and of executing " the law martial." The
army at Tilbury under Leicester consisted of 1,449 horse and
11,000 foot, and the names of his subordinate officers are given.
He also had under him " the forces of Kent," 6,000 in number,
which were assembled at Sandwich.

There is also a copy of the commission to Lord Hunsdon to
be " Lieutenant " of the army for defence of the Queen, with
similar powers to those " lately given " to Leicester, but they
were not to " derogate or diminish the authority " of the latter.
The names of the officers under Hunsdon are likewise stated.

Some counties were ordered to supply the men for one army,
and some for the other army. Sir Thomas Heneage was
appointed " Treasurer at Wars," and the Exchequer officers
were ordered to pay to him 20,000*l.* for the wages of the two
armies; Sir Moyle Finch being Deputy Treasurer.

Wales was entirely excluded from both these commissions,
there being a special commission for the Principality in favour
of the Earl of Pembroke, which is not in the manuscript, but
which may be found on the Patent Roll, under date of 5th
August. The dates of the three commissions seem to show
that the Queen was loth to delegate her authority until the
very last moment, even to her most trusty councillors.

Further statements indicate that the two principal armies
were not so evenly divided as was originally proposed. The
army for the Queen's defence numbered 45,462, besides the
" bands of pensioners," while the army under Leicester numbered
only 18,049. The forces in the Northern counties were not
drawn upon to supply these numbers, but were reserved in case
of any " attempt out of Scotland."

Immediately after the defeat of the Armada, orders were
given for sending back " the footmen " to their respective
counties, owing to the difficulty of providing them with victuals
and lodging, and Leicester's forces were reduced to 6,000 men.
By a further order on 17th August, they were to be still further
reduced, though the Queen was determined to maintain the

Navy at the strength of at least "one hundred great ships"
until she could learn what had "become of the Spanish fleet;"
but this order was "stayed." Another order was drawn up on
24th August, on the alarm being given of the Spanish ships'
expected return through "the Narrow Seas," for the re-assembling
of the troops at Tilbury, but it was never despatched. A fresh
Latin commission was also issued to Lord Admiral Howard
" for returning to the seas," according to the descriptive heading
given to it by the compiler of this portion of the manuscript,
but those words do not appear in the text of the document.
It contains a clause empowering Howard to grant knighthood
and other dignities; a power which had not been comprised in
his previous commission.

At the end of the volume, there is a detailed statement of
the names of the ships under Howard, Drake, and Seymour,
of the ships furnished by the City of London, and of the
"voluntary ships," showing the tonnage and the number of
men.

There are several lists of the noblemen and gentlemen who
took active parts in the defence of the country, and whose
names appear to be recorded only in this manuscript, to their
honour and for the emulation of their descendants. But
it is unpleasant to find charges of peculation brought against
certain captains and officers of the army during this critical
period of national danger (pp. 61, 62).

These instructive contributions to the history of the defeat
of the Spanish Armada are followed by a few papers of the
years 1589 and 1590. The remainder of the manuscript consists of numerous letters and papers connected with the
preparations made against the invasion threatened by the new
King of Spain, Philip III., in 1599. The documents are all
comprised within the months of July and August of that year.

The defensive measures then taken are not so well known,
but appear to have followed almost the same lines as those
which had been taken in 1588. The City of London was
supposed to be "the greatest mark" aimed at by the enemy,
with an intention "to spoil or burn the same;" and the Council
directed the Lord Mayor to take order for defence of the Thames
by furnishing some of "the best ships" in the river with ordnance

and powder. The Earl of Cumberland, having had great experience "in sea causes," was appointed to command the ships in the Thames, and there was a project for "a bridge to be framed for the impeaching of the enemy's access near unto London," and to be defended by ships of war. Another proposal was to sink a number of the least useful ships in the river near Barking. Sundry Lords Lieutenants, including Sir Walter Raleigh in Cornwall, were ordered to send mariners and pilots to Chatham, to serve in "her Majesty's ships royal."

According to further information received by the Council, the Spanish army was "to make a descent in the county of Kent, and from thence to attempt the destruction of her Majesty's Navy or of the City of London." A few days later it is stated that "there hath somewhat been signified to move an opinion of their (the Spaniards') intention to come for Milford and Severn," and precautions were taken for the defence of those parts. Portsmouth and the Isle of Wight were once more objects of the Council's anxious consideration.

The instructions given to Lord Thomas Howard of Walden, who was "sent Admiral to the seas," refer to Raleigh as Vice-Admiral, who was to assist Howard in all his "counsels and enterprises." There were also "divers gentlemen of good quality and sufficiency" serving in the Fleet, who were to be consulted on matters of importance. Charles Howard, Earl of Nottingham, Lord High Admiral, was Captain-General of the Queen's "armies and companies of men" levied for withstanding the invasion, and George Carey, second Lord Hunsdon, was, as his father had been, Captain-General of all "other armies and companies" assembled for defence of the Queen's person.

The methods adopted for the defence of the country in 1588 and 1599 were so elaborate and are described with such minuteness, that they are worthy of attention even in these days, notwithstanding the altered conditions of modern warfare.

(2.) The letters of James, Duke of York, to William, Prince of Orange, printed *verbatim et literatim* (pp. 123–140) cover an important period of the Duke's life, the first of them being dated 29th October 1678, the day on which "Lord Shafsbury" and his gange" made their attempt to get him removed from the Council; this letter is followed by many others written at intervals of a few days referring to the proceedings in both Houses against him and to the alleged popish plots. In March 1679, he writes from Brussels, a few weeks after his withdrawal from England by Charles's order, thanking William "for your kind usage whilst I was with you, of which I shall always be very sensible," an expression worth calling attention to, as a recent biographer of James states, on the authority of Henry Sidney's Diary, that he met with little civility at the Hague on this occasion. The kindly expressions which James continually makes use of when addressing his "sonne" (-in-law) are indeed a noticeable feature of this correspondence.

The Duke remained at Brussels until the beginning of September and wrote occasionally to the Hague commenting upon the news which reached him from the English court and parliament. On his re-call to England in that month, there are a few letters from Windsor chiefly referring to Monmouth's disgrace. In October he writes two letters from Brussels, whither he had gone again to fetch the Duchess of York home; and others from London and Hatfield refer to his intended journey to Scotland to take up his appointment as High Commissioner there. The concluding letter in the series, dated November 27, 1679, reports his arrival in Edinburgh three days previously.

With reference to this correspondence, it will be interesting to note that there is a large collection of James's letters to the Prince of Orange among the State Papers in the Public Record Office, which were formerly kept, with other letters addressed to William, in a sealed bag known as "King William's Chest." A few of these letters are dated between April 1674 and February 1678-9, and then there is a gap until October 1682, from which date there was constant communication between them until the autumn of 1688. Mr. Savile Foljambe's volume therefore fills up a great part of the gap above noted, and it may be added that in one of the volumes of M. Groen van Prinsterer's *Archives ou Correspondance inédite de la Maison d'Orange-Nassau* will be found further letters from the Duke of York to the Prince of Orange written chiefly in the years 1680-82, with a few of earlier and later date. It would thus seem as if the whole of the Duke's letters to his son-in-law and successor on the throne had been preserved, though in places of deposit widely apart.

(3.) MISCELLANEOUS LETTERS AND PAPERS, 1636–1789.

This part of Mr. Savile Foljambe's collection at Osberton requires little detailed notice, though it contains many interesting items. Extracts from it are printed on pp. 141–160. The main portion of it consists of the correspondence of Sir George Savile, of Rufford, for many of the earlier years of George III.'s reign the popular representative of Yorkshire, and perhaps the most esteemed member of the Whig party in his time. Among his correspondents will be found Lord Rockingham, Edmund Burke, David Hartley, Joseph Priestley, and Charles Pelham, referring to political and electioneering matters chiefly; but their letters are too few and detached to be considered as forming any appreciable addition to the material for the history of the period.

The report on the " Book of Musters " was prepared under the direction of the Commissioners by Mr. R. E. G. Kirk. The correspondence and papers of later date printed in this volume were selected and prepared for publication by the Secretary to the Commission.

# HISTORICAL MANUSCRIPTS COMMISSION.

## THE MANUSCRIPTS OF THE RIGHT HONOURABLE F. J. SAVILE FOLJAMBE, OF OSBERTON, NOTTS.

A manuscript on paper, in vellum covers, endorsed :—

> " BOOK OF MUSTERS, 1588."

It also has the following more descriptive title on a fly-leaf, the latter portion being torn off :—

> " *Book of Musters, containing all such directions as have been given for mustering and training of the Forces of the Realm since the year* 1583.
>
> " *Together* w[ith]]
>
> " *The whole m* . . . . . . . . . ."
> *the R* . . . . . . . . . ."

This description is, however, inadequate. The period covered by the volume really begins in the year 1557, and ends in the year 1599, but there are large gaps, especially between 1557 and 1571, and between 1590 and 1599. It relates to both military and naval affairs, the earliest entries dealing with the war with France in 1557, just before the loss of Calais. But the greater number detail the elaborate preparations made by land and sea to resist the invasion of these shores attempted by the Spanish Armada in 1588, and the second threatened invasion in 1599. It is not indeed a " Muster-Book " pure and simple, as the general title would lead one to imagine. Besides the numerous schedules relating to musters and shipping, there are still more numerous copies of most important Royal commissions and warrants, and letters of the Privy Council, addressed to Lords Lieutenants and others, including the Earl of Leicester, Lieutenant General in 1588, Lord Hunsdon, Lord Howard of Effingham, and Sir Francis Drake. The schedules give the names of the captains and officers appointed to take charge in various counties, and the quantities of all kinds of armour and weapons provided for the lances, light-horsemen, petronels, and footmen ; and also the names and tonnage of the Royal Navy and of the other ships employed, and the complements of men in each vessel.

The volume is divided into four portions. The first and principal portion, ff. 1–201, comprises the military matters of the years 1557, 1571–1577, and 1583–1588, and is the compilation of one person. The second portion, ff. 204–213, contains a few letters of 1589–1590, and is in two different hands.* The third portion, ff. 219–251, comprises a large number of letters and papers, of the single year 1599, by another hand. The fourth portion, ff. 294–322, consists of papers relating entirely to naval matters in 1583–1588, and is by the same hand as the first portion. The "table" at the end, written in a neat Italian hand, is

---

* The handwriting on f. 204 is also to be found on ff. 96, 97, 138.

A

also by the principal writer; and the last page of the table, referring to pp. 294 *seq.*, is headed, "The Index for the Sea Causes."

It does not appear that this is a register of documents regularly entered up from time to time. Rather, it is a compilation chiefly made by two persons, probably officials in the Privy Council Office, in the years 1588 and 1599. The principal compiler alludes to himself in a note on f. 172,* but the handwritings have not been identified. To the portion comprising the year 1599 there are careful annotations, evidently made by some high official.

The transcripts contained in this volume were obviously derived from papers formerly existing in the Privy Council Office. The compilers had access to "the Council Chest," but not to papers in the charge of the Secretary of State (ff. 140, 172). All the Council papers, as well as those belonging to the Secretary of State's Office, are supposed to have been transferred to the State Paper Office, and should therefore be found in what is known as "the Domestic Series." (See the Deputy Keeper of Records' Tenth Report, App. I., p. 1.) But the contents of this MS. prove that many valuable Council letters and papers must have disappeared before the transfer took place. It might have been imagined that the missing papers, or some of them at least, would be preserved among the Cecil MSS.; but that is not the case, and in fact there are few governmental papers of the Elizabethan period in that collection. Nor do they appear to have found their way, like many other State Papers, into the Cotton collection. There are, however, copies of a few papers of 1588, and of many others of 1599, in the Harley MS. No. 168, a collection made by Ralph Starkey, probably from the same source. The State Papers and other MSS. have been used by Prof. Laughton in his "Defeat of the Spanish Armada," but not the present MS.

No extracts have been taken from this book where copies are extant among the State Papers, but references are given to the latter in every case of omission, as the official papers frequently consist merely of rough drafts, and the present transcripts may have been made from fair copies. The original warrants and letters were, of course, sent to the persons to whom they were addressed, and some of them may be found in private collections.

A large number of leaves have been cut or torn out of this volume, but they were nearly all blank ones, as shown by the table of contents, which does not refer to them, with the exception of the last two leaves, now wanting.

F. 1. [1557], 3 & 4 Philip and Mary, July 3, Palace of Westminster.—"The Earl of Pembroke's Commission to be Lieutenant General of the army to St. Quintin's."

Philip and Mary, (&c.) "Forasmuch as we have denounced and declared the French King to be our enemy, whose countries and dominions join and border near unto our town and marches of Callis, and other our pieces and territories thereunto appertaining and belonging, and he, being presently in arms, doth not only to th' uttermost of his power annoy us and our subjects, but almost [also?], by all the secret ways, means, and practices he can, seeketh opportunity to obtain and suppress, or at least to annoy and impeach, the said pieces and other parts of our dominion; for the better defence whereof, and for annoyance and invading of our said enemy the French King, his

---

* There is a similar handwriting in State Papers, Domestic, Elizabeth, vol. 209, No. 1.

realm, and dominions, we have resolved and determined to levy an Army or power of our subjects, which we intend presently by God's help to send over into the parts of beyond the seas, to th' intent not only that if any invasion or other enterprise be or shall be by the said French King or his adherents made, purposed, or attempted in that behalf, we may resist and defend the same, but also that we may by all other ways and means annoy and invade him and his dominions, as our mortal enemy, as occasion shall require, and as by our Lieutenant and Captain General by these presents appointed shall be [thought] meet and convenient to be had, made, and done : Know ye, therefore, that for the especial trust and confidence which we have and conceive in the wisdom, dexterity, activity, valiantness, and experience of our dear Cousin and Councillor, we have assigned, made, constituted, and ordained, and by these presents do assign, make, constitute, and ordain our said dear Cousin and Councillor William Earl of Penbrooke as well our Lieutenant and Captain General of our said Army, as also of our said town of Callis, and of all other our forts, castles, and other our pieces, towns, and counties beyond the seas; giving full power and authority to our said Cousin and Councillor, by these presents, to assemble and muster for the purposes aforesaid from time to time, according to his discretion, all and singular captains, petty captains, men-of-arms, archers, soldiers, horsemen, footmen, and all other person and persons of whatsoever estate or degree they be, retained or hereafter to be retained in our said Army, and the same and every of [them] to cause well and sufficiently to be armed and weaponed ; and the same Army not only to lead and conduct for the defence and sure keeping of our said town, pieces, and territories, [and] of our said subjects of the same, during his abode and tarrying in the same, but also with the same Army to invade and give battle or otherwise to annoy and resist the said French King, and his dominions and subjects, and all such as now be or hereafter during the time of this our commission shall fortune to be our enemy or enemies, and his and their countries and dominions, and when or as often as it shall be by our said Cousin thought meet and convenient ; and to make orders, laws, and proclamations from time to time for the leading, order, rule, and government of our said Army ; and of the said Army to make and constitute all and every such captains, officer, and officers, as to his wisdom shall seem meetest, for the better service by him and our said Army to be done unto us. And further we give full power and authority by these presents unto our said Cousin to advance to the degree of a knight, and to give arms or other titles of dignity and honour to such of our said Army as by their deserts and good service shall be thought meet by his discretion to deserve the same, and as to the office of a Lieutenant and Captain General doth appertain.

" We do also give to our said Cousin full power and authority by these presents not only to hear, examine, and determine by himself or his sufficient deputy or deputies, all causes criminal, murmurations, and disobediences and departures from captains, rulers, and governors of our said Army, and all other unlawful acts and deeds of what nature, name, and quality soever they be, done and committed by any person or persons of our said Army, or now being appointed or hereafter to be appointed by us or our said Cousin in our said Army ; and the offenders therein to judge, execute, and punish by death, imprisonment, or other corporal pains whatsoever, according to the quantity and quality of the offence and offences, according to the laws martial ; but also to hear and determine all such contracts, matters and causes, and complaints as shall happen to arise, grow, or be moved between any person or persons of our said Army, and generally to do all and every other thing and things which to the office of a Captain or Lieutenant General doth appertain and belong.

"And also we do give full power and authority to our said Cousin and Councillor, that he, during all the time of his abode in the parts of beyond the seas, as our Lieutenant and Captain General, shall and may from time to time, by his letters or bills signed with his hand, not only cause so much of our money and treasure to be laid [out] and disbursed, but also so much of our artillery and munitions to be employed, set forth, and bestowed for the keeping, aiding, and maintaining of our said towns, fortresses, castles, ports, Army, and things necessary for the same, as to our said Cousin and Councillor shall be thought meet and convenient; and that such warrants and bills signed as our said Cousin and Councillor shall make and direct to any our treasurers or officers for the doing of the premises, shall be a sufficient warrant for them and every of them for the employing and doing of the same, according as by our said Cousin and Councillor shall be appointed, and as to the office of a Lieutenant and Captain General appertaineth and hath been accustomed.

"And we do also straightly charge and command all and singular captains, petty captains, lieutenants, earls, viscounts, marquises, lo[rd] barons, knights, and other estate and estates, men-of-arms, archers, horsemen, footmen, soldiers, officers, ministers, and all other our subjects, and soldiers, of what estate, degree, or condition soever they be, retained or hereafter to be retained in our said Army, to be helping, aiding, assisting, and at the commandment of our said Cousin in the due execution hereof, as they and every of them will answer to us at their uttermost peril; willing, and nevertheless granting, that these our letters patents for the doing, performing, accomplishing of the premises, and of every part and parcel thereof, shall be as well to our said Cousin and Councillor as also to all other earls, marquises, viscounts, lo[rd] barons, knights, captains, and all other our subjects and soldiers whatsoever which shall serve us under the rule, leading, and governance of our said Cousin in our wars as is aforesaid, a good, sure, and sufficient warrant in that behalf.

. "Provided always, and our pleasure, intent, and meaning is, that our said Cousin and Councillor shall not be and stand charged or chargeable with the rule, governance, and safe keeping of our said town and marches of Callis, or of any other our said towns, castles, fortresses, pieces, and counties beyond the seas any longer time than he, our said Cousin, with our said Army shall be and continue his abode within the same; but immediately from and after our said Cousin with our said Army shall remove and depart thence, [the same] shall be and remain in the safe custody of others our accustomed officers and councillors there, in like manner as heretofore hath been used. In witness whereof we have caused these our letters to be made patents."

F. 2. [1557,] 3 & 4 Philip and Mary, July 2, Palace of Westminster.—Letters under the Signet, appointing William Wightman,* esquire, to be Treasurer at Wars.

Philip and Mary, (&c.) "Where we the King intend by the sufferance of Almighty God this present summer to pass the seas in our own person and with an Army Royal to invade the realm of France, the charges of which Army, with the provisions and necessaries for

---

* "Mr. Whiteman" in the heading.

the same, we think meet to **be defrayed by** such persons as we specially trust and know to be men of **wisdom, truth, and** experience, meet to have such charge **committed** unto them; **having** special trust and confidence in the wisdom and fidelity of you, **the said** William Wightman, with your experience in matters of account, **we have named,** appointed, and authorised you **to be** our Treasurer of the English Army presently appointed to attend upon the person of us the King in the **said voyage,** under **the** regiment of our right trusty and right well beloved Cousin **and** Councillor **William Earl of** Pembroke, Captain General **of our said** Army **of the** English nation; willing and commanding you, by **virtue** and **warrant** hereof, that of such our treasure as for this **intent** and purpose shall be delivered into your hands, you content and pay all such particular sum and **sums of** money as shall from time to time during our **said wars be appointed** and assigned to you by the bills, letters, or warrants of **our said right** trusty **and** right well beloved Cousin and Councillor to **be paid by you, as well for** the coats, conducts, **transportations, charges by sea and land, wages** and diets of officers, wages, gifts, and **rewards of chieftains, captains, petty** captains **and soldiers,** hire of **spials, wages of posts and all other ministers in our said English Army, as also** to any **person or persons in prest or otherwise to be expended for** provision of **victuals, carriages, and all other things requisite to be** occupied about **the necessary provisions, costs,** charges, and expenses of the **same** Army, at the **discretion of our** said Cousin and Councillor, for the better service of **us and the better** furniture of the whole regiment, or any part thereof."

**You shall** disburse money for the charges of carriages, provision of tents, trussing coffers, caskets, bags, tables, green cloths, paper, ink, parchment, and all other necessary charges and expenses to be occupied, used, and spent in and upon your office, keeping **one book or** books of parcels and payments. You shall take allowance **of 26s. 8d.** per diem for your own diets, and for **three** clerks under you **16d.** a day each, and and for ten "halberders," **to attend** upon the safe **conveyance of our** treasure, **10s.** a day

**F. 3.** 1557, Sept. **15, at the English** Camp before Hawne.

Warrant by William **Earl of Pembroke,** K.G. &c., Lieutenant and **Captain** General **of** the towns, castles, and pieces in Callis and the county of Gwisnes and marches of the same, as also of the Army prepared against the French King, to William Wightman, esquire, high Treasurer of the said English Army, to pay the wages of bands of horsemen **and footmen** to the several officers named in "the book of regiment"; **viz.—To the** Earl himself, for 150 demilances with officers under the leading of his servant Thomas Highgate, 441l. 15s. Viscount Montague, Lieutenant **of the Army, 52** demilances, under Raphe Elderker, captain. The Lord Gray of Wilton, Lord Marshal of the Field, 99 demilances, under Arthur Grey, esquire. **The Earl of** Rutland, Captain General of the horsemen, under Captain **Norton,** 100. Lord Clinton, Captain General or Coronell of the footmen, **100, under** Capt. Plasteed. Earl of Bedford, 49, under Capt. Craiforde. **Sir Wi. Courtney, 43.** Sir Giles Strangwais, 50.

To **the Earl of** Pembroke, for 47 light horsemen, with their officers, under George Broughton, captain, 95l. 12s. 6d.; 50 under Rowland Vaughan, captain; 48 under William Harberte, captain. Viscount Montague, 76 light horsemen, under Capt. George Browne. Lord Grey of Wilton, 99, under Capt. Plunckett. Lord Clinton, 52. Earl of Worcester, 50, under Captain Powell. Lord Shandois, 47, under Capt. Anto. Bridges. Sir William Courtney, 53. Wi. Edrington, gent., 50.

To the Earl himself for the wages of 491 footmen with their officers, " under the leading of William Clarke, esquire, 100, Roger Jones 200, **Roger** Earth 100, Lewis Pollard 100, Edw. Harbart 96, William Elmer 100, William Harbart 100, and Lewis Aprodeth 95—1,224*l*." Viscount Montague, 300 footmen, whereof under Chr. Morgan 100, Ambrose Digby 100, Roger Michel 100—411*l*. Earl of Rutland, 298, whereof under Roger Mannours 100, Thomas Bambroughe 100, Michael Thompson 98—409*l*. Lord Clinton, 299, whereof under George Devonishe 99, Nicholas Gorge 100, and Sampson Baker 100. Earl of Worcester, 150, under Fra. Somersett. Earl of Bedford, 100, under Edward Catlin, captain. Lord Braye, 300, whereof under Edw. Ludlowe 100, Thomas Woodall 100, and William Bilmor* 100. Lord Shandois, 198, whereof under Jo. Tracy 98, and Richard Dolaber 100. **Lord** Ambrose Dudley, 198, whereof under Robert Thems 98, and John Rogers 100. Sir John Perrott, 98. [Sir] John Finche, knight, 189, under Erasmus Fynche, captain. Sir Roger Vaughan, 259, whereof under himself 87, Thomas Vaughan 85, and William Haward 87. Sir Henry Jones, 94. Sir James Stoomp, 142. Henry Sherington, esquire, 142. Adrian Poyninges, **esquire**, 48, under Thomas Barry, captain. George Speake, esquire, **150.** Chr. Baynham, **esquire**, 192, whereof under himself 98, and **James Hiett 90 (sic).** George **Carleton**, esquire, 100. All **these payments, due for one** month of **30** days, beginning 9 August 57, **and to end 17 [7 ?] Sept., amount to** 8,778*l*. 10*s*

It appears by certificate of Thomas Harvey, esquire, muster-master of the said Army, that divers horsemen and footmen are decayed in service, by death, or by sickness and hurts, some of the latter being discharged and sent home. As they were indebted for victuals and necessaries to the King's victuallers, for which [debts] their captains stood bound to answer, the Treasurer is to make full payment to their captains without deduction, as if they still continued alive or in service; and although the bands of hundreds or fifties remain not full, yet, as the decay cometh by occasion of service, he is to make full payment to the captains.

F. 4 *b*. [1557, Sept. 15.]—"Divers and sundry officers and allowances to be paid by the Treasurer of the King's Majesty's English Army against France."

This is a schedule showing the daily pay of the Captain General (111*s*. 1¾*d*.), the Lieutenant General (66*s*. 8*d*.), the High Marshal (66*s*. 8*d*.), the Captain General of the Horsemen (66*s*. 8*d*.), the Captain General of the Footmen (66*s*. 8*d*.), the Master of the Ordnance (26*s*. 8*d*.), the Treasurer (26*s*. 8*d*.), the Master of the Musters (16*s*. 8*d*.), the Provost (20*s*.), the chief Surveyor of the Victuals (6*s*. 8*d*.), the chief Harbinger (4*s*.), the Master of the Forage (6*s*.), the Master of the Scouts (6*s*.), the Herald (5*s*.), and the officers under them.

The Captain General had under him three chaplains, an English secretary, a secretary for the French, two surgeons, " tronckmen,"† " ten carriages," two trumpeters, a drum, a fife, and 30 halberders. Each of the next four principal officers had a chaplain and a surgeon. The Master of the Ordnance and the Provost each had a chaplain. The Provost also had two judges, two gaolers, a hangman and his man, &c.

Sum total (per diem), 51*l*. 2*s*. 11¾*d*.

---

* Or Bilinor ?      † " Tronchmen " elsewhere.

F. 5b. 1557, Sept. 15, at the English Camp before Hawne.
Warrant by the Earl of Pembroke, Lieutenant and Captain General,
&c., to William Wightman, esq., High Treasurer of the Army, to pay
the noblemen and gentlemen appointed to the offices in "this book"
before mentioned, at the rates "toted," for one month from **19** Aug. to
17 Sept.

**F. 6.** [1557, Sept. 15.]—"The warrant for entertainment **for**
noblemen and gentlemen."
The Earl of Worcester 100 ducats, 32l. 10s. Earl of Bedford **100**
ducats, Lord Graye 40, Lord Shandois 40, Lord Harberte 40, Lord Tho.
Howard 40, Lord Ambrose Dudley 40, Lord Hen. Dudley (for ½
month) 10, Sir Edward Wyndsor 30, Mr. Weste 30, Sir William
Courtney 30, Sir Jo[hn] Parrott 30, Sir Jo[hn] Pollard 30, Sir Peter
Carew 30, Sir Nicholas Throckmerton 30, Sir John Moore 30, Mr.
Jerningham 35, Mr. Farneham 25, Mr. Lauson 25, Francis Browne 25,
Mr. Fitzwilliams (for ¼) 40s. 8d., Mr. Somersett 25 ducats, Mr. Went-
worth 25, Mr. Markham 25, Mr. Fowler 25, Mr. Damell* 25, young
Mr. Harberte 25, Mr. Russell 25, Ferdinando Lignis 25, Mr. Brett 25,
Rowland Vaughan 25, John Harberte 25, William Harberte 25, Anthony
Digby 25, Oswald Wilkinson 25, John Higham 5s. per diem, =
7l. 10s.-[per month], William Edrington, do., Robert Edrington and
John Edrington (together), do.

**F.** 6. 1557, Sept. 15, at the English Camp before Hawne.—Warrant
**by** the Earl of Pembroke to Wm. Wightman, Treasurer, for payment
**of the** sums above mentioned for one month.
*Begins:* "Forasmuch as the King's Majesty hath of his bountiful
liberality granted unto the noblemen and gent[lemen] before named
the several entertainments toted upon every of their heads, and is contented and pleased that the payment thereof shall begin the 19th day
of August last past, and continue for one month of 30 days."

**F.** 6b. Same date. — Similar warrant for payment **to Edward**
Chamberline, **esquire,** his wages for 60 days **from** 20 July **to 17 Sept.,**
at 10s. a day.

F. 7. Same date.—Similar warrant **for** payment to Sir Richard Lee,
captain general of the pioneers, for the wages of himself at 20s. a day,
1,555 pioneers at 8d. a day each, six captains, five at 10s. a day each
and the sixth **at** 6s. 8d., six lieutenants, five at 5s. and the 6th at
**3s.** 4d., six standard-bearers, five at 2s. 6d. and the sixth at 20d., and
**six** drums at 12d. each ; in all, for a month of 30 days from 19 Aug.
to 17 Sept., 1742 [l.] 15[s.] Full payment to be made to Lee although
some of the pioneers are decayed (as before).
*Note in margin:* The most part of all the bands had their **bills**
allowed without checks.

*Ib.* Same date.—Similar warrant for payment **to** Thomas Langford
for the wages of 200 miners at 13d. each by the day, with 100s. over
in the month ; two captains at 5s. 4d. each, and 8 quarter-masters
at 17s. 9¼d., "xxx pars ij d. ob.," by the day ; in all, for one **month,**
372l. 13s. 4d.

F. 7b. [1557.]—"Muster Book containing the form how the forces
were passed musters."
1. The bands of demilances. 2. The bands of light horsemen. 3.
The bands of footmen.

---

* *Qu.* Daniell.

The names of the four captains of each of these divisions, and the numbers of men under each captain, are stated; as also the numbers of the sick, and of those dis[missed] by reason of sickness. " So as the whole army sent out of England to St. Quintin's consisted of—lances 643, light horse 572, footmen 4148, pioneers 1556 (*sic*), miners 200; in all, 6919.

F. 8. 1557, **July 24, Callis** (Calais).—Warrant by William Earl of Pembroke to **Wm.** Wightman.

Pay "**to my servant** Robert Grove for mine **own conduct from** London **to Dover, being 60** miles, at 6*s.* 8*d.* for every mile, 20*l.*; **for** my transportation 10*l.*; for the conduct of 3 chaplains, 2 surgeons, 1 tronchman, 2 trumpeters, 1 drum, 1 piphe (fife), being 12 persons," at 1*d.* each, 60*s.*; for 30 halberders at ½*d.* each, 75*s.*; for the conduct of 200 horsemen from Ruthin, co. Denbigh, to Dover, 210 miles, at 1*d.* each for every mile, 175*l.*; two captains of the same, at 4*d.* a mile, 7*l.*; two lieutenants at 2*d.*, 70*s.*; &c. There are many other items for officers, horsemen, and footmen, marching from various parts of Wales, Devon, Wilts, Monmouth, &c., to Dover; for the transportation of 432 horses, at 2*s.* each; for the coats of 2,109 persons at 4*s.* each; for their transportation, 210*l.* 18*s.* The whole amounts to 1,842*l.* 2*s.* 2*d.*

**F. 9.** 1557, July 20, **Calice.**—Warrant by the **same** [to the same] to pay to the **right honorable the** Viscount Montague, for his "**con**duction" from **London to Dover, at 5*s.* a** mile, 15*l.*, and for his "transportation," **100*s.***

**F. 9*b.*** 1557, July 7, Baynardes Castle.—Warrant by the same to the same to pay to Viscount Montague, for the conduct of 100 horsemen from Coudre to Dover, 100 miles at 1*d.* the mile each, 41*l.* 14*s.* 4*d.*; 325 "men," at ½*d.*, 67*l.* 14*s.* 2*d.*; other sums for sundry officers, halberders, &c.; for the coats of 479 persons at 4*s.*; for the transportation of 479 persons and 108 horses, at 2*s.* "for every man and horse;" in all, 289*l.* 18*s.* 4*d.*

F. 9*b.* "**The like allowances in** every respect **were** made **to the** Companies **for** their **transportation** and conduct homewards." **A** few particulars are given.

**F.** 12. [1571.]—"The Entertainment of **the** Army into Scotland **under** the leading of the Earl of Sussex, a° ——, and in the 13th year of **the** Queen's Majesty's reign."

**The** Earl of Sussex, Lieutenant, and 30 halberders, *Cl.* Lord **Hunsdon,** deputy General, 40*s.* Sir William Drurye, Marshal, 20*s.*; **General** of the forces, 30*s.*; Provost Marshal, 6*s.* 8*d.*; scout-master and harbinger 4*s.* a-piece; gaoler, 12*d.*; tipstaves, 12*d.*; under-gaoler[s], 2 at 6*d.*; (all these under Drurye). Sir Valentine Browne, Treasurer and Surveyor of victuals, 13*s.* 4*d.* "Robert Ardine, deputy Treasurer of the forces **sent** under the charges of Sir Wm. Drurye, himself at 3*s.* 8*d.* and 6 **horsemen at 16*d.*** le piece, **8*s.*"** Sir Robert Constable, serjeant major, **5*s.*; corporals,** 4 at 4*s.* each. Thomas Genison, muster-master, 6*s.* 8*d.*; 6 **light horsemen,** 16*d.*, 8*s.*; 6 demi-lances, 18*d.*, 9*s.* **Thomas Sutton, Master of the** Ordnance, 6*s.* **8*d.*** Rowland Johnson, surveyor of the works, 4*s.*

The wages of the officers, demilances, light horse and footmen under **the** following captains and others are also stated: Sir Henry Clinton, **Sir Geo.** Carye, Henry Anstell, Sir Francis Russell (attending the **Lord** Lieutenant), Sir Wm. Mallary (ut supra), Robert Stapleton, esquire (to attend ut antea), George Deverox, Robert Bowes, esquire,

Edward Turner, gent., George Delves, **gent.**, Henry Harrington, gent.,
Jo. Fortescue, Fra. Killinghall, gent., **Edw.** Grevell, gent., Dionise
Conway, Raphe **Ellerker,** Tho. Barton, gent., [the] **Lord** Lieutenant
(including a surgeon at 18*d.*), the Lord Scroop ("m^d the said Lord
Scroop had further **charge as** occasion served"), **Lord Hunsdon,** Sir
Jo. Foster, **Sir** Wm. **Drury,** Henry Cary, esquire, **Jo. Darringbie,**
Richard Nevell, Wm. Gorley, Robert Bowes, Jo. Warde, **Jo. Dacres,**
**Sir** Wm. Drury (again), Oswold Lambert, Nich. Erington, **Geo.**
**Moore,** Phi. Stirley (*sic*),* Roger Carew, Ric. Pikman, Robert Game,
**Jo.** Carvell, Robert Yaxley, Edw. Woode, Sir Edward Hastinges,
**Sir Wm.** Fairfax, Sir Jerome Bowes, Wm. Knowles, gent., Tho. Cob-
**ham, gent.,** Edw. Turner, Wm. Tuttie, Sir Tho. Manne, Sir Rob.
**Constable, Rob.** Audley, Tho. Bambrough, Jo. Constable, William
**Scoopham, Humfry** Barwicke, Jo. Pragley, Leonard Knap, and Thomas
Morgan.

Each **company of demilances and light horse had a captain,** petty
captain, **guidon, and trumpeter, and many of them a surgeon at** 18*d.*
a day. Each **company of footmen had a captain, lieutenant,** ensign,
serjeant, **and drum, and most of them a surgeon at** 12*d.* **a day.**

"Sum total of the chief **officers, horsemen, and footmen per diem,**
**215*l.*** 19*s.* 7*d.*

"Lances 1,100, footmen 3,900—5,000."

**F. 20.** [1577.]—"Certificate of the Forces of **the Realm upon the**
two general Musters **of** anno 1574 and 1577, **with the increase** and
decrease."

The **numbers** of able men, armed men, selected men, demilances, and
light horsemen **in** each county and principal city or town of England,
and of each county in Wales, in both the years above mentioned, are
compared, and the differences noted. The totals of **men** of all sorts
are given as follows :

| | | | |
|---|---|---|---|
| English counties 1574 | . | . | . | **271,578** |
| „ „ 1577 | . | . | . | **298,068** |
| „ cities 1574 | . | . | . | **11,193** |
| „ „ 1577 | . | . | . | **7,570** |
| Welsh counties 1574 | . | . | . | 10,563 |
| „ „ 1577 | . | . | . | 18,056 |

Herefordshire and **Monmouth are** included among the Welsh
counties.

F. 27. [      ]—"A Note **what** Forces shall repair to the principal
**Havens in** every county upon **the** sea coasts when the Enemy shall
attempt to **take** land ; which Forces are to be taken of the best and best
furnished **men in every shire.**

"The Earl **of Bedford, Lord** Lieutenant."

Then follows **a schedule of** the numbers of men appointed to repair
from certain **counties to** Falmouth, Plymouthe, Poole, Portesmouthe,
"any port **in Sussex,"** the Isle of Sheppye, Harwitche, "any part of
Suffolk," and **Yearmouthe,** when any enemy should attempt to **land.**
The numbers vary **from 11,000 to 20,000 for** each locality.

*Ff 28—35 are **written** cross-wise on sheets which appear **to have**
been inserted, and contain the following schedules.*

1574.—"Hundreds appointed for the relief of the Isle **of** Wyghte."
This is a schedule giving the names of the hundreds **in** Hampshire,
and the numbers, to be furnished **by** each, of (1) able men, (2) corslets,

---

* *Qu.* Shirley.

(3) harquebusses, callivers, and curriars, (4) bows, (5) Almayne rivets, jacks, and coats of plate, (6) bills ; and the names of the captains and petty captains.

Similar schedules of :—

Hundreds for the relief of the town and Isle of Portsmouth.

Hundreds for **the relief of** the sea-coasts from Portsmouth to Hamble Ferry. (Three hundreds).

Hundreds for the relief and guard of **the** Castle of St. Andrew's, Lettley, and the sea-coasts from Hamble to Ichen Ferry (One hundred).

Hundreds for the guard of the sea-coasts from Redesbridge to Limington and the Castle of Callshot. (One hundred.)

Hundreds for the guard of the sea-coast from Limington to Bornemouth **and the** Castle of Hurste. (One hundred.)

The town of Southampton to guard itself unto Itchen Ferry.

Total of able men for the whole shire, 5,483, &c.

" The Beacons to be erected, watched, and warded. Victuals, carts, and carters are appointed in every C. Posts are appointed in every town and village."

Schedule of boats appointed for the transporting of men **into the Isle** of Wight **upon any** attempt ; giving **the** names of **havens and creeks,** the numbers **of boats** and mariners to be supplied by each, **&c.**

*See State Papers, Domestic, Elizabeth, Vol.* 97, *No.* 32 **II., III.**

F. 37. **1583, Dec.** [20].—The Privy Council to the Commissioners for **Musters,** "**for** putting **of some men in** readiness in certain [of] the maritime counties."

*See State Papers, as above, Vol.* 164, *Nos.* 72–74.

F. 39. 1583, Dec.—" Schedule of the numbers of men to be put in readiness in the counties following, viz. :—Cornwall 3,000, Devon 5,000, Somerset 3,000, Dorset 3,000, Wiltshire 3,000, Hampshire 4,000, Sussex 4,000, Kent 5,000, Essex 5,000, Norfolk 4,000, Suffolk 4,000, Surrey 2,000, Berkshire 2,000, Hertford **2,000, Huntingdon** 800, Lincoln 4,000. **Sum** 53,800.

F. 40. 1584, April.—The **Privy** Council to the Commissioners **for** Musters.

*See State Papers, Vol.* 170, *Nos.* 63, 64.

**F.** 40*b*. 1584, April.—" A M[inute] of Instructions for the Mustermasters by her Majesty specially appointed to take a view of the able men, armour, and weapon put in a readiness within the said (*sic*) county, and to train the shot and soldiers in the use of their several weapons, **&c.**"

*See* **State Papers, Vol.** 170, *No.* 65.

F. 42. 1584, April.—" A Note of Entertainments and allowances made to the Muster-masters."

Cornwall, at Lawnston, Capt. Thomas Hoorde. Devon, at Exeter, Capt. James Crwes. Somerset, at Wells, Capt. John Moryce. Dorset, at Blanford, Capt. Lawrence Peacocke. Wilts, at Sarum, Capt. Barnabye. Hants, at Winchester, Capt. William Henworthe. Sussex, at East Grinsteade, Capt. John Vaughan. Kent, at Rochester, Capt. Thomas Churchyearde. Essex, at Chellingston, Capt. Robert Peacocke. Suffolke, at St. Edmondsbury, Capt. Edward Turnour. Norfolk, **at** Norwitch, Capt. Gilbert Haners.* Surrey, at Kin[g]ston, Capt. John Shewte. Berks, at Reedinge, Capt. Barth. Morgan. Herts, **at**

---

* Properly Havers.

Hartforde, Capt. Henry Swane. Cambridge, at Cambridge, Capt. Huddie. Lincoln, at Lincoln, Capt. Thomas Westorpe.

They were paid sums varying from 38*l.* to 29*l.*, for from 58 to 76 days, each. Total, 532*l.*

**F. 44.** 1584, May 20.—[The Privy Council] to [the Commissioners] for Musters in the maritime counties.

*See State Papers, Vol. 170, No. 85.*

**F. 45.** 1584, May.—" An Order for the training of Shot without any waste or great expense of powder."

*See State Papers, Vol. 170, No. 85 III.*

F. 47. 1584.—" An Abstract of the Certificates returned out of the several Shires by the Muster Masters of the men trained."

*See State Papers, Vol. 173, No. 99.*

F. 51. 1584.—" An Abstract of the untrained **men certified.**"

*See State Papers, Vol. 173, No. 101.*

F. 52. 1584.—" Certificate **of the Able men** and Armour in the Cinque Ports." **Totals : able** caliver men 1,701, calivers 1,555, able pikemen 509, corslets 385, able arch[ers] 219, bows and arr[ows] **384,** demilances 1.

[Also to be furnished by the Cinque Ports :] light horse 50, light horsemen 50, halbards with mur. (*sic*) swords and daggers 250, halbert men 215, black bills 984, bill men 240, labourers or pioneers 826, shipwrights 23.

**F. 53. [1584.]** — Commissioners **for** the Muster in the city of Chichester. Philip Earl of Arundel, Anthony Viscount Mountacute, John Lomley, knight, Lord Lombley, Thomas Lord Buckhurst, Henry Merven, esquire, the Mayor for the time being, Richard Lewcknour, esquire, Recorder, Thomas Lewcknour, esquire, John Cooke, William Holland, and Robert Smithe, (the last three) Aldermen.

F. 54. 1584, May.—[The Privy Council] to [the Earl **of Hunting**-don], Lord President [of the Council in the North].

The Queen intends **to** have 10,000 able footmen **and** 400 light **horse** levied in the three Ridings, to be under the charge of your Lordship, the Earls of Rutland and Cumberland, and Lord Darcye, all having houses in the county [of York]. Lord Scroope **is to** attend his charge at Carlisle, and Lord Evers is to have charge **of the** power of the Bishopric [of Durham]. The 10,000 may, it **is** thought, easily be levied out of the 42,000 certified upon the last general musters, for defence against Scotland or any other enemy. The Council there is **to** inquire what state of living and number of tenants each of the said noblemen has in the several Ridings ; and how the 10,000 and the 400 may be furnished. **The** Queen also intends to have a number of men levied in the Bishopric by permission of the Bishop. The state of the forts is to be certified. Proceed to the execution of your commission for the fortifying of the frontiers. Her Majesty blames us greatly that it has not been executed since the making of the statute.

F. 55. 1584, July.—[Extracts from the Lord President's reply to the preceding, with] " Postils to the Lord President's propositions."

He thought the number of 10,000 men was greater than the county could bear.—The Queen may be induced to require only 6,000.

He stated that the county was very meanly furnished with serviceable horses, there being only 356 by the last view. The leading of the 400 horse is to be committed to such gentlemen as can supply the number wanting with their own tenants and **servants.**

In reply to his request for information, he is informed that " the other three noblemen " are to serve under him as principal leaders, and not as generals.

No captain, except some selected men, should have above 100 men committed to his charge, as the gentlemen of the country are of small skill in martial affairs.—Allowed of.

In reply to another request, it is only desired to have an estimate of the able tenants belonging to the three lords, and not the value of the livings.

Musters have always been taken in the Bishopric of Durham, by her Majesty's commission.—The same course shall be continued.

He will give order for executing the two commissions for fortifying the Borders.—The service may be committed to a few well chosen persons.

F. 58. 1584, May 14, Grenewitche.—[The Privy Council] to the Lord President and Council of Wales. " To view and muster the forces of Wales."

*See State Papers, Vol.* 170, *No.* 81.

F. 58b. 1584, 27 (*sic*) Eliz.————.—" M[inute] of her Majesty's letter of thanks to the gentlemen that showed themselves forward at the musters."

" We mean that the said bands shall be employed only for the guard of our person, and the withstanding of foreign invasion."

*No addresses ; see next.*

F. 59. [1584].—" The names of the Gentlemen to whom her Majesty's letters were addressed."

This is a list of sheriffs and gentlemen in 17 counties—from three to five of the latter in each county.

F. 60. 1585, April 9, Greenewitche.—The Lords [of the Privy Council] to the Commissioners for Musters.

*See State Papers, Vol.* 178, *No.* 13 ; *but no particular county is mentioned here.*

F. 61. 1585, April 9.—" Orders to be observed for the training of men by the several Captains to be continued in the Maritime Counties."

The shot to be trained twice every summer on some holidays, in the afternoon, allowing to each harquebusier 1 lb. of powder. The first day they are to be employed in shooting at a mark, the second day in skirmishing, &c. The Lieutenant to appoint a view of the horsemen at such time as he shall take a view of the footmen. Some of the trained shot to be put on horseback, and their callivers to be turned to musquettes.

F. 62. 1585, May.—" Instructions for the Muster Masters to be sent into the counties of Berks, Hertford, Cambridge [and] Hunting-don."

The Muster-master shall repair to the Sheriff, and require him in her Majesty's name to assemble the Commissioners for the Musters, and the captains of the trained men in the county. At their assembly he shall signify to them her great care to avoid unnecessary charges, &c.

*See State Papers, Vol.* 180, *No.* 60 (*July*) ; *omitting the first two paragraphs.*

F. 63b. [Same date ?].—Directions for the Corporals, as to shooting at targets. *Ib. No.* 61

F. 64. 1585, Aug.—The Queen to Lord Cobham. Thanks the gentlemen of the Lathe of St. Augustine's, Kent, for the readiness they have shown to be enrolled and mustered in the band of light horse under the charge of Sir James Hailes.

F. 64b. [1585].—" M[inute] of a letter for John Killegreue, esquire, for the mustering of certain parishes for the defence of Pendennis Castle, in Cornwall."
*See State Papers, Vol.* 185, *No.* 54.

F 66. 1585, May.—" Copy of a Commission of Lieutenancy."
1. Warrant to Sir Thomas Bromley, Chancellor, to make out commissions [of Lieutenancy] to certain noblemen in certain counties.
*See State Papers, Vol.* 179, *No.* 51 (*June* 30).
2. Form of Commission to a Lord Lieutenant. *Ib.; and see Nos.* 46–49 *See also Patent Roll, divers years, Elizabeth, No.* 20 (*June* 15).

F 68. [1585.]—" A form of deputation for the Lords Lieutenants." This is copied from a deed of F[rancis] E[arl] of B[edford] appointing Deputy Lieutenants, whose initials are given.

F. 68b. [1585, June.]--List of the names of the Lords [and] Deputy Lieutenants in the said counties.

F. 69b. 1585.—Names of the Lieutenants and their Deputies.
*These two lists are similar to those in State Papers, Vol.* 179, *Nos.* 52, 53, *but are not copies of them.*

F. 72. 1585, June.—Orders to be observed by the Lords Lieutenants.
*See State Papers, Vol.* 179, *No.* 55.

F. 72b. 1585.—Names of the Counties not under Lieutenants, with the number of lances and light horse in each.

F. 73. 1585, Sept.—" M[inute] from the Lords to the Counties to forbear the general musters in respect of the unseasonableness of the weather."
This copy is addressed to the Lord Lieutenant of Derby and Stafford. The Queen, considering that too many hands cannot be employed in reaping the fruits of the earth, commands the musters to be deferred till the latter end of September. In towns, a register only is to be made.

F. 73b. [1585 ?].--" Powder needful to be in readiness within every of the Cinque Ports and their members incorporated." Total, 136½ barrels=5¼ last and 4½ barrels.

F. 74. [1585.]—" The names of the privileged Towns in England that shall have a store of powder always well kept, and as any part thereof shall be issued and spent, the same to be renewed within two months."
*Begins:* The City of London—powder, 20 lasts; match, 5000 weight.
Totals: Powder, 95 lasts; match, 47500 weight.
6 *pages.* (*Not same as State Papers, Vol.* 179, *No.* 57.)

F. 78. 1585, Aug. 7.—" Instructions given to Brian FitzWilliams, esquire, being sent by her Majesty's commandment to the Earl of Sussex and to Portsmouth."
*See State Papers, Vol.* 181, *No.* 26.

**F. 78***b***.** [1585.]—" An Estimate for the fortifications of the town of Portsmouth, according to the new platt to be taken in hand and finished this year."

Refers to the Green Bulwark, the Bulwark at the four houses, the walls or curtains, the East Bulwark, the Gate Bulwark, the trench, the vauntmures, trenches about the Bulwark, two dams for preserving the water, the Bridge, and the Gates. Total charge, 1,640*l*.

**F. 80. 1585, Sept. 15.**—" A Commission for the survey of the Isle of Sheppey."

*See Patent Roll, divers years, Elizabeth, No.* 8, *dorse (Oct.* 25).*

F. 81. [1585, Sept.]—"Instructions for the Commissioners appointed to survey the Isle of Sheppey, with the Islands thereto belonging, compassed with the salt water."

Perambulate the said isle and islands. Cause a view to be taken in every parish of the number of men between 16 and 60; how many of **them** are able to wear armour and use weapon, as a bow and arrows, or harquebus, or bill, or pike. Rolls to be made of them, marking who are householders, and who are servants. Learn what armour and weapons are in the possession of any there residing. View the persons having such, and cause them to be instructed how to use the same. In every parish or hundred appoint some to train them. Consider what houses, lands, &c., yielding profit, belong to any person not inhabiting in the island, and what persons meet to carry arms dwell on such lands. Inquire what are such profits, and treat with the owners to find able persons with armour and weapon to reside there. Inquire what houses are decayed since 1 Edward VI., and who occupies the grounds belonging thereto. Also what ships able to brook the seas are in those islands, and if there be any decay thereof; how many mariners and fishermen there are; what landing-places there are convenient for landing any number of people; what beacons, and who ought to maintain them; whether the forts decayed are meet to be restored; what orders have formerly been taken for succour of able men from the main land of Kent, and by what means the same may be renewed. Certify us (the Council) of your doings without making them known to others, for so is it meet that the state of those isles should not be known to any stranger.

F. 82. 1585, October.—"M[inute from the Queen] to the Bishops to furnish lances;" with a list of them.

*See State Papers, vol.* 183, *No.* 72.

F. **84.** [1586, Feb. 2.]—"M[inute from the Queen] to certain principal gentlemen in Cornwall to execute the place of Lieutenancy upon the death of the Earl of Bedford;" with lengthy Instructions for the same, in case of invasion.

*See State Papers, Vol.* 186, *Nos.* 50–52.

F. 88. 1585[-6], Feb. 27.—[The Privy **Council**] to the Marquis of Winchester

Her Majesty for divers considerations found it convenient, in these times of jealousy, to appoint Lieutenants for the maritime counties of the realm. The county of Dorset was committed to the charge of the Earl of Bedford, on whose decease she has made choice of your Lordship to supply that charge. Letters patent are directed to your Lordship, and we send you the instructions which were then set down and

---

* The Patent Roll includes Thomas Fludd among the Commissioners, but his name **is not given in** this MS. *See* State Papers, Vol. 182, No. 46.

delivered to the Lords Lieutenants, and you have the like for the county of Southampton. Inform yourself from the Deputy Lieutenants of what has been done in the performance of the instructions sent from hence. Her Majesty is very desirous to understand what order is taken in the maritime counties for withstanding foreign attempts.

F. 88b. 1586, April 16.—[The Privy Council] to the Earl of Derby.

In the estimate you sent hither of the charges for furnishing and training 600 footmen in the county of Chester, we find some of the rates to be over large, and some not needful. Instead of 2,062l., we think the whole charge will not exceed 1,041l. The soldiers "appointed to be trained should be selected and chosen from gent[lemen's], farmers', and good yeomen's sons, being of good haviour, and able to bear the charge of their own diets for the six days of their training." If these are not sufficient in number, or if allowance must be made to any of them, the pay need not be more than 8d. a day, the ordinary pay of a common soldier in her Majesty's present services beyond the seas. The charge for their furniture is set down in the note enclosed. 3 lb. of powder is allowed for each man for the six days, and no more, " because the first three days of the training of the shot is appointed to be only with false fires, to assure their eyes to the use of the harquebus." Wages will not be given to captains and officers, as you are to make choice of principal knights and gentlemen, as has always been observed in the rest of the maritime counties, who, for their own reputations, this service being for the defence of their own country and habitations, would not look for any sold or pay ; and considering that the charge of the muster-master is born by the Queen. The charge thus not being much more than 1,000l., it is not doubted but the country will be ready to yield thereto, by your good means and furtherance.

P.S.--As the like number of 600 is to be furnished and trained in co. Lancaster, the like course is to be taken there.

F. 89. [1586, April 16.]—" A Note set down by the Lords, containing the charges of the furniture and training of 600 men appointed to be armed and trained in Cheshire and Lancashire."

420 callivers, with swords and murryons, at 26s. 8d. = 560l.

180 corslets, with pikes and swards, at 32s. = 288l.

Powder, 3 lb. for each man for six days, 63l.

Match and lead, 10l.

The diet of 600 men at 8d. a day for six days, 120l.

Sum, 1,041l. " This is to follow the rate sent up by Sir John Savag[e] on the other side.

F. 89b. [1586, April 16.]—" An Estimate of the Charges of furnishing and training 600 soldiers in the county of Chester, as it was set down by Sir John Savag[e]."* With "the Lord Treasurer's postils."

Total charge, 2,062l. The letter on f. 88b was partly based on the " postils."

F. 90. 1586, May.—[The Privy Council] to the Earl of Derby.

Although you received direction for the training of 600 soldiers in cos. Lancaster and Chester, of which you are [Lord] Lieutenant, yet, as you inform us that by means of this last unseasonable winter and spring-time, with the greath dea[r]th of cattle and sheep in those shires, corn and all other victuals are grown to such high prices that the counties are hardly able to furnish the said 600 men, we have set down the

---

* " Foster " struck out.

enclosed rates and notes for the ease of those counties. **Chester** and **Liverpool** are however to be furnished with the powder **and** match formerly set down. If you have levied higher rates, the **moneys are to be** repaid. The captains are not to be paid [*as before*]. The Queen **has** no intention to employ either them or the men abroad, but only for the defence of those counties.

F. 90*b*. 1586, May.—[The Privy Council] to the Captain of the Isle of Alderney.

We understand that there is an end of the differences between you, John Chamberleine, and you the inhabitants of Alderney, and that orders have **been set down** by Sir Thomas Leighton, Captain of Garnesey, and Thomas **Wigmour**, esquire, his lieutenant. We require you to conform to **the same, for the** service of her Majesty and security of yourselves. **Other** good **orders** shall be set down by you "for any necessary service **to be** done with your boats, carriages, and persons, in such sort as is **used** and yielded unto in the Isle of Jarnsey (*sic*) by the inhabitants there, for the better strengthening of the same against foreign invasion." Many persons having possessions in the Isle have withdrawn from the same, but enjoy the rents and fruits thereof, so that it **remains** unfurnished of defenders. If, upon admonition by you the **Governor, they** do not speedily return, you shall assemble yourselves and **cause a perfect** survey to be made of all such lands, and **assess them towards the main-**tenance of gunners and other public uses. By reason **of the number of** barques daily employed out of that **Isle** in foreign voyages, **it is** often left unfurnished of defenders. No more than two barques shall be suffered **to** depart at **one time,** and **no** others shall **go** forth till their return. Licences **are to be given by you,** the Captain, or **your** deputy, without charge.

F. 92. 1585[-6], Feb. and March.—"Abstract of the certificates of the Lieutenants of their proceedings **in** the execution of the orders sent from my Lords of the Council to be observed by them in June 1585."

*Kent*, 20 Feb. 1585[-6], Lord Cobham.—"There are trained in this county 2,500 **men,** and put under captains : **to** which his Lordship hath added 700 more, with the good liking of the country. 300 horse put in readiness under captains ; to each captain 50, with a lieutenant, trumpet, and cornet, all **in** suitable cassocks. There are appointed to each company **of 300** trained men, 50 pioneers, and to every company of 200 men, **39** pioneers, furnished under the leading of the head constables of the place where they are levied ; and to every company two carts. The Justices of the Peace will **see** 300 shot mounted upon ordinary nags, for **firing of the** beacons, **viz.** out of every Lath 50. The Justices of **quorum and** th'other Justices have agreed to find petronells, but such **of them as** have the leading either of horse or foot desire to be eased there of, **in** respect they are otherwise employed. All other points performed."

*Essex*, 9 Feb., Earl of Leicester. *See State Papers, Vol.* 186, *No.* 70. (19 Feb., Deputy Lieutenants.)

*Lancashire and Cheshire,* Earl of Derby, **2 March.** *Ibid. vol.* 187, *No.* 5.

*Derby and Stafford*, 11 March, Earl of Shrewsbury. *Ibid. No.* **31.** *Herts*, 21 Feb., Earl of Leicester, *Ibid. Vol.* 186, *No.* 74.

*Lincoln*, 28 Feb., Earl of Rutland. *Ibid. No.* 77 (*misprinted 23 Feb.*).

*Somerset*, 29 March.—"The petronells are only furnished by the **Justices** of Peace. The lances, light horse, and trained **men** viewed, mustered, and trained, and put under several captains. In **the six Rapes**

of that county: lances 26, lighth[orsemen] 281, footmen 2,000. Pioneers,
furnished with mattocks, shovels, and spades, 600. Shot, on horseback,
under captains appointed to have the leading of them, 300. No mention
at all made what order is taken for the petronells to be furnished by the
Justices of quorum and peace." *Not same as State Papers, vol.* 187,
No. 68 ; *cf. Nos.* 36, 37.

*Sussex* (no date).—" They desire that for the better furnishing of the
trained shot their Lordships would appoint 1200 weight of corn powder
to be appointed and laid in store in certain places in that county, with
the like proportion of match and lead for bullets.

|  | Lead. | Powder. | Match. |
|---|---|---|---|
| At Lewes | 200 | 200 | 150 |
| „ Brighthempsten | 100 | 100 | 100 |
| „ Steyninge | 100 | 100 | 100 |
| „ Eastgreinstede | 100 | 100 | 100 |
| „ Hersan [Horsham] | 100 | 100 | 100 |
| „ Petworthe | 100 | 100 | 100 |
| „ Arrundell | 100 | 100 | 100 |
| „ Chichester | 200 | 200 | 150 |
| „ Battle | 200 | 200 | 150 |
|  | 1200 | 1200 | 950 (*sic*) |

" All other points in their Lordships' order performed."

*Dorset, Devon, Cornwall.*—" Have not received any such articles to
be put in execution by them, but desire that the said articles, and like
instructions as the late Earl of Bedford had, might be sent to them.
And where beforetime in the county of Dorset there have been to the
number of 700 horse, they are not now able to make 200."

Counties not as yet certified : (*names not given*).

F. 96. [1586.]—" The beginning of the letter [from the Privy
Council] to the Earl of Bathe, Lieutenant of the county of Devon."[*]

On the death of the Earl of Bedford, her Majesty authorised Sir
Wm. Courtney, Sir Robert Denes [Denys], and Sir John Gilbert, with
Sir Arthur Bassett and Sir John Chichester, since deceased, to take
views of the forces of the county.[†] She has now appointed your Lordship Lieutenant of the county, for executing such things as should be
thought meet for the safeguard and defence of the realm. The said
parties can inform you of the special directions received by them, and
what they have done thereupon. " Her Highness having of late
" entered into consideration how necessary it was, &c. The rest
" following as in the former ordinary letter."

F. 96. [1586.]—" The beginning of a letter [from the Privy Coun-
cil] to Sir Fra. Godolphin, Sir William Mohun, Mr. Peter Edgcombe,
and Mr. Carew of Anthony, Cornwall."

Last year her Majesty directed her letters to Godolphin and Mohun
for viewing and putting in readiness a certain company of footmen and
horsemen in Cornwall.

" Her Highness is for sundry good considerations both touching
herself and the general weal of her whole realm, is (*sic*) very desirous
that the same course which was appointed to be holden last year should
be continued this year also." A commission is sent to you under the

* He was appointed in 1585 according to the list on f. 69b; but see ff. 96, 100b.
† *See* State Papers, 2 Feb. 1585-6.

Great Seal accordingly. "And further, you the Commissioners shall understand that her Majesty having of late entered into consideration, &c. *The rest following as in the ordinary letter.*"

F. 96*b*. [1586.]—"The beginning of a letter [from the Privy Council] to the Lords Lieutenants of the counties of Stafford and Derby, Chester and Lancaster."

Last year the Queen appointed you Lord Lieutenant for viewing and putting in readiness certain forces. By your letters of — March last we perceive that certain numbers of footmen were only sorted and enrolled, **but** not trained, by reason **of** the unseasonableness of the weather; **and** that the horsemen **were** also only viewed, but not as yet furnished **with cassock,** nor captains appointed over them. The foot-**men should be chosen** of men resident in the shire, being of ability to **furnish themselves** with the least expense to the shire, and known to be **well** affected to her Majesty and the State. We could wish them "to be elected of the eldest sons of some of the chiefest gentlemen, or some others of like behaviour, in every shire; to whom some others **more** skilful in martial services might be appointed as lieutenants and officers." The viewing and training to be performed **at times** least burthensome to the subjects. The views of the several bands **may be** taken apart, and afterwards the whole number assembled. **Her** Majesty chiefly desires the training of the shot; **over** every 20 and **[or?] 30** of them a corporal shall be appointed, who **may** instruct them on **the** holidays, after evening prayer, to use and **exercise** their piece[s] by shooting at a **mark. We** doubt not this may be done with the good contentment of **all** well affected subjects, and without taxation of the country if the bands be composed of men of ability. "And whereas we are informed of certain evil affected persons to this **public** service, &c. *The rest following as in the ordinary letter.*"

F. 97. [1586.]—"Postscript to the letter from [for?] Kent." [The Privy Council to the Lord Lieutenant of Kent.]

"We heartily thank your Lordship for the great pains which we perceive you have taken by the certificate of your doings returned unto us. . . . Touching watch and ward, which in ancient times was (*sic*) wont to be kept towards the Isle of Shepic, Rumney Marsh, and **other** places upon the sea coast, and have of late years been discontinued, **we** like well of [that?] such orders as by the records and precedents remaining with Sir Thomas Scott and Mr. Lambarde appear to have been used **in** former times, should be renewed and put in practice." **If** any person oppugn the same, appoint him to appear before us.

F. **97.** [1586.]—" Postscript to the letters of the counties of South-ampton, Dorset, Wiltshire, and Somerset."

We have not received any certificate from your Lordship of the execution of the article[s] sent with your commission of Lieutenancy, whereat her Majesty doth not a little marvel.

F. 97. [1586.]—"Postscript to the letters for the counties of Stafford and Derby."

The certificates received from your Lordship since your commission of Lieutenancy do not in all points particularly answer the articles then sent to you, as her Majesty looked for. In your next certificate let them be fully answered, as also these our letters, so as her Highness may have cause to be satisfied with your doings.

F. 98. [1586.]—"Postscript to the letter for the county of Lincoln." Similar to the preceding. "Touching powder and match, we think it reasonable that the towns of Grimsbie, Grantham, and Stamforde should make a proportionable part of the provision, as the city of Lincoln and other corporate towns do."

F. 98. [1587.]—[The Privy Council] to the Marquis [of Winchester] and the Earl of Sussex.

" Upon advertisement we received of late of certain preparations by sea set forth by the King of Spain to attempt somewhat on some part of her Majesty's dominions, we wrote unto you the Earl of Sussex to pray you to have an especial regard to your charge, and so to dispose the forces of that country (*sic*) to be in a readiness to meet with any inconveniences that might happen. The like advertisement likewise we sent unto Sir George Carye, Captain of the Isle of Wight, being a place also of great importance and especially to be looked unto. Now forasmuch a[s] heretofore an order was set down by some of us, directing the division of that county, for the defence of that Isle, whereof upon occasion the last year we wrote to your Lordships, that we thought it most necessary the same should be continued, and in no case altered; and that we do understand your Lordships have a meaning to alter that course, and to dispose of some of the divisions appointed for the defence of that Isle, to other use; we cannot but as we have done heretofore pray your Lordships in any wise to forbear to make any innovation or alteration in that established order, both because the importance of that place requireth that necessary succour, and for that a new course would be subject to many inconveniences, every man knowing already by continuance of this order whither to repair, which by the sudden change might breed confusion. And where your Lordships may doubt the forces of the rest of the shire not sufficient for the defence of that coast, order shall be taken to have the same supplied out of the counties next adjoining. We think it convenient likewise that the Captain of the Isle of Wight should be present at the mustering of those divisions which are destinate for the aid of that Isle, because he may the better take knowledge both of the conductors and of the forces appointed for his succour, and they likewise know under whom they are to serve."

F. 98b. 1586.—" Numbers of men to be put in readiness in the counties where no training hath been."

Seventeen counties are mentioned. " Sum total, 16,800; whereof—callivers 6,720, bows 3,360, corslets 3,360, bills 3,360." Also, 1,000 men from Lancashire, and 1,000 from Cheshire, in the same proportions.

F. 100. 1586, Oct. [5], Windsor Castle.—" Letter to the several Inland Counties," &c.

*See State Papers, Vol.* 194, *No.* 6 (*date of place not stated*).

At the end is a list of " men," " shot," " pikes," and " bows and bills " to be supplied by London, Middlesex, and 11 other counties.

F. 100b. 1586, Oct.—[The Privy Council] to the Earl of Bathe.

Her Majesty has chosen you to supply the place of her Lieutenant of that county [Devon], and wills us to signify to you that as, by reason of your young years, your Lordship is not furnished of sufficient experience, you shall use the counsel of the gentlemen named in your commission to be by you appointed to be your deputies, who with others by her special letters last year had the chief charge of that county. Follow the instructions sent to them, and of which we send a new copy with the commission.

**F. 101.** 1586[-7], Feb. [19].—[The Privy Council] to **Sir George Car[e]y.**

*See State Papers, Vol.* 198, *No.* 52.

F. 101*b.* [Same date.]—" Hundreds appointed for the relief **of the** Isle of Wight."

*Ibid. No.* 53.

F. 102. 1586[-7], **Feb.** [19].—[The **Privy Council**] to the Lords Lieutenants of Hampshire and Wiltshire.

*Ibid. No* 50.

F. 102*b.* 1586 [-7], **Feb.** [24].—" Letter to certain **Lieutenants** of the Inland Shires."

*Ibid. No.* **69.**

**F, 102*b.*** [1587, Feb. 23.]—" Orders for putting in strength the **power of the** Realm in the Inland Counties."

***Ibid.*** *Nos.* 66, 67.

F. 104. 1586[-7, Feb. 23].—" Orders for putting **in** strength the power of the Realm in the Maritime Counties."

*Ibid. Nos.* 63-65.

F. 106. 1586[-7], Feb. 24.—[The Privy Council] to **the Earl of** Bathe [and the Deputy Lieutenants of Devon].

By your letters of 14 Dec. we perceive how carefully you have proceeded in executing the orders sent to you in October. You allege that 700 horses are imposed on that county by this new taxation, being 500 **more than were ever** laid upon it, while it is " unfurnished of means **to** maintain horses, as also the use of them, by reason of enclosing and straights that the said county is subject unto, though not so necessary to defence"; yet you offer to furnish 200 shot on horseback, and to turn 200 of the trained shot into musquetiers. We never meant to charge so great a number of horse upon that county, "considering it affordeth not that store nor breed of horses, neither great provision **to** find them, as other counties do." The number may be reduced to 200, as heretofore. The shot and musquetiers are to be furnished out of the able men, **and** not out of the trained bands. Touching **your** request for certain pieces of ordnance to be placed upon divers **weak** places along the sea coasts, we have ordered Sir Richard Greenvill to view **" the places of that and other counties westward along the coast,"** **and how** they may **best be** fortified. We appointed a quantity of **match and** powder to be **brought into** the realm, and to be issued out **to the** principal **towns, but we** have not heard whether any provision **has been** made by the towns of **that** shire. Certain advertisement has since **been** received of great preparations in foreign parts, and her Majesty commands us to require you to deal with those towns, for their better defence, to provide themselves with match and powder, as in the schedule enclosed. We understand that the justices of quorum and peace, appointed to find certain petronells on horseback, show themselves unwilling, which we find strange in so dangerous a time, as the charge is so small, and the justices of all other counties have willingly agreed to find them. Certify the names of such as refuse.

F. 106*b.* 1586[-7], March 5.—[The Privy Council] to [the Earl of Pembroke,] the Lord President of Wales.

" Whereas her Majesty hath thought it convenient in this **time** of jealousy, considering the great preparations made in foreign parts, to commit to your Lordship's charge, as her Lieutenant, the counties as well English and [as] Welsh **as** are annexed unto the Presidentship

(Gloucester alone excepted, which is appointed to our very good Lord the Lord Chandois), to th'end that the able men in those parts might be viewed and put in readiness for their better defence : her Majesty now finding it needful that a certain selected number in every one of the said counties should be trained and reduced into bands under the conducting of the principal gentlemen of the said Com' [counties] known to be well affected, we have thought good to let your Lordship understand that we think meet, there should be trained in the four English counties such number sorted with weapons as are contained in the enclosed schedule, and in the Welsh counties such numbers as your Lordship, upon conference with the principal Commissioners of the last Musters, shall find the said counties may be able to bear. And therefore we think it convenient that your Lordship, at your return into those parts, should with all convenient speed send for some of the principal Commissioners of the last Musters, residing in the said counties, such as are known to be well affected in religion, and to confer with them as well what numbers (with the reasonable contentment of the inhabitants of the said counties) may be trained, as also what further numbers may be put in a readiness, enrolled, and reduced under captains, to be employed for the defence of those countries upon any invasion or descent of th'enemy.

" We think it very meet at the said conference, you should take some course for the choice of certain principal gentlemen in every of the said counties (such as are well known to be of sound disposition towards her Majesty and the State) to have chief charge under your Lordship to serve as your Deputy Lieutenants, and of other gentlemen in like sort to have the leading of the footmen, appointing to every of them such numbers of men as to their places and qualities shall appertain, wherein especial care is to be had that the selected numbers appointed to be trained (considering they are to be used for the defence of the said country, and not to be employed in any foreign service) may consist of well affected householders, such as for their personages shall be found serviceable, and for their livings able to bear the charges of training without any burden to the country. And to th'end that the same uniform order may be used and observed throughout the realm in the training of the foot bands, and to be done with as small charges as may be, we send unto your Lordship herewith such orders as have been observed as well in the maritime as inland counties, that such as your Lordship shall appoint muster-masters in the said counties may follow the like directions in the form of their training.

"And whereas we find by the last certificate that the numbers of horse in the said counties are very scant, in such sort as if any occasion of service should require, the country is in manner bare and unfurnished of such numbers as for the defence of the said counties were requisite, we have thought good to put your Lordship in remembrance that special care may be had that the numbers of horse may be increased, and those defects [supplied], appointing such as are to find either lances or light horse, to have them in a readiness in their stable, and such as are as yet unfurnished to provide themselves against a day by you to be limited, to th'end they may be trained, and reduced into bands, and so made more apt and ready for service.

" We have also given order to our very good Lord the Lord Chandais (sic), her Majesty's Lieutenant in the county of Gloucester, that as in other the maritime counties of the realm, upon landing of any foreign enemy in any part thereof, there be certain numbers in the counties next adjoining unto them appointed to repair to the places of descent, for his better defence, that his Lordship in like manner, **if** anything should be attempted by th'enemy, either at Milford Haven or **the** coast thereabout, that upon notice thereof to be given to him from your Lordship or your Deputy Lieutenants he shall send thither the number of —— out of that county appointed to be [in] readiness under captains of the country, to be disposed into such places as your Lordship shall address them unto; as we doubt not but your Lordship will in like sort have care that such other competent numbers may be appointed in the rest of the counties of your Lieutenancy to give assistance unto each other, and to repair to the places or havens of descent, where th'enemy shall attempt to land."

> " Hereford, 600.      Worcester, 600.
> Monmoth, 600.      Sallop, 600."

F. 108. 1586[-7]. March 5.—[The Privy Council] **to** the Lord Chandos.
*See State Papers, Vol.* 199, *No.* 11.

F. 108. 1586[-7], March.—[The Privy Council] to Sir Richard Greenvill.
" Whereas it hath been already signified unto you, that her Majesty's pleasure was, that you should take a view of the places of descent in the countie[s] of Devon and Cornwall, and thereof to make report unto us, together with your opinion what defence might conveniently be made **in every of** the said places either for preventing or impeaching the landing of a foreign enemy : we are now further to signify unto you that her Majesty's pleasure also is, that before your coming up, you do take a view of the trained bands of the said two counties, as well of the person[s] of the men, as of their furniture, and see them exercised and mustered in your presence, to th'end you may be able to make report both of the sufficiency of the armour, and of the profit they have made of this exercise of the training, and also what defects you do find either in the armour, or in the choice of the persons, or their skill in the use of their weapons, whereupon order may be taken for the repairing of **the** said defects. And of this her Majesty's pleasure we have given knowledge by **our** letter, as well to the Earl of Bathe, Lord Lieutenant in **Devon**, and also to the Lieutenant in the county of Cornwall, requiring **them** to afford you their best assistance for th'executing of this charge that is enjoined you."

**F. 108***b***.** 1586[-7], March 8.—" M[inute] of a letter sent to the Earl **of** Bath, Lieutenant of Cornwall" (*sic*).
*See State Papers, Vol.* 199, *No.* 19.

F. 108*b*. [1587.]—" Instructions for the Muster-masters sent into the Inland Counties ; as also to the Warden of the **Stannary,** for the mustering of the inhabitants of the said Wardency
" Having made choice of an apt man to supply the place of muster-master there, he shall enter into a muster-book the names and surnames of the persons of every band enrolled, with their several weapons.
" He shall likewise certify to you the aptness of the persons enrolled, and in what sort they be furnished with several weapons, to th'end be may give order for the reformation of th'one and th'other.
" And whereas the charge of the training doth chiefly consist in two things, th'one in the oft assembling of the said bands, th'other **in** expense of powder ; for avoiding of this inconvenience, concerning the first point, it is thought meet that the shot of every band **shall be** trained at such time as——(*sic*).

"And to th'end the training of the shot apart may be the better performed to the ease of the country, every captain shall make choice of 4 or 5 of those which shall be appointed to be shot in the several bands, such as he shall think most apt to be instructed by the said captain and muster-master, in such sort as they be thoroughly taught and made **sufficient to** train the rest of the shot according to such direction as they shall receive from the muster-master, who shall also deliver unto these selected persons for train[er]s the form and manner in writing, to th'end one uniform order may be generally observed therein.

"The said chief trainers shall carry the title of corporals, whereof, **in** every band consisting of 80 or a 100 persons, 4 corporals shall **be** appointed, each to have under him 20 or 24 shot.

"For the more ease of the country, every captain shall appoint his **corporal** to train his shot in some such place as may be most fittest chosen near to the habitation of the shot allotted to him, according to a direction sent herewithall to be observed by the corporals.

"It is also thought meet that the muster-master himself shall take a view of the whole bands, at such times as they shall be mustered together by your order, at the least two several times, which for **the** ease of the country may very well be done on some holiday in **the** afternoon after the Common Prayer, but not on the Sabbath day.

"At the first time he shall take view of their persons and weapons, and if he find any defect of th'one or the other he shall admonish and warn them to see the same reformed against the next general assembly

"The second time he shall instruct them in such martial exercises as by himself shall be thought meet, and take an account of the several corporals how they have profited the shot committed to their charge.

"And if any of th'enrolled men shall happen to decease, or by sickness or otherwise made unable to serve, order must be taken that their places may be supplied with able men, sorted with like weapon, so **as the like** number may be always complete and furnished.

"**And to** th'end a special choice be made of fit and able men, it **is** not meant that the service of any person whatsoever shall be excuse **to** any retainer to be exempt or spared, if otherwise he be thought fit.

"The oath also of the Supremacy shall be ministered to the captains **and other** officers **and soldiers under them.**

"**It is** also thought meet that you, or the corporals appointed over the **shot,** may have the charge and oversight of the pieces committed to them, to be better kept and had in readiness."

F. 109*b*. 1586[-7], March 10.—Warrant [by the Queen] to the Master of **the** Ordnance.

"Right trusty and right well beloved Cousin and Councillor, we greet you well, and let you wit, that our pleasure and commandment is, you deliver or cause to be delivered to our right trusty and well beloved Cousin, Henry, Earl of Sussex, Captain of our town of Portesmouthe, out of our Store within our Tower of London, and of provision otherwise to be had, for the better fortification and defence of our said town, **these** parcels hereafter following, viz.:—demiculvering[s] of cast **iron,** mounted and furnished with ladles, sponges and rammers, twenty-five; sacres of cast iron mounted, and with like furniture, seven, whereof 2 upon wheels shod with iron[;] portpieces of brass, with two chambers a-piece, well stocked and mounted, 4; portpieces of iron forged, with 2 chambers a-piece, in like manner stocked and mounted, 28; round shot of iron for demi-culverings, 625; round shot for sacres, 175; cross-**barred** shot for sacres, 14, **and** for demi-culverings, 50[;] stone shot **for** portpieces, **480** ; common corn-powder for the said pieces, **3 lasts, and britchinge** rope, of 6 inches of scantling, 3 coils : all which **to be sent** by sea to our town of Portesmouthe, in good and serviceable order, to be placed **and** bestowed only upon **our** new erected bulwarks there.

" Moreover our further will **and** pleasure is, that forasmuch as we are disposed to furnish certain **our** maritime counties bounding upon the sea coast, that is to say, our countie[s] of Kent, Sussex, Southampton, Dorset, Devon, and Cornwall, **ye** deliver or cause to be delivered out of our said Tower, viz. **: to every of our** said counties, 2 sacres, 2 minions, and 2 fawcons of cast **iron, being in** all 36 pieces, to be well mounted upon carriages with **wheels shod** with iron, and furnished with ladles, sponges, and **rammers, and with all** other necessaries incident for travel, and **service where they are** employed ; spare extrees (*sic*) for the said pieces, **36 ; spare wheels,** shod also with iron, 18 pair ; bullets, or shot, **or iron for the said pieces**, 720, viz., **of** each sort to serve every of the **pieces** aforesaid, 20 ; common corn-powder for the said pieces, one last di., distributing to every the said counties 600 weight ; fine corn-powder, viz., for the county of Kent, 9000 weight, for Sussex, 4800 weight, for the county of Southampton, 4800 weight, for the county of [Dorset]*, 4620 lb. ; for Devon, 7200 weight, and for Cornwall, 3000 weight—in all, 14 lasts, 420 lb.; lead for the said **counties, 17 ton 20** lb.; and match, 34,020 lb. ; so much **in poyse and quannity as is set down** before in the title of fine corn-powder. **And that the portions** aforesaid allowed to the said counties be delivered to **such person or** persons as shall be directed to you by letters of six of **the hands of our** Privy Council. And for the delivery **of the premises, etc.**"

**F.** 110. **1586[-7], Feb. 16.**—" A proportion of Match and Powder **and** Ordnance to **be sent into** the Maritime Counties at her Majesty's charge."

*See State* **Papers,** *Vol.* 198, *No.* 43.

F. 111. **1587, Aug.**—" The Ordnance and Munition appointed for the Maritime Counties."

*See State Papers, Vol.* 203, *Nos.* 17, 18 (*Aug.* 25).

F. 113. 1587, **Aug.** 25.—" M[inute] to the Lieutenants [of the same counties] for **the** receiving of the ordnance and munition **sent out** of her Majesty's Store."

*Ibid. No.* 19.

**F.** 113. **1587, Aug. 20.**—[**The** Queen] to Lord Cobham.

" **Right trusty, &c.** We find it very strange that the inhabitants of our **Cinque Ports,** seeing **the** great spoil[s] that have of late years been committed by **those** of Dunkircke upon the subjects of this realm, for the most part upon the coasts of Kent, whereof also some part of the said spoils hath lighted on themselves, pretending to have such large privileges above the rest of our subjects of this our realm, which were **at** the first granted unto them in consideration of services to be done by them upon our narrow seas, whereof there is, at this present, no use, neither have they been called upon to perform the same ; all which notwithstanding they have not at any time made offer unto us in respect of the benefit they receive by the pretence they make to the said privilege, as to employ themselves for the defence of our sea-coasts upon our narrow seas, or take revenge of the spoils done by these [those] of the said town of Dunkircke. And therefore our pleasure **is that** you, calling unto you such as are the principal governors and

---

* Omitted.

officers of the said **Ports, shall** give them to understand how hardly we conceive of their **lack of care** and remissness in **that** behalf; and admonish them that **unless** they shall make offer and **provision** to employ themselves **hereafter** for the defence of the said **coasts in** some part of acknowledgment of such other services as for th'use **of their** privileges they are bound unto, we do not mean to suffer them **in such** a fruitless manner to enjoy **the** [same]."*

**F. 125.** The following is written **as a title-page :—**

"*Upon sundry advertisements of **the** preparations made by* **the** *King of Spain, with intention, as it was' **said**, to invade **this** Realm, directions were given for the speedy putting the forces in readiness throughout the Realm. And the Counties wanting Lieutenants were supplied, **and** thereupon these directions sent unto them which follow.*

"**There were** *in like sort divers **directions given for the arming** and setting forth to the Seas, **whereof the particulars** appear together in the end of **the** book.*" ⟍

F. 125*b*. [1587].—" The names of the Lieutenants and their Deputies throughout **the Realm.**"

Lord Chancellor. **Northampton: Sir Tho. Cecil, Sir Ry. Knightly,** Sir Edw. **Mountagu.**

Lord **Treasurer. Lincoln : Sir** Willoughby of **Parham, Sir Tho.** Cecil, Sir **Edw.** Dymock, **Sir Anto.** Tharrold (*sic*). **Essex : (***blank***),** Hertford **:** (*blank*).

Marquis [of] Winchester. **Dorset :** Sir Jo. Horsey, Geo. Trenchard. Marquis Winton [and] Earl of Sussex. Hampshire **: (***blank***).**

Earl of Shrewsbury. Stafford : Sir Walter Aston, **Mr.** Bagott. Derby : Jo. Manners. Nottingham : Lord Talbott.

Earl of Kent. Bedford **:** (*blank*).

Earl of Derby. Lancashire : Sir **Jo. Byron, Sir Ry. Sherburn.** Cheshire : Sir Jo. Savag, Sir Hugh Cholmley.

Earl **of** Huntingdon. Leicester : Sir George Hastinges, **Fra.** Hastinges. Rutland : **Sir John Harrington, Sir Andro Noel.**

Earl **of** Huntingdon. Yorkshire : (*blank*). Northumberland : (*blank*). Cumberland : (*blank*). Westmoreland : (*blank*). B. of Durham **: (***blank***).** Villa Hull : (*blank*). Villa Newcastle : (*blank*).

Earl of **Peimbroke.** Somerset : Sir **George** Sidenham, Sir Hen. **Barckley. Wilts : Sir Hen. Knevit, Sir Charles Danvers.** Villa Bristoll **:** the mayor for the time being.

Earl of **Bathe. Devon : Sir Wa. Ranley, Sir Wm.** Courtney, Sir **Ro.** Dennys, **Sir Jo.** Gilbert, **Hugh Fortescue,** Geo. Cary. Villa Exon. the mayor [and] recorder, **with certain** other townsmen.

Lord Admiral. Surrey : William **Haward, Sir** Tho. Brown, Sir Wm. More, Sir Fra. Caro.

Lord Admiral, Lord Buckhurst. **Sussex : Sir Tho. Shurley,** Sir Tho. Palmer, Wa. Covert, Ni. Parker.

Earl of Warwick. Warwick : Sir Foulk Grevil, Sir Tho. Lucy, **Sir** Jo. Harington

Lord Chamberlain. Norfolk : **Sir** Art. Hemington, Sir Edw. Clere, Sir Jo. **Payton,** Sir Wm. Heydon. Suffolk : Sir Ro. Wingfeld, **Sir** Phil. Parker, **Sir** Ro. Jermin, Sir Jo. Higham.

Lord Cobham. Kent : Sir Hen. Cobham, Sir Tho. **Vane,** Sir Thomas Scott.

Lord Graie. Buckingham : (*blank*).

---

* Omitted.

Lord Shandois. Gloucester: (*blank*). Villa Gloucester: the mayor, recorder, with some of the townsmen.

Lord St. John. Huntingdon: (*blank*).

Lord Northe. Cambridge: (*blank*).

Lord Norris. Oxford: Sir Wm. Knoles, Sir Hen. Umpton.

Sir Fra. Knoles. Berkshire: Sir Hen. Nevil, Tho. Parry.

Sir Wal. Rauley Cornwall: Sir Fra. Godolfin, Sir Wm. Moon, Peter Edgcomb, Ry Carew, Sir Ry. Grenvil.

Earl of Pembroke. Radnor: Tho. Wigmor, Jo. Vaughan. Brecnock: Geo. Price, Tho. Vaughan. Glamorgan: Sir Wm. Herbert **de** Swansey, Tho. Lewes of Van. Carmarthen: Sir Tho. Jones, Edw. Dunlo. Pembroke: Sir Jo. Perrott, Geo. Bowen. Cardigan: Ry. Price, Morgan Lluyd. Merioneth: Jo. Win ap Cadwalider, Jo. Lewis. **Carnarvon: Jo.** Win **ap** Guider, Wm. Morris. Flint: Tho. Mostin, Ro. Puliston. Anglesey: Sir Ry. Buckley, Jo. Griffin. Denbigh: Wm. Ailmer, Ro. Salsbury. Montgomery: Sir Ed. Herbert of Montgomery, Jo. Price of Nenton (*sic*). Monmouth: Sir Wm. Herbert of St. Julian, Edw. Layton of Waltsbury. Salop. Sir Art. Mainwaring, Ed. Layton of Waltsbury. Hereford: Jo. Scudamor, Tho. Commisbye (*sic*). Wigorn.: Sir Jo. Packington, Sir Jo. Russel.

Counties not under Lieutenants Middlesex. (*No others named.*)

F. 127. 1587, Oct. [4].—[The Privy Council] to the Lord Lieutenants.

*See State Papers, Vol. 204, Nos. 5, 6* (*rough drafts in Burleigh's hand*).

*Note in the margin:* "It was at the same time thought meet that the Lord Admiral should be set forth with her Majesty's ships into the narrow seas, and Sir Fra. Drake to be sent to the coast of Spain, whereof the direction[s] follow, fol. 301."

F. 127b. 1587, Oct. 5. — [The Privy Council] to the Vice-Admiral[s].

"The Queen's Majesty, having knowledge by sundry means of the great preparations made in Spain for a navy with an army to come to seas, towards her dominions, hath thought necessary to have due regard **here for a** good defence both by sea and land, and therefore hath ordered that her own Navy should be forthwith made ready to pass the seas, minding also to have the strength of all her subjects' ships **and mariners** to join with her own for defence of her dominions against **all attempts by sea.**

"For that purpose her Majesty's pleasure and commandment is, that all manner of ships and mariners throughout the coasts of the realm, in what ports or creeks soever the same be, shall be stayed and not suffered to depart upon any voyage. And therefore we will and command you, the Vice-Admiral in those parts, with all speed to make your repair to those ports and creeks where any vessels that are able to cross the seas shall be, and charge the owners thereof, in her Majesty's name, as they will answer to the contrary at their uttermost perils, not to depart with the same from that port, until there shall be further direction given from us, or from me the L[ord] Admiral. And furthermore you shall certify the names of the said vessels and their owners, with their tonnage, and what number of mariners are in the same vessels, or appointed for service in the same, and what number of mariners otherwise **are** in the same port[s] and creek[s], how many of them are inhabitants **in** the same ports or creeks, and how many strangers, and of what places they are inhabitants; and of these points to advertise **us** particularly with all the speed that you can. And if you shall find any ships that are ready with victual and men, for any voyage intended, you shall certify us thereof, and yet you shall stay the same until you shall receive further answer. You shall do the like if there be any vessels of any foreign parts there, which, in your opinion, may be serviceable to be made and appointed to serve us as ships for the war; you shall also make (*sic*), assuring the owners that in case the said ships shall be used for service, they shall have such entertainment as shall be in reason due for the same.

"And notwithstanding this general stay, which we do direct, yet where you shall find any crayers, or small vessels, which are used to carry corn or such other vessels [victuals?] from one port to another, if the owners thereof shall require to have th'use thereof for those purposes, you shall not stay them from such necessary services, but yet you shall certify both the names and the owners thereof, with their tonnage and number of sailors; and thereupon **you** shall inform th' officers of her Majesty's Custom-houses, that there may be good bands taken for their repair to such [some?] other ports of the realm, and not to cross the seas, but to bring due certificate of their discharges in the ports limited, in such manner as by the laws of the realm and common usage in their ports they ought to do.

"**And** so **for** the speedy execution **of** all the contents **of** these our **letters,** we require you to use all the speed you can possibly, and to that **end, because** the places may be far distant one from th'other, we remit **it to your** own discretion to use the help of any others near inhabiting to the ports, being of good discretion and disposition to the service of her Majesty, whereby this service may be the more speedily performed, and we also with like speed advertised."

*Note in margin :* "To this there was never any certificate returned from the Vice-Admirals, for the number of ships and mariners belonging to every port."

F. 128. [1587, Oct. 23.]—The Queen to the Marquis [of **Win**chester] and the Earl of Sussex, Lords Lieutenants of Hampshire.
*See State Papers, Vol.* 204, *Nos.* 44, 45. ("*The Council*" should be "*The Queen.*")

F. 129. [1588, Feb. 22.]—"The whole numbers allotted to Sir George Cary by the letters of April 1587"; and "by the letters of the 22nd of Feb. 1587."
*See State Papers, Vol.* 208, *No.* 80.

F. 129*b*. 1587, Dec.—The Queen to Lord Shandois [Chandos].
"Where we have already by our letters and otherways taken order with our Lieutenants, to whom the principal charge is committed of such our counties and shires as do lie most subject to foreign invasion, for convenient numbers of soldiers and trained men to be put in a readiness for the defence of the same : forasmuch as amongst other counties within this our Realm, o[u]r principality of Wales (whereof **our Cousin th'Earl** of Pembrooke is our Lieutenant) requireth a **special** regard **and care to be** had unto it ; we have thought it very necessary, for the **safety thereof** (if any attempt should happen to be given that way), by these presents earnestly to will and require you, that at any time when our said Cousin of Pembrooke shall by his letters require to be assisted with one thousand of those trained men which are within our county of Gloucester, whereof you are our Lieutenant, you do with all expedition possibly (*sic*) send the whole number aforesaid, or such **part** thereof, unto such place **and with such** furniture and weapons as

he shall appoint, under the conduct and leading of such captains and other officers as in your judgment shall seem meetest **to have** that charge committed unto them."

F. 129*b*. 1587, Sept. 2.—The Queen to the Earl of Pembroke.

" We have already by our own letters addressed to the Lord Chandois taken order with him for a supply of 1,000 of able men and trained to be sent unto you at any time to any place you shall require the same or part of them to be conducted out of our county of Gloucester, for your better assistance in our service in that part of the realm. And for that we would not have you also to want the aid of a great[er] number, if you should **see** any good occasion of employment for them, we authorise you by **these** presents **to** increase our forces there with 1,000 more of trained soldiers of **our** county **of** Somerset, being in your lieutenancy, which we doubt **not** but that you have seen provided of such sufficient captains, weapons, and furniture as are meet and requisite for th'advancement of our service."

*Note in margin :* " Upon further consideration **it** was thought meet, that the Lord Admiral should be sent upon the coast of Spain and join with the forces under Sir **Fra.** Dra[ke's] leading ; whereupon letters were written to the ports **to** arm certain ships **to** the **seas,** whereof the directions follow, fol. **312.**"

F. 130. **1587,** Dec. 2,* **Ely House.—The Queen to the** Earl of Shrewsbury.

Right trusty **and right well** beloved **Cousin** and Councillor, we greet you well. Where, by our special commission heretofore in that behalf directed, we have appointed our right trusty and well beloved Cousin the Earl of Huntingdon, to be our Lieutenant in the North parts, where for the furtherance of our service there may fall out occasion for some supply of forces to be had out of other countries (*sic*) adjoining to his lieutenancy, and for such cause our said Cousin of Huntingdon may require some numbers of soldiers to be sent out of the counties of Salop and Stafford, whereof you are Lieutenant : forasmuch as amongst those numbers it is like that a great part be of your tenants or servants and followers, we have thought good, in case the said Earl of **Huntingdon** shall at any time for our service require of you any such **aid** or supply out of the foresaid countries (*sic*) under your Lieutenancy, not **only** to will and will (*sic*) and require you to take order that the same **may be** accordingly **sent unto** him, but also to signify unto you that **as we** ourself think **there can be no** person so meet to have the charge over such **as** you shall send as your son, the Lord Talbot, so we wish and require you to appoint him thereunto, who also may have the leading and charge of any other our subjects, being your tenants within the jurisdiction of the lieutenancy of our said Cousin **the** Earl of Huntingdon, as cause may require."

F. 131 1587, 30 Eliz., **Dec.** 3,† Ely House.—The Queen to the Earl of Shrewsbury, Earl of Derby, Earl of Rutland, Earl of Pembroke, and Lord Treasurer [**Burghley**].

*See State Papers, Vol.* 206, *No.* 3.

F. 132. 1587, Dec. 21, Somerset House.—" A copy of the Warrant for the entertainment of certain Captains which were sent into sundry counties to take view of the forces, with their allowances."

*Ibid. No* 36 *; which does not contain the following schedule —*

---

* " 5 " Dec. at **the top.**          † " 2 " Dec. at the top.

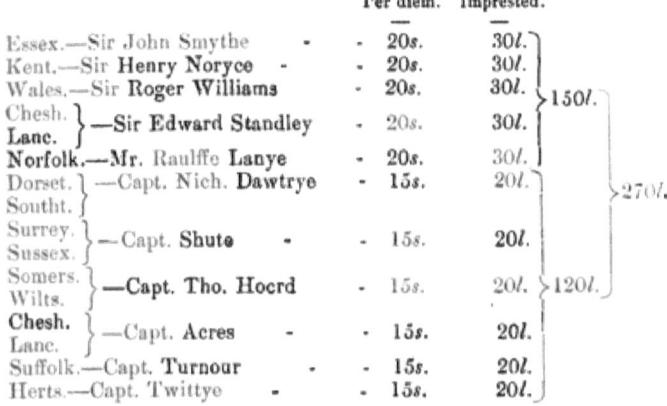

|  |  | Per diem. | Imprested. |  |  |
|---|---|---|---|---|---|
| Essex.—Sir John Smythe | - | 20s. | 30l. | } 150l. | |
| Kent.—Sir Henry Noryce | - | 20s. | 30l. | | |
| Wales.—Sir Roger Williams | - | 20s. | 30l. | | |
| Chesh. } —Sir Edward Standley<br>Lanc. } | | 20s. | 30l. | | |
| Norfolk.—Mr. Raulffe Lanye | - | 20s. | 30l. | | |
| Dorset. } —Capt. Nich. Dawtrye<br>Southt. } | | 15s. | 20l. | } 120l. | } 270l. |
| Surrey. } —Capt. Shute<br>Sussex. } | - | 15s. | 20l. | | |
| Somers. } —Capt. Tho. Hoerd<br>Wilts. } | - | 15s. | 20l. | | |
| Chesh. } —Capt. Acres<br>Lanc. } | - | 15s. | 20l. | | |
| Suffolk.—Capt. Turnour | - | 15s. | 20l. | | |
| Herts.—Capt. Twittye | - | 15s. | 20l. | | |

F. 132b. 1587, Dec. 10.—" Instructions given by her Majesty's commandment to Sir John Smithe, knight, and others, for certain services to be done in the counti[es] of Essex and Hertford."

"The Queen's Majesty being informed of the training and mustering of divers companies of soldiers and other captains and officers within the counties of Essex and Hertford, for the doing whereof her Majesty doth allow of the pains and travail of such as have been Deputies to the Earl of Leicester, her Majesty's Lieutenant General of both the said counties, and hath a desire to be certified of the same by the view of some to be sent thither, being of experience and knowledge in martial services, and therefore have [hath ?] thought good to make choice of you, Sir John Smithe, knight, taking unto you for assistance —— Tuttye, a gent' of that county of Essex, trained also in martial affairs ; and to that end her pleasure is that you have with you in your company the said Tuttye, [and ?] shall repair to those that be Deputies to the said Earl, both in the county of Essex and Hertford, sending unto them our several letters, mentioning the cause of this our commission ; and therewith you may require them aforesaid by your letters to come to some place in the confines of both the shires meet for their assembly, and at one day also certain, whither you shall repair, and there show them these instructions and directions as (sic) have been sent both from her Majesty and her Council for the levying, arming, and training of the forces of those counties, and to inform you how the said directions have from time to time been executed, and where and wherein they have not been, to know of them the impediment thereof, giving you advice how the same defaults may be remedied as the time shall require.

" After you shall be thus informed by the said Lieutenants Deputies in both the shires, of the whole forces of both the shires severally, and, namely, how many have been trained in every shire, and how many also have been armed, though not as yet trained, and how the same have been distributed under captains and leaders in every of those shires, you shall inform the Deputies both of Sussex [Essex] and Hertford, and other principal gentlemen of those shires, whom the Deputies shall think meet to call to that conference, that her Majesty's desire is to have the forces of both those countries (sic) to be better trained and disciplined, for to be more able to encounter with an enemy that is exercised than it hath been possible to be done by certain short musters and trainings, which have served more, as it is thought, for fashion than for substance of discipline; and therefore [she] thinketh it meet that an assembly be made of such numbers of both the counties in some meet places in the confines of the two shires, and being gathered together may make the form of the camp, which is requisite at the least to be with 2,000 men, whereof we think 1,500 may be chosen of the trained men of Essex, and 500 of the trained men of Hertford; and the same to be brought to some fit place for the purpose, where they may be mustered, viewed, arrayed, armed, and weaponed, and afterwards trained as well to make their march as to lodge and to be in camp, and so to be enabled by that exercise and discipline to encounter with th'enemy, that shall offer to assail them, either in marching or in camp. And to the intent they may continue together at the least 16 days, it would be considered that the able people of both the shires, according to the numbers appointed out of each shire, without burthening of such as live upon the hand labour, might be contributory to the daily wages, which we think reasonable to be 8d., of the numbers, for the time of their service, with regard of the days of coming and returning; and that lodging and victuals be provided in villages and towns near to the places of mustering and encamping, where the soldiers may be lodged and victualled at reasonable rates, according to the wages that shall be given them by the country.

" And for that no place may not (sic) be burthened with the continuance of these numbers so long together, it shall be well done to make choice of sundry places for the placing of the camp, somewhat distant asunder, so as they may march from one place to another every third or fourth day, as places may be found meet in either of the shires for the encampage. And because such a camp of footmen would be accompanied with horsemen to be trained with the footmen, it is also desired and thought necessary to have a number of horsemen to accompany the said camp, for which purpose the Deputy Lieutenants, &c., [are] to be dealt withall, that for every 1,000 of footmen there may [be] 100 horsemen, whereof 150 may be taken out of the county of Essex, and 50 out of the county of Hertford; and that the said horsemen may also be [t]here trained for the space of four whole days together, or at three several days in the whole time of service.

" And considering this one kind of service now purposed shall be no[*] more available to enable the forces of the county than all the former trainings, being so lately and imperfectly done, for lack of time, and the charges not much greater, being borne at so many times in the year as they have been with small profit, it is thought that by the wisdom and credit of the Deputy Lieutenants, upon conference by them had with the principal gentlemen of both the counties, this project and intention of her Majesty shall not be misliked, but shall be willingly furthered by all good means. And therefore her Majesty would that you, Sir John Smithe, after this declaration made to the Deputy Lieutenants of both the shires of her Majesty's intention, shall make them to determine of the time and place, and of the manner how to bring these numbers under captains and other officers of knowledge and experience to the places appointed, wherein it is very necessary that no delay be used. And for any particular directions, it shall not need, for that the intention of her Majesty being in this sort known, the prosecution thereof to [may ?] be left to the discretion and good devotion both of the Deputy Lieutenants and other principal gentlemen of the country.

---

* Qu. omit " no."

"Finally, we think it convenient that **for** this service warning be given by the Deputies of both the shires to the muster-masters of the same shire[s], that they **may** give their attendance **and** employ their labours for th'exercising and training of the said numbers allotted out of every the said shires, and your proceedings herein we require you, Sir John Smithe, to advertise us; for we know that her Majesty will be very glad to hear that this service is not neglected nor delayed; and besides these numbers above mentioned to be so thoroughly trained, you shall declare to the Deputy Lieutenants, that she would have them **to** give order that the rest of such as have been trained, not comprised in these former numbers of 2,000, may be also in some other places of the shire brought to musters and to be viewed, to be furnished with armour and **weapon,** [and kept] in good readiness, that if cause of service shall require they may be adjoined to the foresaid two thousand, to increase the forces of the same; and whatsoever number there be of others, being found able men and having armour and weapon, though they have not been trained, her Majesty requireth that they may also be in order under their leaders, with the armour and weapon, to be also called and adjoined to the trained numbers, not doubting but they also, adjoined with the soldiers trained, will shortly become good soldiers and servicable men for the defence of the county [counties].

"And for the continuance of these great numbers **of** footmen to **be** exercised so many days, which continuance may be over-burthenous to any one,* it shall be good to have them change the place of their encamping sundry times, and thereby to march from one place to another, being convenient for the purpose, to train them thereby; and according to such change of places, warning to be given to the towns and villages for to provide for their night lodgings and victualling, upon such reasonable prices to be rated by the authority of the Lieutenants, having regard **to** the wages allowed to the soldier, as well the horsemen as the footmen. .

"We think it necessary that you should see and view the **numbers** appointed by the Lieutenants Deputies to serve for the succour **of** Harwitche, and to consider whether they are trained and made apt, and furnished with armour and weapon meet for such a service; and what **you** shall find needful there to be reformed, and† to give your advice **how** the same may be done; and likewise to see the ground about the town, how it is meet to be entrenched and fortified for strengthening of the town against any sudden surprise, and therein also to give your advice to the townsmen, that have taken upon them the charge thereof, and to whom her Majesty hath given a 1,000*l.* in money for that purpose."

*Two-thirds of these Instructions are to the same effect as the rough draft dated 4 Dec., with corrections in Burghley's hand, in State Papers, Vol. 206, No. 7.*

F. 135. [1587.—The Privy Council to the Earl of Sussex.]

"Upon the return of Bryan FitzWilliams from thence and of William **Peierce** (*sic*) the ingenour there, we have, with conference with some of experience for that respect, considered both the platt of the town of Portsmouthe sent hither from your Lordship, as also the articles containing the several portions of works meet to be done according to the said platt, with the several sums of money required for the perfecting of the same works and other necessaries thereunto belonging, amounting to the total sum of 3,850*l.*; and in like sort the charges of a new bridge, and new gates for the town, with the charges for the same, amounting (besides the timber) to the sum of 190*l.* And for that the season of the year

---

* Place?　　　　† *Qu.* **omit** "and."

meet **for such** works is greatly past, her Majesty is resolved **to** have but certain parts of these works to be taken in hand and perfected before November (if the same may be), so far forth as shall or may amount to the sum of 1,650*l.* and no more. And therefore order is taken that 150 men (as labourers) more than are already, shall be prested, and sent thither out of Sussex and Hampshire ; praying your Lordship, according to this memorial signed by us, containing the portions of the works to be done, that your Lordship will give order to the said William Peerce, Wm. Spicer, and others that are to see the works furthered, that they with pioneers do their uttermost diligence to hasten the said works, with care to have the same well and substantially done, and so as no more of the walls of **the town be** opened at any time than may be speedily reforced (*sic*) **with new** working and fortifying."

F. 135. [1588, March ?]—" The Opinion of the Lord Gray, Sir Francis Knowles, Sir John Norris, Sir Richard Bingham, Sir Roger Williams, and others, what places were most likely the Enemy would land at, and what were most meet to be done to make head against him, with their answer to certain other propositions and heads set down by my Lords of the Council."

This title is written on **a slip of paper,** pasted **over what** was originally written. It differs from **the title of the** similar paper in *State Papers, Vol.* 209, *No.* 49, which **is** however **a** copy made in the 17th century; while *No.* 50, a contemporary copy, **has** a much shorter title, mentioning **no names.**

**The copy in the present** volume **differs** slightly from both the copies **among the** State **Papers, and** has **some** paragraphs which they do not contain, as follow :

" Also for th'increase of armed pikemen in this time of scarcity of armour, we do think it good that all the armed billmen may be converted to be made armed pikemen, and that **able billmen** unarmed should **be** levied and chosen in their places, because **the ranks** of billmen in **order** of battle are always environed and compassed about with pikemen, **for** the billmen serve specially for execution if the enemy in battle shall be overthrown. But here is to be noted that there must be reserved a few armed billmen **or** armed halbards to guard the ranks wherein **the ensigns** and **drums,** &c., are placed, in the order of battle." . . .

"**And** to conclude, when it shall be bruited in Spain **that** there are at **Plymothe** and other places such a number of armed soldiers, under **ensigns** and leaders, the number will be reported to be double or treble, so as **the** King of Spain, upon good probability, may conceive that those soldiers and such as are in other places upon the coast in like readiness are determined to land in Portugal or the Indias; the same opinion being fortified by the preparation of so many ships as are given in charge to be made ready in those parts by Sir Fra. Drake.

" We think it also very necessary, that throughout all the counties of the realm this proportion, as well amongst the armed and trained as the unarmed pikes and bills, may be observed, that is to say, that of every hundred there be 80 pikes and 20 bills.

" We think it is necessary also that some order and provision be taken by their Lordships that her Majesty's ships being at Rochester be not entrapped."

F 138. 1587 [–8], 30 Eliz., March 8, Manor of Greenwich.—The Queen to " the City of London."

" Trusty and well beloved, we greet you well. Whereas upon information given unto us of great preparations made **in** foreign parts with **intent** to attempt somewhat against this **our realm, we** gave present order that our said realm should be put in order of defence, which we have caused to be performed in all parts accordingly, saving in the City of London; we therefore, knowing your readiness by former experience to perform any service that well-affected subjects ought to yield to their Prince and Sovereign, do let you understand that within our said City, our pleasure is, there be forthwith put in a readiness to serve for defence of our own person upon such occasions as may fall out the number of 10,000 able men, furnished with armour and weapons convenient; of which number our meaning is that 6,000 be enrolled under captains and ensigns, and to be trained at times convenient, according to such further direction as you shall receive from our Privy Council under six of their hands, which our pleasure is you do follow from time to time in th'ordering and training of the said numbers of men. And these our letters shall be your sufficient warrant for the doing of the same. Given under our Signet."

F. 138. 1587[-8], March 11, the Court at Greenwich.—The Privy Council to Sir George Bonde, Lord Mayor of London, and his Brethren.

" Whereas the Queen's Majesty, having received divers advertisements of great preparations in foreign parts with intent and purpose to attempt somewhat in this our [her] realm, did providently give speedy order for to provide all things necessary to withstand any attempt or invasion that might be offered, and to that end did direct her letters unto you, thereby willing and requiring you to put in a readiness the number of 10,000 within the City and liberties of the same, being the principal and chief City in all the realm, to serve as well for the defence of the same, as for the safeguard of her Majesty's person, if need should so require, whereof 6,000 were to be enrolled and to be reduced under captains and ensigns; and for the better ordering and disposing of the said soldiers, you were required to follow such directions as you should from time to time receive from us :

" These are therefore to let you understand that we have thought good to require our loving friends Sir Fraunces Knowles, knight, Treasurer of her Majesty's Household, and Sir John Norris, knight, to confer with you in that behalf, to appoint a convenient time for the better training of the said 6,000, and for the better ordering and sorting them with armour and weapons, and reducing the same under captains and ensigns, to th'end that they may be trained and made apt to use their weapons and disciplined, whereby they may be the more serviceable and better instructed to serve, either for the defence of the said City, or to join with that army that shall be appointed for the defence of her Majesty's person, as occasion shall serve; and that th'other 4000 men may also have their several armour and weapons appointed unto them, and to be commanded to be in readiness to serve also in case of necessity for like purposes as is aforesaid ; wherein we are to pray you that you will use th'advice and help of Mr. Treasurer, and omit no care and diligence to see this her Majesty's pleasure put in execution, tending to your own preservation and safeguard, as becometh all good subjects to do, and to advertise us of th'order you have taken as well in the training of the 6,000, as having in readiness the residue."

Signed: Chr. Hatton, Canc., W. Burghley, Ro. Leicester, Fra. Walsingham, Tho. Heneage, Jo. Wolley.

F. 140. 1588, April 2, Greenwich.—The Privy Council to the [Lords] Lieutenants.

See State Papers, Vol. 209, No. 62.

This copy has the following note in the margin:

u 93210.

C

" **There is** answer made to this letter by all the Lieutenants (saving the **Earl of** Huntingdon, for the North parts), whereof the certificates **remain** in the Council chest, and an abstract with Mr. Secretary."

F. 140. 1588, April 2, **the Court at** Greenwich.—Mr. Secretary to the Lords Lieutenants.

*See State **Papers, Vol.** 209, No.* 63 (*addressed to those of Sussex only*).

This copy has the following note in the margin :

" To this there is answer made by some few of the **Lieutenants,** whereof the certificates remain with Mr. Secretary."

F. 140*b*. 1588, April 6.—The Queen to the [Lords] Lieutenants.
*See State Papers, Vol.* 209, *No.* 73.

This copy has the following notes in the margin :

" To this letter Sir John Norris hath delivered his answer in writing **for** the counties of Dorset [and] Southampton, but not for Sussex and Kent, being hindered by the approaching of the Spanish fleet and assembling of her Majesty's army at Tilbury.

" Sir Thomas Laiton [Leighton] hath likewise made his report for the counties of Norfolk and Suffolk, but not for Essex, being called away by a pres (*sic*); and their **reports remain** with Mr. Secretary." (*See also* f. 143.)

F. 140*b*. 1588, April 6.—Warrant for **Sir** John Norris, Sir Thomas Laiton, and Sir Thomas Morgan.
*See State Papers, Vol.* 209, *No.* **72.**

**F. 141.** 1588, April.—" The Names of the Captains chosen by Sir John Norris to go with him in his Journey to Sussex, Dorset, Hampshire, [and] Kent :—

" Capt. Wilson, Capt. Crispe, Capt. Dawtrye, Capt. Antonie Wingefeilde, Capt. Ric. Wingefeilde, Capt. Harte, Capt. Geo. Pettye, Capt. Greene, Capt. Sampson.

" The Names of such Captains as are chosen by Sir Thomas Laiton to accompany him in his Journey to Essex, Suffolk [and] Norfolk :—

" Capt. Havers, Capt. Elmes, Mr. Edmonde Yorcke, Capt. Westrope, Capt. Piper, Raulf Lane, Capt. Twittie, Capt. Barnishe, Capt. Smithe, Capt. Tanner."

" Note, that **Sir Tho. Morgan,** appointed **to repair to Somerset,** Gloucestershire, **and** Wales, did not go."

**F. 142.** 1588, April 12.—" Instructions given to Sir John Norris **and** other Martial men sent into the Maritime Counties."

" Forasmuch as it is greatly to be doubted that, in case th'enemy should attempt to make any descent into any of the maritime counties, for lack of some good established orders, both for the impeaching of his landing and descent, and the choice of **some** apt and fit places for retreat of forces to withstand him, and **for the** erecting of a body of an army to make head against him, **great confusion** is like to fall out, to the dismaying of the good subjects **and the** encouraging of th'enemy : It is thought meet **by** her Majesty that **some** persons of skill and judgment should **be sent down to** confer with the several Lieutenants of the **mari-time** counties **for the** establishing of some such good orders, whereby **the** confusion **likely to ensue** may be avoided. And for that there hath **been** special **choice** made of you in respect of your skill in martial affairs, to take a view of the counties of A. B. and C.* D., you shall, with as **much** speed as you may, make your repair to the said counties,

---

* Should be " C. and."

beginning at the county of C., and so to **continue and** proceed in the viewing of the said several counties, until you shall **have** finished the service, according to the directions hereafter following. .

" First, you shall receive our **letters directed to** the several Sheriffs of the counties committed to your charge, by the which **they** are required to notify unto the Lieutenants of the several counties that her Majesty's pleasure is, that they repair to the shire town of each county, **or** to the principal place in the said county usually accustomed for such assembly, to meet with you at such time as by your particular letter shall be signified unto the said Sheriff. You shall at the assembly make the **said** Lieutenants or their Deputies acquainted with the cause of you repair thither, and require them, by virtue of such letters as you shall receive from her Majesty for that purpose, to assist you in the service committed to your charge.

" And first, for the viewing of the places of descent, you shall let them understand that her Majesty's pleasure is, that both they and you shall repair to the said places accompanied only with such persons as are men of skill and trust, for it is thought convenient that there should not be many acquainted with the danger and weakness of the **said** places.*

" And after a view taken of the said places, you shall, after conference had with the said Lieutenants, deliver unto the said Lieutenants, in writing, your best advice for the impeaching of th'enemy's descent, as also how the forces of the country may make their retreat with safety and honour to such places of strength as by you shall be thought meet.

" Amongst other things it shall be very requisite that some of the best trained bands within that county, and best furnished with martial men, be appointed to impeach the said descent, to be executed according to such direction as by you shall be given to the said Lieutenants, with the advice of such captains as you shall **leave** there to assist the **Lieutenants**, and to see due execution of such **advice as** you shall leave **with** them in writing.

" After the view of the said places of descent, you shall then consider of some fit place within the said counties that by situation with the help of some rivers **or** other straits shall be most fit, with use and assistance of the pioneer, **to be put in some** such strength **as** may be able to make head unto the enemy, and to stay his incursions until such time as the forces of other counties appointed to yield assistance shall repair thither, **as also** until they shall receive order and direction from her Majesty, **how to** proceed and deal with the enemy.

" And forasmuch as nothing will be more necessary for the strengthening of **such** places of defence upon the sudden, than the use of many pioneers and other necessary artificers ; you shall require the said Lieutenants in her Majesty's name to take a special care to have such numbers of pioneers in a readiness as by you shall be thought sufficient for **the** strengthening of the said places of retreat, and to see that there may **be provision** made of mattocks, spades, shovels, and all other necessaries **fit to be used** and employed in that service by the said pioneers.

" You **shall also** give direction unto the said Lieutenants, how such horsemen as are within the said counties may be best employed in the champion and plain places of the said counties as well for the annoying of

---

* *Note in the margin :*—Because the **Isles** of Sheppie **and Tenet** are of most **danger,** you shall let them understand that her Majesty's pleasure is, that both they **and you** should repair —— (*blank*) Isles and other places of descent upon that **coast.**

the enemy as for the defence in the retreat of such bands as shall be used in the impeaching of th'enemy's descent.

" You shall also take a view in the said counties of the several bands both of horsemen and footmen; and in case you shall find them not sufficiently trained, or not that choice made of the men, or so sufficiently furnished with armour and weapon, as appertaineth, you shall require the said Lieutenants in her Majesty's name to see the said defects speedily reformed, and to take order with the said captains, whom you shall leave in the said counties, as well to put the said Lieutenants in mind to see speedy redress of the said defects, as also to employ themselves in the training of the said bands, as well horse as foot.

"Amongst other matters of importance fit to be ordered, you shall confer with the said Lieutenants, in case th'enemy shall take footing a-land, how there may be good order taken for the removing into the inland parts of the county of all manner of cattle, victuals, and other necessaries that may in any sort relieve th'enemy, and to see the places of retreat furnished with a convenient portion of victuals for the number of the forces that shall be there placed.

" For execution whereof it shall be meet that some special persons be appointed that shall be men of some credit and discretion, fit for that service, for that otherwise it is likely there will fall out great confusion. You shall also confer with the said Lieutenants about the due execution of some necessary points contained in [such] former instructions as have been heretofore given unto them, (whereof you shall have a copy,) so far forth as they shall not be found repugnant unto these present instructions.

"And for her Majesty's satisfaction in the mean time until your return, you shall certify from time to time how you find the state of the said several counties, after you have taken a view of them, and shall send a copy of such directions as you shall leave with the said Lieutenants.

"And whereas this service might seem to require many other particular directions, forasmuch as by these instructions it might appear unto you, that her Majesty's intention is to have the forces of those counties to be made apt and in a readiness for service, and all things necessary for defence provided accordingly upon conference with the Lords Lieutenants or Deputies and view of the forces and state of the country, you shall be able to consider and conceive what you think further meet to be done in that behalf; wherein, and in all things meet to adorn* this service, you shall give your best advice to the said Lieutenants, and direction for th'executing of that which shall be thought requisite."

F. 143. *Note:* "Here wanteth the return of Sir John Norris['s] answer to these Instructions above recited for the counties allotted to him, and likewise Sir Thomas Leighton's for the counties allotted to him, and Sir Richard Grenfield's for Cornwall and Devon." (*See also f.* 140*b.*)

*The rest of f.* 143 *is cut off.*

F. 144. 1588, April [or later].—"Abstracts of the Certificates returned from the Lieutenants of the able men and trained men in the several counties upon letters from their Lordships in April 1588."

The number of able men in each county is stated, and how many of them were " furnished." The latter were divided into " trained " and " untrained," each class being subdivided into companies, the names of whose Captains are stated. The forces are further distinguished as " men," " shot " (partly calivers, partly muskets), " corslets," " bows,"

---

* *Qu.* advance.

and "bills." Particulars **are also given of the** quantities of arms, ammunition, carts or carriages, **nags, &c. At the end** of each county are the numbers of lances, light-horsemen, and petronels. Pioneers and musq[ueteers] are mentioned under some counties. The Captains' names are as follow :—

*Sussex :* Tho. Palmer, Tho. Leuknor, Tho. Stanny, Tho. Bushop, Hen. Shelley, Wal. Coverte, Rich. Shelley, Nic. Parker, Jo. Lunford, Jo. Culpeper, Adam Ashburnam. Lances, 20, Capt. —— ; lighthorse, 204, Capt. —— ; petronels, 30, Capt. Anto. Shirley.

*Surrey* Sir Tho. Browne, Geo. Morte (or More), Wiᵐ Gainsford, Poynings Heron, Nicho. Munger, Rich. Hill, Rich. Leiford, Tho. Gardener. Lances 8, and lighthorse 98, Capt. Rich. Broune ; petronels 29, Capt. James Lugler.

*Berks :* Sir Hen. Nevie [Nevil ?], **Tho. Parry,** Hum. Forster, Edw. Umpton, Chr. Lideot. Lances 10, **Capt.** —— ; lighthorse 95, Capt. —— ; petronels 2, Capt. ——.

*Gloucester :* Charles Bridges **and Jo.** Tracie ; Sir Henry Poole and Ant. Hungerford ; Sir Rich. Barckley and Tho. Throgmorton ; **Tho.** Baina (*sic*) and Wm. **Bridges** ; Gilbert Reade, Hen. Winston, Geo. Huntley, Jo. Banham. Lances 20, and lighthorse 180, [Captains] Wm. Ducton, Hen. Bridges, Geo. Huntlie, Tho. Lucy ; petronels 35, Capt. ——.

*Essex :* Sir Jo. Peter, Sir Tho. Lucas, Maxy, Wrothe, Purton, Weston, Harrys, Barrington. Lances 50, Capt. Capel ; lighthorse **50,** Capt. Smithe ; do. 50, Capt. Leighe ; do. 50, Capt. Barnish ; do. 50, **Capt.** Walgrave.

*Southampton :* Lord Marquis [of Winchester], Earl [of] Sussex.

*Norfolk :* Sir Hen. Woodhous, Christopher Heiden, Ed. Cleeres, esq., Henry Doylie, esq., Tho. Townesende, Jo. Rippes, esq., Basingb. Gawdy. Lances 80, Captain Gressam, esq. ; lighthorse 321, under captain[s] of 50 ; petronels 374, under captain[s] of 50 ; petronels of the Just' (*sic*), 53, Captain Fra. Clere, gent.

*Suffolk :* Sir Robert Wingfeilde, Sir Philip **Parnar, Sir Robert** Jermyn, **Sir** Arth. Henningham, Sir Nicholas Bacon, **Sir Jo. Heygham,** Sir Tho. Barmaidon (*sic*), Sir Wm. Springe, Sir Wm. **Walgrave,** Robert Forde, esq. Lances 70 ; lighthorse 230.

*Kent :* Sir Hen. Palmer and Ed. Boise, esq. ; Sir Tho. Scott ; Sir Ric. Baker and Jo. Cobham, esq. ; Sir Tho. Fane, Tho. Fane, esq., and Jo. Loueson,* esq. ; Justin Campney, Ed. Stile, esq., and Tho. Willoughby ; Hen. Crispe, Ed. Crispe, Erasm. Finche. Lances 64 ; .ighthorse 80, Capt. Tho. Palmer ; do. 45, Capt. Tho. Scott ; do. 40, .Capt. Wm. Cromer ; do. 50, **Capt.** Roger Twis[d]en ; do. 50, Sampson Leonard ; aryolets 300, under **captains of 60** a-piece ; petronels 84, to attend the Lord Lieutenant.

*Lancaster :* (*blank*). Lances 20 ; lighthorse **50.**

**Cheshire** : (*blank*). Lances **30** ; lighthorse 50.

**Lincoln :** Sir Wm. Wray, Geo. St. Pooles (or Poole), Charles Bolles, Valentius (*sic*) Browne, Charles Hussey, Barth. Armyn (or Armine), Robert Carre, junior, Rich. Ogle, Wm. Thumbleby. Lances 30, Capt. Charles Dimock ; lighthorse 150, —— ; petronels 91, ——.

*Oxford :* **Geo.** Pettie, Jo. Doily, Owen Ogelthorpe, Rich. Ferris, **Ed.** Braie. Lances **23** ; lighthorse 130 ; petronels 37.

*Dorset :* **Sir** Henry Asheley, Sir Jo. Horsey, Sir **Rich. Rogers,** Geo. Trenohe [Trenchard].† Jo. Shongwas [Strangways].† **Lances** 120,

---

* "Tho. Leueson" in another place.
† *Cf.* State Papers, Vol. 209, No. 1.

Captain[s] Ralph Horsey, Tho. Hussey; lighthorse 0; **petronels** 40, Capt. Tho. Earle.

*Devon :* Sir Wm. Courtney, Sir Robert Dennis, Hugh **Fortescue,** Hugh Pollard, Antony Monk, **Sir Jo.** Gilberte, Rich. Champernon, Tho. Fulforde. **Lances ——;** they **find not** but musquets instead of them; lighthorse **150.**

*Derby:* Wm. Kinveton (*sic*), Wm. Millward. Lances 18, Capt. Tho. Grasly; lighthorse 50; petronels 22.

*Stafford :* Ralph Sneede, Tho. Horwoode. Lances **18,** [and] lighthorse, 50, Capt. Walter Harcourt; petronels 26.

*Bucks :* Wm. Burlacy, Alexander Hampden, Tho. Pigotte, Ed. Tirrell. Lances 18, Capt. Rich. Craiford; lighthorse 83 , petronels 20.

***Nottingham :*** **Jo.** Basset, esq., Wm. Sutton, **esq.** Lances 20 ; lighthorse 60 **[and] petronels** 20, Robert Markham, esq., capt.

*Cornwall :* **Sir** Richard Greenvile, Rich. Carewe, Ed. Coswarthe, Wm. Bevil, Jo. Carminowe, Jo. Arundel. Lances 4 ; lighthorse 96.

*Somerset :* Sir Geo. Sidnam, Sir Hen. Barckley, Sir Jo. Stowel, **Sir** Jo. Clifton, Arthur Stopton (*sic*). Lances 50 ; lighthorse 250 ; petronels, 60.

*Wilts :* Sir Jea. [James] Marvin, Sir **Tho.** Wroghton, Sir Jo. Davers, Sir Hen. Knevet. Lances **15** ; lighthorse **100** ; petronels **10.**

*Cambridge :* Jo. Cotton, Sir Fra. Hinde, **Tho.** Northe. Lances 14 ; lighthorse 40 ; petronels 80.

*Northampton :* Robert Knolles, **Thomas** Barnaby, Fra. Nicols, Wm. **Browne.** Lances, 20 ; lighthorse 80.

*Huntingdon :* Geo. Wanton (*sic*), Oliver Cromwel.

*Middlesex :* Robert Wrothe, Wm. Fleetwood. Lances 19 and lighthorse 65, Capt. John Machel of Hack (*sic*).

*Hertford :* Jo. Leventhorp, **Edw.** Poulter, Roul. Litton, Sir **Jo.** Cuttes, Edm. Varney. **Lances 20, Tho.** Sadler, capt.; lighthorse **60,** Ed. Newport.

F. 151. [1588.]—"**London.** A perfect collection made out of **the** general Certificates, delivered under the hands of the Aldermen, of **all** the able **men for** service from the age of 17 years to 60, as well English as Strangers, resident within the several Wards in the City of London; together with the number of such persons suspected for religion within the same Wards."

The number of men **in each Ward is specified** ; total, 17,083. (The number of persons **suspected is *not* stated**.)

**F. 151*b*.** [1588.]—"The particular how every Ward in London **was charged** for the furnishing of the first 6,000 men to be trained, and **the 4,000** men that were only armed."

The total number required from each **ward** is stated, and is then separated into two portions, one under the head of " For the first charge of 6,000 men," the other under the head of " For the second charge of 4,000." The first division is further subdivided into shot, corslets with pikes, and corslets or jacks with bills. The second division consisted of calivers, bows, bills, and pikes.

**F. 152*b*.** [1588.]—"The distribution of the whole 10,000 men put in readiness in London, reduced into bands under Captains, **and** how they **were** sorted with weapons."

Able men, 20,000, whereof furnished 10,000, **viz.,** trained 6,000, untrained 4,000.

The trained men were divided into **four** Regiments, each of 1,500, and are distinguished **as shot**, pikes, and bills. The names of their Captains are **as** follow :

1st Regiment: Gawen Smith, Portsoken Ward ; **Benjamin** Anis, Algat Ward ; John **Audley**, Tower Ward ; Nicholas Stoderd, **Tower** Ward ; **William** Towerson, Billingsgat ; Chr. Webb, **Billingsgat**; Richard Morris, Bridg Ward ; Jo. Joles (or Jolles), Langburn ; **Tho.** Ferris, Limestret ; Thomas Smith, Bushopsgat.

2nd Regiment : William Bouser, Cornehil ; Mr. Barrett, Brodstret ; George Barnes, Colmanstret ; Robert Offeley, Bassingshaw ; Jerrat Gore, Criplegat ; Baptist Hasel, Creplegat ; Anto. Gall, Criplegat ; James Anton, St. Martin's ; Martin Bond, Aldersgat ; Samuel Saltonstall, Cheap.

3rd Regiment : **William Becher**, Farington without ; Tho. Parvish, Farington without ; Geo. Leister, Farington without ; Mr. Loo (or Loe), Farington without ; Mr. Swinerton, Farington [with]out ; Wm. Meggs, Farington without ; Mr. Martin, Farington within ; Anto. Wolcoke, Farington within ; **Jo. Martin, Farington within** ; Hugh Loo (or Loe), Bainard **Castle**.

4th **Regiment** : Edm. **Person**, Castle Baynard ; Arnold Rote, Quenhive ; **Wm. Powel, Bredstret** ; Baptist Hicks, Bredestret ; Michael **Pollison, Vintry** ; **Nicholas Heth** (or Heath), Cordwainer ; Mr. Dobson, **Cordwainer** ; **Henry Campion**, Dougat ; Wm. Chambers, Walbrook ; **Wm. Bloum, Candlewick** stret.

**The untrained men** were divided into four Regiments of 1,000 each, **and are distinguished** as calivers, pikes, bows, and bills. **The names of their Captains are precisely** the same as those given above, each **captain having 150 trained and 100** untrained men under him.

F. 154. [1588.]—" Abstract **of the** Certificates under the Presidentship of Wales, upon letters written the 2nd of April 1588."

This is similar in form to the Abstract **on f. 144** *seq.* **The names of** the Captains are as follow :

*Salop :* Edmond **Scriven**, esq., Fra. Bromley, esq., **Wm. Olladd**, esq., Ro. Needham, Ro. **Corbet**, Ed. Hussey.

*Denbigh :* Kenrich Tyton, **esq.**, John Winedward, Ed. Loyde, esq., Peiers Salisbury, Joh. Jones, esq., Wm. Bowen, gent.

*Flint :* Tho. Evans, esq., Rich. Trevor, esq., Wm. Mostin, esq.

*Carmarthen :* Char. Vaughan, Tho. Powell, Redds (*sic*) Gwyn de Roose, Lewes (*sic*) William, James Puthrogh, Fra. Loyd, Ed. Donlee.

*Radnor :* Tho. Lewes, esq., Clement Price, esq.

*Anglesey :* (*blank*).

*Worcester :* Geo. **Winter, Robert Acton**, Fra. Ketley, Tho. Brydges.

*Montgomery :* Ric. **Harberte, esq.**, Oliver Loyd, **esq.**, Tho. Innos (*sic*), esq., Morgan Gwyn, esq.

*Pembroke :* Wm. Warren, John ap **Rice, Hugh Butler, Jo.** Phillipps, **Jo. Butler**, Wm. Wogan, villa Haverford **West**.

F. 159. 1574–1588.—" Abstract of the lances **and** light horse throughout the realm from anno 1574 to anno 1588."

The numbers in 48 counties of England and Wales, the Cinque Ports, the cities of Gloucester and Chester, and the towns of Southampton and Colchester, are stated.

F. 161. 1588.—" Certificate **of lances, light horse, and** petronells throughout the realm."

The numbers in 34 counties of England and Wales are stated.

F. 164. [1588.]—"Abstract of the Certificates of the Noblemen and others of such numbers of horse and foot as they made offer to furnish, to attend upon her Majesty's person."[*]

Lord Chancellor : lances 50, light horse 50, footmen 300.

Lord Treasurer : la. 50, li. 50.

Earl of Warwick : la. 100, li. 50, f. 20.

Earl of Essex : lances 180, petronels 64, foot 50.

Lord Chamberlain : la. 80.

Earl of Worcester : la. 6, li. 24.

Lord Mountague : la. 20, li. 60, p. 20, f. 148 [238 ?], the last including corslets 100, calivers 72, bows 30, bills 36.

Lord Morley : li. 10, f. 100 (incl. calivers 70, musq. 30).

Lord **Lumley** : la. 10, li. 30, p. 10, f. 20.

**Lord** Sturton : **la.** 6, li. 14.

Lord Sandes : la. and li. 10.

Lord North : la. 30, p. 30, f. 80.

Lord Dacres : la. 10, li. 10, p. 10, f. 80 (incl. corsl. 40, cal. 20, musq. 20).

Lord Darcy : la. 10, li. 10, p. 10.

Lord Windsor : la. 24, li. 10.

Lord Compton : la. 8, li. 20, **p. 10.**

Lord Mordant : la. 20, li. 10.

Sir Tho. Henneag : la. 40, p. 10.

Sir Fra. Walsingham : la. 50, **p. 10, f.** 200.

Sir Wa. **Mildmay :** la. 5, li. 15, p. 8.

Mr. Wolley : **la.** 10, li. 14.

Mr. Fortescue : la. 20, li. 20.

Sir Hen. Cromwel : la. 15, li. 15.

Sir Edw. Wingfeld : la. 20, f. 150.

Sir Hen. Godere : la. 10, f. 150.

Mr. Pointz : la. **20.**

Sum of the **lances, 1,029**; light horse, **422**; petronels, 159 = 1,610. Footmen, 1,448. In all, 3,058.

"Beside the **ordinary bands of** the Pensioners, and her **Majesty's** household servants."

F. 166. [1588.]—"Abstract of the Certificates of the Clergy of such numbers of horse and foot as they made offer to furnish, to attend upon her Majesty's person."

It shows the numbers, to be supplied from 17 dioceses, of lances, light horse, petronels, and foot, the last including corslets, calivers, musq[uets], bows, and bills, "holberds" being mentioned in some cases. The Bishops of London, Salisbury, and Coventry and Lichfield made separate contributions, in addition to the numbers furnished by their dioceses. "Men in all, 4,444."

F. 168. [1588, June.]—"The names of the **Martial** men certified from the several counties.

This schedule is arranged under the heads of " counties "—" names "—" quality "—" places of service."

*Sussex :* Thomas Lewcknor, lieutenant ; hath served a lieutenant in Ireland and the Low Countries. John Vaghan, captain and muster-master. Wm. Henworthe, captain ; an old soldier.

*Berkshire :* Wm. Bowyere. Henry Drury, captain. —— Rowles. **Hen.** Shippam. Branch'in (*sic*) Lovell.

---

[*] *Cf.* f. 172, 172*b*.

*Gloucester :* Charles Bridges, esq., captain ; **served** the Emperor Charles in Germany, with charge of horsemen and **footmen**. Sir John Tracy, knight, captain ; at St. Quintines, and in Low **Countries**. Henry Bridges, esq., captain ; at Liethe served with charge **of** footmen. George Blockley, lieutenant ; at St. Quintines. John Izod, lieutenant ; a lieutenant in Flanders. John Stubbs, gent., lieutenant ; at St. Quintines. Hugh Powell, gent., lieutenant ; in Scotland under Colonel Morgan. Henry Poole, gent., lieutenant ; in Ireland almost 14 years. Arthur Powell, gent., lieutenant ; in the Low Countries. Rich. Thomas, gent., ensigner (*sic*) to Sir John Tracie ; in the Low Countries. **Wm.** Churchey, corporal ; in the Low Countries. Ed. Draper, corporal ; **in** Ireland under Captain Cornewall.

*Devon :* Sir Thomas Dennis, knight ; in Flanders. Wm. Birckham, esq. ; **at Newhaven and in** Ireland. Gawen Champernon, esq. ; **in** France **and Ireland. Arthur** Champernon ; **in** France and the **Low** Countries. **Humfrey More** ; in France and Flanders. Hugh Earthe ; at Newhaven. **Lewis Argenton** ; at Newhaven and in Ireland. Roger Gifford ; **in** France. **Thomas Predeaux** ; **at Newhaven** and in Ireland. Thomas **Courtney** ; **in France and Ireland. Arthur Harte** ; **in Ireland** and Flanders. **Wm. Harte** ; **in Ireland. Wm. Yere** ; **in Ireland.** Arthur Gifford ; **in Ireland. Giles Carpenter** ; **in Ireland and Flanders.** Wm. Stowford ; **in Flanders.**

*Derby :* Sir Tho. Cockain ; **an old man.**

*Stafford :* **Sir** Walter Aston, knight, captain ; at Liethe with charge **of 300.** Richard Aston, esq., captain ; in the Low Countries, 200. Tho. Gresley, lieutenant ; at Lyethe. Richard Greene, ensign ; at Lyethe, **to** Sir Walter Aston. Ed. Harcourt, captain ; in Ireland and the Low **Countries**. Tho. Rigley ; in Ireland under the Earl of Essex. Francis Grymes ; **in** the Low Countries hath had charge. Nicholas Brereton ; in the Low Countries. Roger Stamford ; at Boloyne.

*Essex, Worcester, Norfolk, Suffolk, and Kent,* not certified.

*Buckingham :* Henry Drury, lieutenant ; in the Low Countries. John Oplett, corporal ; in the Low Countries. Richard Dollen, corporal, in the **Low** Countries. Thomas Tucker, ensign ; in the **Low** Countries. George Walter, ensign, at Newhaven. Henry Cannon, serjeant ; **in** the Low Countries, the same office. John Owen, serjeant ; in the Low Countries. Sherington Ardis, an ensign ; in the Low Countries. Mathew Tedder, an ensign ; in Ireland. George Cockney, **serjeant** ; **in the Low** Countries. James Kinge, serjeant ; in the Low **Countries. Michael** Harcourt, esq., captain ; at Leythe, in France, and **in the Low Countries.** Edward Harcourt, lieutenant ; in the Low Countries. **William Jackson, serjeant** ; in the Low Countries. Richard Craiford, esq. ; ———.

*Surrey :* John Nelson, **a** serjeant. Baldwin Hurst, a serjeant. Thomas Kinge, corporal. Edward Plasted, a lieutenant. Henry Drury, captain. George Waters, corporal. Thomas Baldwin, serjeant. Garret Rombol, serjeant. Thomas Carpenter, lieutenant. Wm. Sares, serjeant. John Wines, serjeant. Wm. Monday, ensign. Peter Versant, **a** serjeant. James Johnson, lieutenant. John Thomas, a corporal. Rowland Hampson, a serjeant.

*Oxford :* Michael Dorner, gent., captain ; in Flanders, of horse. Wm. Cornewall, gent., captain ; in the Low Countries. Edmond Bray, gent., captain ; hath had charge of footmen in the Low Countries. George Pettie, gent., captain ; of foot **in** the **Low** Countries. ——— Roper, **gent., lieutenant** ; **of horse** in **the Low Countries.** Ralph Doilee, gent., lieutenant; of foot in the Low Countries. John Edge, gent., lieutenant; of foot in the Low Countries. Nicholas Paine, ensign; ———. John Hall, serjeant; in the Low Countries.

*Cornwall:* ——— Dowdall, captain. ——— Hewes, captain. John Chamonde, gent., captain, hath had a charge in the Low Countries by the Prince of Orenge. Justinian Tackarne (*sic*), lieutenant; was a lieutenant at Newhaven.

*Southamᵖton:* Anthony Deeringe, gent., captain; a soldier of 10 years' continuance. Hambden Powlet, gent., captain; hath had charge in the Low Countries. Ed. A Baroughe, gent., captain; hath served 5 or 6 years in the Low Countries, and Ireland; thought meet for a charge. Ed. Deeringe, gent.; hath served both in Ireland and Flanders. William Cotton, gent.; hath served in Ireland. Ed. Norton, gent.; hath served both in Ireland and Flanders. Wm. Abarre, lieutenant; hath been a lieutenant both in Ireland and Flanders. William Wroughton, gent.; a forward gent. Wadham Foster, gent., lieutenant; was a lieutenant a short time in Flanders. Gilbert Tichborne, a very sufficient man of long service, but a Papist obstinate.

F. 170*b*. A schedule, over which a blank leaf is pasted.

F. 171. 1588, June 15.—[The Queen] to the Lord President of Wales.

*See* **State Papers, Vol. 211, Nos. 23, 24.**

**F. 171. 1588, June 15.—The Queen to Sir John** Perrott. *Ibid. No. 25.*

**F. 171*b*. 1588, June 15.—[The Privy** Council] to the Lords Lieutenants.

" The Queen's Majesty being certainly advertised, that the King of Spain's navy is already abroad on the seas, and gone to the coast of Biscaie, whereby it is to be doubted the same may take some course to make some attempt on such part of the realm as shall be thought fit for his purpose, whereof as yet we cannot know any certainty; for which respect her Majesty hath thought it convenient your Lordship should be advertised thereof, to th'end you may give present order to all the gentlemen that are captains and leaders of men in that county, in no wise to be absent out of the shire, and to have especial care that the numbers of the several bands be full and complete, to which end notice shall be given, and straight commandment to all the soldiers of the trained bands in like manner to remain in the country, and no wise to be out of the way, that upon an hour's warning there [they] may be in a readiness to be employed as occasion shall serve, upon pain to be committed to prison the space of ——— days, and further punished at the discretion of your Lordship or your Deputy Lieutenants ; of which bands it is thought expedient that there should be a present view taken, that they and their furniture may be certainly seen to be complete and thoroughly furnished.

" We are likewise to pray your Lordship, that the like care be had to see the beacons watched in such sort as hath been appointed, and those other orders put in execution and duly observed with all speed and diligence, which have been set down and devised for the better defence of the realm, and for preparing and putting in readiness with convenient speed the forces of the said county.

" And because in such doubtful times it falleth out commonly that divers false rumours and reports are given forth and spread abroad, which do distract the minds of the people and breed confusion, it is thought very requisite a care should be had thereof, and that the authors of such rumours and tales should be diligently **found out** from time to time, and severally and speedily punished. For better **execution** whereof, because there are very many vagrant **and** idle persons, that go about the country fit to be evil instruments of **all** bad actions, it is also thought very requisite at this present, for the chastising **of** such lewd persons, and preventing these inconveniences that by them may any ways arise, that you shall appoint a Provost Martial [Marshal], according to the authority your Lordship [hath?] by your commission of Lieutenancy, to peruse the country, and to be arrested [assisted?] in all places by justices and constables, for the apprehension and stocking **and** imprisoning of them if they will not give themselves to labour; wherein, praying your Lordship that speedy direction be given in this behalf, **we** bid your Lordship heartily farewell, for at this time **no** delays, nor **any** slackness is to be used."

**F.** 172. **1588, June 2,** Greenwich.— [The Queen] to "sundry Noblemen." (**See next** entry, f. **172** b.)

" Right trusty **and well** beloved, we greet you well. Being credibly given to understand that the great preparations of foreign forces, whereof heretofore **we** have had sundry advertisements, and [are?] certainly intended to be employed against this our realm, not only for invading **the** same, but also with full resolution and a tyrannous intent to make a conquest thereof, and all under the colour and pretence of the advancement of the Romish and Papistical Religion: We have therefore thought necessary to put our realm in some more speedy order of defence, generally, not doubting but, through the goodness of Almighty God (who, from the first entrance into our kingdom, hath as it were miraculously preserved us and our dominions against all the malicious attempts and designs of our enemies, which have been many), **we** shall be able, with the fidelity, valour, and constancy of our natural good subjects, to withstand anything that shall be attempted against us and **our** realm, to his high glory, and their confusion.

"And for that we have always assured ourselves, amongst the rest **of** our nobility, of your faithfulness towards us and our service, and knowing how greatly it importeth those of your degree and calling, having that interest that you have in the honour, liberty, and surety of the state of this our realm, **to** employ **both** your lives and goods in defending and preserving the same from the intended conquest; considering the infinite and unspeakable miseries that do always fall out upon any such accidents and change, if the same should not in time be withstood; **which miseries** do well appear by the cruel and tyrannous government **in other** countries not far distant, what pretence soever is made otherwise **for** the cause of religion; we doubt **not** but **that** you will make it apparent and manifest to the world, how greatly **you** are devoted unto us and the service of our realm, your natural country, and how ready you are to employ yourself and all your forces in so necessary and dutiful an action. For which purpose we do look that **you** should put yourself in a readiness to attend upon our person, with such a convenient number of lances and lighthorses as may stand with your ability, to be ready **to** repair hither at such time as you shall receive notice of our pleasure **by** our Privy Council. And so nothing doubting of your forwardness herein, we require you, as soon as you may, to signify to our Privy Council what numbers of horsemen you shall be able to have in readiness furnished, as well of your household as of others **that are** retaining to you. Given under our Signet."

*Notes in margin*: (1) " Penned by Mr. Secretary."

(2) " **To this** the answer of some few noblemen **was** returned to Mr. Secretary, and a certificate of their trains, which remain with him, but I think the perfect certificates was [were] delivered **to the** Lord Chamberlain." *

F. 172*b*. [1588, June.]—"The names of the Lords to whom her Majesty's letters were directed, requiring them to attend on her person.

| | | |
|---|---|---|
| L. Audley | cert. L. Sandes. | L. Compton. |
| cert. L. Morley. | cert. L. Windsore. | **E.** Hereford. |
| cert. L. Dacres of the | L Weintworthe. | **E.** Northumber- |
| South | L. Mordante | land. |
| cert. L. Dudley. | cert. L. Riche. | cert. E. Worsester. |
| cert. **L. Sturton.** | L. **Darcy.** | cert. E. Lincolne. |
| L. **Lumbley.** | | cert. L. Montague." |

**F. 172*b*. 1588,** June—, Manor of Greenwich.—The **Queen to** the **Lords** Lieutenants.

" Right trusty and right well beloved Cousin and Councillor, **we greet** you well. Whereas heretofore, upon advertisement from time to time and from sundry places of the great preparations of foreign forces, with a full intention to invade this our realm, and other our dominions, we gave our directions unto you for the preparing of our subjects within your lieutenancy to be in readiness and defence against any attempt that might be made against us and our realm; which our directions we find so well performed, as we cannot but receive great contentment thereby, both in respect of your careful proceedings therein, as also of the great willingness of our people in general to the accomplishment of that whereunto they were required, showing thereby their great love and loyalty towards us, which as we accept most thankfully at their hands, acknowledging ourself infinitely bound to Almighty God in that it hath pleased him to bless us with so loving and dutiful subjects, so would we have you make it known unto them : Forasmuch as we find the same intention not only of invading, but of making a conquest also of this our realm, now constantly more and more detected and con-firmed as a matter **fully** resolved on, an army being already put **to the** seas for that **purpose,** although we doubt not, by God's goodness, the same shall prove frustrate, we have therefore thought good to will and require you forthwith, with as much convenient speed as **you** may, to call together, at some convenient place or places, the best **sort** of gent[lemen] under your lieutenancy, and to declare unto them that, considering these great preparations and threatenings now burst out in **action** upon the seas, tending to a purposed conquest, wherein every man's particular estate is in the highest degree to be touched in respect of country, liberty, wife, children, lands, life, and, that which is specially to be regarded, for the profession of the true and sincere religion of Christ, we do look that the most part of them should have upon this instant extraordinary occasion of† larger proportion of furniture, both for horsemen and footmen, but specially horsemen, than hath been certified, thereby to be in their best strength against any attempt whatsoever, and to be employed both about our own person and other-wise, as they shall have knowledge given them : the number of which larger proportion, as soon as you shall know, we require you to signify **to** our Privy Council. And hereunto as we doubt not but by your good endeavour they will be rather conformable, so also we assure ourself that Almighty God will so bless these their loyal hearts borne towards

---

* *Cf.* f. 164.      † " Of " for " a " ?

us, their loving Sovereign, **and** their natural country, that all th'attempts of any enemy whatsoever shall be made void and frustrate, to their confusion, your comforts, and God's high glory. Given under our Signet."

*Notes in margin :* (1) "Penned by Mr. Secretary."

(2) "Few **of** the Lieutenants **have** made answer to these **letters,** and those that have, remain **with** Mr. **Secretary.**"

**F.** 173. 1588, June **27.—[The Privy Council]** to the Lords Lieutenants.

"Whereas her Majesty hath thought it convenient that as well such **numbers** of trained bands and others as by former order have been erected in **the several** counties in the realm, should be disposed and divided, some to repair to the sea coast, **as** occasion may serve, to impeach the landing or [for the?] withstanding of th'enemy upon his first descent ; some other part of **the** said forces **to** join with such numbers as shall be thought convenient to make **head** to th'enemy after he shall be landed (if it shall so fall out) ; and an other principal part of the said trained numbers to repair hither to join with the Army **that** shall be appointed for the defence of her Majesty's person :

"**These** shall **be to pray** your **Lordship** to give present order, that **of** those numbers which were appointed to be levied in that county, the number of 2,000, sorted with weapons according to such proportion as hath been heretofore set down unto you, and reduced into bands, may **be** in **a readiness** with convenient armour, furniture, and other necessaries, agreeable with the direction heretofore given, upon an hour's warning, to repair either to the Court to attend on her Majesty's person, or to such place as shall be appointed to join with **the** Army which shall be specially assembled for the making head to th'enemy, upon notice given you either from her Majesty or from us, or **from** such a person of quality as shall be notified to you to be appointed by her Majesty to be the General of the Army, either to attend upon **her** Highness' person or to go against th'enemies. The like order is **also to** be taken that these lances and lighthorse which have been **certified** already may be in a readiness to join with the foot-bands in these armies, according as you shall **have** direction. Wherein nothing doubting but that your Lordship **will give** speedy **and special** direction, we bid your Lordship very heartily farewell."

**F. 175.** [1588.]—" Projects.—Numbers of Men appointed to be **drawn** together **to** make an Army **to** encounter th'enemy."

**This shows the** number of **foot to be supplied** by certain counties, **with the names** of their Colonels.

*Foot.*—Cornwall, 2,000, **Sir Richard Greenvil.** Devon, 3,000, Sir Wm. Courtney. Somerset, 3,000, **Sir** Henry Barckley. Dorset, 2,000, Mr. Trenchard. Wilts, 2,000, Sir Robert Cunstable. Southampton, 4,000, **Sir** Thomas West, Hambden Poulet. Berks, 2,000, Sir **Henry** Norris. Sussex, 4,000, Sir John Burrowe, Sir Charles Blunte. **Kent,** 4,000, **Sir** Robert Sidney, Sir Edward Moore. Surrey, **1,000, Sir** Thomas Manners. Sum, 27,000.

*Horse.*—**Lances and** lighthorses (*sic*) to be drawn **out of** certain shires for the said Army."

Cornwall, lances 4, light horse 96. Devon, la. 0, li. 200. Dorset, la. **120,** li. 40. Somerset, la. 50, li. **300.** Wilts, la. 19, li. 150. Southampton, la. 100, li. 50. Sussex, la. **20, li.** 240. Kent, la. 64, li. 330,

harqueb[uses] 263, petronels 84. Berks, la. 10, li. 87. **Surrey, la. 8,
li. 127.** Sum, la. 407, li. 2,011 (*sic*).

" Pioneers to be levied out of certain Shires for the said Army."

Cornwall, 0. Devon, 600. Somerset, 0. Wiltshire, ——. Dorset,
600. Southampton, 1,000. **Sussex, 1,300.** Kent, 1,077. Berks, 115.
Surrey, 200. Sum, 4,692.

" The proportion of Ordnance for **the Army,** that is to encounter
th'enemy."

Demicannons 4, 18 horse. Culverins 4, 14 h. Demiculverins 3, 12 h.
Sacres, 3, 7 h. Falcons, 2, 3 h. Minnions, 2, 6 h. " Each of the
said pieces, so many horses."

" The numbers remaining in the counties for the guard thereof,
besides the forces drawn thence."

Cornwall, 3,000. Devon, 3,200. Somerset, 0. Dorset, 1,300.
**Wilts, 0.** Southampton, 2,600. Berks, 0. Sussex, 0. Kent, 1,100.
**Surrey, 72.**

F. 176. 1588, March and April.—(1) " Projects.—Places appointed
to levy certain numbers of Men for an Army for her Majesty's person,
April 1588."

The numbers to be furnished **by London and 16 counties are stated ;**
total, 23,900.

(2) " Taxation of Horse to be **levied** in certain Counties for an
Army to attend her Majesty's person, March 1588."

The numbers to be furnished by 18 counties are stated ; totals,
lances **389,** lighthorse 1,032.

(3) " Numbers of Men appointed to be drawn together to make an
Army for the defence of her Majesty' person."

The numbers to be furnished by London and 17 counties are stated,
differing from those given above. The names of some of the [Colonels
or Captains] are given, as follow :

| | | |
|---|---|---|
| London - - - | 10,000. | |
| Middlesex - - | 1,000 | } Sir Wm. Hatton. |
| Northampton - - | 1,000 | |
| Oxford - - | 1,000 | } Sir Wm. **Knolls.** |
| Gloucester - - | 1,500 | |
| Bedford - - | 500 | |
| Buckingham - - | 1,000 | |
| Hertford - - | 1,500 | } Sir Fra. Knolls. |
| Cambridge - | 500 | |
| Essex - - | 2,000 | Sir John Smithe. |
| Kent - - - | 2,000 | } Sir Thomas Cecill. |
| Surrey - | 800 | |
| Suffolk - - - | 2,000 | Sir Ed. Cary. |
| Norfolk - - | 2,000 | Sir John Peiton. |
| Warwick - - | 600 | |
| Leicester - - | 500 | } Sir Henry Goodyeere. |
| Huntingdon - - | 400 | |
| Worcester - - | 600 | |

Summa, **28,900.** Reg[iments,] 14.

Horse (from 14 counties) : 371 lances, 2,114 light horse.
Pioneers (from 6 counties), 2,000 (2,300 ?).

F. 177b. 1588, April 2.—" Certain numbers appointed to be drawn
out of the Inland Counties unto London, there to be trained."

Nine counties—4,000 men.

"A proportion of Ordnance for the Army for defence of Her Majesty's person."

| | | | |
|---|---|---|---|
| Cannons | - | - 6 | 24 [horses] |
| Demi-cannons | - | - 6 | 18 |
| Culverins | - | - 6 | 14 |
| Demi-culverins | - | - 6 | 12 |
| Sacres | - | - 6 | 7 |
| Minions | - | - 6 | 6 |
| | | — | — |
| Summa | - | - 36 | 81 |

"Provisions to be made for the Armies described"; viz.:—
Pikes, 10,000. Tools for pioneers, 10,000. The Lieutenant of the Ordnance to take view of the gunners. Last of corn powder, 20. Last [of] corn powder [for] great ordnance, (*blank*). Lead fodder, 20. Match, (*blank*).

F. 178. [1588.]—"The principal Officers belonging to the Camp." 1. Her Majesty's Lieutenant-General. 2. The Marshal. 3. The General of the Force. 4. Lieutenant of the Lances. 5. Lieutenant of the Lighthorse. 6. The Master of the Ordnance. 7. The Colonel of the Infantry. 8. Colonels of particular regiments.

Inferior officers: Serjeant Major. Muster Master of the Army. Chancellor, or Secretary. Trench-master, or Colonel of the pioneers and gunners. Provost Marshal of the Army. Corporal of the Field. Scout-master. Quarter-master. Master of the carriages and tents. Master of the conductors and guides. Divine minister. Herald-at-arms. Pursuivant, or messenger. Trumpeter.

2. "Names of Marshallmen [Martial men] which are presently to be used."
*Sir Wm. Fitzwilliams, *Sir John Norris, Sir Walter Rawleighe, *Sir Henry Goodyeere, Sir Henry Ley, Sir Ed. Wingfeild, Sir Henry Harington, *Sir Roger Williams, *Sir Ed. Stanley, Sir Henry Norris, Sir Geo. Bourchier, Sir John Smithe, *Sir Thomas Manners, *Sir Robert Cunstable, *Sir Henry Knyvet, Sir Jerome Bowes, Sir Ed. Hastinges, Sir Thomas Gorge, Sir Henry Palmer, *Brian FitzWilliams *Captain Carlel, Captain Wilson, Captain Merreman, *Captain Turner, Captain Shute, Captain Hoord, Captain Doudall, *John Vaughan, Captain Scudamore, Captain Peacock, Captain Westrope, Captain Henworth, Captain Newton, Captain Wm. Selbie, *Sir Richard Greenvile, *Captain Ed. Barckley, Captain Piper, *Captain Gilbert Yorck, Captain Hitchcock, Captain G. Moore, Captain H. Drury, Captain Warde, Captain Roger Carewe, Thomas Marckham, Captain Highefeild, Captain Parckinson, *Captain Geo. Carleton, *Captain John Wattes, Captain Twittie, Captain Plott, Captain Marchant, Captain Wheeler, Ralph Lane, Gawen Champernon, Captain Price, Captain Crewes, Captain Dawtrie, Captain Sidnam, Somer[set]; Captain Ma. Morgan, Wil[t]s; Captain Ellis; Captain Staunton th'elder, [and] Captain Staunton the younger, Warwick; Captain John Bingham, Captain Spindola, Captain John Roberts, Bristowe; *Captain Fra. Allene, Thomas Roper, Edward Philpott, John Couper, Thomas West, —— Strange, Wm. Goodwine, *Captain Ed. Yorck, Captain Geo. Acres, at Lirpoole; Roger Hussey, Captain Jo. Riggs, Captain Goringe, Sir Edward Moore, Captain Pwe (*sic*), Captain Barton, Hambden Paulet, Anthony Wingefeilde, Captain Bealinge, *Sir Henry Goodyeere, Captain Woodhowse, *Edmonde Yorck, Morgan Woolfe, *Captain Huntley, Captain Harte.

---

* Marked for selection?

F. 180.   1588, July 23.—"M[inute] of a letter from the Lords [of the Privy Council] unto [the Lords Lieutenants of] the Counties underwritten."

"After our hearty commendations to your good L[ordship]. Whereas the Spanish fleet hath now of late been discovered again on the seas, and it is doubtful what course they may take, and in what places of the realm they may attempt to land : These are to give your Lordship knowledge of them, to the intent with all diligence the forces under your Lordship's lieutenancy be directed to come to such place or places as have been heretofore thought convenient, or as you shall think fittest, to be in a readiness upon firing of the beacons to resort, to impeach such attempt as th'enemy may make to set on land his forces in any place, according to such directions as your Lordship hath heretofore received in that behalf.

"We pray you likewise to give special directions, for the avoiding of confusion, that no other persons be suffered to assemble together besides the ordinary bands, and that good order be given to see watches be kept in every thoroughfare town, to stay and apprehend all vagabonds, rogues, and suspected persons, that are like to plod up and down to move disorders ; and if any such be found with any manifest offence, tending to stir trouble, or rebellion, to cause such to be executed by martial law.

"And because the greatest doubt presently is th'enemy will attempt to land in some part of Essex, to which place her Majesty hath sent our very good Lord, the Earl of Leicester, Lord Steward of her Majesty's Household, and Lieutenant of that county, to have the charge of such an Army as is appointed to encounter them there in that county, her Majesty's pleasure is that you should forthwith send into Essex, unto the town of Brentwood, the number of —— lances and lighthorse, to be conducted by such as have the charge of them, to be there the 27th of this month, where the said Earl of Leicester shall take them in charge, &c.

"Furthermore upon farther resolution her Majesty's pleasure is, that you shall send from thence the number of [——?] foot, to be led by the captains and officers, to be at Stradfford of the Bowe, near London, by the 29th of this month, and that some special person may have the general charge to conduct them."

"The number of Lances and Lighthorse, sent for by the said letter to come to the Lord Steward."

Bedford, lances, 17, lighthorse, 40.  Buckingham, la. 12, li. 83. Hertford, la. 25, li. 60.  Kent, la. 50, li. 100.  Suffolk, la. 50, li. 200. Essex, la. 50, li. 200.  Middlesex, la. 30, la. 88.  Surrey, la. 8, li. 98. Essex, la. 50, li. 200.  Sum, la. 253, li. 796.  Sum of horse, 1,449 [1,049 ?].

F. 180b.  [1588, July.]—"The number of Footmen drawn out of the shires for the Army under the Lord Steward assembled at Tilbury."

| | | | |
|---|---|---|---|
| Bedford | - | - | 500 |
| Buckingham | - | - | 500 |
| Hertford | | - | 1,000 |
| Surrey | - | - | 1,000 |
| Berkshire | | - | 1,000 |
| Oxford | - | - | 1,000 |
| Essex, the whole force of the armed men by reason the cam[p] was assembled there | | - | 5,000 |
| London, sent directly to Gravesend | | - | 1,000 |

To be at Stratford Bow by the 29th of July.

49

" Sum of the Army there : horse 1,449, foot 11,000 ; total 12,449.
" Beside the forces of Kent, to the number of 6,000, assembled at Sandwich."

F. 182.  **1588, July.**—" Copy of a Commission given to the **Earl of Leicester to be** Lieutenant General of her Majesty's Forces **in the South parts.**"*

" Elizabeth, by the grace of God, &c., To our trusty and well beloved Cousin and Councillor Robert, Earl of Leicester, Lord Steward of **our** Household, greeting. Whereas we have lately directed and sent forth our several commissions under our Great Seal of England, authorising thereby divers and sundry of our nobilities (*sic*) and others to be our Lieutenants within sundry of the counties of this realm, as well for the **mustering** and **choice** of our loving subjects meet and apt for the wars, as **also for** the **doing and executing** of divers and sundry things mentioned in the same **our commission**, as **by the same** our commission more plainly doth **and may appear: As we will signify to** our said Lieutenants th'effect **of this our commission to you our** Lieutenant† over our **Army** that shall **be provided to withstand all** manner of **invasion of our** realm by sea, so **we will** charge **them accordingly to send unto you from** time **to time** such **numbers of** our **loving, able, and apt subjects for the wars, as** well horsemen as footmen, **sufficiently armed** and furnished **in** all points, to such place **or** places **and** at such time as **you** shall by your wisdom appoint and require from any our said Lieutenants to be brought unto you.

" And **where also we** have already assigned and appointed and mean hereafter **to assign and** appoint sundry of **our said** special Lieutenants to send **or cause to** be sent unto you, as our said Lieutenant **and** Captain **General over** our said Armies (*sic*), from time **to time, such** number **of our loving** subjects, apt and able men for **wars, as well** horsemen as footmen, well and sufficiently furnished **in all** points, to such place and places, and [at] such time and times, **as** you **by your** wisdom and discretion for our better service shall require of or‡ from any of our **Lieutenants** to be sent, brought, or conducted unto you :

" Know ye **that** we, trusting of your assured fidelity, wisdom, and circumspection, have constituted, ordained, and appointed you to be **our** Lieutenant and Captain General over all men of our Armies as shall **be** levied in all counties of the South parts of this our realm, to stay th'invasion of our realm by **any** foreign forces, and to order, govern, and command, not **only** all **and** singular our subjects, which be or shall be levied **or assembled together** by you within the counties of Essex **and** Hertford, **and the town** of Colchester, whereof you are our special and several Lieutenant,† but also§ all and singular other our subjects which are already, **or at** any time hereafter shall be, sent, brought, conducted, or otherwise shall come to you from any of our special Lieutenants, or from any other place of the realm, or by any other order or direction from us, or by any order, commandment or direction from **you,** by the virtue of this our commission and authority given unto **you** as Lieutenant General over the said Armies.

* *See* Leicester's **acknowledgment of the receipt of this** Commission, July 24, State Papers, Vol. 213, No. 21. It is **not in the State Papers, nor** on the Patent Rolls, nor among the Chancery **Signed Bills, the Privy Seals, or** the Privy Signet Warrants.
† " Lieutenants " in MS.      ‡ " Any " is put for " or " in MS.
§ " Of " occurs here in MS.

"And further we have given you full power and authority,[*] the same persons so levied or assembled, or so to be levied or assembled, by you, or sent, conducted, or brought, or that otherwise shall come to you, either by our special order, or by authority of this our[†] commission, as aforesaid, to try, array, and put in a readiness, and them also and every of them, after their abilities, degree[s], and faculties, well and sufficiently cause to be weaponed and armed, and to take or cause to be taken the musters of them from time to time, in places most meet for that purpose, after your good direction [discretion?]; and also the same our subjects so arrayed, tried, and armed, as well men-of-arms as other[‡] horsemen, archers, and footmen, of all kind[s] and degrees meet and apt for the wars, to govern, lead, and conduct, as well against all and singular our enemies attempting any invasion, as also against all and singular rebels, traitors, and other offenders and their adherents attempting anything against us, our Crown and dignity,[§] within any part or place where our said Army shall be [conducted] by you from time to time, as oft as need shall require, by your discretion; and with the said enemies, rebels, and traitors to fight, and them invade, resist, repress, and subdue, slay, or kill, and put to execution of death, by all ways or means, by your said good direction [discretion?]; and to do, fulfil, and execute all and singular other things which shall be requisite for the leading, government, order, and rule of the said Army and subjects, and for the conservation of our person and peace; and further to do, execute, and offer against the said enemies, rebels, traitors, and such other like offenders and their adherents, as necessity shall require, by your discretion, the law called the Martial Law, according to the Law Martial; and of such offenders apprehended, or being brought in subjection, to save whom you shall think good to be saved, and to slay, destroy, and put to execution of death such and so many of them as you shall think meet by your good discretion to be put to death, by any manners of ways, to the terror of all other offenders.

"And further our will and pleasure is, and by these presents we do give unto you full power and authority, that in case any invasion of enemies, insurrection, rebellion, riots, routs, or unlawful assemblies or any like offences been happened or shall happen to be moved in any place where our said Army by you levied and conducted against any invasion shall be and remain, that then and as often as you shall perceive any such misdemeanour to arise, you, with all the power you can make, shall with all diligence repair or send convenient forces to the place where any such invasion, unlawful assembly, insurrection, or rebellion shall happen to be made, to subdue, repress, and reform the same, as well by battle or other kind of force as otherwise, by the laws of the realm, or the Laws (*sic*) Martial, according to your discretion.

"And further we give you full power and authority, for the executing of this our commission, to appoint and assign within our said Army a Martial or Provost Martial [Marshal], to use and exercise that office in such cases as you shall think requisite to use the said Law Martial."

"And also we give unto you, our said Lieutenant General, full power and authority by these presents to hear, examine, and determine, as well

---

* "That" occurs here in MS.                    † "Your" in MS.
‡ "Our" in MS.  *Cf.* the commission to Lord Hunsdon, f. 191
§ See the Queen's proclamation against the Bull of Pope Sixtus V., and "traitorous libels, books, and pamphlets." (Chancery Signed Bills, 1 July, 1588; and Patent Roll, 30 Eliz., part 18.)

by yourself as by your sufficient deputy **or deputies,** all criminal causes growing or arising within **the** said Army, as **well** concerning the death of any person as loss **of** member, and all causes civil, whatsoever they be, which shall happen or chance within the said Army.

"And also **we** give unto **you** full power and authority **to** make, **constitute, and** ordain statutes, ordinances, and proclamations **from** time **to time, as the** case* shall require, for the good government, order, and rule **of our** said Army, and **the** same and every of them to cause **to be** duly proclaimed, performed, and executed; and whomsoever you **shall** find contemptuous, disobedient, or disordered in our said Army **to** attach, apprehend, and imprison, and them and every of them **to** chastise and punish; and such as you shall imprison, you shall cause them to be proceeded against according to the quality of the offence, **as** well by pains of death as by loss of member, or otherwise, according **to** your directions (*sic*); and to deliver **and set** at liberty any person so imprisoned, as by you shall **be** thought convenient; **and** generally to do all and every thing and things which to the office **of** Lieutenant and Captain General **over our** said **Army doth** belong **and** appertain, and which for the **good and safe government of our** Army and subjects shall **be** thought expedient and necessary.

"And ther[efore] we will and command you our said Lieutenant General that with all speed you do execute the premises with effect. Wherefo[re] **we** will and command all and singular lieutenants special, marquises, **earls,** viscounts, barons, knights, sheriffs, bailiffs, constables, captains, petty-captains, soldiers, and all other [our] officers, ministers, and loving subjects, of what estate, degree, or condition soever he or they be of, that they and every of them, with their power and servants, from time to time shall be attendant, aiding, and assisting, counselling, helping, and at your commandment in the due execution hereof, as they and **every** of **them** tender our pleasure **and** will **answer to the contrary** at their perils.

"And further our pleasure is that whatsoever you shall do **by virtue** of this com[mission] and according to the tenor and effect of **the same,** touching th'execution of the premises or any part thereof, you **shall be** discharged in that behalf against us our heirs and successors. Provided always that this our present commission or anything therein mentioned shall not in anywise extend to levy or send for any forces out of the principality or dominion of South Wales and North Wales, **the** Marches thereof adjoining, nor out of the several counties of Worcester, Monmouth, Hereford, and Salop, nor from any corporate or privileged places within the limits or precincts of the principal[ity?], dominions, marches, and counties aforesaid, or from any of them, or the liberties thereof, [or] to levy or send for any forces out of the counties of York, Northumberland, Cumberland, and Westmoreland, the bishopric of Durham, the city of Yorcke, the town of Kingeston upon Hull, and Newcastle upon Tyne, or the liberties thereof, nor out of the counties of Lincoln, Derby, Lancaster, or Nottingham, or the liberties thereof, or out of **any** corporate or privileged places within the limits or precincts **of the** said counties or any of them. In witness whereof, we have cause[d] these our letters to be made patents, and to continue during our pleasure."

F. 1836. [1588, July.]—"Captains appointed **to** attend on the Lord Steward" [the Earl of Leicester].

Sir John Norris, Sir Henry Goodyere, Sir Roger Williams, Sir Ed. Stanley, Sir Henry Norris, Sir Ed. Moore, Capt. Westrope, Capt.

* "Cause" in MS.

Piper, Capt. Tutty, Capt. Dawtry, Ralph Lane, **Sir John** Roper, Ed.
Philpott, Roger Hussey, Capt. Goringe, Capt. Barton, Edmond Yorck,
Morgan Woolfe, Capt. Dudley, Capt. Harte, Capt. Tanner, Capt. Brere-
ton, Captain Barnishe, Capt. Walgrave. Capt. Cooke, Captain Judge,
Capt. Careles, *alias* Wrighte, Capt. Xpñas [Christmas], Capt. Raines,
Capt. Peacock, Capt. Latham, Capt. Pettie.

F. 184. 1588, July.—"**The** Names of **the** Officers of the Army
assembled at Tilbery under the **Earl of** Leicester."

Lord Lieutenant General, Earl **of Leicester.**

Lord Marshal, Sir John Norris, knight.

The Earl of Essex, General: Captain of the lances, Sir Roger
Williams, knight; Captain **of the** lighthorse, Sir Robert Sidney, knight.

Colonel General of the footmen, Sir Thomas Leighton, knight.

Serjeant Major, Capt. Nicholas Dawtry.

Corporals of the Field, 4 : 1, Capt. Wilson; 2, Capt. Acres; 3,
————————; 4, ————————.

**Master of** th'Ordnance, Sir Fra. Knolls, jun.; James Spencer, lieutenant.

Muster-master, Ralph Lane, esq.

Provost-marshal, Capt. Cripse.

Quarter-master, Capt. Ed. Yorck.

Trench-master, Lederico Jembel [**Federico** Jenibelli].

Scout-master, Edmond Pettye.

Judge of the **Army,** Edmond Sucklif.

Master of the **Carriages,** ————————.

Treasurer, **Sir Moile Finche,** deputy to Sir **Thomas** Hennadge.

F. 185. [1588, July.]—"**Rates for** the entertainment of the Officers
of the Camp, set down by my Lords" [the Privy Council].

This is similar to the schedule **on** f. 188, but gives **no** names, and
does not specify all the "inferior **officers.**"

F. 187. [1588, July.]—"**Warrant from her Majesty for Sir Thomas**
Henneage, for 20,000*l.,*" &c.

"Elizabeth, &c., To the Treasurer and Chamberlains of our Exchequer,
greeting. Whereas we have ordained our trusty and right well beloved
Councillor, Sir Thomas Hennea[ge,] knight, our Vice-Chamberlain and
Treasurer of our Chamber, to be also now our Treasurer [of] Wars, as
well for the payment of our armies and companies of men levied or to
be levied for the withstanding of any foreign invasion of our Realm
and under the condu[ct] of our right trusty and right well beloved
Cousin and Councillor, the Earl of Leic[ester], our Lieutenant and
Captain General over the said armies and companies, as also for the
payment of all such other armies and companies of men as shall be
assembled for the defence and surety of our Royal person and under
the conduct of our right trusty and well beloved Cousin and Councillor
the Lord of Hunsdon, Captain General and Lieutenant over them;
And whereas also we have appointed our trusty and well beloved Sir
Moyle Fynche, knight, to be Deputy Treasurer at Wars unto the sai[d]
Sir Thomas Henneage, for the payment of all such armies and companies as [are] or shall be under the conduct of the said Earl : We will
and command you that out of our treasure, being or that shall be in the
**Receipt** of our said Exchequer, [you] pay or cause to be paid unto the
**said Sir** Thomas Henneage or his as[signs] the sum of 20,000*l.,* whereof
**such** part as shall come to the hands of the said Sir Moyle **Fynche** to
be issued out by him from time to time according to such order as shall
be prescribed unto him by warrant of the said Earl **of** Leicester, and
the residue to be issued out from time to time by **our** said Treasurer

at Wars b[y] warrant of the said Lord of Hunsdon, or else by such order and direction as he s[hall] receive in writing under the hands of six of our Privy Council, whereof [you,] our said Treasurer, or our Principal Secretary,* to be one. And there, &c."

F. 188. [1588, July.]—"The Entertainments (sic) of the Officers of the Camp, as it was paid by the Treasurer, by warrant from the Lord General."

This is similar to, but not a copy of *State Papers, Vol.* 215, *No.* 86, there being some differences. The Earl of Leicester is here stated to have had 30† halberds under him (instead of 20). The Provost's name is here given as G. Acres (instead of Peter Crispe). The muster-master was Raulfe Lane, at 13*s.* 4*d.* a day, with four clerks under him at 2*s.* each. The commissary of the victuals was —— Arden, at 6*s.* 8*d.*, with one clerk at 2*s.* The trench-master's name is here given as Fedrik Jenebellj (instead of Frederick Gembell).

F. 190. 1588, July 27.—[The Privy Council] to the [Lords] Lieutenants of Norfolk and Suffolk.

"Whereas the Spanish fleet hath now of late been discovered again on the seas, and it is doubted what course they may take and in what places of the realm they may attempt to land : These are to give you knowledge thereof, to th'intent that with all diligence the forces of that county, under your Lordship's Lieutenancy, may be put in a readiness to be employed as occasion may serve upon an hour's warning. We pray you likewise to give special direction, for the avoiding of confusion, that no other persons be suffered to assemble together, besides th'ordinary bands ; and that good order be given to see watches kept in every thoroughfare town to stay and apprehend all vagabonds and rogues that [are] like to pass up and down to move disorders ; and if any such be found with any manifest offence tending to stir trouble or rebellion, to cause such to be executed by martial law"

F. 190. 1588, July 27.— [The Privy Council] "to the Counties underwritten " (*names not given*).

"Whereas, upon the discovery of the Spanish Navy upon the coast of this realm, it is thought meet and convenient that sufficient number of horses (sic) should presently repair to the Court, to attend upon her Majesty's person : These are therefore to signify unto your Lordship, that her Highness' pleasure is that, with all convenient speed that may be used, you shall send hither such number of lighthorses as was contained in your last certificate sent hither, under the conducts of those gent[lemen] to whom the leading of the said horses was committed ; praying your Lordship herein not to fail to give order that they may be here by the —— of the month."

F. 191. 1588, Aug. [July ?]‡—"Copy of the Lord Chamberlain's [Lord Hunsdon's] Commission of Lieutenant General for defence of her Majesty's person."

"Elizabeth, by the grace of God, &c., To our right trusty, &c. Know ye that we, greatly trusting in your approved fidelity, wisdom, valour, and circumspection, have chosen, ordained, and appointed you

---

* Lord Burghley and Sir Francis Walsingham.
† So also on fol. 185.
‡ See State Papers, Vol. 213, No. 68. This commission is not in the State Papers, nor on the Patent Rolls, nor among the Chancery Signed Bills, the Privy Seals, or the Privy Signets. The commission to Henry, Earl of Pembroke, to be Lieutenant in Wales, dated 5th August, *is* among the Signed Bills, and on the Patent Roll, 30 Eliz., part 4.

to be our Lieutenant, principal Captain, and Governor **of and over** all our Army, levied and to be levied and assembled near unto **us,** for the defence and surety of our own Royal person against th'attempts and powers of any manner foreign forces, or any the malicious and traitorous enterprises of any our rebellious or undutiful subjects; and do give you full power and authority, by the tenor hereof, all and singular our subjects which are or shall be so levied and assembled together by the command-ment of us or of our Privy Council, or shall **be** by you by force of this our commission levied and assembled for the defence of our person, of what estate or degree soever they be, being meet and apt for the wars, to call and gather togethers, and the same to array, try, and put in readiness, and them also and every of them, after their abilities, degrees, and faculties, well and sufficiently cause **to** be armed and weaponed, **and to** take **or cause** to **be** taken **the** musters of them from **time to** time, in **places most meet for that** purpose, after your good discretion **;** and also **the same our** subjects so arrayed, tried, and armed, as **well** men-of-**arms as** other horsemen, archers, and footmen, of all kinds and degrees meet and apt for the wars, to govern, lead, and **conduct,** as well against all and singular our enemies attempting any invasion, as also against all and singular rebels, traitors, and other offenders and **their** adherents attempting anything against us, our Crown and dignity, **within** any part or place where our said Army, so assembled for our defence, shall be by you conducted from time to time, as often as need shall require, by your good discretion, for the safety of our person; and with the said enemies, rebels, and traitors to fight, and them to invade, resist, repress, subdue, slay, kill, and put to execution of death, by all ways and means, by your discretion ;[and] to do, fulfil, and execute all and singular other things which shall be requisite for the leading, government, order, and rule of our said Army and subjects, and for the conservation of our person and peace ; and further to do, execute, and use against the said enemies, rebels, traitors, and such other like offenders and their adherents, as necessity [shall] require, by your good discretion, the law called the Martial Law, according to the Law Martial ; and of such offenders apprehended or being brought into subjection to save whom you shall think good to be saved, and to slay, destroy, and put to execution of death such and so many of them as you shall think meet **by your good** discretion to be put to death, by any manner of ways, to the terror **of** all other offenders.

**And** further our will and pleasure is, and by these presents we do give unto you full power and authority, that in case any invasion of enemies, insurrection, rebellion, riots, routs, or unlawful assemblies, or **any such** like offences been happened or shall happen to be moved **in any** place where our said Army so assembled for the safeguard of our person shall be and remain, that then and as often as you shall perceive any such hostility or rebellious attempts to arise to the danger of our person, you, with all the power you can make, shall with all diligence repair or send convenient force to the place where the danger shall appear to our person by any such invasion, unlawful assembly, insurrec-tion, or rebellion, and the same you shall to the best of your power subdue, repress, and reform, as well by battle or other kind of forces **(sic)** as otherwise, by the laws of our realm, or the Law Martial, according to your discretion.

" And further we give you full power and authority, for th'execution of this our commission, to appoint and assign within our said Army a Marshal or Provost Marshal to use and exercise that office in such cases as you shall think requisite to use the said Law Martial.

"And also we give unto you, our said Lieutenant, principal Captain, and Governor of our said Army, full power and authority by these presents to hear, examine, and determine, as well by yourself as by your sufficient deputy or deputies, all criminal causes growing or arising within the same Army, as well concerning the death of any person as loss of member, and all causes civil, whatsoever they be, which shall happen or chance within our said Army.

"And also we give unto you full power and authority to make, constitute, and ordain statutes, ordinances, and proclamations from time to time, as the case shall require, for the [good] government, order, and rule of our said Army, and the same and every of them to cause to be duly proclaimed, performed, and executed ; and whomsoever you shall find contemptuous, disobedient, and disordered in our Army to attach, apprehend, and imprison, and them and every of them to chastise and punish ; and such as you shall imprison, to cause them to be proceeded against according to the quality of their offence, as well by pains of death as loss of member, or otherwise, according to your discretion, and to deliver and set at liberty any person so imprisoned, as by you shall be thought convenient ; and generally to do all and every other thing and things which to th'office of a Lieutenant, principal Captain, and Governor of our said Army doth belong and appertain, and which for the good and safe government of our said Army and subjects shall be thought expedient and necessary.

"And therefore we will and command you, our said Lieutenant, principal Captain, and Governor, that with all diligence you do execute the premises with effect. Wherefore we will and command all and singular lieutenants of any special counties, and all marquises, earls, viscounts, barons, knights, justices, mayors, sheriffs, bailiffs, constables, captains, petty-captains, soldiers, and all other our officers, ministers, and subjects, of what estate, degree, or condition he or they be of, that they and every of them, with their power and servants, from time to time shall be attendant, aiding, assisting, counselling, helping, and at your commandment in the due execution hereof, as they and every of them tender our pleasure, and will answer to the contrary at their perils.

"And further our pleasure is, that whatsoever you shall do by virtue of this our commission and according to the tenor and effect of the same, touching the execution of the premises or any part thereof, you shall be discharged in that behalf against us our heirs and successors. Provided always that this our present commission or anything therein contained shall not derogate or diminish the authority of our commission lately given to our right trusty and right well beloved Cousin and Councillor th'Earl of Leicester, being thereby authorised to lead an army to withstand the landing by sea and invasion of our realm by any foreign forces, except we shall by our special warrant in writing for any cause necessary limit any special matter to be done by you, our Lieutenant, principal Captain, and Governor of our Army, that may in some sort be derogatory or repugnant to the foresaid commission given to our said Cousin the Earl of Leicester."

F. 192. [1588, July.]—"The Captains appointed to attend the Lord Chamberlain [Lord Hunsdon].

"Sir Edward Wingefeilde, knight. Sir Henry Knivet, knight. Sir Richard Grenevile, knight. Sir Henry Barckley, knight. Capt. Willson. Capt. Turner. Capt. Shute. Capt. Doudall. Capt. Henworthe. Capt. Roger Carew. Capt. Parckinson. Capt. John Watts. Capt. Wheele. Capt.

Hoord. Capt. Staunton, th'elder. Capt. Staunton, the younger. Capt. Acres. Capt. Edward Yorck. Capt. Anthony Wingfeilde. Capt. Woodhoure. Capt. Tristram Trevit, Tyrwhitt.* Capt. Smithe."

F. 193. 1588, July, **August.**—"**The** Names of the Officers of the Army for the guard of her **Majesty's person** under the Lord Chamberlain, began to be **assembled at St. James's.**"

The Lord Lieutenant General, **the Lord Hunsdon**, Lord Chamberlain.

The Lord Marshal, the Lord Gray **of Wilton.**

The Earl of Essex, General : Captain **of the lauces, the** Lord Norris ; captain of the lighthorse, the Lord Northe.

Treasurer, Sir Thomas Hennage, knight.

Master of **the** Ordnance, Sir Robert Cunstable, knight.

**Colonel General of the** Foot, Sir **Fra.** Knolls, knight, Treasurer of the **Household.**

**Serjeant** Major, Sir William Reade, knight.

"No more named."

F. 193b. [1588, July.]—" Forces appointed to **repair up to London,** out of sundry shires, for **an** Army **for to attend upon her Majesty's** person."

**Gloucester 1,500, Somerset 4,000, Sussex** 2,000, Wilts 2,000, **Cambridge 500, Northampton 600, Leicester** 500, Warwick 500, **Dorset** 1,000, **Suffolk** 2,000, **Norfolk** 2,000, Huntingdon 400. **[Total,] 17,000. Besides** 9,000 of the bands trained in London.

*Cf. State Papers, Vol.* 213, *No.* 37.

" Horses appointed for the Army appointed to attend her Majesty's person."

Gloucester, lances 20, lighthorse **100.** Somerset, la. 50, li. 100. Sussex, la. 20, li. 100. Wilts, la. 25, **li. 100.** Cambridge, la. 13, li. 40. Northampton, la. 20, li. 80. Leicester, **la. 9, li.** 70. Warwick, la. 17, li. 76. Dorset, la. 120, li. 0. Suffolk, la. **70, li. 230.** Norfolk, la. 80, li. 32. Huntingdon, la. 6, li. 26. [Totals,] **la. 481 ; li. 1,431.**

F. 194. 1588, **July 26.**—"**The** numbers of armed and trained [Men] in **the several** Counties, and how they are distributed to furnish the **Army** for the Queen's Majesty, and that under the Lord Steward with **the remains** " (*sic*).

1. Counties **to repair to the** Lord Steward [Leicester] : viz., Bedford, Bucks, **Herts,** Surrey, **Berks,** Oxford, Essex, Kent, London. The numbers are **stated** of (*a*) **the** armed men in the county, (*b*) those sent to the Lord Steward, (*c*) those remaining in the county, and (*d*, in four cases) supplies to come to the Queen out of the remains.

2. Counties that furnished men to attend her Majesty's person : *viz.*, Glouc., Somerset, Sussex, Wilts, Cambr., Northn., Leic., Warw., Dorset, Suff., Norf., Hunt., London, Middx. The numbers are stated of (*a*) armed men, (*b*) those to attend her Majesty, (*c*) untrained, and (*d*, in six cases) new supplies sent for.

3. Counties not charged, viz., Worcester, Hants, Derby, Staff., Linc., Chesh., Lanc., Salop, Cornw., Devon. (The numbers of armed men in each, and supplies sent for from three, are stated.) " Besides the Welsh shires [and] the Presidentship of York."

---

* **Both these** last two surnames are written opposite to " Tristram."

F. 194b. [1588, July.]—" The Supplies sent for out of the Counties of the remains of the trained bands for the reinforcing of the Army for Her Majesty's person, as appeareth on the other side." *

| | | | | |
|---|---|---|---|---|
| Hertfordshire | . | . | 500 ⎫ | |
| Surrey | . . . | . | 500 ⎪ | To be at London by the |
| Berkshire | . | . | 500 ⎬ | 6th of August. |
| Oxford | . . . | . | 150 ⎪ | |
| Gloucestershire | . | . | 1,000 ⎭ | |
| Sussex | . . . | . | 500 ⎫ | London, the 8th August. |
| Wilts | . | . | 300 ⎭ | |
| Cambridge | . . . | . | 200 | 7 Aug. |
| Suffolk | . | . | 1,000 | 8 Aug. |
| Norfolk | . . . | . | 1,000 | 9 Aug. |
| Worcester | . | . | 400 | 9 Aug. |
| Hampshire | . . . | . | 2,000 | 7 Aug. |
| Devon | . | . | 2,000 | 10 Aug. |

Sum . . 10,050

*Cf. State Papers, Vol. 213, No. 68.*

F. 194b. 1588, July 29.—" Letters written to the Lords Lieutenants of Kent, Dorset, Hertford, and Suffolk, to this effect. That whereas their Lordships were required by late letters from the Lords of her Majesty's Privy Council, to have a certain number of lances and lighthorse that were levied in those counties, to be sent to Brentwood, by a certain day: their Lordships were now prayed that all the rest of the lances and lighthorse that were levied in those countries (*sic*) might be sent up hither to London, under the conduct of such gentlemen as had the charge of them."

The lances and lighthorse of ⎰ Kent, Dorset, Hertford, Suffolk, ⎱ to be at London by the ⎰ 7 8 6 7 ⎱ of August.

The lighthorse of . . ⎰ Gloucester, Sussex, Somerset, ⎱ to be at London the ⎰ 8 6 9 ⎱ of August.

F. 195. [1588, July.—Summary of foregoing papers.]
" So as the Army appointed for defence of her Majesty's person consisted of :—

| | | | |
|---|---|---|---|
| Companies first sent out of the counties - - | 17,000 | 481 | 1,431 ⎫ |
| Out of the counties sent for by the second letters - - | 10,050 | 0 | 0 ⎪ |
| Out of London - | 9,000 | 0 | 0 ⎬ Men, 45,362. |
| Noblemen's voluntary bands - | 1,448 | 1,029 | 581 ⎪ |
| Forces furnished by the Clergy - | 3,883 | 21 | 538 ⎭ |
| | 41,381 | 1,531 | 2,550 |

---

Sum  -  -  - { Horse, 4,081, } 45,362 [45,462].
{ Foot, 41,381, }

Beside the bands of Pensioners, her Majesty's household servants.
The Army under the Lord Steward :—

The foot appointed
out of sundry
shires to repair to
his Lordship  - 11,000
The whole forces of
Kent, encamped at } Foot, 17,000.
Sandwich  -  - 6,000
Lances attending his
Lordship  -  - 253 } In all, 18,049.
Lighthorse attending } Horse, 1,049.
his Lordship  - 796

Sum **total of** both { Horse, 5,130, } **In all, 63,511.**
Armies  -  - { Foot, 58,381. }

" **It is** to be remembered that the forces of the Presidentship of the
North were not drawn forth, but reserved **to answer the** service if anything were attempted out of Scotland.

" The like was also for the forces of the Presidentship of Wales.

" Beside no forces drawn out **of** these English shires :" Derby,
Stafford, Lincoln, Cheshire, Lancaster, Salop, Cornwall.

" As also out of the shires appointed to the service, some of the
enrolled forces and others of the able and armed [were] left Derby,
**defence of** the county, as appeareth."

F. 196. 1588, Aug. 7.—" Letters [from the Privy Council] to the
Counties underwritten, for the sending back of the footmen that were
appointed to repair hitherward **out of** those Counties."

" Whereas you were directed **to have the conduction of those**
companies which are sent hither **out** of the county of ——— ;
forasmuch as the forces which are to repair hither out of divers **other**
counties of the realm to furnish those armies which her Majesty **hath**
prepared, **as** well for the resisting and withstanding the attempts **of**
th'enemy **as for the** safeguard and defence of her Majesty's person,
doth grow to so great numbers as that speedy provision cannot be
**made** for the victualling of them here, and convenient lodging, as so
**great** forces will require, in so short time as was first limited by our
**letters** for their repair hither : we have thought good to let you know
that it **is** her Majesty's pleasure, and so by virtue hereof in her Majesty's
name **we** do require you upon the sight of these our letters, to return
again **into** the said county with those forces you have brought from
thence, and that nevertheless order be taken that they may be in good
readiness with all their armour and weapons **upon** such directions as you
shall receive from hence **upon** a new **warning to repair hither.**"

The **names of** the counties, viz. : Devonshire, 2,000. Somerset,
4,000. **Gloucester,** 1,500. Worcester, 400. Dorset, 1,000. Wiltshire,
2,000. Hampshire, 2,000. Sussex, 2,000. Norfolk, 3,000. Hertford,
500. Berkshire, 500. Oxford, 150. Surrey, 500. Huntingdon, 400.
Cambridge, 700. Leicestershire, 500.

F. 196b. 1588, Aug. 14.—The Privy Council to the **Lord** Steward
[Leicester].

" Her Majesty did think it convenient, as before your Lordship's
departure from hence she did let you understand, that whereas the Army

under your Lordship's charge doth consist of 16,500 footmen, the same should be reduced to a lesser number of 6,000. Her Highness, continuing still in that resolution, hath given us charge to signify her pleasure unto your Lordship for the dismissing of the rest, retaining only 6,000 footmen, which are referred to your Lordship's discretion to licence for the most part those which are of the counties nearest unto you, because they may in a short space, upon any new warning, repair again to your Lordship, as occasion shall serve ; and to retain those for the number of 6,000 which shall remain with your Lordship, which came out of the remote counties, in respect that besides their travel in going and coming they cannot with that speed and readiness be assembled together as may be required. We have thought it not amiss also to put your Lordship in mind that you will be pleased not only to give straight charge and commandment to the captains and leaders of those companies that your Lordship shall think fit to discharge, to cause the soldiers to have a special care to keep their armour, weapons, furniture, and coats, that the same may be forthcoming to serve them at such times as they may be called again hereafter; but also to write your letter to the Deputy Lieutenants of those counties of the which the said footmen were levied, giving them to understand that her Majesty, considering the great charge the said country (sic) have been at to furnish armour, weapons, and coats, hath thought good they should give special order that some of the leaders and chief persons of those several bands may be charged to have care to the particular soldiers, that they keep in good order the armour, weapons, and other furniture ; and also that the said Lieutenant (sic) do cause the said companies to be always in readiness upon new warning to repair either to your Lordship or to any other place as they may be directed, and to suffer no change to be made of those which have been now trained and sent up hither, for others unexperienced and untrained, and most especially of such as are shot ; but if any happen to decease, then to cause other able men to be chosen in their places ; for which purpose we think it meet that every captain should deliver unto your Lordship a note of the names of the soldiers under his charge, with their several weapons and furniture, which he shall be charged to see kept and preserved accordingly as he will answer for the same ; the which notes of* the names of the soldiers with their furniture your Lordship shall cause to be put into a book by the mustermaster. And as concerning the horsemen, her Highness's pleasure is, according as she signified to your Lordship, that they shall be continued still in pay."

F. 197. 1588, Aug. 17, the Court at St. James's.—The Privy Council to the Lord Steward [Leicester].

"Her Majesty being advertised by letters from Sir John Conwey, knight, unto some of us of her Privy Council, that the Duke of Parma hath withdrawn his forces from Dunkircke and Neweporte, and hath sent some of his forces towards Boua (sic) and some other parts toward Berganupsone (sic) ; her Highness, upon this advertisement, doth not think it needful that your Lordship should retain so great forces about you, considering that her Majesty's meaning is that the Navy shall remain still upon the seas in good strength, at the least 100 great ships, until she shall certainly be informed what is become of the Spanish fleet, as also to impeach any attempt the Duke might make. These shall be therefore to let your Lordship understand that her Majesty doth think it meet, your Lordship shall diminish your numbers in such sort

---

* "For" in MS.

as they [there] may remain in the county of Kent the number **of** 1,000
footmen **and** 250 horsemen, and the like numbers in the county **of Essex,**
to be placed in such places in the said counties and under those captains
and in such sort as by your Lordship shall be thought meet ; and that
the said numbers of horsemen and footmen thought necessary to be continued, shall be of those which have been sent hither out of other counties,
for that the forces of Kent and Essex may **upon any** occasion of service
join with the other forces that are thought meet **to be** continued in the
said counties. And when your Lordship hath **taken order** herein for
the bestowing of **the** said numbers accordingly, then **her** Majesty's
pleasure is that **your** Lordship should repair hither."

*Note in margin:* " Stayed."

**F. 197. 1588,** Aug. 24.—[The **Privy Council**] to the Lords Lieute-
**nants of the** several Counties, " for **the repair again** of the horse and
**foot that before** were at Tilbury."

" Whereas her Majesty hath received advertisement the Spanish fleet,
being chased and driven to flee northwards from all the coasts of her
Realm by her Majesty's Navy, should have. some intention to return
again through the Narrow Seas, and so intend **to** give a new attempt for
invasion of the same ; her Highness, upon this intelligence, hath thought
it meet to gather together again some convenient **forces** (by God's
favour) for the withstanding of those attempts that may be made by the
said fleet, or by the Duke of Parma and his forces joining with them
upon his* return. **For** which **respect** our pleasure is that you shall presently, **upon the** receipt **hereof, cause** with **all** diligence and speed that
may be **used,** that those **forces** as well of horse as of foot which was
**[were]** sent out of the county of late furnished and sorted with armour,
weapons, and other necessary provision, as of late the same were† very
well informed, to be put in readiness **and sent up** under the conduct and
leading of those gentlemen, captains, and **other** officers to **whom the**
charge of them was lately committed, so **as the foresaid captains, as well**
of horsemen as footmen, may be at ——— by the ——— of ———— ; and
order shall be taken at their coming thither both for allowance of conduct
money unto them for their repair out of that country (*sic*) to the **said**
place, [and ?] that they shall be received into pay and entertained presently
upon their arrival, after a view taken of them. Wherefore we most
**earnestly** require you to take order herein accordingly, that there may be
**no default,** considering the importance of this service tendeth to the
**safety of the whole** realm."

*Note in margin:* " Stayed."

**F. 197b. 1588,** Aug. 25.—[The Privy Council] " to the Lieutenants
of sundry counties, to examine certain abuses complained of, &c., and
to advertise their Lordships what they find."

*See State Papers, Vol.* 215, *Nos.* 50, 53.

" Of the first part of this letter, touching money collected, there is
yet no answer come, saving only of two shires.

" Of the other part, touching the abuses of Captains, the certificates
remain with Mr. Secretary."

**F. 200.** [1588, July.]—" The Supplies sent for out of the Counties,"
&c. This is a duplicate of F. 194b.

**F. 200.** 1588, July 29.—" Letters written to the Lords Lieutenants,"
&c. **This is** a duplicate of f. 194b., but omits the schedule.

---

* *i.e.* its.          † " weare," *qu.* **we are.**

F. 200*b*. [1588.]—" Abstract of the certificates from the Lieutenants of the abuses committed by the Captains and Officers, upon the letters from the Lords of the 25th of August.

*Com. Surrey.* — Captains Heron, Hill, Gardiner, Gainesford, Courthopp.

Heron received for discharges of men, in number twelve, 32*l*. He made no pays to Budonn (?) for his whole service, Walker for ten days, Collier for 5 days.

Hill discharged of his men, before he delivered them over to Gardinner (*sic*), 17, and retained in money for those discharges 13*l*. 16*s*.

Gardiner discharged 27, and received of them 22*l*. 12*s*. 2*d*. And received more at the camp when his companies were dissolved, 12*l*. 14*s*. 4*d*. His companies lacked of their pay 22*l*. 13*s*. 4*d*. There was armour lost—corslets 8, Alman rivets 9, muskets 5, calivers 25.

Gainesford, for exchanges or dismissions of soldiers, took nothing; detained of pay from every soldier, upon pretence of wastes and fees, twenty pence. Gainesford had hundreds: Tanridge, Bryxton, Wortington (*sic*).* There was armour taken away by Pannet, from the soldiers levied within the Hundred of Tanridge : calivers 2, headpieces 4, muskets changed 1, headpieces changed 2, sword and dagger 1. By Rogers, his serjeants : bills 1, dagger 1, gorget 1, sword changed 1. In the Hundred of Brixton : calivers changed 4, flasks and touchb[oxes] 3, headpieces 11, swords and daggers 11. Coats of plate 2, headpieces 1, swords 1. In Worlington Hundred, armour lost: calivers 1, flasks 2, touchbox[es] 2, murrions 5, swords 4, daggers 5, coats 1. Calivers 2, flasks 3, touchbox[es] 2, murrions 1, swords 1, daggers 1, pikes 1.

Courthopp, from his soldiers levied within the hundred of Kingeston, took no money for discharges, kept no pays back from his soldiers. There was missing in furniture under him: coats 6, murrions 6, swords and daggers 6, calivers 2. All the same said to be taken by Sir Ed. Stanley's officers. From his soldiers levied within the Hundred of Tanridge, detained out of every man's pay, upon pretence of wastes and fees, 20*d*.; for exchanges or dismissions, nothing taken. Of armour taken away by Garret, headpieces 3. In the Hundred of Wallington : coats 2, murrions 1, flasks 1, touchbox 1.

*Com. Essex.*— Captains : Wrothe.

Wrothe discharged nine men, and received in money for them 4*l* 11*s*. Furniture lost under his charge : coats 1, bufierkin (*sic*) 1, musq. fur. 1, sword and dagger 1. Days' want of pay not made to his soldiers, 79.

*Com. Bedford.*—Certified by the Earl of Kent, that restitution is made to the country of the remainder of the moneys collected. That the gentlemen captains are without spot or blemish of corruption. That some inferior officers, found faulty, are accordingly punished. That there are no pays behind due to the soldier. That small defects in armour shall be redressed.

*Com. Hertford.*—Certified by Sir Henry Cock, that they proceed not, by reason of the death of the Lord Lieutenant [Earl of Leicester].

*Com. Berks.*—1. Within the division of Redinge, levied 227*l*. 3*s*. 5*d*. in all. Disbursed ———. Armour wanting : corslets 20, rivets 7, calivers 40, bows 22. Dismissed soldiers for reward, 20. Ran away with their armour, 25. Unpaid for service : 29 for 6 days, and 6*d*. the piece over ; and 46 for three days, and each 6*d*. a-piece over.

2. Within the division of Neuberrie, levied, 276*l*. 9*s*. 4*d*. Whereof disbursed, 208*l*. 14*s*. 10*d*. Remaineth undisbursed, 48*l*. 2*s*. 6*d*. Armour

---

* Wallington Hundred ; Worlington and Wallington below.

wanting: corslet 1, calivers 8, bows 13. Dismissed for reward, none. Run away with armour, 1. Unpaid for service, 30, for 4 days; the captains took order for present satisfaction.

3. Within the division of Abington,* levied, 229l. 18s. 10d. Disbursed, 210l. 4s. 7d. Remaining, 19l. 14s. 3d. Armour wanting: corslets 1, rivets 2, musq[uets] 4, calivers 10. Dismissed for reward by Captain Cooke, 6.

4. Within the division of the Forest, levied, and wholly disbursed, the sum of 130l. Armour wanting under Captain Lovelace: musquet 1, calivers 2, bows 3. Dismissed, none. Run away 2, with calivers. Unpaid under Captain Dockney, 30, for 2 days.

[5.] Within the division of Fanchington (sic),† levied 261l. 15s. 4d. And thereof disbursed, 215l. 19s. Remaineth 45l. 16s. 4d. No armour lost. None dismissed for money. None run away. None unpaid."

*Cf State Papers, Vol. 217, No. 77.*

F. 204. 1589, May 14, the Court at Whitehall. The Privy Council to the [Lords] Lieutenants. [This copy was addressed to Lord Burghley.]

"Where her Majesty hath authorised your Lordship by her commission under the Great Seal of England to be her Lieutenant General over those her counties of Hertford, Essex, and Lincoln, as by her said commission very largely appeareth, and for the good execution of the same commission your Lordship hath had, by divers letters and other writings both from her Majesty and from us, as her Councillors, sundry instructions and orders for the mustering, arming, arraying and putting in strength all the forces of those counties in your charge both on horseback and on foot; according whereunto your Lordship did this last year, as we have well understood, employ great labours, partly by yourself and partly by your Deputies, with a occurrence (sic)‡ in travail of sundry gentlemen employed, some as captains and some otherwise, in that service, so as her Majesty had cause to think your Lordship worthy of the trust committed to you.

"But now, considering that not only a whole winter season, but all the spring time of the year is past, and the summer season being well entered, and nothing done for the renewing of the former orders concerning the having of the forces of the country in a readiness, as were most necessary, her Majesty, having a special care that her whole realm without delay should be put into good readiness for defence of the same against the attempts of the enemy, whatsoever the same shall be, hath expressly commanded us to notify her pleasure to all her Lieutenants throughout her whole realm, of the which your Lordship is one for those counties, and so divers of us have the like charge in other places, that presently, according to the authority given to your Lordship and us, all such directions, instructions, and orders as were§ either the last year or some years precedent for the viewing, mustering, arming, arraying, and putting in a readiness of the forces heretofore limited and prescribed, both for horsemen, footmen, and pioneers, and also for provisions of powder, match, carriages, and such like, should be now diligently again renewed; and in cases where any lack then was the last year or now shall be, either of men, armour, weapon, horse, and other provision of powder or munition of war, or what other necessary things appertaining to

---

* Abingdon.                    † Qu. Farringdon.
‡ Qu. concurrence.             § i.e. were given.

these services, the same should be repaired, supplied, and made perfect.

" And therefore, in the accomplishment of her Majesty's princely care and direction, tending to the honour and safety of this realm, we do most earnestly pray your good Lordship, and in her name will and require you, that upon the receipt of these our letters your Lordship do, according to the authority of your commission, forthwith send for and assemble such of the Justices of Peace of those counties as either heretofore you have used in that kind of service, or shall forthwith now think meet for the same, and therefore [thereupon ?] enter into some good determination how the forces of those shires, both for horsemen and footmen, with their cap[tains] and other officers, may be warned to be ready at convenient places, at some one or several days without long delays, to be fully furnished, and to be viewed and mustered; at which places and days we will and require you, as far forth as with your own presence the same may be, or otherwise by your deputies, [that] the same forces may be mustered in places convenient, to be with least trouble or travail* of the people ; and upon those musters and views to take present order to supply all lack of captains and officers and of the numbers of the soldiers that were last year put into bands, if any either be dead, or by infirmity or removing to dwell in other countries (sic) or by any other accident shall not be ready to serve ; and then to cause all the said forces to be put into bands under captains and officers, with furniture of all things warlike, as by former directions have been appointed.

" And because we mind not to enlarge our letters with so many particularities as for this service are by your Lordship to be considered, we remit you to all former orders and instructions tending to the accomplishment of this service, both for the strength and furniture of the people to be armed, both on horseback and on foot, and for the provision of such store of powder and munition to be in staple for a store, and for the watches in the country and the maintenance and guarding of beacons in places usual ; and generally to see all other things appertaining to your authority as her Majesty's Lieutenant, for the good order and strength of those countries (sic) and for maintenance of peace, and suppression of all great riots and rebellions, as shall to your Lordship as her Majesty's Lieutenant, with assistance and advice of the best sort of the Justices, seem convenient.

" And because it hath seemed a thing very chargeable to the country to continue the multitude of people in trainings, as was in sundry places the last year used, we remit the consideration thereof to your discretion, to be used or to be forborne, so as you foresee that at your musters the persons of the men may be seen to be men able to use their weapons, and their armour and weapons also to be sufficient, and the horse and their riders well furnished and ready to serve therewith ; which being sufficiently fulfilled and perfected, wet† may be the better forborne ; and these your musters to be so taken in several places and at several times, as may be both meet for the service and least troublesome to the people to repair thither. Thus, nothing doubting of your Lordship's accustomed care in performing of these public services importing the state of the realm, we wish your good Lordship right heartily well to fare.

[P.S.]—" We pray your Lordship to certify us of the state of the forces in your charge, as was prescribed the last year."

Signed : C. Hatton, Canc., H. Derby, C. Haward, Hunsdon, Buckhurst, Knoules, Perrot, Wolley, Jo. Fortescue.

---

* i.e. travel.                    † Sic ; qu. the trainings.

F. 204*b*. 1589, Sept. 15.—Mr. **Secretary [Walsingham] to** the [Lords] Lieutenants.

" Whereas in May last, by her Majesty's especial commandment, letters were written unto you from my Lords and others of her Majesty's Privy Council, whereby you were required to review, muster, arm, and put in readiness the forces of foot and horse within the county of your Lordship's Lieutenancy, and to return certificate thereof in due time ; albeit her Majesty nothing doubteth by [but] that you have performed the contents of the said letters, yet forasmuch as hitherto nothing is certified of your proceedings, her Majesty hath commanded me, in her name, to write unto **you**, and to require your Lordship forthwith to send hither the certificate **of your** doings, following therein the directions you have in that **behalf received**, whereof I trust your Lordship will have care."

F. 206. 1589[-90], Jan. 3.—The Privy Council to the [Lords] Lieutenants.

*See State Papers, Vol.* 230, *No.* 1 (Jan. 1).

"There was a clause added in those letters which were sent into **the** co[unties] appointed to furnish men into Ireland, to have the first appointed numbers in readiness, and a new supply also, as appeareth **in** the schedule entered in the Irish book,\* and in the little memorial **of** muster causes."

*The rest of the MS. is in several **different** hands.*

F. 211. 1590, June 29.—**[The Queen] to the** Marquis of **Win**chester.

" Right trusty, &c. **We** have lately caused our Council to confer with our Cousin of Sussex, as Captain of Portesmouth, and with Sir George Carie, knight, as Captain of the Isle of Wight, for some certain orders to be established for sufficient succours of men well furnished for the war, to be put in readiness with[in] that country (*sic*), to serve for to repair to Portesmouth, and to be transported to our said Isle, for defence of the same, upon occasion of any danger of invasion by any enemy to be made against our said town of Portesmouth, or our said Isle of Wight ; whereupon, with the consents of our said Earl **as** Captain of Portesmouth, and Sir George Carie, as Captain of the Isle, there **are appointed** certain numbers of men to be levied and mustered **in certain hundreds** within that county of Southampton, whereof by the **said order it is** limited what numbers and in what places the same shall **be always** in readiness under the levying of able captains and officers **to repair to** Portesmouth for defence thereof; and in like manner what numbers and in what places the same shall be always in readiness under captains and leaders, to be transported into the Isle of Wight. And in like sort **by** the said order there are numbers appointed to be taken out of certain hundreds, to resort to divers places upon the sea coasts, where danger may be of landing of the enemy, for defence against them. So as these orders are to be duly observed, whereof we have commanded our Council to send you in writing the copies thereof signed with their hands, which we will and require you, and also do charge you, being one of the Lieutenants of that county, to see duly observed ; and that all the said forces so limited and appointed may with speed be furnished with armour and weapon, and committed to the charge of captains and other officers ; and that our said Cousin the Earl of Sussex, being both jointly Lieutenant with you and Captain of Portesmouth, may have from time to

---

\* **This book** does not appear to be extant. Among the State Papers (Ireland) there **is** an Entry Book for 1597-9. The earliest Irish letter Book (Signet Office) begins in 1627.

time the musters and commandment of the numbers to be always ready within the hundreds limited to Portesmouth; and Sir George Carie in like manner the musters and commandment of all the numbers limited to the said Isle of **Wight**; so as hereafter there be no default for the speedy sending of the same to the said town and **the said Isle,** as by the orders are limited."

F. 212. 1590, **June** 29.—The Queen to the Earl of Pembroke, [Lord Lieutenant of Somerset and Pembroke].

"Right trusty, &c. Whereas we have heretofore given order for the defence of our Haven of Milford, within our county of Pembroke, that there should be allotted to repair thither in times of danger and doubt of invasion the number of 1,000 men out of our county of Gloucester, and **one** other 1,000 **out** of our county of Somerset, whereof you are our Lieutenant, armed and **furnished** in **such sort** as is convenient : like as **we** have now lately given order **to our right trusty** and right well beloved **the** Lord Chandos, our Lieutenant **in** our **said** county of Gloucester, to see the said **number of 1,000 men to be** presently mustered, armed, and put in readiness to **march upon** any sudden warning that may **be** given : so have we also thought good **to** require you to do the like for **the** other 1,000 within our said county of Somerset, giving order, either **by** yourself or your Deputies, that the said number may be presently **mustered, armed,** enrolled, and allotted out of places of the shire lying **most** convenient for the succour of our said Haven of Milford, and **so to be** kept in a readiness to march thither upon any occasion that shall **fall** out, **to** join with the rest of the forces of our counties of Pembroke, Caermarthen, and the other shires of South Wales.

"And whereas we have been given to understand by information **from** yourself, that your Deputy Lieutenants in **the** said county of Pembroke are **now** absent out of **the** shire, so **as you** are destitute of that help **that** you ought to have in the execution **of our** service within the said county, whereby our said service suffereth great hindrance, we have thought good to nominate unto you certain other meet persons to supply the same place of your Deputies there, which are Sir William Herbert of Swansey, knight, Sir Edward Stradling, knight, **Edward** Kerne, esq., and ——- Maunsell, esq., whom we have appointed **to be** your Deputies within the said county of Pembroke; and therefore we require you to give unto them such warrant and authority as other Deputy Lieutenants in other places have, and withall to give them in charge, as from us, that our pleasure is that they give their attendance in that place of your Deputies by turns, as monthly two of them at one time, and two at another, **so** as there may be always two of them resident **in** the shire to do such things as to the said place of Deputy Lieutenants appertaineth, or as by direction from us or from you shall be enjoined them, to the end that our forces in the said county may be always kept in such readiness **as** the danger of that place requireth.

"We do also think it meet that you appoint your said Deputies in the said county of Pembroke above named, to join with your Deputies in other counties of South Wales next adjoining to the said Haven **of** Milford in the mustering and viewing of the forces of the said counties, to the end **that** they may be acquainted what numbers there **are in** the said **counties to be** drawn **unto** the said Haven in time of danger, and also that **they may be held in** convenient **readiness to** march thither when occasion shall require. And these our **letters shall be** unto you a sufficient warrant **for doing** hereof."

F. 213. 1590, June 29.—[The **Queen] to the Earl of** Pembroke, [Lord] Lieutenant of Wiltshire.

"Right **trusty**, &c. Whereas we have lately taken order what numbers of men shall be put in bands under captains and **officers** fully furnished and in readiness within our county of Southampton **to** resort to **our town** of Portesmouth and the Isle of Wight for the defence of the **same** against the invasion of any enemy : we, finding that, besides **the** numbers appointed for the service of the Isle of Wight, it is requisite **to** have some further numbers to be in a readiness out of some other shire near to the said Isle, we (*sic*) have therefore determined that as heretofore there was order given, so the same shall be now duly put in execution, for certain numbers to be put in readiness in the south parts of that shire, where you are Lieutenant, and from whence the same numbers may most speedily be transported by sea into the said Isle for defence thereof, when cause shall require. And therefore we have commanded our Council to signify to you out of what places and hundreds the same shall be levied, according to the which we will and require you, and by virtue hereof do authorise you with speed, either by yourself **or** your Deputy Lieutenants, to cause all the forces of able men within the hundreds named to you by our said Council to be levied, mustered, armed and weaponed, and put into bands under sufficient captains and officers, and thereof to advertise Sir George Carie, our **Captain** of Wight, so as he may by himself or his deputies have the view **and** mustering of the said bands, and be well acquainted with the captains ; **and** that there be such order taken betwixt him and the said captains **and you or** your Deputy Lieutenants, as upon all usual warnings by beacon or otherwise given out of the said Isle by order of our said Captain for calling of the said **numbers to his succours, they may be** readily sent into the said Isle, in like manner **as other forces are** appointed to be sent to the said Isle out of our county of Southampton. For the doing of all which, these our letters shall be your sufficient warrant, &c."

F. 219*b*. 1599, Aug. 21.—"*Upon advertisement and intelligence that the King of Spain made great preparations both of ships and galleys, and of great forces, to employ the same against this her Majesty's kingdom, there were divers orders, letters, and directions given for putting the forces of the realm in readiness, and for other necessary preparations for defence of the same, which are entered in this book.*"

(**This is** written as a title on a separate page.)

F. 220. 1599, July 22, the Court at Greenwich.—"Minute of their Lordships' [the Privy Council's] letters to the Counties hereunder named, being Maritime Counties."

"Your Lordship* shall understand that her Majesty hath lately received advertisements that the King of Spain doth renew his preparation by sea, and doth add to his other forces of shipping a number of galleys, and [they] are by this already arrived, or very shortly to arrive, at the Haven of Brest, in Brittany, which is an evident argument that he hath a purpose to make some attempt on some part of the coast of this realm. And therefore her Majesty, in her princely wisdom and provident care for the defence of her kingdom, and of her loving subjects, doth foresee by timely provision to withstand and prevent his malicious attempts. For which purpose we are to put your Lordship in mind of those special directions you have received from us by her Majesty's commandment, at such time as the like danger was threatened and expected, wherein particular directions were set down, in what sort your Lordship **was to** govern yourself, and to employ the forces of that county upon

---

* The Lord Lieutenant of each of the counties named below.

any doubt of appearance of landing or purpose of the enemy to make descent in any place, either in that county under your Lordship's Lieutenancy or near unto you, and with what number you were to be supplied out of other counties adjoining, and what helps you were to afford them, if the enemy should bend his force to those parts. Wherein heretofore having given so large and particular directions, we need to add nothing at this present, but that you peruse the same diligently, and cause all the forces and other preparations to be in a readiness for defence of the country. And amongst other things, it is thought requisite that as well all the horse which are enrolled in that county, whereof you are Lieutenant, shall come with your force of foot in repair to the place of landing, as also that the other counties that are to yield supplies unto you, shall in like manner send all their horse unto you, or so many of them as you shall require, according to the occasion which shall be offered unto you ; and you shall do the like to your neighbour counties upon like request made by them. So, referring you to those directions you have formerly received from us in that behalf, we bid your Lordship very heartily farewell."

| Cornwall, | | Kent, |
| Devon, | | Essex, |
| Dorset, | . | Suffolk, |
| Southampton, | | Norfolk. |

F. 220b. [1599], July 22.—[The Privy Council] to the Counties that must send supplies to the Maritime Counties."

(*Same as preceding, down to "malicious attempts."*)

" **For** which purpose we have written our letters to the Maritime Counties, to have the forces of horse and foot in a readiness ; and we are also to put you in mind of those special directions you have received from us by her Majesty's commandment at such time as the like danger was threatened and expected these lat[t]er years, wherein particular directions were set down in what sort your Lordship was to govern yourself, and to direct the forces of that county of (Wilts), upon notice given you from the Lieutenants of Dorset, Devon, and Southampton, in sending two thousand men unto either county, as you shall be required, upon appearance and intended course of the enemy discovered to land in any of those counties ; to whom, besides the foresaid number of foot, and horse, you are to send also all the horses that are enrolled in that county, or so many as shall be required of you, with such other necessary provisions as by our former direction hath been prescribed unto you ; whereunto we do refer you, and especially require of you, for the furtherance of her Majesty's service, to peruse diligently our former directions and instructions given you in that behalf, that there may no default be found in you in these occasions concerning the necessary defence of the realm and withstanding the attempts of the enemy."

"The schedule doth set down the forces of foot every county is to furnish, and to what counties."

| | | | |
|---|---|---|---|
| Wilts | - | 2000 | ⎱ Devon. Dorset. Southampton. |
| Somerset | - | 4000 | Devon. Dorset. |
| Berks - | - | 3000 | Southampton. |
| Sussex | - | 4000 | Southampton. Kent. |
| Surrey | - | 3000 | Southampton. Kent. |

E 2

| | | | |
|---|---|---|---|
| London - | - | - 3000 | { Kent. <br> { Sussex. |
| Hertford | - | - 1,000 <br> 500 | { Essex. <br> { Suffolk. |
| Cambridge | - | - 500 | { Suffolk. <br> { Norfolk. |
| Huntingdon | - | - 500 <br> 300 | { Suffolk. <br> { Norfolk. |
| Lincoln - | - | - 3,000 | Norfolk. |

F. 221. [1599,] July 23.—[The Privy Council] to the Lord Mayor of London.

"Whereas her Majesty hath received divers advertisements that the King of Spain doth make preparations by sea, both of ships and galleys, which are drawing towards these seas: as her Majesty hath a princely care to prevent, by all provident means, the design the enemy may make to attempt anything upon any part of the sea coast, so in her princely wisdom, and in regard of the City of London, the chiefest and principal part of the realm, and the greatest mark whereat they shoot to spoil or burn the same, her Majesty is not unmindful to provide for the withstanding those attempts they may make of the River of Thames. For which purpose, although her Majesty is no way minded to have you put to any unnecessary charge (yea, though it be for your own natural defence), nevertheless she hath thought fit to command us, in her name, to require you to call unto you the owners of the best ships that lie now in this river, and to take such order as this* ordnance and powder may in some good proportion be brought aboard some twelve or sixteen of them, whereby they may be the readier for defence upon any sudden occasion or attempt. This being a matter which can put them to no loss (in which no prince can be more respectful than her Majesty is) further than the necessity of the times requires it, we doubt not but you will use the matter with that discretion and expedition which shall be thought convenient."

F. 221. [1599,] July 27.—[The Privy Council] "to the Lords Lieutenants, their Deputies, Commissioners for the Musters, and the Vice-Admirals of the several Counties hereunder named."

"Whereas certain of her Majesty's ships royal are to be set to the seas with all expedition, and there shall be occasion to use a good number of mariners to serve in them, her Majesty's pleasure is, you shall cause notice and public proclamation to be made that all the mariners, pilots, and seafaring men that are fit for service, from the age of 16 unto 60, that may be found in all that country (*sic*), shall be imprested and taken up, and charged upon pain of death to make their present repair with all expedition unto Chattam, so as they may be there within —— days after this warning given them, not staying for any other. For the more expedition and advancement of this service you shall cause imprest of 12*d.* to be given to every man, after the rate of one halfpenny the mile, from thence where they shall be imprested to Chattam, the charges whereof shall be again answered unto you. And further you shall cause a roll to be taken of the names of those which shall be imprested, to th'end, if any of them shall withdraw themselves and shall not be there at the time appointed, they shall be assured of the foresaid punishment to be inflicted upon them. So, &c.

"Postscript. You shall cause stay to be made of all shipping in every port of that country (*sic*) upon pain of death."

* Qu. that.

| Counties. | | The time limited. |
|---|---|---|
| Suffolk | within | 6 days. |
| Norfolk | „ | 6 days. |
| Somerset | „ | 8 days. |
| Devon | „ | 8 days. |
| Cornwall | „ | 10 days. |

F. 221b. [1599, July.—The Privy Council] "to Sir **Walter** Rawleighe, knight, her Majesty's Lieutenant of the County **of** Cornwall."

"Although we wrote very lately unto you that you should take up and imprest, with all expedition and care, all the mariners, seafaring **men**, and pilots within that county,* directing them to be at Chattam within ten days after you had given them notice ; and we doubt not but you have taken order therein as you were required, according to the importance of the occasion, which caused us to write in such earnest manner : nevertheless, because we hear nothing as yet of the coming of the men, nor yet from you, what order you have taken, we do again will and command you, in her Majesty's name, if those mariners be **not** already sent away according to our former direction, that you will **use** all means and care to hasten the men unto Chattam with all speed **that** may be used ; and that you appoint some discreet and trusty persons to come in their company, to hasten them in their coming hither, and **to** see that none of them do run away. The expedition of the service is such as we can give you now no other order for imprest and conduct money but to charge you to see the same delivered to the mariners, as by our former direction you were appointed **to do,** which shall be presently answered and paid again to such **as** you shall appoint to receive the same. Thus, charging you upon your allegiance to **use** such expedition, as if the mariners be not already departed from **thence,** they may be at Chattam within ten days after these our **letters shall** come to your hands, **we** bid you, &c.

" Like letters **written** to the **counties** of :—

> Devon, 8 days.
> Somerset, 8 days.
> Norfolk, 6 days.
> Suffolk, 6 days."

F. 222. [1599, July 25, Greenwich.]†—The Queen **to** Sir Francis Vere.

"**Trusty and well** beloved, we greet you well. You shall understand **that we** have received credible intelligence from divers places that the King **of Spain hath** drawn down a fleet of ships and galleys so far hitherward as they are daily expected at Brest in France, the galleys being (as some reports do deliver) already arrived in the Passage the 5th of this month. We leave it to your judgment to consider whether it be not evident (if this be true) that they have a design either upon our coast, or upon the Low Countries, seeing there is no other argument why they should be drawn down thus far, where they fear no enemy, **nor** from whence they have no parts to assail but England **or the Low** Countries. These things do little trouble us, because we know what it is to despise the Spanish attempts, when they were made of another manner of force ; although it may be that they are carried on with

---

* " and " occurs here, in MS.
† This date, and the last eight **lines of the letter, are struck out.**

some opinion that we, that have great numbers in **Ireland both of** commanders and soldiers, may be easily induced to leave **that work** unperfected, **if we** should be attempted nearer hand, or may be less provided to **resist** their malice. Secondly, it is not unlike but from some ill affected subjects here they may be informed, that we have no great fleet **in** readiness fit to encounter them; **a** matter surely (if it were less forward than they shall find it) **wherein** we cannot but represent unto you two observations which we have made of the strange proceedings of the Low Countries this summer, which (we can be content the States should know) have proved far contrary to our expectation.

" First, in the beginning of their preparations, we were assured from them, that they were resolved to keep a fleet upon the Spanish coasts all this year, and to have attempted some things of good moment, especially for the destruction of his navy, of which we have found the effects so contrary as they have passed so clear of all the coast of Spain as they have made thereof great triumph, to see that such a navy after such an expectation should engage themselves no further in action. Secondly, we do conceive that they have used a little too much reservation to make us so great strangers to any of their particular purposes, as to **this** hour we are, whereby we have remained uncertain in such proceedings divers ways as we would have taken, if **we** had **not** expected **some** better correspondency from **them, who know that we do never** forget them, neither in our counsel **or actions.**

" To th'intent that **you may** know some particulars considerable in this matter, and thereby **the better** fashion things for our service, we think it not amiss to say **thus much unto** you, that although the fleet of **Spain be** smaller than heretofore, yet the mixture with galleys in the summer time will be a great furtherance to their ships in the calms, when ours cannot stir; in which case, because there is no invasion from Spain which can annoy us to any purpose without the assistance of the army of the Low Countries, we think it not fit to neglect the consideration of that point, and therefore find **it** not improbable but that they may, having now the coast of France to their friend, pass over in short passages the Spanish forces from the Low Countries in their galleys, whilst their ships may be of sufficient force to encounter with **any** of ours **which they may** imagine we can be able on the sudden to set **forth.** And therefore **we** have written, first a letter to the States of credit for you, as also **another to** Count Maurice, of both which you may make use for warrant **of those** things which **you** shall find necessary to declare unto them.

" And for your better direction, these be the points whereof we would have you bethink yourself : first, to learn by all means possible, whether this siege of Ostende be likely to prove resolute, for it is not impossible but it may seem [serve?] for a colour to draw down their forces nearer to the place of embarking. We would also have you above all things to seek to understand, whether the army that is there, do carry itself so, as if it come not to Ostende, that it do keep itself wholly to be drawn down upon warning, or come lower to be quartered nearer the seaside, or else engage itself some other where. For of these things shall you be able to gather some light the better to advertise us.

"And for the matters that you are to propound to the States; we require you to let them know, that to resist the Spanish fleet, if it come into **the** Narrow Seas, we will expect that,* according to the Contract such numbers of ships as may join with our fleet, which we are setting

---

* " that " is superfluous.

out to the seas for the defensive, which shall consist of forty sail of ours and our subjects'; and further to* let them know that we do make ourselves [ourself?] secure also, if his purpose of invading us with any power or army demonstrate itself, that besides those forces which are under your commandment, they will assist us with such convenient numbers as we shall require; considering well, that if that army or any part thereof be employed here, that in that case there is no fear of any prejudice to their fortune, till the matter be tried between us. Of which we are so far from fear, as we do rather wish they would be so unadvised as to attempt us, that it might make an end of the quarrel, for if it had not pleased God already to give us experience what they could do against us, yet our confidence in the justness of our quarrel would sufficiently assure us against him [them?].

"Now have we delivered you what we are advertised, which we require you to impart to the States, and to Count Maurice, rather to prepare their minds and hear what will come from them, than that we do apprehend this in any other form than as a prince ought to do, who hath not been used to receive a scorn by her enemies, and therefore hold it wisdom to use prevention, having a state and people whose good is dearer unto us than our own."

F. 223. 1599, Aug. 4, Nonesuche.—The Queen to the Lord Mayor of London.

"Right trusty and well beloved, we greet you well. Whereas by good advice we hear that the King of Spain draws to head at the Groine all those forces which he had prepared to defend his coast all this year against the States' fleet, with a large increase both of men and munitions, provisions, ships, and galleys, of purpose to assail our kingdom near to our State,† and to make a spoil of that our City of London, presuming to find us at this time unprovided, when a great part of our forces are necessarily employed out of this our realm: yet as a prince that hath more care and feeling of the honour and preservation of her realm, the safety of that City, and loss of her good subjects, than of herself, we are resolved so far forth to employ our own means, and so well otherwise to provide, as with the assistance of Almighty God we shall be able to meet with his malicious designs to his great dishonour and loss, and therefore have given order for the levying of sufficient companies of horse and foot in divers of our counties with all speed ; and so likewise do will and command and hereby authorise you to levy within that our City the number of three thousand able footmen, to be armed and sorted with weapons, as in like levies hath been used, and them to put into orderly bands by the 12th of this present August, ready to be delivered to the charge of such commanders and leaders for the service, as by our Privy Council you shall understand our further pleasure. And in case we shall find necessary to levy any more numbers of foot or of any other companies in our said City for this service than the said 3,000, then we will and authorise you likewise by these our letters to levy and put in order in our said City the same, according to such further direction as you shall receive from our said Council."

*There is a brief note of the foregoing letter among the State Papers (Docquets).*

F. 223b. [1599,] July 28.—[The Privy Council] to the Lord Mayor [of London].

"We have had conference at large with the Aldermen, your brethren, which your Lordship sent hither this morning; by whose report you

---

* " do " in MS.   † *Sic.*

shall understand upon what ground and respects we are **moved to have** extraordinary care at this time for the defence of the River **of Thames,** and to hasten those preparations which shall be necessary for that purpose. Therefore, where we wrote lately unto you to cause 12 or 16 ships that were at that present in **the** River, to be made ready and to be furnished with ordnance, powder, and other necessary provision, you shall now understand that we have made choice of **16,** which we think fit for this purpose, and have given **direction to these your** brethren, what further provision we have thought **meet to be added** and had in a readiness for the furnishing those ships, and in what sort they shall **be** employed if occasion shall serve, and what we have further considered of for the **defence of** the City. For the better performance whereof, we **do hereby authorise your Lordship, or** such as you **shall** depute and appoint **to have the care and** charge, **to** direct, attend, and execute these services, as well for the taking up **of** men and all other necessary **provisions** that may be incident unto the same, as for the doing of any other thing that shall be requisite for the advancement of this important service. And considering the chiefest respect that **is sought** and desired by **these** provisions, is for the defence of that City (**being** a principal part and member of the realm, and **whereat the** enemy doth chiefly level), we pray your Lordship **that you will with all** speedy **direction** cause good numbers of men **to** be **made ready and** sorted with armour and weapon, that **they may (if occasion** serve) **be** put into bands under fit captains to **serve for the defence of** the City; and that you will likewise give direction **that all inhabitants** and citizens of ability within the City and liberties **of the same, that** are appointed and ought to find armour **and** weapon, may **be** required to have the same in present readiness. Because we have conferred with the Aldermen that were before us at large in these matters, **we refer** you unto their report, being men of discretion, and that **have** been **used by** you in like services."

F. 223*b*. [1599,] July 28.—[**The Privy** Council] **to the Officers** of the Ordnance.

"Whereas there hath been request made unto **us by our very good** Lord the Lord Hunsdon, Lord Chamberlain of **her Majesty's House-**hold, **for certain munitions** for the Isle of Wight: these **shall be** to req**uire** you to deliver or cause to be delivered out of her Highness' [Store] within the Tower of London, unto the said Lord Hunsdon, **or** to such as he shall appoint for the receipt thereof, for the better supply and **defence of the same** Isle, **these** parcels of iron shot and munition following; **that is to say, round** shot for demi-cannon, twenty; for culvering, twenty; **for** demi-culvering, six hundred; for sakers, fifty; and for minion, thirty; long pikes, two hundred; match, six thousand weight; ladle-staves, forty-eight; heads and rayners (*sic*), forty-eight; waddhookes staved, twelve; black bills, one hundred; lead for shot, two tons; copper plate, one hundred; sheepskins, twenty-four; ginne complete, one; ginne reape spare (*sic*), fifty pound weight; draught rope, four coils; shovels and spades, two hundred; pickaxes, fifty; and crows of iron, twelve. For all which these shall be, &c."

F. 224. [1599,] July 29.—[The Privy Council] to the Archbishop of Canterbury.

"Her Majesty receiving daily and certain advertisements that the King of Spain maketh great preparations by sea both of ships and galleys, with purpose to invade some part of this realm, **as** there is direction to the Lieutenants of the Maritime Counties to put the forces both of **horse** and foot in readiness to withstand th'attempts of the **enemy, so it is** thought fit that there should **be** forces both of horse and foot to attend the defence of her Majesty's person, as the like was done in the year '88. At which time there was offer made by the Bishops and the rest of the Clergy of the realm, of the number of 559 lances, lighthorse, and petronels, besides a good number of foot, to attend her Majesty's person. We pray your Lordship, therefore, considering the great preparations the enemy doth make at this present, that you will direct your letters at this time unto all the Lords the Bishops within your Province, requiring them, in her Majesty's name and for the defence of her sacred person, to have in a readiness as well their own horses, as to procure (with all speed) all the Deans and Clergymen within their diocese[s] to do the like, and to see them furnished with necessary furniture, and with riders to serve with the horses ; and to certify to your Lordship the number of horse they have in readiness, and how many are lances, lighthorse, and petronels, as also of the foot, that we may understand from your Lordship what the number is they do provide, how many of each sort there are, how they are furnished, and in what readiness they are ; that upon any occasion they may be directed to repair to such place as shall be appointed for the rest of the forces and Army that is intended for the defence of her Majesty's person. Herein we doubt not but they will shew all forwardness and good example, both to increase the number, and to send able and sufficient horses and men, considering the enemy doth colour his malice under pretence to advance the Romish religion. So, &c.

"Postscript. We pray your Lordship to use all expedition herein because the army of the enemy is expected within 15 days."

F. 225. [1599,] July 29.—[The Privy Council] to the Earl of Pembroke.

"Whereas her Majesty hath of late received divers and certain advertisements, that the King of Spain maketh great preparations by sea, both of ships and galleys, with purpose and intent to invade some part of this realm ; as we have written our letters, by her Majesty's express commandment, both to the maritime and sundry inland counties of the realm, to have all the horse and foot in a readiness to withstand the attempt of the enemy, with direction how the maritime counties shall be supplied out of other counties adjoining, as occasion may require , so we have thought good likewise to give your Lordship notice hereof, and do pray you to cause all the numbers of horse and foot within the several counties in the principality of Wales (especially in the maritime counties) to be likewise in a readiness, as hath been in former time, and to see the beacons duly and carefully watched alongst the sea coast, and meet places near the sea coast, the better to discover any attempt, navy, or number of shipping, that may come towards any part of that coast, and to have special regard of Millford Haven ; to which end you shall give directions, that one of the Deputy Lieutenants may be there in person. Wherein, praying your good Lordship to take present order, &c."

F. 225. [1599,] Aug. 1.—[The Privy Council] to the Lord Mayor of London.

"You shall understand that her Majesty, in regard of the knowledge and great experience that our very good Lord the Earl of Cumberland hath in sea causes, hath appointed his Lordship to have the command of those ships that are to be placed in the River of the Thames, for the defence of the same and withstanding the attempts of the enemy, and to consider of and direct all those necessary provisions that shall be fit for that purpose. To whose opinion, in regard of his Lordship's experience and judgment, we pray your Lordship to attribute that

confidence and credit which is meet, and to follow such directions as he
shall advise you to take in that behalf; his Lordship being by us
appointed to confer herein with your Lordship, and to use the advice
also of some person of skill and knowledge, and for the better directing
those ships, forces, and provisions that are to be employed at this present
in this action."

F. 225. **[1599,] Aug. 1.**—[The Privy Council] **to** the Earl of
Cumberland.

" Whereas her Majesty hath thought good, in regard to your Lordship's knowledge and experience in sea affairs, to appoint your Lordship
to take the charge to direct those ships which are to be placed in the
River of the Thames, for the defence of the same, considering the importance of this service, being intended to prevent the designs of the
enemy's, that are most to be doubted, whereby he may find resistance even
in the entry to his chiefest attempts: her Majesty's pleasure is, your
Lordship shall call unto you Sir George Caro,* Lieutenant of the Ordnance, and the Lieutenant of the Tower, being gent[lemen] of good
knowledge and judgment in martial affairs, and confer with the Lord
Mayor of the City, and such of the committees as are appointed by him
for these causes, both for the furnishing and employing of the shipping
that are to be placed in the **River** of Thames, and for all other things
that may be thought requisite **for** defence of the River and the City, that
present **order** may be taken **to see** your resolution in the same put in
execution ; wherein **we pray your** Lordship to acquaint us with those
**things you shall, after consultation had,** agree upon."

F. 225*b*. [1599,] Aug. 1.—[The Privy Council] to Lord Cobham,
**her** Majesty's Lieutenant in Kent.

" We have thought good to let your Lordship understand that it is
thought requisite that an Army of 12,000 [10,000 ?] foot should be
drawn together to such place in the county of Kent, under your Lordship's lieutenancy, as [they] might be conveniently lodged and quartered,
and where they might be in a readiness to be directed to such place as
the enemy should attempt to put men on land. Of these, 6,000 **are to**
be drawn out of the ordinary bands of that county, and the other 4,000
shall be **sent** unto you out of the county of Sussex. Therefore we **desire
to know** your Lordship's opinion where the 6,000 soldiers of that county
**may be** conveniently placed, that they may be directed to be there by
some certain day of this month ; for which purpose we think the city of
Canterbury to be a very fit place. And because these men are to be
drawn to an head, and to be employed as occasion shall serve, we desire
to understand from your Lordship how you are furnished of skilful and
experienced captains to have charge and conduction of them, that we may
think on such as your Lordship shall want to be supplied and recommended
unto you.

" We have also entered into consideration of some special and necessary
officers for that Army, when it shall be assembled together, for the better
ordering and governing of them ; whereof Sir Thomas Wilforde, one of
your Deputy Lieutenants, is thought a meet man to be Marshal of the
Army, and Sir Richard Wingfeilde to be Serjeant Major, and the
Colonels may remain as already they are, if it shall so like your Lordship. For the 4,000 which are to be drawn out of Sussex, we think
Sittingborne to be a fit place for their rendezvous, though we leave
the same to your Lordship's choice and ordering, to whom the country
is best known.

---

* Carew.

" **In** these points, as we desire to have your Lordship's opinion, so, because matters cannot as well be handled and all doubts satisfied by writing as by conference, which by reason of your indisposition we cannot have presently with your Lordship, as we chiefly **do** desire, we pray you that your Lordship will, with all expedition, send for Sir John Leveson, and acquaint him with your mind and opinion **in** these things, and send him presently to us, that we may know the **same.** And for the victualling and other provisions for the Camp,* or **a greater** (if need shall require), and so by him send our resolutions, **and such further** directions as shall be thought meet in that behalf."

F. 226. [1599,] Aug. 2.—[The Privy Council] to the Lord **Trea**surer [Burghley] and the Lord Admiral [Nottingham], her Majesty's Lieutenants in Sussex.

" Whereas it is thought meet that there should be an Army assembled in **Kent,** to consist of 10,000 foot, besides horsemen, whereof 6,000 are drawn out of that county, and 4,000 out of the county of Sussex, with all the horses that are enrolled and certified : because there is that expedition to be used as the 4,000, that are to be levied in Sussex, may be at Syttingburne by the 10th of this present month, we do pray **your** good Lordships that you will give present direction unto your Deputy Lieutenants to levy with all speed the number of 4,000 foot of the enrolled bands in that county, to be sorted with armour and weapon, as hath been generally prescribed to be observed throughout all the counties of the realm ; that is, the one half pikes, armed with gorgetts, curattes, and murrions, and the other half shot, whereof half to be muskets, saving a few short weapons ; and the horse to be sent also with them. These men are to be sent under the conduct of such gentle**men** of the country as are appointed ordinarily to have charge of them, so as they may be at Syttingburne by the 10th of this month, where there shall be direction given **to see** them placed, lodged, **and** dieted in such sort as shall be convenient.

" Therefore we pray your good Lordships **to give speedy direction** herein, as we for more haste do write **our** letters unto you **to** advance the service, wherein for your better warrant your Lordship[s] shall have her Majesty's letters under her hand signed. In the mean season your Lordships will be pleased to use all care the service may be performed, and to see the soldiers may have conduct money delivered unto them at their entering into march, which shall be answered again to the country ; and at their arrival at Syttingburne they shall enter into pay. **Your** Lordships knowing how this doth import her Majesty's service, being for the defence of the realm, we do not doubt but your Lordships will cause all diligence and expedition to be used, and that you will see them furnished with apparel as shall be meet for soldiers, if upon the sudden you cannot provide them of coats."

F. 226*b*. [1599,] Aug. 2. — [The Privy **Council**] to Sir Robert Sidney, Governor of Vlishinghe (Flushing).

" Her Majesty having occasion to gather together some good numbers of men in the county of Kent, to be there in a readiness to be disposed of, to withstand such attempts as the King of Spain's army may **make,** of whose preparations by sea we doubt not but you have heard long sithence ; because it is not doubted but you have in that garrison many good and experienced soldiers, her Majesty's pleasure is you shall make choice of 300 of the best and most ancient soldiers in that garrison and to (*sic*) send them over, with their captains and officers, with all

---

* A clause seems to **be wanting here.**

expedition, directing them to land at Margett, or the Downs in Kent, where order shall be taken to receive them, and for their weekly imprests. Herein we pray you to have care in the choice of the companies, whereby though your numbers there shall seem to receive some diminution, yet considering they are to be employed in so necessary a service, and we hope the time will not be long that shall require their stay here, we doubt not but you will shew that dutiful forwardness which is expected of you to perform this her Majesty's pleasure. For the charge of their transportation, we will take order the same shall be allowed upon your account shewed unto us of the charges disbursed. Herein we require you to take speedy order."

F. 226b. [1599,] Aug. 2.—[The Privy Council] to the Lord Mayor of London.

"Because we receive daily advertisements, confirming the great preparations of the King of Spain, and all likelihoods that he intendeth the same against the City of London, and therefore all care is to be had and used to strengthen the River of Thames, and to advance those provisions that are to serve for that purpose; wherein we doubt not but your Lordship hath already had conference with our very good lord the Earl of Cumberlande, and that you will use all care and speed [to] put in execution those things that upon conference with his Lordship shall be concluded and agreed upon: for the] better defence of the River, and for divers necessary respects, it is thought meet your Lordship shall make choice of some discreet person, who shall be authorised to repair to the places alongst the River of Thames hereunder written,* and to take up in those places to the number of ten Western barges, and to cause them to be brought up to London, to be employed as there should be occasions; and that you will also cause to the number of twenty lighters of the greatest burthen to be taken up, and to be sent unto Gravesende, to lie and attend there to serve for the transportation of men that may be sent out of Essex into Kent. Herein we pray your Lordship to use all care and expedition."

F. 227. [1599,] Aug. 2.—[The Privy Council] to Lord Cobham.

"Her Majesty, by advice that cometh from sundry parts, finding the intelligence your Lordship hath heard of the Spanish preparations to be confirmed, and that it is greatly suspected, by the manner of their preparations, correspondency held with his forces of the Low Countries, and by advertisements and other reasons, that he will attempt to land his forces either in the Downs or at Margett: her Majesty's pleasure is, your Lordship shall presently send to Sir Thomas Wilforde, being one of your Deputy Lieutenants for the East part, and to command him forthwith to consider where and how some provision may be made, by casting up trenches or any other way or [of?] impeachment, at their likest landing places, either in the Downs or at Margett, which may serve also for defence of those forces which shall be used against them; the performance whereof we pray your Lordship to leave to his consideration, so it be done with all expedition. And further, as we doubt not but your Lordship will have all the foot companies in a readiness, so, besides your ordinary horse-bands, we pray your Lordship to foresee that the numbers of horses may be increased, by moving the gentlemen to bring as many (sic) of their servants well horsed, to such place of rendezvous as shall be appointed."

F. 227. [1599,] Aug. 3.—[The Privy Council] to the Lord Mayor of London.

---

* The names are not given in the MS.

"We have considered of your Lordship's letter sent this day unto us, whereby we perceive the pains you take for the defence of the City, and providing those things that are necessary for that purpose, and, amongst other things, that you have appointed captains for those 3,000 men that you have already levied. Wherein as we do allow of your care, so we are to advise your Lordship to consider that those 3,000 men are to serve for the defence of the River of Thames, or to be sent to defend the coast, if occasion be offered by attempt of the enemy either on Kent or Essex; and therefore, how requisite it is that the leaders and conductors of them should be men of skill, knowledge, and charge, we leave it to your consideration. Because we do hear nothing from your Lordship of the rest of the forces of the City you were required to have in a readiness, which specially are desired for the good and defence of the City, we would be glad to hear what the numbers are, how they are furnished, and in what readiness they be. Lastly, for the warrant your Lordship requireth from her Majesty for your further authority and indemnity, we doubt not but you have received the same before these shall come to your hands. Thus, praying your Lordship to go forward with all necessary preparations as you have had upon conference with our very good lord the Earl of Cumberland, we bid, &c."

F. 227*b*. [1599,] Aug. 3.—The Privy Council to Lord Cobham.

"We have received your Lordship's letter and opinions in those things we wrote unto you, and have seen the list of the names of those your Lordship thought fit to have charge as Colonels and Captains over the 6,000 men that the county of Kent doth furnish. Considering your Lordship is to venture your life amongst them, we doubt not but your chiefest respect shall be to make choice of such as for their ability and knowledge are worthiest to be preferred, and therefore we do allow of those your Lordship hath named; and if your Lordship shall find want of any captains, we will be glad to supply you with such as at this present may be had; a great number, as your Lordship knoweth, of principal leaders being out of the realm at this present. We do also yield to your Lordship's request for Sir Calisthenes Brooke to be Serjeant Major; and where your Lordship doth recommend Mr. George Wiatt to be Master of the Ordnance, he may have charge (if so your Lordship shall think good, and he be willing) of the Ordnance that is there, but that title is not to be allowed to any as yet for the present time.

"In the mean season we pray your Lordship that the field pieces that are at Canterburie may be viewed, and that you will consider and certify us what is wanting for them, which shall be supplied out of her Majesty's Store, of those kinds that are there to be had. But for the wheels and carriages, if they be decayed, we pray you to cause carpenters to be taken up out of hand, and the best stuff you may readily find, and to see the same forthwith sufficiently repaired, the charge whereof shall be answered to such as your Lordship shall appoint to receive the same.

"Now, for the quartering of the forces, we concur with your Lordship, that Canterburie will be the fittest place for those of Kent to make their head, howbeit those numbers that are appointed for the defence of her Majesty's ships are not to be removed until other 2,000 shall be come unto you out of Surrey, who are directed to be there by the twelfth of this month, and to be bestowed at Gravesende with the 4,000 out of Sussex; and because we find there are only 100 selected men in the Isle of Thannett under the charge of John Ascoughe, they may very well serve and be appointed, as occasion shall serve, **to** come to the ships that are under Sheernes[s].

" Lastly, because we do find, both by the view of your muster rolls and other information, that there are divers gentlemen and other persons of good ability in that county, that have no charge in **the** country, and **are not** assessed to find horses ; in this occasion we think it meet, and so **require** your Lordship, that they may be commanded to repair to such **place** as shall be appointed for the rendezvous of the Army, with **all the** lances, light horses, or petronels they shall be able to bring, with **their** whole retinue, wherein we doubt not but they will shew all forwardness to come in good sort with good numbers, and furnished, **seeing** it is for **the** defence of themselves and the country where **they inhabit** and their livings doth lie. The rest we refer to the report **of Sir** John Leveson, because it would be tedious in writing to set down every particular direction, being sorry your Lordship hath no better health at this time, whereof we do wish speedy recovery; and yet, if your Lordship's indisposition will [not] permit you to repair into the country so soon as we wish, we think it meet that Sir Thomas Wilforde, being Marshal in your Lordship's absence, may have the chief **charge** and command over those numbers that are to be assembled **there, and** give order for all things that are to be done **in** this **behalf, and to see** those directions which shall be sent from hence put in **execution.**"

F. 228. **[1599,]** Aug. 4.—" Minute of her Majesty's letters to the Counties **following,** for the sending up of Voluntary Horse."

" Right trusty and well beloved,* we greet you well. If we were now **to** require a matter that needed persuasion, or did make choice of persons of common understanding, then should we peradventure mistrust some excuse or delay; but when we consider what a matter these our letters bring you, we assure ourselves that you will receive great comfort, and we speedy satisfaction—you, to perceive our extraordinary care for you, with the opinion we have of your forward disposition, and we, to receive from you the fruits of our desires, which tend to your own preservation. For, seeing it is so fresh in memory that in all the attempts from Spain against this kingdom, slaughter and servitude was prepared for you (as by their own proclamations **did** appear), when by the powerful hand of God, and the endeavour of our ministers, you were preserved, and they in their pride confounded ; it were **now a** lack of consideration, when opportunities may invite such an **enemy to assail us, that these†** things should be omitted which are necessary **to resist** attempts **on** the sudden, seeing we so little need to care for any **of his** declared purposes.

" Being therefore by very good advice assured that he draweth to head all those forces at the Groine which he prepared to defend his coasts all this year against the States' fleet, with purpose now to assail us, when he presumes we are least provided for him, hoping thereby to divert that work which we have chargeably begun for the suppression of the Irish Rebellion, and that he meaneth to make a sudden descent, even in the inner parts of our Kingdom nearest to our City and Navy ; forasmuch as we have resolved to have him impeached by all convenient means at his landing with such numbers of foot and horse especially as shall be thought needful : we have thought fit hereby (seeing time will not suffer us to write to all particularly) to command you to give present notice to these† whose names are underwritten to send unto

---

\* *i.e.* the Lord Lieutenant of the county
† *Qu.* those.

————---- so many horses, furnished **as is hereunder** written, to be there by the ———— of this present August, **where we will give** order to have them disposed, requiring every man to provide **for the** maintenance of themselves and their horses for the space **of one** month. Wherein, though this commandment tendeth to no other purpose **than** to move **you to** defend yourselves, yet will we take more feeling **of this** dutiful **part of** yours being performed at this time without delay, **than** of a far greater matter, because it shall thereby appear to the **world** that those advantages that our enemies might hope to find by prevention of time, shall be recompensed by the resolution and expedition **of** our good subjects, **for whom** we will spare nothing that God hath given **us** here on earth, **to** preserve them from falling into the hands of those **who have so** long thirsted **after the** destruction of this kingdom. And **these,** &c. Given, &c."

## "'The Schedule."

(The **first** figure after **each name shows the number of** "**lances,**" the second figure the number **of** "lighthorse.")

*Berks :* Thomas Vachell, 1, 1. **Francis** Winchcombe, 1, **1. Hugh** Speake, 1, 1. Sir Humfrey Foster, 2, **3.** William Hide, **1, 2. Sir** Thomas Parrye, 2, 3. Alexander Choke, 1, 1. John Norreis, **1,** 1. Samuel Backhouse, 1, 2. Richard Warde, 1, 2. Bessells Fettiplace, 1, 2. **Thomas** Reade, 2, 3. Richard Hide, 1, 1. Sir Michael Mollins, 2, 3. Edmond Duncke, 2, 3. William Essex, 2, 3. Edmond Phettiplace, 2, 3. ———— Sherley, 2, 3. Lances, 26. Lighthorse, 38.

*Bedford :* John Dive, 1, 1. Anthony Tirringham, 2, 2. George Smithe, **1, 1.** John Burgoine, 1, 2. William Goswicke, 1, 1. John Osborne, **1, 1.** Nicholas Luke, 2, 2. William Duncombe, 1, 1. Richard Charnocke, **1,** 1. George Wingate, 1, 1. Geo. Rotheram, 1, **2.** Henry Butler, 1, 1. Richard Conquest, 1, 1. Sir Edw. Radcliffe, 2, **3.** Miles Sands, 2, 2. William Fleetwood, 2, 3. Lances, 21. Lighthorse, 25.

*Buckingham :* Edward Tirrell, 1, 2. Sir Edm. Varney, 1, **2.** William Andrewes, 1, 1. Paul Darnell, 1, 1. Robert Mordant, 1**, 2.** Henry Longvile, 2, 2. Thomas Denton, 1, 1. Thomas Throgmorton, 2, 2. Francis Curson, 1, 2. Francis Cheney, 1, 1. John Temple, 2, 2. Rowland Litton, 2, 3. John Crook, seg$^r$ (*sic*), 1, 2. Thomas Tafforde,* 1, 1. Thomas Pagett, 2, 2. Sir Ro. Dormer, knight, 4, 6. Sir Jo. Packington, 2, 3. Alexander Hambden, 1, 2. John Cotton, 1, 1. Henry Drurye, 1, 1. Richard Ingolsbye, 1, 1. William Burlacie, **1, 2.** Francis Goodwin, 2, 2. William Garrard, 1, 1. William Totill, **1, 1. Sir** Tho. Tasborough, 1, 2. Christopher Barker, 1, 1. ———— **Jarney, 1, 1.** Lances, 41. Lighthorse, 55.

*Cambridge :* Sir John Peyton, 2, 3. Sir John Cotton, 2, 3. Thomas Sutton, 2, **3.** Sir Horatio Pallav[icini], 2, **3.** Giles Alington, 2, 2. John Skinner, 1, 1. Ferdinando Paris, 2, 3. Sir John Cuttes, 2, 3. Mark Steward, 1, 2. William Hinde, 1, **1.** William Mallorie, 1, 1. Anthony Cage, 2, 2. Thomas Wendy, 2, 2. Thomas Marshe, 1, 2. John Batsforde, 1, 2. Lances, 24. Lighthorse, 33.

*Essex :* Edw. Bagges, jun., 0, 1. Francis Barrington, 1, 1. Richard Frank, 0, 1. John Wright, 0, 1. Gamaniell (*sic*) Capell, 0, 1. Francis Stonard, 0, 1. William Smithe, 0, 1. Robert Leighe, 0, 1. Sir Edw. Denny, jun., 2, 3. Andrew Joiner, 0, 1. Richard Jenings, 0, 1. Thomas Josseline, 1, 1. Rook Greene, 1, 1. Edw. Waldegrave, 1, 1. Edw. Grimstone, 0, 1. John Darcie, 0, 1. Peter Tuke, 1, 1. Thomas Wilde, 0, 1. Edward Fage, 0, 1. Henry Appleton, 1, 2. Richard

---

* *Qu.* Trafford.

Campion, 1, 1. Sir John Peeter, 6, 9. Thomas **Knightley**, 0, 1.
Gabriel Pointz, 1, 2. John Hurlestone, 0, 1. Anthony **Browne**, 0, 1.
William Ailoffe de Chissell, junior, 1, 2. Richard Cutts, 0, 1. **Edward**
Hubbarde, 1, 1. William Wiseman, 1, 1. Thomas Meade, ar., 0, 1.
George Nicholls, 0, 1. **Francis** Rame,* 1, 1. Anthony Radcliffe, 0, 1.
Edward Jackman, 0, 1. John **Parke**, 0, 1. John Hare, 1, 1. Miles
Sandes, ar., 0, 1. Bernard Whitstone, 0, 1. Oliver Skinner, 0, 1.
William Gamage, 1, 2. John Paschall, 0, 1. Benjamin Gonson, 0, 1.
Thomas Gardiner, 1, 1. Humfrey Mildmaie, 1, 1. **Sir** Tho. Mildmaie,
2, 2. William Perte, 1, 1. Edward Suliarde, 1, 1. Richard Cannon,
1, 1. **Jerome** Weston, 0, 1. Thomas Mildmaie, ar., 1, 1. Giles Allen,
0, 1. **Henry** Mildemaie, 1, 1. William Harris, 1, 2. Sir Thomas
**Lucas**, 4, 4. **Sir** Edm. Huddl[e]stone, 2, 4. William Nuttbrowne,
1, 1. **William Tifferne**, 0, 1. John Ive, ar., 1, 1. Roger Harelakenden,
0, 1. **Samuel** Elmer, 0, 1. Edmond Allen, ar., 0, 1. Rafe Wiseman,
1, 1. William Ailoffe **de** Braxted Magna, 1, 1. Jo. Wentworth de
Bocking, 1, 1. Edward Thursby, 1, 1. Thomas Waldgrave, 0, 1.
Thomas Bendishe, 1, 2. William Bendlowes, 1, 1. William Kempe,
1, 1. Jo. Wentworthe de Gosefeilde, 1, 1. Arthur Breame, 1, 2. Tho.
Frenche, senior, 0, 1. Henry Maxey, 0, 1. Henry Smithe, 0, 1.
Thomas Harris, 0, 1. **Jo.** Tasboroughe, 0, 1. John Sammes, 1, 2.
Tho. Rawlins, 1, 1. Lances. 50. Lighthorse, 105.

*Hertford:* Sir Philip Butler, **2**, 4. **Sir** Arthur Capell, 2, 3. **Sir**
Tho. Sadler, 2, **2**. Thomas Harris, 1, **2**. John Brograve, 1, 1. Humphrey Coningsbye, **0, 1**. Rowland Litton, **1, 1**. William Purvey, 1, 2.
Richard Spencer, **1, 2**. **John** Gill, 0, **1**. **Tho.** Dockwraie, 1, 1. Jo.
Lenthroppe, 1, 1. **Fran.** Heidon, **1, 1**. Robert Chester, **1, 1**. Edward
**Poulter**, 1, 1. Tho. Pope **Blont** (*sic*), ar., 1, 2. Tho. Hanchett, 1, 1. Geo.
Knighton, 1, 1. Henry **Pranell**, 1, 1. John Colte, ar., 1, 1. Thom.
Fanshawe, 2, 3. John Goodman, **0, 1**. Henry Maime (*sic*), **1, 1**.
Robert Hide, 1, 2. John Luke, 0, 1. **Ralph** Connisbye, **1, 1**. **Henry**
Mewtis, 1, 1. William Newce, 0, **1**. **Jo.** Tasboroughe, 0, **1**. **Jo.**
Crowche, 0, 1. Leo. Hide, 1, 1. Edw. Newporte, 1, 2. Edw. **Lucie**,
1, 1. William Thurgood, 1, 1. John Cage, **1**, 1. George Perient,
0, 1. Tho. Crompton, 2, 2. Geo. Needham, 0, **1**. Lances, 35.
Lighthorse, **52**.

*Huntingdon:* Sir **Hen.** Cromwell, 4, 6. Sir **Jervis** Clifton, 4, 6.
Sir Rich. Dier, 2, 3. **Oliver** Cromwell, 2, **3**. Robert Sapcotts, 2, 3.
Robert Bevile, 2, 2. Robert Brunell, 1, 2. **Rich.** Trice, 1, 1. Robert
Cotton, 1, 2. Robert Price, 2, 2. John **Bedell**, 1, 2. Thomas Marshe,
1, 2. Lances, 23. Lighthorse, 35.

*Lincoln:* Philip Tirwhitt, 2, **3**. William Heneage, 1, 2. Sir Henry
Dimocke, 1, 2. Sir George St. Polle, 2, 3. Sir William Wraie, 2, 3.
Robert Carre, 1, 2. Arthur Halle, 1, 2. Henry Halle, 1, 1. Tho.
Grantham, 1, 2. Sir Tho. Mounson, 2, 3. Charles Hussey, 2, 2.
William Savile, 1, 1. Charles Dimocke, 1, 1. Edm. Tarpolde, 1, 2.
William Pelham, 1, 2. Edw. Askewe, 1, 2. Andrew Gedney, 1, 1.
Valentine Browne, 1, 2. William Hickman, 2, 2. Richard Ogle, 1, 1.
Lances, 27. Lighthorse, 39.

*Middlesex:* John Roche, 1, 2. Rich. Peacocke, 1, 1. Arthur Atie,
**1, 1**. Sir Re. Wrothe, 2, 4. Rich. Paine, 1, 2. Tho. Fowler, 1, 1.
Ambrose Copping[e]r, 1, 1. ——— Franklin, 1, 2. ——— Arrundell,
2, 3. William Reade, 2, 2. Tho. Slidolphe (*sic*), † 0, 1. John Page of
Welmly, 0, 1 William Shidolphe (*sic*), † 0, 1. Christopher Hoddesdon,

---

* *Qu.* Raine.            † *Qu.* Stidolphe.

1, 1. —— Brownloe, 1, 1. George **Kempe**, 1, 2. —— Cholmley, 1, 1. Sergeant Harris, 1, 2. William Flettwode, **2, 3.** Tho. Foster, 0, 1. Lances, 22. Lighthorse, 35.

*Northampton :* **Sir** William Clarke, **1, 2. Samuel Davers,** 1, 1. George Sherley, **1, 3.** Rich. Chettwoode, 1, 1. Thomas **Kirton,** 1, 1. John Wake, 1, 1. Francis Foxley, 0, 1. Edward Cope, **0, 1.** Erasimus Dreidon, 1, 1. Sir Geo. Farmer, 2, 2. Sir Arthur Throgmorton, 1, 3. Valentine Knightley, 1, 1. Francis Bernarde, 0, 1. Tobias Chauncye, **1, 1.** John Reade, 0, 1. Sir Thomas Thresham, 4, 4. Robert Osborne, 1, 1. Edward Villars, **1,** 1. Edward Griflin, 2, 4. Thomas Tresham, 0, 1. Charles Norwiche, 0, 1. Edmond Sands, 0, 1. Humphrey Stafford, **1, 2. John** Brudnell, **2,** 2. Edward Watson, 0, 1. John Freeman, **0, 1. Roger Charnocke,** 0, 1. Arthur Jenkinson, 1, **1.** Ambrose Agard, **0, 1. Thomas Isham,** 0, 1. Eusebius Isham, 1, 2. **Thomas** Muksho **(*sic*),*** 0, 1. **Edward Elmes, 1,** 2. Gilbert Pickering, 0, 1. **Thomas Lawe,** 0, 1 **George Line,** 0, 1. Tobie Houghton, 0, 1. **Henry** Beecher, 2, 2. **William Hacke,** 0, 1. **Richard** Worsley, 0, 1. **James** Cleapoole, 1, 1. **Edmond Mountstephen,** 0, 1. **William** Samuell, 0, 1. **Sir** Edw. Montague, 2, **3. Sir Richard Knightley,** 1, 2. Sir John Spencer, 4, 6. Lances, 40. **Lighthorse, 75.**

*Norfolk :* Sir Edward Cleere, 1, **2. Nathaniel** Bacon, 1, 2. Henry Jerningham, 1, 1. Sir Tho. Knevett, **2, 3.** Sir William Paston, 4, 4. Edward Paston, 1, 1. Ralph Hare, 1, 2. Sir **Arthur** Heveningham, 1, 2. Sir Miles Corbett, 2, 2. Sir Philip Woodhouse, 2, 2. Sir Bass. Gawdie, 2, 2. Henry Gawdie, 1, 1. William Rugge, 1, 2. Martin Barne,† 1, 1. Wm. Blenerhassett, 1, 1. Edw. Moundford, 1, 2. Clement Spilman, 1, 2. Richard Kempe, 1, 2. Ed vard Doiley, 1, 1. Tho. Oxboronghe, 1, 1. Wentworth, the Attorney, **2,** 2. Thomas Hewar, 1, 2. —— Sidney, 1, 2. Lances, 31. Lighthorse, 43.

*Suffolk :* Henry Warner, **1, 2.** Sir Tho. Kidson, 4, **4. Anthony Bull,** 1, 1. Sir Philip Parker, **2, 3.** Lionel Tallmage, 1, 2. **Edward Bacon,** 1, 2. John Browne, 1, 1. Edward Suliarde, 1, 2. Edward Rookewooke (*sic*), 2, 4. Sir William Springe, 2, **2.** Thomas Eden, 1, 1. Sir William Waldgrave, 2, **4.** George Colte, **1, 1.** John Gwrdon (*sic*), 1, 1. Sir Edmond Withipoole, 1, **2.** Thomas Rouse, 1, **2.** John Prettiman, 1, 1. Sir Thomas Cornwallis, 2, 3. Sir Thomas **Barner**diston, 1, 2. Edward Lewkenor, 1, 2. Francis Cowlbye, 1, 1. Robert Forthe, 1, 1. Anthony Felton, 1, 1. Thomas Croftes, 1, 2. Robert Barker, 1, 1. William Clapton, 1, 1. Richard Brooke, 1, 1. Sir Anthony Wingfeild, 2, 3. Sir Robert Jermin, 2, 2. Sir Nicholas **Bacon,** 4, **8.** Sir John Heigham, 1, 2. Robert Ashfeild, 1, 1. Francis **Jermye,** 1, **2.** Philip Tilney, **1, 2.** Jo. Jermin of Debdry(?), 1, 1. Tho. **Stutevile,** 1, 1. —— Crane, **1, 2.** Lances, 49. Lighthorse, 72.

*Oxford :* George **Pudsey, 1, 1** George **Broome,** 1, 2. Francis Curson, 1, 2. William **Denton, 1, 1.** Sir Richard **Wayman, 1, 2.** Sir Michael Blont, 2, 3. Francis Ploidon, 1, 2. **Richard Lide, gent., 1,** 1. Thomas Vachell, 1, 1. William Mollins, 0, 1. **John Symmons,** 1, 2. Francis Stoner‡, 2, 2. Robert Chamberlaine, 2, 2. **Edmond Phetiplace,** 2, 3. William Masham, 1, 1. Thomas Tipping, 1, 2. **John Arden,** 1, 1. Thomas Reade, ar **, 2,** 3. William Napper, 1, **2. Richard** Owen, **1,** 1. William Freere, 1, 1. Sir William Spencer, 2, 3. **William Moore,** 1, 1. Lawrence Tanfeilde, 1, 1. Sir Richard **Fynes,** 2, **3. Sir** Anthony Cope, 2, 3. William Pope, 2, 2. **Owen** Oglethorpe, 1, 2. William Greene, 1, 1. Lances, 33. Lighthorse, **52.**

---

* *Qu.* Mulsho.  † *Qu.* Barue (Barrow).
‡ " Sr " is **written opposite to** this name **in** the margin.

*Sussex:* Thomas Sherley, 1, 1. Thomas Leedes, 1, 2. Henry Shelley, 1, 1. Edward Apsley, 1, 1. Thomas Bishoppe, 1, 2. John Ashburnham, 1, 1. John Culpepper, 1, 1. Thomas Maie of Pashley, 1, 1. George Chute, 1, 1. Sir Walter Covert, 2, 2. Henry Bowier, 1, 1. Thomas Eversfeild, 1, 2. Ralph Hare, 1, 1. Edward Culpepper, 1, 1. Peter Garton, 1, 1. William Goring, 2, 2. William Bartlett,* 1, 1. Thomas Stanley, 1, 1. John Michell, 1, 1. Richard Blunt, 1, 1 Adrian Stoughton, 1, 1. Richard Earnley, 1, 1. Richard Stanney, 1, 1. Richard Lewkenor, serjeant-at-law, 1, 2. Edward Carrell, 2, 3. Thomas Dike, 1, 1. Nicholas Fowle, 1, 1. Edward Gage, 1, **2.** Thomas Eversfield, 1, 1. John Shurley, 1, 1. Herbert Morley, 1, 1. Charles Howard, 1, 1. Jo. Lunsford, 1, 2. Sir Nicholas Parker, 1, 2. Herbert Pelham, **1,** 2. John Gage, 2, 2. Lances, 42. Lighthorse, 51.

*Surrey:* William Forster, 1, 1. Robert Skerne, 1, 1. Richard Bostocke, 1, **1.** William Widnell, 1, 1. William Brend, 1, 1. Thomas Gresham, 1, 1. Richard Lenchford (*sic*),† 1, 2. Sir Thomas Palmer, 1, **2.** William Milles, 1, 2. Julius Cæsar, 1, 1. Sir Francis Caroe, 2, **2.** Oliver Leighe, 1, 1. John Eveline, 1, 2. Thomas Brend, **1,** 2. Thomas Vincent, 1, 2. Thomas Stidolphe, 1, 2. William Stidolphe, 1, 1. Henry Slyfeilde, 1, 1. Lawrence Stoughton, **1, 1. Francis** Singer (?), 1, 1. Sir Richard Weston, 1, 1. Francis **Browne, 1,** 2. Sir Matthew Browne, 1, 2. Edward Aleford, **1, 1. William** Morgan, 1, 2. Richard Lechforde, 1, 2. Sir George Moore, 1, 1. Edward Bowier, 1, 1. Bartholomew Scotte, 1, 1. Francis Muschampe, 1, 1. John Arrundell, 1, 1. Robert Linesey(*sic*),‡ 1, 1. Edward Bollingham, 1, 1. Edward Bannister, 11. John Lacie, 1, 1. John Whittbrooke, 1, 1. Matthew Locke, 1, 1. Lances, 38. Lighthorse, 49.

(Some of the totals given at the end of each county are inaccurate.)

*There is a brief note of the foregoing among the State Papers (Docquets.)§*

F. 231. [1599,] Aug. 4.—"Minute of their Lordships' [the **Privy** Council's] letters directed to the Lieutenants and Commissioners **for the** Musters in divers Counties."

"You shall receive herewithall her Majesty's letters, whereby **you** are directed to send to those persons in that county whose **names are** contained in a schedule, and to give straight commandment unto them to send with all expedition so many horses as is required of them, unto the place limited, and [by] a day limited. We send you also our letters unto certain principal gentlemen named in the schedule, because the time serveth **not** to write to all, and yet it is expected that no man shall pretend at this time any excuse or delay, (the cause being duly weighed for which they are demanded,) as there is no horses demanded of any whose ability may not bear a greater number; so in these occasions, if any person should go about to be forborne, he may be assured such backwardness would be hardly censured. Now because it may fall out that some persons contained in this schedule are assessed to find horses in the country, and thereby some confusion might happen, it is meant that these which are now speedily to be sent for this service shall not excuse any man of those which they are to furnish in the country, which numbers are to be kept complete, to be used together as they shall be directed with the forces of the shire. For the rest, we doubt not but considering these forces are to withstand the attempts of the enemy

---

* *Qu.* Bartelott.   † *Qu.* Lenchford.   ‡ *Qu.* Livesey.
§ In the Calendar, 1598–1601, p. 277, line 5, "footmen" should be "footmen and horse."

here at home, whereon the state of the **whole** realm dependeth, but that every man will shew his zeal and affection in hastening the horses demanded of them, and to see them well set forth, **of** choice horses and men fit for service."

[The Schedule.]

Bedford, Berkshire, Buckingham, Cambridge, Essex, Hertford, Huntingdon, Lincoln, Middlesex, Norfolk, Northampton, Oxford, Suffolk, Surrey, Sussex.

F. 231*b*. [1599,] Aug. 4.—"Minute from their Lordships to such Gentlemen as were to send up Horse, inhabiting in the Counties aforesaid; their names and number of horse being contained in a Schedule following."

" Forasmuch as her Majesty at this time being advertised of a purpose in the King of Spain to send an army to make a descent in the county of Kent, and from thence to attempt the destruction of her Majesty's Navy or City of London; in which respect her Majesty, being to use the service **of many, cannot** conveniently, in case of this expedition, write to all whom it concerneth, but hath directed her letters under **her Signet** Manual to the Lieutenants and Sheriffs of divers counties, containing a schedule of such men's names within that **shire, at** whose hands she expecteth full accomplishment of the same letters: we doubt not but this which you shall receive from us, being testified under our own hands by her Majesty's express commandment, shall draw the same effect from you as if you had received particular letters from her Highness, seeing it is derived from the commission which she hath given us, and shall be reported by us with all the recommendation possible which your forwardness herein shall deserve ; **whereof** you shall **more** particularly see the causes by the letters **which her** Majesty **hath** written **us** aforesaid ; her Majesty having for this present commanded us **to deliver** you thus much, that she expecteth, upon those reasons therein contained, that you should send to ———, by the 12th of August, —— horses furnished, to remain for the space of **one** mouth at your charge, where her Majesty will cause them to be received and disposed of, as occasion shall serve. Herein requiring you not to fail, so &c."

" The **Schedule.**"

(The first figure after each name shows the number of "lances," the second figure the number of "lighthorse.")

*Berks :* Sir Thomas Parrie, 2, 3. Sir Humphrey Foster, 2, 3. Sir **Michael** Mollins, **2, 3.** Thomas Reade, 2, 3. Edmond Duncke, 2, 3. **Edmond** Phettiplace, **2,** 3. —— Sherley, 2, 3. William Essex, 2, 3. **Lances** and lighthorse, **40.**

*Bedford :* Sir Edw. Ratcliffe, **2, 3.** William Fleetwoode, 2, 3. Anthony Tirringham, 2, 3. **John Burgonie (***sic***),** 1, 2. Nicholas Luke, 2, 2. Miles Sands, 2, 2. Lances and lighthorse, **26.**

*Bucks :* Sir Jo. Paggington, 2, 3. Sir Robert Dormer, **4, 6. Sir** Tho. Tasborough, 1, 2. Miles Sands, 2, 2. Fran. Goodwinne, 2, **2.** Anth. Tirringham, 2, 3. John Temple, 2, 2. Thomas Paget, 2, **2.** Henry Longevill, 2, 2. Thomas Throgmorton, 2, 2. Rowland Litton, 2, 3. Lances and lighthorse, 52.

*Cambridge :* Sir Jo. Cuttes, 2, 3. Sir Horatio Pallav[icini], 2, 3. Sir Jo. Peiton, 2, 3. Sir Jo. Cotton, 2, 3. Jo. Batsforde, 1, 2. Tho. Wendy, 2, 2. Tho. Marshe, 1, 2. Mark Steward, 1, 2. Giles Allington, 2, 2. Tho. Sutton, 2, 3. Ferdin. Paris, 2, 3. Antho. Cage, 2, 2. **Lances** and lighthorse, 51.

*Lincoln:* Sir Edw. Dimocke, 1, 2. **Sir** Geo. St. **Poole**, 2, 3. Sir William **Wray**, 2, 3. Sir Tho. Monson, 2, 3. Edm. Tarrolde, 2, 2. Charles Hussey, 2, 2. William Heneage, 1, 2. Arthur Hall, 1, 2. Philip Tirwhitt, 2, 3. Lances and lighthorse, 37.

*Middlesex:* Sir Robert Wrothe, **2**, 4. Tho. Crompton, 2, 2. Arthur Atye, 1, 1. **Richard** Paine, 1, 2. **John** Roche, 1, 2. Ambrose Copping[e]r, **1, 1.** —— Frankelin, **1, 2.** **John** Arrundell, 2, 3. Lances and lighthorse, 28.

*Norfolk:* Sir Bassingh. **Gawdy, 2, 2.** **Sir Miles** Corbett, 2, 2. **Sir** Arthur Hevin[i]ngham, **1, 2.** **Sir William** Paston, **4, 4.** Sir **Tho.** Knevett, 2, **3.** Sir Edw. **Clere, 1, 2.** **Sir** Philip Woodhouse, **2, 2.** Henry Sidney, 1, 2. —— **Wentworth, 2, 2.** Nathaniel Bacon, **1, 2.** Lances **and lighthorse, 41.**

*Northampton:* Sir **Thomas Thresham, 4, 4.** Sir William Clarke, 1, **2.** Sir **Edw.** Mountague, 2, 3. Sir **George Fermor,** 2, 2. Sir Antho. Mildmaie, **2,** 3. Sir Arthur Throgmorton, **1,** 2. Sir John Spencer, 4, 6. Sir Richard Knightley, 1, 2. John Brudnell, 2, 2 Edw. Griffin, 2, 4. Lances and lighthorse, 51.

*Oxford:* Sir Michael Blonte, 2, 3. **Sir** Richard **Fines, 2, 3.** **Sir** William Spencer, 2, 3. Sir Anthony Cope, 2, 3. **William Pope, 2, 2.** Edm. Pettiplace,* 2, 3. Thomas Reade, 2, **3.** **Robert Chamberlaine,** 2, 2. Francis Stoner, 2, 2. Lances and lighthorse, **42.**

*Huntingdon:* Sir Henry Cromwell, 4, 6. Sir Richard Dier, 2, **3.** Sir Jervis Clifton, **4,** 6. Oliver Cromwell, 2, 3. Robert Sapcotts, 2, 3. Robert Bevyle, **2, 2.** Robert **Price, 2, 2.** Lances, 18. Lighthorse, 25.

*Surrey:* Sir **Thomas** Palmer, 1, **2.** Sir Matthew Browne, 1, 2. **Sir Richard Weston, 1, 1.** **Mr.** Doctor Cæsar, 1, 1. Lances, 4. Lighthorse, **6.**

*Sussex:* Sir **Nicholas Parker, 1, 2.** Sir Thomas Palmer, 1, 2. Sir Walter Covert, **2, 2.** **Edward Currell, 2, 3.** John Gage, 2, 2. William Goringe, 2, 2. **Lances, 10. Lighthorse, 13.**

*Hertford:* Sir **Philip Butler, 2, 4.** **Sir** Arthur **Capell, 2, 3.** **Sir** Thomas Sadler, **2, 2.** **Thomas Fanshawe,** 2, 3. Lances, 8. **Lighthorse, 12.**

*Essex:* Sir **John** Peeter, 6, 9. Sir Thomas **Lucas, 4, 4.** Sir Edward **Denny,** junior, 2, 3. Sir Edmond Hurlestone, 2, **4.** **Sir** Thomas Mildmay, 2, 2. Lances, 16. Lighthorse, 22.

*Suffolk:* Sir Anthony Wingfeild, 2, 3. Sir Robert Jermin, 2, 2. **Sir** Thomas Kitson, 4, 4. Sir William Waldgrave, 2, 4. Sir Nicholas Bacon, 4, 8. Lances, 14. Lighthorse, 21.

*Cf. State Papers (Docquets), under " Aug.* **5 ? "**

F. 232b. [1599,] Aug. 4.—"Minute of their Lordships' letters to such Noblemen as were to provide troops of Horse to attend her Majesty's Person."

" Her Majesty having received **divers advertisements** from sundry places of the King of Spain's **purpose, with a** fleet of ships and galleys, to make descent in **the parts adjoining to her** Majesty's Navy and City of London, **and having given order for all** things necessary for the making of **an Army** to encounter **them** where they shall seek to come on shore : Forasmuch as her Majesty knoweth that you are no **way** ignorant, but that the scope of the enemy's designs is wholly to **subvert** the state of this Kingdom, which God hath blessed with so great **peace and** tranquillity these many years, and further assureth herself **that you** that are a nobleman and a Peer of the realm (besides your

---

* *Qu.* Fettiplace.

natural inclination as a true English subject do [to ?] take yourself further interested in the honour and state of this Kingdom than persons of other quality) will always be ready to your uttermost power to withstand their malicious attempts, who seek to bring the estate of this flourishing Kingdom into servitude and confusion, together with the destruction of her Majesty's most Royal person: It hath pleased her Majesty, in respect of her good opinion and experience of your affection and fidelity towards her (who hath been the minister of God's blessings, so many years bestowed upon us), to command us in her name to require your Lordship (without any other delay) to repair unto her Court, to attend her person, amongst other[s] of the nobility, by the 20th of this month, with such troops as you can conveniently make, both for lances and lighthorsemen. Wherein, to the intent the want of great horse or geldings (whereof the more you bring the better it shall be taken) may be supplied otherwise, her Majesty requireth you to increase your numbers by providing able men with petronels upon horses of smaller stature than is need for a lance or staff, the same to remain about her as long as she shall think convenient. Herein we little doubt but your Lordship will, with all expedition and resolution, make manifest to the world your affection to her safety and preservation, who never thought anything too dear that she possessed (were it life or fortune), so it might be thought fit to be employed for the good of her kingdom and people. And thus, being ready for our parts also (to our best power) to unite ourselves in all things with you that may frustrate their ambition, whose power this kingdom doth contemn, having so just a quarrel and such a Prince to defend, we commit you to God, &c."

[List of the Noblemen and others written to:—]

"Lord Marquis of Winchester, Earl of Darbie, Earl of Huntingdon, Earl of Shrewsburie, Earl of Worcester, Earl of Pembrooke, Earl of Hartforde, Earl of Lincolne, Earl of Rutlande, Earl of Bedforde, Earl of Kent, Viscount Mountague, Lord de la Warre, Lord Sandes, Lord St. John of Bletsoe, Lord Darcy of Chitche, Lord Compton, Lord Dudley, Lord Barkley, Lord Lumley, Lord Norreis, Lord Mordant, Lord Sturton, Lord Morley, Lord Windson (sic), Lord Riche, Lord Chief Justice, Sir Henry Lea, Sir Anthony Mildemay."

F. 233. [1599,] Aug. 4.—[The Privy Council] to the Archbishop of Canterbury [Whitgift].

"Whereas we did of late signify the necessity unto your Lordship of the employment of the horses of the Clergymen at this time, and did pray your Lordship to give order accordingly throughout the province of Canterburye, that the said horses might forthwith be furnished and put in readiness to repair unto such place as should be appointed by direction from us: Forasmuch as we have since that time been informed, that the horses of the Clergymen in the county of Kent have been certified in the Roll of Musters for the whole county, and so are esteemed as a part of that account, we have thought meet not to sever them from the rest of the horses of the said county in their meetings, but do hold it to be more convenient that they be joined together with them, and sent to such place or places as by her Majesty's Lieutenant of that county shall be appointed. For the rest of the horses of all other counties, we do think Lambeth and Southwarke to be the most convenient places for their repair and assembly, and do therefore pray your Lordship that forasmuch as our late advertisements of the enemy's designs are daily more and more confirmed, and it is to be doubted that their coming will now be very speedy and sudden, your Lordship will give order accordingly for the repair of the said numbers of horses to Lambeth and Southwarke by the 12th of this instant, there to remain until they shall otherwise by direction from us be disposed of and employed. Whereof not doubting but your Lordship will take special care, we bid, &c."

F. 233. [1599,] **Aug.** 4.—[The **Privy** Council] to the Lord Admiral [Nottingham].

" Whereas order and direction hath **been given of** late that the 2,000 foot and 80 horse appointed at this time to **be** levied in the county of Surrey, for **the** compounding of an Army **to** resist any invasion **or** attempt of the enemy, should repair **to** Lewsam* by the 12th of this instant : Forasmuch **as,** upon further deliberation, we have found it more **convenient for the** said number **to** repair unto Gravesend, where **they may** readily **and** speedily **be** employed in such sort as there shall **be best** use of them ; **we** have therefore thought meet to alter the place **of their** rendezvous, and **to** assign it to be at Gravesend, and do pray your Lordship to give present order to your Deputy Lieutenants accordingly that the said 2,000 foot and 80 horse may not fail to make their repair thither by the time aforementioned, to be disposed of as the service shall require, which we doubt not but your Lordship will forthwith see performed, &c."

F. 233. [1599,] Aug. 4.—[The Privy Council] **to the Lord** Chamberlain [Hunsdon] and Lord Montjoye, her Majesty's **Lieutenants** in co. Southampton, &[c.]†

" Whereas there is dail**y confirmation** by advertisement of the great **preparation** continued by **the** King of Spain, intending, in all appearance of reason, a strong invasion by the forces he prepareth of shipping, galleys, **and men,** which he hath gathered out of all parts of his dominions, to execute his malicious designs with greater forces, and that his whole fleet and army is in a readiness to take the first wind, which is not to be thought he will neglect ; for that her Majesty disdaineth to take any scorn or affront by want of timely provision to resist any attempt, and knowing, if they shall surprise the Isle of Wighte, by the benefit of the galleys, they may be able to impeach the passage of any forces **to come** out of the Main in their supply‡ ; her Majesty hath therefore commanded **us to let you know that it** is her pleasure that you do send all the forces **both** of horse and foot appointed and by former directions allotted for supply of the Isle of Wighte, with their captains, leaders, carriages, and victuals for **15 days,** (or money to serve for provision of such, or so much victuals,) **to be** in the Isle of Wight, under the conduct of Sir Thomas Weste, at the furthest, by the 10th of this present, there to be in a readiness to preserve the Island, and impeach their landing ; and likewise that for the better strenghthening of the town of Portesmouthe, you cause the number of 500 of those forces formerly appointed for the supply of that place, with their captains and leaders, to be sent thither under the conduct of Mr. Hambden Pawlett by the 10th of this instant at the furthest, with 15 days' victual, or money to provide it ; and likewise cause all the rest of the Hundreds appointed to strengthen that place to be trained, and put in a readiness to answer all alarms as occasion shall require ; and further that as well in their marching as in their residence within the Island, no time be omitted by the captains **to** train the soldiers and to teach them the use of their weapons. Hereof we pray your Lordships' care and diligence."

---

* Lewisham, Kent.
† *Cf.* Patent Roll, 41 Eliz., part 24, dorse (their commission).
‡ *i.e.* from the main land (Hampshire), for supply of the Isle.

F. 233*b*. [1599,] Aug. 5.—[The Privy **Council**] **to the** Archbishop of Canterbury.

" Whereas by our late letters we prayed your Lordship **to** give order and direction unto the Bishops and other men of quality that **are** of the Clergy, to send up the horses (which they are to find) unto Southwarke and Lambeth with all possible speed out of the counties that are within the Province of Canterbury, the county of Kent only excepted : Now, forasmuch as upon consideration of the far distance of the counties that are **in** Wales, and likewise of the counties of Cornwall and Devon, it **is** thought convenient that the horses of the Clergy of those counties shall be forborne; we do therefore pray your good Lordship to renew **your** direction to the Clergymen of the said counties of Wales, Cornwall, and **Devon,** and to let them know that they **may** be spared and forborne **from** making their repair up as formerly **they** were appointed, and that **it** shall suffice for the present to keep their **horses in a** readiness within the **counties,** to be employed **as** there **shall be use of them** for her Majesty's service, and that they in the mean while **shew or** cause them to be shewed to the Deputy Lieutenants or Commissioners of the Muster-in the counties, whereby notice may be taken of their readiness, and accordingly certified. And forasmuch as by former letters there hath been no order or direction given that the horsemen should come furnished with coats, albeit we suppose that those by whom they shall be sent will cause them to be well and fitly apparelled as becometh for service, yet for the more assurance we do pray your Lordship to give order that they come furnished of horsemen's coats of some such colour as your Lordship shall think good to prescribe, and to **be** at Lambeth and Sout[hwark] by the 15th of this instant **at the furthest.**"

F. 234. [1599,] Aug. 5.— [The **Privy Council] to Sir** George Carewe, Lieutenant of the Ordnance, **and to the rest of the** Officers there.

" Whereas we understand that the **two Forts of Gravesende and Til-**burie are unfurnished of powder, shot, and other necessaries, and **that** their ordnance be dismounted ; these are to pray and require [you] to cause them to be supplied with such munitions and other necessaries as in your discretions shall be thought meet according to the necessity of the time ; and to cause delivery **to** be made of powder, shot, and other habiliments, to furnish them, according to a proportion set down and hereunto annexed, subscribed under our hands, taking the captains' **hands** for the receipt thereof, according to the custom of the office. And **these** shall be, &c."

F. **234.** [1599,] Aug. 6.—" Minute of letters from their Lordships to the several Counties hereunder named."

" **Because by our** late **letters in** the **beginning of** this summer we gave direction unto you to take **order a perfect view should be** taken of the forces of that county, and by **your letters and certificate we** perceive you **have** carefully performed **the** same, **we make no doubt** but the forces of that county be in a readiness, **and the wants** and defects also supplied ; and therefore we shall not need in that behalf, to give you any new direction, but in regard of the great preparations the enemy doth make by sea, to require you to have in mind our former directions ; and if there be any defects in the bands of that county, to see them speedily and effectually amended, that they be in a readiness, so as upon any warning they may be employed as there shall be occasion **for** the defence of the realm or the royal person of her Majesty. For which respect we do think it meet, that general order and straight commandment be given throughout the whole shire, that none of the captains of horse and foot be absent out of the country, but by direction from hence, and in defence against invasion, according as by our former letters hath been ordered, or that hereafter may be directed; and in like sort that no trained soldier of the ordinary bands depart from his habitation, without special leave of the captain, or some public employment, for the space of six weeks; and that all such as do furnish horse may be enjoined to keep them in their stables. And because the enemy doth make account to have the assistance of the evil affected subjects of the land, as there is direction given to restrain the Recusants of ability, so we think it meet, that you cause all the horses or geldings in the possession [of] or belonging to any Recusant to be for this present time sequestered from them, and committed to the custody of some well affected gentlemen, their neighbours, that their service may be used if there be occasion; and in the mean season, they shall be kept and maintained at the charge of the owners, and restored safely again.

"Moreover, as we doubt not of your vigilant care to look to the quiet government of the country, and to see the Beacons kept with good watches, so because in like times there are often rumours and reports spread to distract and discomfort the minds of her Majesty's subjects, your Lordship shall be careful to apprehend and commit to prison the authors and spreaders of such false, idle, and mutinous reports. For the suppression whereof and the punishment of idle and vagrant persons, whereof there are very many in all parts of this realm, that take all occasions to commit outrages, it is thought meet that your Lordship according to the authority given you by her Majesty's commission shall appoint a Provost Marshal, who may have authority to apprehend such sturdy and vagrant persons, that go up and down the country, living loosely without labouring, and to see them committed to prison (especially suspected persons), as also to have care to prevent all unlawful assemblies.

"Lastly, where the clergy and ecclesiastical persons do find certain number[s] of horse and foot, which are meant for the guard and defence of her Majesty's person, because it may fall out they shall stand in need of men to ride their horses, and wear their armour, we pray your Lordship to give your best assistance and aid in helping them to men sufficient and fit for the purpose, if they shall require the same, not being retained by others, nor enrolled in the ordinary bands."

"The Counties to which these letters were written: Bedford, Berks, Buckingham, Cambridge, Chester, Cornwall, Devon, Dorset, Derby, Gloucester, Huntingdon, Hertford, Hereford, Kent, Lincoln, Lancaster, Leicester, Nottingham, Oxford, Rutland, Salop, Somerset, Stafford, Wilts, Worcester, Warwick."

F. 234b. [1599,] Aug. 6.—[The Privy Council] to Sir George Carewe, Lieutenant of the Ordnance.

"Whereas we are given to understand that there is good store of saltpetre at this present in her Majesty's Store, forasmuch as her Majesty shall have occasion to use great quantity of powder, it is thought meet, and so we require you, that you will cause such saltpetre as is at this present remaining in her Majesty's Store, to be delivered by indenture unto John and Robert Eveling, esquires, that they may convert the same towards the making of gunpowder for her Majesty's present service; and they are to deliver again the like quantity they shall receive of you into her Majesty's Store within six months after warning given them by me the Lord Treasurer, or the Master or Lieutenant of the Ordnance.

Moreover, where **we** are given to understand **that** there is great quantity of gunpowder in her Majesty's Store that is decayed and unserviceable, and may **by new** making be made good and fit for service, we pray you therefore that you will confer with the said Evelinges, **and** make some bargain and agreement with them as reasonable as you can, **to new** make the said powder, that it may be made serviceable, and thereupon **deliver** such quantities unto them, out of her Majesty's Store as is not fit **for** use, and to receive the same again after it shall be amended and reformed upon such agreement **as** you shall make **with them**. And **these** our letters shall be sufficient warrant unto you in that behalf, for delivery of the said saltpetre, **and decayed** and unserviceable gunpowder, unto the said Evelinges, **in such sort as** is hereby appointed."

**F. 235. [1599,] Aug. 6.—[The Privy Council]** to the Lord Mayor [of London].

" That whereas divers complaints had been made to their Lordships, by divers Deputy Lieutenants in some counties of the realm, who, having **occasion** to make provision of sundry sorts **of armour** and furniture, &c., to serve for the use of the soldiers that were now to be employed, **were** to provide the same in London; the armourers, bearing hereof, **began** to enhance and sell the same at higher rates than usually they **were** wont to do: his Lordship therefore was required to send for them, and to take such order as they might be compelled to afford the **same at as easy and reasonable** prices as in like occasions of service they were accustomed to do, &c."

F. 235. [1599,] Aug. 6.—[The Privy **Council**] to the Earl of Kent, her Majesty's Lieutenant in **co.** Bedford.

" Whereas your Lordship hath already received **direction** to have the forces of that county in a readiness, we are now **to let you** understand her Majesty's pleasure **is**, your Lordship shall take present **order** to cause 500 of the trained soldiers of that county and 60 horse to **be for[th]** with **levied, and** sorted with armour and **weapon** in such sort as **formerly** hath **been prescribed** unto you, and to be **sent** up hither under **the conduct of such gentlemen** of the country as have the ordinary charge of **them, so as they may be at** Hackney and Stepney by the —— of this month. **Considering this service is** for the defence of the realm, and the royal **person of her Majesty, the destruction of both** being greedily thirsted **after and sought by the enemy, we** doubt not but your Lordship **will use all care and diligence to see these** numbers set forth, both **of choice men and well furnished with armour**, weapon, and apparel **as becometh soldiers, and to be there by the day** appointed, allowing **conduct money unto them according to the distance of** the mills [miles?], **which shall be repaid unto** the country at **their arrival** at the foresaid **place[s], where they shall enter** into her Majesty's pay. For your Lord-**ship's further warrant** you shall receive her Majesty's letters **very** shortly. In the mean season we pray you with all expedition to advance the forces **according to** this direction."

F. 235b. [1599,] Aug. 6, from the Court at Nonesuche.—[The Privy Council] **to Sir** Ferdinando Gorges, Captain of the Fort at Plimouthe.

" We perceive by your letter the pains you take with the rest of the gentlemen and inhabitants of that country to set all things in good order for defence of the same, and to withstand th'attempts of the enemy, wherein as you shew the care that becometh **men** of your sort and quality, and put in trust by her Majesty, so you may be assured the like care shall not be wanting here in us, as there shall be occasion, to see **you** supplied both with forces and all other necessary provisions, if the enemy shall bend his forces to land in those parts. But where you inform us that you have already assembled the forces of that county, and that they do expect some order from hence to ease the charge of the country therein, though you do shew great forwardness, and good foresight to your own defence, yet the same being done before you had special direction and the men remaining still in their own country, it would be an excessive charge to her Majesty if other countries bordering upon the sea coast should, in doing the like for their own safety, look to have their charges borne by her Majesty ; **for** the forces you have assembled being of the country people do consume no more victuals than if they had remained at their own houses; and therefore, until there shall be **an** army assembled under a General and officers in orderly **manner,** her Majesty is wont never to be **put to** any charges. We are **sorry to** hear **the want you** have of martial men, of whom we can hardly spare any from hence, yet if **we** find the enemy shall, as you conceive, shall (*sic*) make descent there, then you shall not need to doubt but besides those forces appointed to come unto you for your assistance, our whole care and direction shall bend likewise with the forces prepared in these parts to succour you.

"Touching the inconvenience you do conceive that may come by former orders set down in the general directions you have received, to appoint some persons for the defence of certain sand bays and creeks, we do think meet that you acquaint our very good Lord, the Earl of Bathe, her Majesty's Lieutenant in **that** county, therewithall, and that upon conference with the Deputy Lieutenants and other gentlemen of knowledge, his Lordship may take that course therein that shall be thought convenient for the defence of the country, and they are to be commanded to follow the resolution that upon considerate advice shall be taken by his Lordship.

"For those of Cornwall, you know **there is** direction in what sort they are to repair to your assistance, if **the** enemy attempt to land in the county of Devon; otherwise we see **no** necessity as yet to draw them forth of their own country, being so near unto you as upon any warning they may come to assist you. Thus having answered your letters in all those points that **are** material, we bid you heartily farewell."

F. **236**. [1599,] Aug. 6.—"A letter to the Lord Admiral [Nottingham], that where the 2,000 levied in the county of Surrey were appointed to be sent to Gravesend, the place of their rendezvous, his Lordship was now required they might repair to Croidon and Stretham, to be there in a readiness, either to be sent unto the foresaid county of Kent, or to such other place of the realm where it should be most likely the enemy would make invasion."

Same date.—"A like letter to the Lord Treasurer, that the 4,000 in the county of Sussex might likewise repair to Eltham and Lewsam, to remain there until they should be otherwise disposed of by direction from their Lordships."

Same date.—"A letter to the Lord Mayor, and the Earl of Cumberland. Seigneur Genebelly recommended unto them for his help in the finishing of the Bridge over the River of Thames, in regard of his great skill and practice in those matters."

F. 236. [1599,] Aug. 7.—"Minute of a letter [from the Privy Council] to the Mayors of the several Ports and Towns hereunder written."

"You are not ignorant of the daily advertisements that are brought hither of the great preparations the King of Spain doth make by sea, not only of ships of war, but of a good number of galleys, to invade some part of this realm; **and** therefore you can consider how behoofful and necessary it is to have certain intelligence of their approach in the Narrow Seas, and **what** course they do hold. **For** which purpose we do, in her Majesty's name, will and command you forthwith to set some two or three nimble vessels unto the seas out of that harbour, that may go and ply up and down between the coast of France and ours, to learn what they may discover of the coming of the said fleet, and use all diligence to advertise the same unto you, that we may by post receive from time to time such news as you shall understand from them. Herein requiring you to take present order, we bid, &c.

" Postscript. We think it meet that you should keep these pinnaces and vessels at sea, as you are directed, for the space of 6 weeks.

" Perin [Penryn], Plimouthe, Portesmouthe, Linne, Dartmouthe, Southampton."

**F. 236b.** [1599,] Aug. 7.—[The Privy Council] to Sir Christofer Heidon.

" We have received your letter sent by this bearer, written in some length, **unto which we must in few** words make you **answer to the** chiefest **matter** concerning the mariners, masters, and pilots with the seafaring men, we so earnestly required by two several letters to be taken up and sent to Chattam. And although you have forborne for some respects, which is enlarged in your letter, to follow our directions in sending so many as we desired, considering how it importeth the defence of the realm that her Majesty's ships should speedily and presently be manned, **we** do therefore again require you to take present order that a greater number be with all possible diligence sent thither; and if you make choice of good masters, pilots, and skilful mariners, the number of 100 shall for the present be accepted, which is the least number that of necessity must be had out of that county and town; hoping out of the rest of the seaports there may as many be had as can be gotten, according to our former direction, and sent up with all possible speed. Wherein requiring your care, we bid, &c."

**F. 236b.** [1599,] Aug. 7.—[The Privy Council] to the **Earl of** Pembroke.

" Among many **other** advertisements that have **and** do come daily unto **her** Majesty and **us of** the great preparations **and** speedy purpose of the King of Spain's forces to make descent upon **some** part of this realm, there hath somewhat been signified to move an opinion of their intention **to come** for Milforde **and** Severne; whereof though we do not conceive **so great likelihood as of other places,** nevertheless, because, in such a case **as this is, too much care cannot be** taken for assurance of all parts, her Majesty's pleasure is, **and** we do accordingly pray and require your Lordship, that order be taken forthwith, by your direction **to** your Deputy Lieutenants, for the forces of the country to be kept and had in a readiness **in** those parts to make head together and in good order **for** defence and resistance, if it shall be found needful.

" And therefore, concerning Milforde and the country thereabouts, it shall be very meet that your Lordship do write and give order **to** Sir John Wogan and the rest of your Deputy Lieutenants and other gentlemen of quality, carefully and diligently to provide against any such attempt as may be made, and to put in execution such directions as heretofore upon like occasion have been prescribed. The like course **we** do pray your Lordship to take for the country about Severne, and especially about Bristoll. Howbeit we do not think it needful, as yet, for **any forces to** be in either of **those places** assembled, but only as is before mentioned to be put and kept in readiness, so as they may be upon very sudden warning assembled and employed (if need shall require).

"And forasmuch as the weakness of your Lordship's health is such as may well and justly require more help and assistance in such trouble-some business, and we think your Lordship would be pleased therewith, and our very good lord, the Lord Chandois, her Majesty's Lieutenant of the county of Gloucester, is by his lieutenancy so near adjoining unto the parts about Severne and Bristoll, as he may very conveniently assist your Lordship upon any occasion in those parts, for the better perform-ance of any service there; her Majesty therefore doth like very well that your Lordship shall use his help and assistance in the said service, as you shall find cause, both for advice, and for the putting in execution such things as to the said service shall be appertaining; not prejudicing hereby or impeaching the authority of any of your Deputy Lieutenants in those places. For which cause her Majesty is likewise well pleased to spare his (sic) Lordship from coming to the Court, to attend here, as the most part of the noblemen are appointed to do, especially since your Lordship's son, the Lord Herbert, is appointed amongst those that are to attend her Majesty's person; and we have accordingly certified the Lord Chandois of her Majesty's pleasure in that behalf."

F. 237. [1599,] Aug. 8.—[The Privy Council] "to the Lords Lieutenants, High Sheriffs, and Commissioners for the Musters in the Counties hereunder written."

"Whereas your Lordship received her Majesty's letters for the levying of —— foot and —— horse within that county, because that time may seem somewhat short, and our desire is that good choice be made of these soldiers that are to be employed at this instant for the defence of the realm against foreign invasion; we have thought good to put off the day for their rendezvous, at the place appointed, and defer it until the —— of this month. And therefore, in respect your Lordship hath more time to levy the men, and to see good choice made of them, we pray you likewise that you will have care to see them trained in the mean season, that they may come the better appointed, furnished, and instructed."

The Schedule.

| Counties. | Foot. | Horse. | Places of Rendezvous. | Times first Assigned. | Alterations of the Times by later Directions. |
|---|---|---|---|---|---|
| Kent | 6,000 | And a number of horse | Canterburye | 10th of August | |
| Norfolk | 2,000 | 300 | Ingerstone and Brentwoode. | | |
| Suffolk | 2,000 | 200 | Ingerstone and Brentwoode. | | 16th August |
| Hertford | 1,000 | 80 | Tottenham and Newington. | 12th August | |
| Huntingdon | 500 | 50 | Blackwall | | |
| Middlesex | 1,000 | 60 | Stratford Bowe | | |
| Buckingham | 500 | 100 | Brainforde | | |

93

| Counties. | Foot. | Horse. | Places of Rendezvous. | Times first Assigned. | Alterations of the Times by later Directions. |
|---|---|---|---|---|---|
| Essex - - - | 3,000 | 200 | Roinham* and Barkinge. | 13th August | |
| Surrey - - | 2,000 | 80 | Croydon and Stretham. | | |
| Cambridge - | 500 | 50 | Islington - - - | 15th August | 17th August |
| Bedford - - | 500 | 60 | Hackney and Stepney. | | |
| Oxford - - | 500 | — | Southworke - - | | |
| Sussex - | 4,000 | And a number of horse | Eltham and Lewsam. | 12th August | 15th August |
| Northampton - | 500 | 50 | London - - | 16th August | No alteration made of the first direction. |
| | 24,000 | 1,230 besides the numbers of Kent and Sussex. | | | |

* *Sic.*

F. 238. [1599,] Aug. 8.—[The Privy Council] to the Lord Mayor of London.

"We have heard by the Aldermen your Lordship sent hither this morning, and reported to her Majesty, the proceedings of the City at this time in making provisions, with so great willingness, against the designs of the enemy, and for their own defence, wherein though there be nothing that may seem strange and unexpected unto her Majesty, whose often proofs of the zeal and affection of the City to her Majesty's person have made an assurance in her mind of their uttermost endeavours with all dutiful affection, and procured the like care to be taken by her again for the City's safety, as the most precious place, and as it were the Chamber of this Realm; nevertheless the relation of these particularities, whereby her Majesty understandeth the forwardness of their minds, the readiness of their preparations, and their willing offers to undertake such necessary charges as this important occasion shall require, are so well pleasing unto her Majesty, as she doth most graciously profess her thankful acceptation thereof, and her desire to make known to the City, that while her Majesty shall have residence here in earth, (which both we and you, and all well disposed persons do wish many years prolonged,) she will have care to employ her best means to prevent any misfortune or danger that may be intended to that place which she holdeth so dear, or to you that are so good members of it, and so loving subjects unto herself.

"And as this doth concern the generality of your proceedings, so in particular, whereas a project was made and a purpose conceived of a Bridge to be framed, for the impeaching of the enemy's access near unto London, and of certain ships to be in a readiness and manned for defence of the said Bridge; first, the willingness of the City to confer to the charge so largely as was intended, and to **employ their industry to** the accomplishing thereof, was and is much commended, **and very** thankfully accepted; and secondly, forasmuch as the variety **of** occasions doth justly make alterations of counsels, and we, upon earnest and diligent consultations both among ourselves, and with such **noblemen** and others as are thought meet to be of Council for War, do **find** some other course meeter to be taken for impeachment of the enemy's access by river, as namely by sinking and drow[n]ing a sufficient number of such ships as are of least use in the River near Barkinge (a matter conceived and propounded from yourself and devised by one Adye, that hath with good allowance delivered his opinion this morning before us), we **have** thought good to lay aside the former purpose of the Bridge, and have resolved of this concerning the **sinking** of **the** ships (if it shall be needful) **as** a matter of more **security and less** charge, **and** therefore as **we** suppose the better to be **liked of by yourselves,** whom we doubt not **to** find as ready in the **furtherance of** this as you were of the former resolution. And therefore it is thought more available for the service that you do hasten the readiness of the twelve ships **of** the City to join with **her** Majesty's Fleet; which if you procure speedily to be done, we do conceive very great hope that the strength and speedy employment of them towards the sea will either prevent **the** use of other preparations, **or be a** means of such further respite **unto** us, as we shall be able to **take the** best courses from time to **time to** meet with the **enemy's designs,** according as **we** shall **have intelligence of** them.

" **We** will **end our letter with this** remembrance only, that having **understood of** some disturbance in the City, the last night, upon certain **misreports and** rumours, whereupon some inferior persons assembled themselves with great disorder and clamour, which is a thing unsufferable in such a City, especially in these times, when all ill disposed persons are ready to shew their malice ;. we have thought it very convenient to require you to take precise care and order for preventing and suppressing any such disorders, and to give straight direction that no confused arming or assembly be made upon uncertain news, but that you do only proceed upon good cause, and upon advertisements from us, who are no less careful for all things that do concern **you in** particular, (besides our public respect,) than we are for our own well doings. And so we wish, &c.

" Postscript. Her Majesty expecteth that the ships of the City be put in a readiness and dispatched away with all possible speed ; and therefore we pray and require your Lordship to take order therein accordingly."

**F.** 238*b*. [1599,] Aug. 10.—" A letter to the Lieutenant of the Tower, charging him to take great care that very diligent watch be kept about the store of powder and other munition, lest any evil disposed persons practice any mischief about it."

Same date.—" Letters written this day to the several Counties for the hastening of all the forces as well horse as foot, to their places of rendezvous, which they were required to do with all expedition, in respect of the certain intelligence and advertisement that was now given of the discovery **of the** enemy's fleet upon the coast of France."

Same date.—" A letter to the Lord Mayor, that the 6,000 men levied in the City might be in a readiness. Good numbers of **ships** and barks in the Thames, to lie at Barking Shelfe overthwart **the** River. Good watch to be kept in the City. To look **to** disorderly persons, tumults, and lewd bruits."

[Same date.]—" A letter to the Lord Keeper, **for** watch to be kept for safeguard of the Rolls in Chauncery Lane."

Same date.—" A like to the Lord Mayor to give order that the inhabitants thereabouts may keep watch and ward there, so long as he should think meet."

[Same date.]— " A like letter to the Lord Treasurer for **watch and** guard to be kept for security of the Exchequer, Treasury, **and other** places about Westminster."

[Same date.]— " A like to Mr. Secretary, to give order that the inhabitants of Westminster might also keep sure guard and watch for the better security of the abovesaid places, from any danger that might be practiced by lewd and mischievous persons."

F. 239. [1599,] Aug. 10.—[The Privy Council] to Sir Thomas West and Hambden Powlett, esquire.

" Forasmuch as there is newly advertisements come to us of the arrival of the Spanish fleet upon the coast of Brittanie, so as it is to be thought, ere this time, they are near the coast of this realm to execute what their intention is, we have therefore thought good to require you that with such expedition as you see the necessity of **her** Majesty's service requireth, you do cause to be put into Portesmouthe such numbers of men as to you is known to be allotted out **of that** county for the guard of that town ; and likewise to send away to be transported into the Isle of Wighte such numbers of horse and foot as are assigned for supply thereof upon like occasions, lest the coming of the galleys may hinder their transportation. And if they cannot be altogether shipped away so soon as were to be wished, you shall do well to send over the next adjoining to the Isle first, and the rest after so soon as conveniently may be, to th'end her Majesty's subjects there may **see** her princely care of them. And herein **we recommend unto you to use** such diligence as the case requireth, and may make appear **to her Majesty** your care in her service upon such urgent occasions."

F. 239. [1599, Aug.]—" A letter to the Lord Mayor of **London,** that the captains of the ships set out by the City might be appointed **by** the Admiral of the Fleet."

F. 239*b*. [1599,] Aug. 12, from the Court.—The Privy Council to the Earl of Bathe, her Majesty's Lieutenant in co. Devon.

" By your late letters we do very well perceive (as we have ever observed) an honourable care in your Lordship in all things concerning her Majesty's service, worthy of the place you do hold, and answerable to the trust reposed in you by her, which you have at this time made now **manifest**, by **the** extraordinary care and pains you have taken to attend the defence of that country, with your continual endeavours, direction, and encouragement to others, to your Lordship's great commendations, and **the** gentlemen which attend you ; all which is graciously accepted of by her Majesty, to whom we have imparted the same **at** large. And **where your** Lordship desires to know from us, when we do think the forces there may be dismissed which you have already gathered together, we have thought fit to make you this answer.

" First, that we do well consider the trouble to which **the country is** put, and would be as glad as any to free it from the same ; **but w**hen we consider that they do know it is but the duty they owe to their Sovereign and Country, and that it is nobody's good so much as their own, we doubt not but they will with all comfort endure the same.

" Secondly, for answer to your request, that you may understand **whether** we know anything that may give you any occasion to dismiss

**the** forces which your Lordship hath assembled ; this we say, that those **advertisements** which are brought **us** (if they be true) doth rather give **us cause to the** contrary ; for we do hear from Garnezey **and** Serke that the fleet is in Conquett Road, and hath been there since **W**ednesday night ; a matter which, if you do understand there, (as it is strange but you should,) then we know it requireth still that the course be kept still which you have holden ; but if it should be otherwise, for which purpose we require you presently to send over some pinnace from Plimouthe, to discover the truth either in Brest or Conquett, then have we thought fit to write thus **much** unto you for the point of ease of the country, that in regard these late warnings cannot but have made the country much more able to prepare themselves than they were, and that it cannot be but **that** he shall find all things now in good order, your Lordship **may do well, for the ease of the** country, only to give direction that all **the villages near to the** Island of **St.** Nicholas and the Fort may be in a **readiness** upon **an hour's** warning to put themselves into that place, which being kept, will **be** a great safety for the Harbour.

" And where because Sir Ferdinando Gorges (to whom particularly **her** Majesty committeth the charge of that place,) hath affirmed often that the wind may be in such a corner that men cannot be **put at** all times into that Island with expedition, we do hereby give **your Lordship** authority, upon conference with Sir Ferdinando Gorges, **to consider of** some numbers that may be put in to remain there, to prevent all sudden surprise ; to which place because her Majesty hath already (besides the standing numbers that hath been therein maintained) allowed 50 more in her Majesty's pay than was before ; your Lordship may do well (if it appear necessary) to strengthen **Sir** Ferdinando Gorges' authority, to take in presently so many more **as** may be thought necessary to make good that place, till supplies from the main may be had, when there shall be any attempt.

" If your Lordship shall do this, when we receive certificate of the numbers by poll[*] that are maintained for some time in those two places, and of the charges for their entertainment, there shall be money paid unto any such person here as shall be assigned by you to receive the same, it being now impossible for us to send down money in specie.

" And for the **rest** that you have drawn together in the country **far** from **their** dwellings, we do think your Lordship shall do well (except **you** find that this last report of their being in Brest or Conquett be true,) **to send** all back to their dwellings, upon commandment to march to their rendezvous **at an** hour's warning. For if the other places of landing **be** guarded, **we** doubt **not** but the rest shall have time given for their coming.

" Thus **do** you see how, between care of safety, and desire to ease the **country** as much as may be, we are drawn to give you conditional answers, which may easily be reconciled by you, if you **do** cause some small boats to be sent to that coast directly **to try** this particular, and that you do also give straight direction **that** always some boats lie to the westward, towards the mouth **of the Sleeve,** [so] as they may still be able to give an **alarm to the** country by fires, shooting off, or any other signal, as shall be agreed upon at their departure. That will be surely a very good means to give time for the country to repair to the landing places, though they be not kept together in head. What your Lordship shall do herein, we desire to understand, and what numbers **you** do retain in those places where the enemy is likest to land.

---

* " Pole." in MS.

" We may not omit to let your **Lordship know, her** Majesty having understood diversely how great **scarcity there is in those** countries of Marshal [martial] Commanders, **and** knowing **how** acceptable it will be unto **you to** have the assistance of such a sufficient gentleman as Sir William Russell is, being also so nearly allied **unto you, it** hath pleased her, out of former experience of his valour **and knowledge** in martial services, to send him down with authority **to command** under you all such forces as shall be found necessary for **the** defence of **that** country ; whose advice, **as** an assistant unto you, she doubteth not but you will **follow, and** upon conference **with** Sir Ferdinando Gorges, **and** others, **direct** and order all things to the good of her Majesty's service. And so we commit you to God's favour."

F. 240*b*. [1599, Aug.]—"Minute **to** Sir John Peyton, knight, Lieutenant of the Tower of London."

*A blank space is left for this letter.*

F. 240*b*. [1599,] Aug. 14.—"**A** Minute of **letters this day** directed to such noblemen (to whom their Lordships had **formerly written to** provide numbers of lances and lighthorse to attend **her Majesty's person,)** to stay their repair hither to the Court, until the **25th of this month,** and then **not to** fail."

F. 240*b*. [1599,] Aug. 16.—"Another Minute written **this** day **for** their further stay until the 5th **of** September, and afterwards other letters for their stay till such time as they should be directed to the contrary."

**F. 240*b*.** [1599.] Aug. 25.—"Upon advertisement of six galleys **that** were arrived in Conquett Haven and **discovery of a fleet** which was suspected to be the Spanish army, letters **were written to** the several counties for recalling of the forces **with all expedition, and** like direction for the horses of the Clergy **and the Voluntary (*sic*), which** the next day following were stayed again upon **further** intelligence that the ships which were discovered on the seas were part **of the Flemish** army, which arrived at Plimouthe to the number of —— sail."

F. 241. 1599, Aug. 18.—"A Warrant and List for the payment **of** the Army levied for withstanding of Invasion as followeth.

"Whereas her Majesty's pleasure is, that of the Army which was lately levied to withstand invasion, the number of one thousand horse **and** seven thousand foot, with their officers and captains, shall be con**tinued in** her Majesty's pay, until some further knowledge may be had **of the** enemy's purpose : It is therefore ordered that payment be made **to Sir John** Stanhope, knight, Treasurer at Wars, or to William **Meredith, his** deputy, after the **rate** contained in **this** list as followeth, **viz. :**

1,000 horsemen :—

The **pay of** 100 lances per diem, viz., **captain, 8*s*.,** lieutenant, **4*s*.,** guidon, **2*s*., a** trumpetor, a smith, a farrier, **and** 100 lances at 18*d*. le piece, 7*l*. 14*s*. 6*d*., in all per diem 8*l*. 8*s*. **6*d*.** And so the pay of **four** bands of **lances** of a 100 a-piece amounteth to 33*l*. 14*s*. which is for **a** week, 235*l*. 18*s*.

The pay of 100 lighthorse per diem, viz., captain, 6*s*., lieutenant, 3*s*., guidon, 2*s*., a trumpetor, a clerk, and a smith, at 18*d*. a-piece, 4*s*. 6*d*., and one hundred lighthorse at 16 pence a-piece, 6*l*. 13*s*. 4*d*., in all per diem 7*l*. 8*s*. 10*d*. And so the pay of six bands of lighthorse of 100 a-piece amounteth per diem to 44*l*. 14*s*., which is for one week 312*l*. 11*s*.

[Total,] 548*l*. 9*s*.

G

7,000 footmen distributed into bands, viz. :—

The pay of seven colonels at 13s. 4d. a piece, per diem, and seven lieutenant colonels, at 6s. 8d. a piece, per diem. And so in **all per** diem, 7l. and so for a week, 49l.

The pay of 200 footmen, per diem, viz.: captain, 8s., lieutenant, 4s., ensign, 2s., two serjeants, two drums, a surgeon, and a clerk, at 12d. a piece, 6s., and 200 footmen at 8d. a piece, 6l. 13s. 4d.; in all per diem [amounteth] to 7l. 13s. 4d. And so the pay of fourteen bands amounteth, per diem, to 107l. 6s. 8d., which amounteth for one week to the sum of 751l. 6s. 8d.

The pay of **150 footmen** per diem, viz., captain, 6s., lieutenant, 3s., ensign, 18d., **two serjeants, two** drums, a chirurgion, and a clerk at 12d. a piece 6s., and 150 footmen at eight pence a piece, 100s., in all per diem [amounteth] **to** 116s. 6d. And so the pay of 28 bands, per diem, **amounteth to** 163l. 2s., which for a week is 1,141l. 14s.

[Total,] per hebdom., 1,942l. [0s.] 8d.*

### Deputy Treasurer :—

The entertainment of the Deputy Treasurer at 10s. per diem, and two clerks at 2s. a-piece per diem, which amounteth for one week to the sum of 4l. 18s.

### Commissaries :—

Two Commissaries of Musters at 5s. a piece per diem, amounteth, **per** hebdom., to 70s.

The sum of the ordinary entertainments is: per diem, 352l. 19s. 4d.; **per hebdom., 2,498l.** 17s. 8d.

### Extraordinary Payments :—

**For money** to be given in reward, as to the Lord Lieutenant General shall be thought fit, to divers captains and officers which have attended upon this service, for their better encouragement to come at other times, 300l.

Furthermore, payment is to be made for the conduct money of the number of horse and foot afore mentioned by the warrant of the Earl of Nottingham, General of the said Army, or of six of the Privy Council, whereof the said Earl to be one, as well for their conduct to the Army as in discharge, which, being estimated at one week's pay for **the said** footbands, cometh to 1,893l. [0s.] 8d., and for the horsebands at four days' pay 297l. 13s. 4d. And so in the whole, by estimate, the **sum** of 2,410l. 14s."

F. 242b. [1599,] Aug. 22.—The Queen to the Lord Admiral [Earl of Nottingham], Lord General of her Majesty's Forces assembled in the South parts.

" Right trusty and right well beloved Cousin and Councillor, we greet you well, &c. Having caused our Council to consider of divers particular things fit to be remembered when we should please to dissolve or dismiss our forces, of all which they have written to you; we do now, by this our letter under our own hand, fully authorise you to dismiss our loving subjects assembled together by virtue of our former commandments, and therein do require you to take great care, when you shall dismiss them, that they may be conducted by such persons as will do it with order and discretion; that you do also make known unto them, that although we have no cause to think otherwise, but that the enemy will make some attempt, if by visitation of sickness in his kingdom, or other accident, his designs be not diverted; yet when we considered that this their keeping together could not be but to their

---

* Qu. 1,893l. 0s. 8d.; see **below.**

trouble and charge (a matter in which we have ever sought to ease them as much as we could), we were contented both (sic) to prepare a great fleet to set out with no small care nor common expedition, by which occasion we might have better cause and upon better ground to give our people some ease, that have so willingly performed our commandment, though for their own especial preservation, as well as in regard of the duty they owe to us their sovereign, to whom they have and ever shall be most dear.

"And therefore you shall make it known by your letters to the Shires, that we, upon these considerations, have dismissed them for the present until they shall receive our new commandments, with this declaration, that we do expect at their hands to be still ready at a day's warning to make their repair hitherwards, with such speed and such order as they shall be directed. In which case we doubt not but they will take good heed that have the setting of them forth, to see all these defects whatsoever which have been found (and which we impute rather to the sudden sending for them, rather (sic) than to any lack of duty) carefully reformed and repaired, against such time as they shall be commanded to come again together, of which it is necessary that they do all stand in expectation, as things are yet disposed; though we do use the best means we can (even to our excessive charge) to give them as much ease and time as the cause will permit, before they be put to trouble. For the rest we do refer you to such things as we have commanded our Council to deliver unto you."

F. 243. [1599,] Aug. 19.—The Privy Council to the Lord General [Earl of Nottingham].

"Whereas there were good numbers of horse and foot levied in divers counties of the realm, of which an Army was to be compounded, for defence against invasion, whereof as yet there are to the number of six or seven thousand foot, besides the horse, in such places near to the City of London as was appointed for their rendezvous; forasmuch as her Majesty hath now sent out a Fleet to the seas, to encounter such forces as may be likely to make their descent in these inner parts of her Kingdom, and that she hath always sought to put her people to no charge, but in cases of apparent necessity; for avoiding whereof she is now at great expense out of her own coffers; it hath pleased her to command us in her name to signify to your Lordship, that she is contented that for the present you disperse* those forces that are assembled, back again to their habitations, and to the several counties out of which they were levied; according to the which we pray your good Lordship to take present order that payment be made unto the several companies of horse and foot of such moneys as shall appear to be necessary; which being done, your Lordship may dismiss them under the charge and conduct of those gentlemen and conductors that brought them hither, who are straightly to be charged and commanded by your Lordship to have special care, that the armour, weapon, furniture, and coats of the soldiers (which have been provided at the charge of the country,) may be safely delivered back again at their return, to be kept in the several towns, there to be ready as occasion shall serve. For the better effecting whereof, we pray your Lordship to write your letters to the Lieutenants or Commissioners for the Musters of those several counties, signifying unto them the order and care your Lordship hath taken herein, and what the numbers are that are now dismissed, requiring them that there may be no change of these men that were now sent up, and have been

* "Dismiss," written over.

viewed and trained (especially of the shot), saving such as **have** now or shall be found insufficient; a matter whereof her Majesty doubteth not but they will have some more care against a new warning. **For** which purpose you must let them know, that it is expected, though the said companies are now for their ease returned back for this time to the counties, yet they are to be kept in such readiness as they may hereafter march forthwith, and repair to such places as shall be appointed unto them, with all speed. Herein praying your Lordship to take speedy order, according **to** her Majesty's resolution and direction, we bid, &c."

F. 243b. [**1599,** Aug.]—"Instructions given **to the Lord** Thomas Howard, **being sent** Admiral to the Seas.

"Although you have **received a** commission from us enabling you to execute upon the enemy whatsoever shall seem necessary for the defence of **our** kingdom, either **by** impeachment of his forces from landing, or using any other means to the overthrow of any fleet of the King of Spain's; yet we think good hereby to direct you (with the advice of such of our Council as we have used in the like occasions) what **course** it **is** which we hold fit and proper for those our services, leaving **it notwith-**standing to your good discretion to change for the good **of our service as** you shall see cause, who shall be better able to fashion your resolutions (by the consideration and observation of such accidents as shall fall out) than we shall be able precisely to direct you from hence. Only this **we** recommend **unto you, as** a main point to be carefully obeyed, that you take special **care not to** engage our Royal Ships in any fight or in any **port in** such sort but that you may come off from them again from the danger of either firing, boarding, or sinking. For we consider that if you should be entangled by the enemy's ships, that as they exceed you in number and greatness, so they are filled with great store of soldiers and musketeers, whereas for the sudden (*sic*) and haste of our; setting forth we could not so provide you, **nor** furnish victuals for them without further time.

"Next, if you shall follow the ships **of our** enemies into any **straight** port, they having galleys to draw and conduct fire unto you, **you shall** not be able **to** shun it; and therefore our pleasure is, that you **shall** take special **care** thereof, and that you hazard (if need require) those ships which are of less charge, and such other crumpsters and hoys as shall be added **unto** the fleet under your command.

"For **your** going to the Westward, we must leave that **to** your dis-cretion, **as you** shall find necessary cause for the good of our service. But this **we must** let **you** know, that we do think that the greatest peril **is** like to **be by** those men that shall be received out of the Low Countries to be transported over, which is the matter that must be looked unto above all things else; for which purpose we do command you still to be sure that you have special care to lie in such sort as to be able to discover all ships that come to the eastwards, lest, whilst you be on the shore, the enemy borrowing [burrowing?] on the other do pass by hitherwards.

"Whensoever you shall hear anything of the enemy's coming and designs, you shall diligently advertise us, and if you find any certainty at any time of approach you shall give the alarm to the coast, to th'intent that our forces may be in a readiness to answer such places **of** descent as are most likeliest to be attempted.

"If you at any time shall meet with any of our ships **in** the Narrow Seas, we do command **both** those and all others **of our** subjects' ships to obey **your commission and** commandments.

" Further, because we **know how fit it is** in **all** these cases to
nominate unto you some **selected** persons in **whose** discretion and fidelity
we do repose extraordinary confidence, being **such as we** hold fit to give
advice in matters of importance, we do hereby command **you** (having by
our commission already under our Seal nominated our **servant** [Sir
Walter] * Rawleighe, knight, Captain of our Guard, Lieutenant of our
**county of** Cornwall, to be our Vice-Admiral, and to be aiding **to you in
all** your counsels and enterprises,) that you do also use the advice and
opinion of our servant Foulke Grevill, our Treasurer of our Navy, **and
our** servant Henry Palmer, knight, Comptroller of the same, in all your
**and our** servants' consultations and resolutions concerning the attempts
**upon the** enemy or resistance of the **same**, or any other matter **of
importance** for the good of our service.

" **We do** also require you to take great care, both during your being
**abroad** to avoid all needless wastes of **our** munition and other sea stores,
and towards your return to give careful direction that nothing be
embezzled by the inferior ministers; **a matter** which we do also recommend especially **to** the care of our Treasurer of our Navy, whom we do
hereby constitute our Rear-Admiral **of** this Fleet, in regard of **our good**
opinion of him.

"Further, where **we have** assigned **some** portion of money **to** be
carried aboard **with** (*sic*) our said Treasurer of our Navy, to be bestowed
and laid out as occasion shall serve, for our necessary services, lest by
the lack of any such payments any prejudice should grow **to** our service
upon accidents that may fall out either for the preservation of our fleet,
or for the destruction of our enemy's: our will and pleasure is, that for
all such sums so to be expended, the same be done by direction of you
our Admiral, and calling to you our Treasurer of **our** Navy and the
Comptroller of the same, or any one of these two. In which **case** we do
hereby declare to you our Treasurer, that **we** do give **you** warrant
to make payment of all such sums of money **as** shall be **found necessary**
upon the direction of you, the Lord Howarde of Walden, **our Admiral of**
this Fleet, whose warrant, signed by you our said Admiral, **and sub-**
scribed by the hands **of** our Vice-Admiral, and the Comptroller **of our**
Navy, **or any** one **of them** in case of the others' absence, **shall be a**
sufficient warrant **to** you **our Treasurer** for your discharge.

" Lastly, whereas there **are** now serving in our Fleet divers gentlemen
of good quality and sufficiency, although **we** have hereby only constituted
these three abovenamed **to** be of the council with **you** ; yet we do
further authorise you (as any occasion shall offer itself) **to** debate any
**matter** of importance for the good of our service, [**and ?**] to call unto you
**such of our captains** and servitors **as** you **shall** think **fit**, to th'intent that
upon due **consideration in matters** of difficulty your resolutions may be
**executed upon the better advice and** deliberation."

F. 244*b*.    1599, 41 Eliz., **Aug. 11, Manor of Nonesuche.**—
" Commission for Sir John **Stanhope, kt., and Mr. Meredith, to be**
Treasurers **at** Wars.†

" Elizabeth, by the grace of God, &c., To our trusty and well beloved
Sir John Stanhoppe, knight, Treasurer of our Chamber, greeting.
Upon the special trust we repose in your fidelity and acceptable good
service, we do by these presents name and appoint you **to** be our
Treasurer at Wars, and to receive and issue such our treasure as shall

---

* Omitted in MS.
† This is not in the Signet Office **Index, the State** Papers, or the Patent Rolls.
**There is** a docquet of it under Aug. 12.

be employed as well for the payment of our armies and companies of men, levied or to be levied for the withstanding of any foreign invasions of our realm of England, under the conduct of our right trusty and right well beloved Cousin and Councillor, the Earl of Nottingham, our High Admiral of England, and Captain General over the said armies and companies; as also for the payment of all other our armies and companies of men as shall be assembled for the defence and surety of our Royal person, and under the conduct of our right trusty and well beloved Councillor, the Lord Hunsdon, our Chamberlain, Captain General, and Lieutenant over them. And we do also appoint our trusty and well beloved William Meredithe, esquire, to be Deputy Treasurer at Wars unto you, for the payment of such armies and companies as are or shall be under the conduct of the said E[arl]. We will and command therefore that such part of our treasure as shall come to the hands of the said William Meredithe, shall be issued forth from time to time by him, according to such order as shall be prescribed unto him by warrant of the said Earl of Nottingham, or any other our Lieutenant over that Army, by our commission under our Great Seal of England to be named; and the residue of our said treasure to be issued from time to time by you our said Treasurer at Wars, by warrant of the aforesaid Lord Hunsdon or any other our Lieutenant over that Army to be by us appointed, or else by such order and direction as you shall receive in writing under the hands of six of our Privy Council (whereof our High Treasurer of England, our Principal Secretary, [and] our Chancellor of our Exchequer, to be always two). And of all such sums of money, as you or the said William Meredithe shall issue or pay by warrant, order, and direction as above is said, we do by these presents authorise our High Treasurer of England, Chancellor and Barons of our Exchequer to give you and the said William Meredithe, and to either of you, a full discharge upon your account at any time hereafter. And our further pleasure is, that for the execution of the said office of Treasurer at Wars by you, and of Deputy Treasurer of [by ?] the said William Meredithe, there shall be allowed unto each of you from time to time, out of such sums of money as shall come to your hands, or his, for the payment of our said armies, such several entertainments and allowances as by a list of the numbers and change of our said armies to be established by our Privy Council under six of their hands (whereof the said Earl of Nottingham and Lord Hunsdon, as Generals of our said several armies, to be two) shall be assigned unto each of you. And these our letters shall be their and your sufficient warrant and discharge in that behalf. Given under our Signet."

F. 245. [1599,] 41 Eliz., Aug. 11, Manor of Nonsuche.—"Privy Seal for Sir John Stanhope, knight, to be Treasurer of the Army."

This is a Royal warrant to the Treasurer and Chamberlains of the Exchequer, referring to the appointments made by the preceding, and commanding them to pay to Stanhope 10,000l., to be expended by Meredith and himself, as above.

"And forasmuch as it is uncertain how long time we may have cause to continue both our said armies, or either of them, in our pay, we do therefore will and command you to pay or cause to be paid unto the said William Meredithe, out of our treasure in the Receipt of our Exchequer, from time to time, such further sums of money as by six of our Privy Council under their hands (whereof you our said Treasurer, our Principal Secretary, or Chancellor of our Exchequer to be always two,) you shall be required to pay for the use of our said armies, according to such several lists of the numbers of **men and** rates of entertainments meet to be by us allowed, as from time to time our said Council shall send unto you, under their hands, according to the increase or decrease of the numbers of our said armies ; and further to make payment to the said Meredith of any other sums of money for the coat and conduct of our said forces, either coming to our said **army** or upon their discharge, or for rewards of captains or other persons serving or attending to serve us in our said Army, as by any six of our Privy Council or else by the said Earl of Nottingham, our Lieutenant General, shall, under his or their hands, be set down and appointed. And these our letters shall be your sufficient warrant and discharge in this behalf. Given under our Privy Seal."

*(Not among the Privy Seals.)*

**F.** 246. [1599, Aug.]—"Commission for Sir William Russell, knight, to be assistant to the Lieutenants in the counties of the South and Western parts, where Lieutenants are, and to the Sheriff[s] and Commissioners for the Musters, and to **be** the chief Commander of the forces there, &c.

"Elizabeth, by the grace of God, Queen **of** England, France, **and** Ireland, Defender of the Faith, &c., To all Lieutenants of our counties, Deputy Lieutenants, Sheriffs, Commissioners for the Musters, and to all other our officers, ministers and subjects in the South and West parts of our realm, to whom it shall or may appertain, and to every of them, greeting. Forasmuch as it may fall out that the enemies may make their descent upon some of the coasts of the Southern and Western parts, **whose** forces and attempts are by all means to be speedily impeached and resisted, both at the landing, and otherwise also, in case they shall proceed further within land ; and for that we consider how requisite and necessary it is for the speed and advancement of **this present service** that some person of ability, quality, and experience in **martial causes** should be assistant with our Lieutenants **in** those our **counties** that **be** within their charge, and with their Sheriffs and Commissioners for **the** Musters in such other counties where no Lieutenants are, **for better** orders to be given for the employing and disposing of our forces **that** are to be used against the enemy's attempts, and for the directing of all other things any way requisite for this service, in any the South or Western parts :

"Know ye that we have made special choice, to this purpose, of our **trusty** and well beloved Sir William Russell, knight, as of a personage **who**[m], in respect of his lineage, experience, and knowledge in martial **affairs**, (by reason of his former employments divers ways in sundry our services,) we do think very meet thereunto. And therefore we have and by these presents do constitute him the said Sir William Russell to be General and Chief Commander, Ruler, and Director, under our Lieutenants in those counties where Lieutenants are, and in those also where there are only Sheriffs and Commissioners for the Musters, **of** all such our forces, both of horse and foot, in such manner as he shall think **fit** and convenient for the performance of this service of impeaching and withstanding the enemy's attempts any way ; giving him **hereby** full power and authority to that end, excepting that he shall **not deal** within the precincts of the charges that **we** have appointed **to Sir** Ferdinando Gorges at Plimouthe, and to **Sir Nicholas** Parker **at Falmouth.**

"We will and command **you**, therefore, **our** Lieutenants, Deputy **Lieutenants,** Sheriffs, and Commissioners for **the** Musters, not only so to receive and accept the said Sir William Russell in **such sort as by** these presents we have named and constituted him, and to join **him with** you in advice and execution of anything that shall concern **this service,** but also to follow the directions and orders he shall give and prescribe for the same upon your consultations had with him, and to cause all persons resisting or disobedient herein to be punished according to the quality of their offence; and that all mayors, sheriffs, bailiffs, constables, and all other our officers, ministers, and subjects be aiding and assisting and obeying unto him with all their powers and means in anything that he shall appoint, require, or ordain for the performance and advancement of this important service; as you and they tender our pleasure, and will **answer** for the contrary at their uttermost perils. In **witness whereof we have** caused these our letters to be made patents, **to continue during our pleasure.** Witness ourself, &c."

(*Not on the Patent Rolls, nor among the Privy Seals, &c.*).

F. 247. [1599, Aug. 10.] Nonesuche.—" Commission given to the Earl of Nottingham, Lord High Admiral of England, to be Lieutenant General of her Majesty's Forces in the South parts."

*See Patent Roll,* 41 *Eliz., part* 24, *m.* 24, **dorse.**

F. 248b. [1599, Aug. 10, Nonesuche.]—" Commission given to the Lord Thomas Howarde, being Admiral of her Majesty's Navy and Fleet sent to the Seas."

*Ibid., m.* **23,** *dorse.*

F. 250. 1599, Aug.—" **A** list of the trained Horse of the several Counties, with their numbers, and time of their entrance into pay.

| Counties. | [Captains.] | The Day of Entrance. | Lances. | Light Horse. | Petron[els]. |
|---|---|---|---|---|---|
| Bedford | Oliver Harvey | 14th | 32 | 18 | 0 |
| Bucks | Francis Cheney | 15th | 48 | 0 | 45 |
| Cambridge | John St. George | 14th | 20 | 30 | 0 |
| | Sir Edmond Hurleston | 14th | 45 | 0 | 0 |
| Essex | William Smithe | 13th | 0 | 92 | 0 |
| | John Sammes | 13th | 0 | 35 | 0 |
| | Robert Leighe | 14th | 0 | 29 | 0 |
| Huntingdon | Sir Jervis Clyfton | 15th | 20 | 20 | 10 |
| | William Gresham | 19th | 42 | 0 | 50 |
| Norfolk | Anthony Drurye | 18th | 0 | 50 | 0 |
| | Thomas Barney | 19th | 0 | 32 | 50 |
| | Thomas Grosse | 19th | 0 | 48 | 0 |
| Suffolk | George Brooke | 18th | 22 | 51 | 0 |
| | John Harvey | 17th | 63 | 31 | 0 |
| | Thomas Sherley | 15th | 4 | 44 | 16 |
| Sussex | Henry Goring | 13th | 5 | 49 | 10 |
| | Thomas Challenor | 15th | 10 | 41 | 0 |
| Surrey | Sir John Morgan | 12th | 0 | 31 | 0 |
| | Thomas Forthe | 11th | 0 | 33 | 0 |
| | | | 311 | 638 | 181 |

The whole number of these horse—1,126 (*sic*).

F. 250*b*. 1599, Aug.—"A list of the Footbands of the several Counties, with the time of their entrance into pay.

| Counties. | Captains' Names. | The Day of their Entrance. | Foot. | |
|---|---|---|---|---|
| Bedford - - | Richard Conquest - - | 15th | 200 | |
| | Robert Newdigate - | 15th | 150 | 500 |
| | John Cocken - - - | 15th | 150 | |
| Bucks - - - | William Burlacye - - | 15th | 150 | |
| | Tho. Piggett - - | 15th | 200 | 500 |
| | Alex. Hambden - - | 15th | 150 | |
| Cambridge - | Albury (*sic*) Yorke - - | 15th | 300 | 500 |
| | Mich. Gubbidge - | 15th | 200 | |
| Huntingdon - - | Rob. Throgmorton - - | 13th | 200 | 400 |
| | Millicent (*sic*) Smithe - | 13th | 200 | |
| Oxon, being of the Regiment of Sir Francis Knollis. | Henry Warde - - - | 19th | 300 | |
| | James Yarworthe - - | 19th | 200 | 500 |
| | Thomas Adams - - - | 19th | | |
| Norfolk - - | The Regiment of Sir Jo. Townsend, knight. | Sir Jo. Townsend, Colonel - | 16th | 200 | |
| | Sir Bass. Gawdye, Lieut.-Col. | 16th | 200 | |
| | Roger le Straunge - - | 16th | 150 | 1,000 |
| | Thomas Townesend - - | 16th | 150 | |
| | Francis Spilman - - | 16th | 150 | |
| | Henry Holdiche - - | 16th | 150 | |
| | The Regiment of Sir Christopher Heidon, knight. | Sir Chris. Heydon, Colonel - | 16th | 200 | |
| | Sir Philip Woodhouse, Lt.-Col. | 16th | 200 | |
| | Tho. Corbet - - - | 16th | 150 | 1,000 |
| | James Colthroppe - - | 16th | 150 | |
| | William Barrowe - - | 16th | 150 | |
| | Clipsbye Gaudye - - | 16th | 150 | |
| Suffolk - - | The Regiment of Sir William Woodhouse. | Sir William Woodhouse, Colonel | 16th | 200 | |
| | Gilbert Lea - - - | 16th | 200 | |
| | Robert Bacon - - | 16th | 150 | 1,000 |
| | Thomas Waldgrave - - | 16th | 150 | |
| | Tho. Minshawe - - | 16th | 150 | |
| | Tho. Hide - - - | 16th | 150 | |
| | The Regiment of Sir Clement Heigham. | Sir Clement Heigham, Colonel | 16th | 200 | |
| | William Marche, Lieut. - | 16th | 200 | |
| | —— Dacres - - - | 16th | 150 | 1,000 |
| | Jo. Germin - - - | 16th | 150 | |
| | George Waldgrave - - | 16th | 150 | |
| | John Prettiman - - | 16th | 150 | |

The whole number of the Foot is—6,400.

F. 251*b*. [1599, Aug.]—"Counties out of which men were to be drawn for an Army for the defence of her Majesty's person."

| Foot. | Horse. | Counties. | Men. |
|---|---|---|---|
| 2,000 | 300 | Norfolk - - - - | 200 |
| 2,000 | 200 | Suffolk - - - | 200 |
| 3,000 | — | London - - - | 300 |
| -- | — | Berks - - - - | 1,500 |
| 500 | — | Oxford - - - | 500 |
| 1,000 | 50 | Hertford - - - | 500 |

| Foot. | Horse. | Counties. | Men. |
|---|---|---|---|
| 500 | 100 | Bucks - - - | 500 |
| 500 | 60 | Bedford - - - | 300 |
| 2,000 | 80 | Surrey - - | — |
| 3,000 | 200 | Essex - - - - | 1,000 |
| 500 | 50 | Northampton - - | 1,000 |
| 500 | 60 | Cambridge - - - | — |
| | | Warwick - - | 2,000 |
| | | Leicester - - - | 1,000 |
| | | Gloucester - - | 2,000 |
| | | Nottingham - - - | 1,000 |
| | | Rutland - - | 500 |
| | | Derby - - - | 1,000 |
| | | Somerset - - - | 3,000 |
| | | Wilts - - - - | 1,000 |
| | | Lincoln - - - | 2,000 |
| | | | 36,100 |

*Ff.* 252-293 *are cut out.*

### [NAVAL AFFAIRS, 1583-8.]

F. 294. [c. 1583 ?]—" The Names of the Officers of the Navy, with their places and feos belonging to them.

Lord Admiral—200 marks [per annum].

Vice Admiral—feo 100*l.*; his diet 10*s.* per diem; 2 clerks, one 12*d.* the other 10*d.* per diem; 10*l.* for his boathire per annum—Faict per annum 325*l.* 19*s.* 2*d.*

Master of the Ordnance—feo 100 marks; diet 6*s.* 8*d.* per diem; two clerks 8*d.*; and 8*l.* boathire per annum.—Faict per annum 220*l.* 13*s.* 4*d.*

Treasurer of the Navy, Sir John Haukins—feo 100 marks; diet 6*s.* 8*d.* per diem; two clerks 8*d.*; and 8*l.* boathire per annum.—Faict per annum 220*l.* 13*s.* 4*d.*

Comptroller, Wm. Holstock—feo 50*l.*; diet 4*s.* per diem; 2 clerks 8*d.*; 8*l.* boathire per annum.—Faict per annum 155*l.* 6*s.* 8*d.*

Surveyor—feo 40*l.*; diet 4*s.* per diem; two clerks at 8*d.* per diem; 8*l.* boathire per annum.—Faict per annum, 145*l.* 6*s.* 8*d.*

Clerk, Wm. Bouroughe—feo 33*l.* 6*s.* 8*d.*; diet 4*s.* 4*d.*; 8*l.* boathire—Faict per annum 102*l.* 3*s.* 4*d.*

Keeper of Store, Chr. Baker—feo 25*l.* 6*s.* 8*d.*; diet 2*s.* 6*d.* per diem. Faict per annum 72*l.* 5*s.* 10*d.*

Surveyor of the Victuals, James Quarles—feo 58*l.*; diet 5*s.* per diem; and one clerk at 8*d.* per diem.—Faict per annum 161*l.* 8*s.* 4*d.*

Qu[een's] merchant for Danske, Mr. Thomas Allen—feo 30*l.* without other allowances.—Faict per annum 30*l.*

Pilot, Thomas Graye—feo 20*l.*—Faict per annum 20*l.*

The Master Shipwright—12*d.* per diem.—Faict per annum, 18*l.* 6*s.* 8*d.*

William Barnes, for grounding—6*d.* per diem.—Faict per annum 9*l.* 2*s.* 6*d.*

The ordinary yearly charge by the Treasurer of [the] Navy, 5,714*l.* 2*s.* 2*d.*

The ordinary charge by the Victualler, 1,000[*l.*]

F. 296. 1583.—"The number of Ships throughout the Realm; collected out of the Certificate returned anno 1583."

| | Vessels above 100 Tons. | Under 100, above 80. | Under 80. |
|---|---|---|---|
| London | 62 | 23 | 44 |
| Essex | 9 | 40 | 145 |
| Norfolk | 16 | 80 | 145 |
| Suffolk | 27 | 14 | 60 |
| Cornwall | 3 | 2 | 65 |
| Devon | 7 | 3 | 109 |
| Dorset | 9 | 1 | 51 |
| Bristow and Somerset | 9 | 1 | 27 |
| Wight | 0 | 0 | 29 |
| Southampton | 8 | 7 | 47 |
| York | 11 | 8 | 36 |
| North parts | 17 | 1 | 121 |
| Lincoln | 5 | 0 | 20 |
| Sussex | 0 | 0 | 65 |
| Kent | 0 | 0 | 95 |
| Cinque Ports | 0 | 0 | 220 |
| Cumberland | 0 | 0 | 11 |
| Gloucester | 0 | 0 | 29 |
| Chester | 0 | 0 | } 72 |
| Lancaster | 0 | 0 | |
| Summa | 177 | 74 | 1,383 |

Cf. State Papers, Vol. 156, Nos. 45, 46 (undated).

F. 297. 1583.—"The number [of] Masters, Mariners, and Fishermen belonging to every Shire throughout the Realm, certified anno 1583."

| | Masters. | Mariners. | Fishermen. |
|---|---|---|---|
| London | 143 | 991 | 191 |
| Essex | 115 | 578 | — |
| Norfolk | 145 | 1,438 | — |
| Suffolk | 69 | 198 | — |
| Cornwall | 108 | 626 | 1,184 |
| Devon | 150 | 1,915 | 101 |
| Dorset | 85 | 460 | 100 |
| Bristow | 48 | 464 | — |
| Southampton | 25 | 133 | 64 |
| Isle [of] Wighte | 21 | 94 | 119 |
| York | 81 | 292 | 507 |
| North parts | 29 | 372 | 450 |
| Lincoln | 20 | 195 | 334 |
| Sussex | 70 | 371 | 122 |
| Kent | 0 | 243 | 0 |
| Cinque Ports | 200 | 604 | 148 |
| Cumberland | 12 | 180 | 20 |
| Gloucester | 19 | 100 | 23 |
| Chester | 85 | 253 | 36 |
| Lancaster | 5 | 0 | 0 |
| Summa | 1,484 | 11,515 | 2,299 |

Wherrymen between London Bridge and Gravesend—957.

**Sum** of $\left\{\begin{array}{lr}\text{mariners} & 11,515 \\ \text{fishermen} & 2,299 \\ \text{watermen} & 957\end{array}\right\}$ men, beside masters, 14,772 (*sic*).

F. 298. [1587?].—" The Names of the Queen's Majesty's Ships and Pinnaces, with their tonnages, numbers of marines, gunners, and soldiers.*

| Tonnage. | [Ships.] | Mariners. | Gunners. | Soul[diers]. | Men in all. |
|---|---|---|---|---|---|
| 1,000 | The Triumphe | 340 | 30 | 130 | 500 |
| 900 | The Eliza : Jonas | 340 | 30 | 130 | 490 |
| 900 | The White Beare | 340 | 30 | 120 | 490 |
| 800 | The Arke Rauley | 290 | 30 | 110 | 430 |
| 800 | The Victory | 290 | 30 | 110 | 430 |
| 650 | The Hoape | 175 | 25 | 76 | 270 |
| 500 | The Non Parley | 150 | 24 | 76 | 250 |
| 500 | The Mary Rose | 150 | 25 | 76 | 250 |
| 500 | The Lion | 150 | 24 | 76 | 250 |
| 500 | The Bonadventure | 150 | 24 | 76 | 250 |
| 500 | The Revenge | 150 | 24 | 76 | 250 |
| 500 | The Vantguard | 150 | 24 | 76 | 250 |
| 500 | The Rainbow | 150 | 24 | 76 | 250 |
| 360 | The Dreadnaught | 120 | 24 | 40 | 190 |
| 330 | The Suifte Sure | 120 | 20 | 40 | 180 |
| 300 | The Antelope | 120 | 20 | 30 | 170 |
| 300 | The Swallow | 120 | 20 | 30 | 160 |
| 260 | The Forsighte | 110 | 20 | 20 | 150 |
| 180 | The Aide | 90 | 16 | 14 | 120 |
| 160 | The Teigar | 80 | 12 | 8 | 100 |
| 160 | The Bull | 80 | 12 | 8 | 100 |
| 120 | The Scoute | 55 | 8 | 7 | 70 |
| 120 | The Tremontany | 55 | 8 | 7 | 70 |
| 100 | The Achates | 45 | 8 | 7 | 60 |
| — | The Gallie Bonauoglia | 200 | 8 | 62 | 270 |
| 70 | The Charles | 36 | 4 | 9 | 40 |
| 60 | The Moone | 34 | 4 | 0 | 38 |
| 35 | The Makshift | 31 | 4 | 0 | 35 |
| 35 | The Spie | 31 | 4 | 0 | 35 |
| 35 | The Advice | 31 | 4 | 0 | 35 |
| 35 | The Marlion | 20 | 4 | 0 | 24 |
| 40 | The Sune | 26 | 4 | 0 | 30 |
| 30 | The Truste | 18 | 2 | 0 | 20 |
| — | The Brigandin | 33 | 2 | 0 | 25 |
| 15 | The Grayhound | 10 | 0 | 0 | 10 |
| 10 | The Georg | 16 | 4 | 0 | 20 |
| | Sum | 4,302 | 555 | 1,465 | |

*In the margin :* Men, 6,322.

Wages - $\left\{\begin{array}{l}\text{For the wages of the said 6,322 men for one month} \\ \text{of 28 days after 14s. every man for diets, dead shares,} \\ \text{and rewards per mensem, —— (blank).}\end{array}\right.$

Victuals $\left\{\begin{array}{l}\text{For sea victuals of the said 6,322 for one month of} \\ \text{28 days at 16s. 8d. every man, ——- (blank).}\end{array}\right.$

Half numbers $\left\{\begin{array}{l}\text{The wages and victuals for half the foresaid numbers} \\ \text{for one month of 28 days, —— (blank).}\end{array}\right.$

* This differs from State Papers, Vol. 199, No. 98.

F. 301. [1587,] 29 Eliz., March 25 (*sic*), **Westminster.**—" Copy of Sir Francis Drake his Commission, being sent **to the Seas in** December 1587 (*sic*), to repair to the coast of Spain."

*See Patent Roll,* 30 *Eliz., part* 13, *m.* 1 *dorse* (*dated March* 15, *i.e.* 1588).\*

F. 305. 1587, Dec. 16.—" A copy of the Lord Admiral's [Charles Lord Howard of Effingham] Commission, being sent to the Sea with certain of her Majesty's Navy."

*See Patent Roll,* 30 *Eliz., part* 17, *m.* 7 *dorse* (*Dec.* 21) ; *and State Papers, Vol.* 206, *No.* 41 (*Dec.* 21).

This is in Latin.†

**F. 307.** 1587, Dec. 15.—" Minute of the Instructions given to the **Lord** Admiral, being appointed to go to the Seas."

" Being sundry ways most credibly given to understand of the great and extraordinary preparations made by sea, as well in Spain by the King there, as in the Low Countries by the Duke of Parma, and that it is also meant that the said forces shall be employed in some enterprise to be attempted either in our dominions of England and Ireland, or **in** the realm of Scotland, tending principally to the disquieting of **our** estate : we have thought it very convenient to seek by all such good means as God hath given us, to put ourselves in order of defence for the better withstanding of the said attempts.

" And therefore, finding that the withstanding of the said intended attempts can in no sort be so well performed as by arming by sea, we have thought it therefore most necessary to have as well our own ships as certain ships pertaining **to** our subjects **set** forth **to serve** us under your conduction, in **respect** of the place **you hold and the zeal and** sufficiency you have to serve us.

" Now, forasmuch as it is to be **doubted that the forces prepared as** well in Spain as in the Low Countries **may be employed in sundry** attempts, some in Ireland or Scotland **and** some against **this realm : we have** therefore thought **good** that our servant, Sir Francis **Drake, with** some of our own ships, **such** as you shall think meet, and others **per**taining to our subjects, **should** be ordered by instruction as well **from** yourself as others of our Privy Council to ply up and down between our realm of Ireland and the Isle of Scilly and Ushent, and the entrance of the Sleve, [in the] south-west part of this our realm, as well to impeach any descent that may be made in the said realm of Ireland, or on the south-west parts of this our realm, as also to intercept and distress such forces as **may** be sent into Scotland.

" **And for** yourself, **in** respect of **the preparations** made by the Duke of Parma in the Low Countries, **we think it meet,** as well for the withstanding of any attempt that may be made **against this our realm, as** also for the intercepting of such forces as by **the said Duke** may **be sent** into Scotland, you should ply up and down, sometimes towards **the** north, **and** sometimes towards the south, as to you in your own discretion and judgment shall be thought may tend best to the impeaching of attempts and designs of the said Duke, or the Spanish forces.

" And for that some of our greatest ships, for lack of convenient harbours, cannot with so convenient safety be continued in daily service

---

\* The commission is not under either date in the State Papers. The Patent Roll altogether omits the opening words, " Elizabeth, **by** the grace of God, &c.," beginning " To our loving and faithful subject."

† *Cf.* f. 317 *b*.

by the Narrow Seas as other of our ships that draw not so much **water**, we refer the bestowing of them, either under the conduction **of our** Vice-Admiral, the Lord Henry Seamer, or some such other **as by you** shall be thought meet, in such harbours where they may **be in most** safety, and may also be ready to be employed at such time as **you shall** find it expedient for our service.

"And if during the time of our service on the sea, you shall receive any certain advertisement that the navy of Spain shall repair into these parts with such force and strength **as** the ships committed to the conduction of our servant, Drake, shall not be able to make head against them, then you **shall either** give order unto him, if you shall certainly understand **that the** said navy shall have an intent to come into the Narrow Seas to join his forces with the Duke of Parma's, to repair with **all** speed **to** you, **to** th'end you may join both your forces together, or else, if you shall in your discretion so think it meet, send so many other of our ships as you may well spare for the reinforcing of him, for that, as we conceive, the forces of the Duke of Parma will not be such but that you may with a convenient number of our own ships be able to impeach and withstand anything that he shall attempt either against this realm or Scotland.

"And further, if during your being on the seas you shall happen to **meet** any ships coming out of the East parts bound for Spain, we think it meet that you do make stay of all the said ships in some courteous* and favourable manner, and send them hither into this our realm, **to** th'end that search may be made whether they be laden with victuals or munition.

"And forasmuch as we have given order for the moving of the States (according to the Contract between them and us) to send also some of their ships to the seas, we think it meet that you should also take charge of them accordingly as it is agreed on by the said Contract, and employ them together with ours as you shall see cause, for the common defence as well of our own realms as those Countries.

"Also if, during the time of your continuance on the seas, you shall understand of anything to be attempted against our two cautionary towns, Briell and Flushinge, or the towns of Ostende or Bergen up Zone (sic), where our subjects are placed in garrison, you shall do your best endeavour to impeach any such attempt, and to yield them any convenient relief that you may.

"Lastly, forasmuch as there may fall out many accidents that may move you to take another course than by these our instructions you are directed, **we** therefore **think** it most expedient to refer you therein to your own judgment and discretion, to do that thing you may think may best tend to th'advancement of our service. And of all your doings and proceedings in the said service, and such intelligence as you shall receive, we require you to advertise us from time to time."

F. 308, 1588[-9], Jan. 3.†—"The Rates of the Officers' Wages attending upon the Navy."

"The Lord Admiral hath for his diet, every day, 3*l.* 6*s.* 8*d.* All other Admirals and Vice-Admirals are to be paid by warrant from the Lord Admiral by his discretion.

"**The** Captains of all other ships and pinnaces have per diem 2*s.* 6*d.*"

---

* "Curtouse."
† This date is given at the beginning, but another appears at the end.

(1.) "The Eliz. Jonas, 500 men. The **Triumphe,** 500. The Beare, 500. The Victorie, 400. The Arcke, 400."

| [Officers.] | Month. £ | s. | d. | Week. s. | d. | Day. s. | d. |
|---|---|---|---|---|---|---|---|
| The Master | 3 | 2 | 6 | 15 | 6½ | 2 | 2¼ |
| 2 mates, each at | 1 | 10 | 0 | — | | — | |
| A pilot | 1 | 10 | 0 | 7 | 6 | | 12½ |
| A boatswain | | 30 | 0 | — | | — | |
| Mates, each at | | 17 | 6 | 4 | 4½ | | 7½ |
| Quarter masters, each at | | 25 | 0 | — | | — | |
| Quarter mates, each at | | 17 | 6 | — | | — | |
| 4 yeomen of { The jeer[i]e, The halyards, The sheets, The tacks } each at | | 17 | 6 | — | | — | |
| A master carpenter | | 25 | 0 | 6 | 3 | | 12½ |
| 2 mates to use both axe and mallet | | 17 | 6 | — | | — | |
| If any more caulkers or carpenters be appointed, each to have | | 13 | 9 | 3 | 5¼ | | 5½ |
| A purser | | 20 | 0 | 5 | 0 | | 8½ |
| A steward | | 17 | 6 | — | | — | |
| A cook | | 17 | 6 | — | | — | |
| 2 mates | | 13 | 9 | — | | — | |
| A surgeon | | 20 | 0 | — | | — | |
| 2 sergeants* in common pay | | — | | — | | — | |
| 4 trumpeters, each at | | 20 | 0 | — | | — | |
| A drum } A phiphe } each at | | 15 | 0 | — | | — | |
| A coxswain | | 17 | 6 | — | | — | |
| His mate | | 13 | 9 | — | | — | |
| A skyse (*sic*) swain | | 17 | 6 | — | | — | |
| His mate | | 13 | 9 | — | | — | |
| 2 swabbers, each at | | 13 | 9 | — | | — | |
| An armourer | | 18 | 8 | — | | — | |
| A gunmaker | | 18 | 8 | — | | — | |
| A master gunner | | 15 | 0 | — | | — | |
| 2 mates, each at | | 11 | 3 | 2 | 9¼ | | 4½ |
| 4 quarter gunners, each at | | 11 | 3 | — | | — | |
| 4 quarter gunners' mates, each at | | 11 | 3 | — | | — | |
| Yeoman of the powder-room | | 11 | 3 | — | | — | |

(2.) "The Marirose, 250 men. The Bonaventure, 250. The Lyon, 250. The Hope, 250. The Nomperlie (*sic*), 250. The Revendge, 250. The Vauntgard, 250. The Rainbowe, 250."

| [Officers.] | Month. £ | s. | d. | Week. s. | d. | Day. s. | d. |
|---|---|---|---|---|---|---|---|
| A master | 3 | 0 | 0 | 15 | 0 | 2 | 1 |
| 2 mates, each at | 1 | 5 | 0 | — | | — | |
| A pilot | 1 | 5 | 0 | 6 | 3 | | 10½ |
| A boatswain | 1 | 5 | 0 | — | | — | |
| 2 mates, each at | | 17 | 6 | 4 | 4[½?] | | 7½ |
| 4 quarter-masters, each at | | 17 | 6 | — | | — | |
| 4 quarter-masters [mates?], each at | | 13 | 9 | 3 | 5¼ | | 7½ |
| 4 yeomen of { The jeerie, The halyards, The sheets, The tacks } each | | 14 | 0 | 3 | 6 | | 6 |
| A master carpenter | 1 | 5 | 0 | — | | — | |
| His mate, a caulker | | 17 | 6 | — | | — | |
| If any more carpenters or caulkers be appointed, each to have | | 13 | 9 | — | | — | |

* "Servants" in other cases below.

| [Officers.] | Month. | Week. | Day. |
|---|---|---|---|
| | £ s. d. | s. d. | d. |
| A purser - - - - - | 16 8 | 4 2 | 7½ |
| A steward - - - - | 17 6 | — | — |
| One mate - - - | 13 9 | — | — |
| A cook - - - - - | 17 6 | — | — |
| One mate - - - | 13 9 | — | — |
| A surgeon - - - | 1 0 0 | 5 0 | 8* |
| A servant and gromet in common pay - | — | — | — |
| 3 trumpeters, each at - - - | 1 0 0 | — | — |
| If an Admiral, 4 trumpets - - | — | — | — |
| A drum } each at - | 15 0 | 3 9 | 6½ |
| A phiphe } | | | |
| A coxswain - - - | 17 6 | — | — |
| His mate - - - - - | 13 9 | — | — |
| A swabber - - - | 13 9 | — | — |
| His mate - - - - - | 11 3 | 2 9¾ | 4¼ |
| An armourer - - - - | 18 8 | — | — |
| A gunmaker - - - | 18 8 | 4 8 | 8 |
| A master gunner - - - | 15 0 | — | — |
| 2 mates, each at - | 11 3 | — | — |
| 4 quarter gunners, each at - - | 11 3 | — | — |
| 4 quarter gunners' mates, [each at] - | 11 3 | — | — |
| Yeoman of the powder-room - - | 11 3 | — | — |

(3.) "The Dreadnought, 200 men. The Swiftesure, 180. The Antellope, 170. The Swallow, 160. The Foresighte, 160."

| [Officers.] | Month. | Week. | Day. |
|---|---|---|---|
| | £ s. d. | s. d. | d. |
| A master - - - - | 2 10 0 | 12 6 | 23¼ |
| One mate - - - | 1 5 0 | — | — |
| A pilot - - - - - | 1 5 0 | 6 3 | 10¼ |
| A boatswain - - - | 17 6 | — | — |
| One mate - - - | 13 9 | — | — |
| 4 quarter masters, each at - - | 17 6 | 4 4½ | 7½ |
| 4 quarter mates, each at | 13 9 | — | — |
| 2 yeomen of { The jeerye and halyards } | 14 0 | 3 6 | 6 |
| { The sheets and tacks - } | | | |
| A master carpenter - - - | 6† | — | — |
| His mate, a caulker - - - | 13 9 | 3 5½ | 5½ |
| If any more caulkers or carpenters be | | | |
| appointed, each to have - - | 13 4 | — | — |
| A purser - - - | 13 4 | — | — |
| A steward - - - - | 17 6 | — | — |
| One mate - - - | 13 9 | — | — |
| A cook - - - - | 17 6 | — | — |
| One mate - - - | 13 9 | — | — |
| A surgeon - - - | 1 0 0 | 5 0 | 8½ |
| One servant in common pay - - | — | — | — |
| A trumpeter - - - | 1 0 0 | — | — |
| If an Admiral, 3 trumpeters - - | — | — | — |
| A drum } each at - | 15 0 | 3 9 | 6½ |
| A phiphe } | | | |
| A coxswain - - - | 17 6 | — | — |
| His mate - - - - - | 13 9 | — | — |
| A swabber - - - | 13 9 | — | — |
| His mate - - - - | 11 3 | [2] 9¾ | 4¼ |
| An armourer - - - | 18 8 | 4 8 | 8 |
| A master gunner - - - | 15 0 | — | — |
| 2 mates, each at - - | 11 3 | — | — |
| 4 quarter gunners - - | 11 3 | — | — |
| Yeoman of the powder-room - - | 11 3 | — | — |

* *Sic*, usually given as 8½d,  † *Sic*.

(4.) "The Scowte, 70 men. The Handmayde, 70. The Tremontaine, 70. The Archattes (*sic*), 60."

| [Officers.] | Month. | | | Week. | | Day. |
|---|---|---|---|---|---|---|
| | £ | *s.* | *d.* | *s.* | *d.* | *d.* |
| A master | 2 | 0 | 0 | 10 | 0 | 12* |
| One mate | 1 | 0 | 0 | — | | — |
| A pilot | 1 | 0 | 0 | 5 | 0 | 8½ |
| A boatswain | | 17 | 6 | — | | — |
| One mate | | 13 | 9 | — | | — |
| 4 quarter masters, each at | | 17 | 6 | 4 | 4½ | 7½ |
| A master carpenter | | 17 | 6 | — | | — |
| His mate, a caulker | | 13 | 9 | 3 | 5¼ | 5¾ |
| A purser | | 13 | 4 | 3 | 4 | 5¼ |
| A steward | | 17 | 6 | — | | — |
| A cook | | 17 | 6 | — | | — |
| A surgeon | 1 | 0 | 0 | — | | — |
| A trumpeter | 1 | 0 | 0 | — | | — |
| A swabber | | 13 | 9 | — | | — |
| A master gunner | | 15 | 0 | 3 | 9 | 6½ |
| One mate | | 11 | 3 | 2 | 9¾ | 4¼ |
| 4 quarter gunners, each at | | 11 | 3 | — | | — |

(5.) "The Ayde, 120 men. The Bull, 100. The Tiger, 100."

| [Officers.] | Month. | | | Week. | | Day. |
|---|---|---|---|---|---|---|
| | £ | *s.* | *d.* | *s.* | *d.* | *d.* |
| A master | 2 | 5 | 0 | 11 | 3 | 19¼ |
| One mate | 1 | 0 | 0 | — | | — |
| A pilot | 1 | 0 | 0 | 5 | 0 | 8½ |
| A boatswain | | 17 | 6 | — | | — |
| One mate | | 13 | 9 | — | | — |
| 4 quarter masters, each at | | 17 | 6 | 4 | 4½ | 7½ |
| 4 quarter mates, each at | | 13 | 9 | — | | — |
| A master carpenter | | 17 | 6 | — | | — |
| His mate, a caulker | | 13 | 9 | 3 | 5¼ | 5¼ |
| A purser | | 13 | 4 | — | | — |
| A steward | | 17 | 6 | — | | — |
| One mate | | 13 | 9 | — | | — |
| A cook | | 17 | 6 | — | | — |
| One mate | | 13 | 9 | — | | — |
| A surgeon | 1 | 0 | 0 | — | | — |
| A trumpeter | 1 | 0 | 0 | — | | — |
| If an Admiral, 3 trumpet[er]s | — | | | — | | — |
| A drum / A phiphe } each at | | 15 | 0 | 3 | 9 | 6½ |
| A swabber | | 38 | 9 | — | | — |
| An armourer | | 18 | 8 | 4 | 8 | 8 |
| A master gunner | | 15 | 0 | — | | — |
| One mate | | 11 | 3 | 2 | 9¾ | 4¼ |
| 4 quarter gunners | | 11 | 3 | — | | — |
| Yeoman of the powder-room | | 11 | 3 | — | | — |

* *Sic*, for 17*d*.

(6.) "The Marlin, 35 men. The Charles, 40. The Moone, 40. Th'Advyce, 40. The Makshifte, 40. The Spye, 40. The Sonn, 30."

| [Officers.] | Month. | Week. | Day. |
| --- | --- | --- | --- |
| | £ s. d. | s. d. | d. |
| A master | 1 7 0 | 6 9 | 11½ |
| One mate | 17 6 | — | — |
| A boatswain | 17 6 | 4 4½ | 7½ |
| 2 quarter masters, each at | 17 6 | — | — |
| A purser | 13 4 | 3 4 | 5½ |
| One to be both cook and steward | 13 9 | 3 5¼ | 5½ |
| A carpenter | 17 6 | — | — |
| A trumpeter | 1 0 0 | 5 0 | 8½ |
| A master gunner | 15 0 | 3 9 | 6½ |
| One mate | 11 3 | 2 9¾ | 4¾ |

(7.) "The Signet [Cygnet], 16 men. Ketches and small barks, 8."

| [Officers.] | Month. | Week. | Day. |
| --- | --- | --- | --- |
| | £ s. d. | s. d. | d. |
| A master | 1 0 0 | — | — |
| One mate | 17 6 | — | — |
| A boatswain | 13 9 | — | — |
| One for cook and steward | 13 9 | — | — |
| A gunner | 13s. 4d. for the Signet, 11s. 3d. for the Ketches. | | |
| Every common man's wages | 10 0 | 2 6 | 4½ |
| A gromet['s] wages | 7 6 | 1 10½ | 4½* |
| A boy's wages | 5 0 | 1 3 | 2¼ |
| A preacher with the Lord Admiral | 3 0 0 | — | — |
| Preachers with other noblemen | 2 0 0 | — | — |
| A preacher with Sir Robert Southwell | 2 0 0 | — | — |

"Determined by the Lord Admiral, [and] confirmed by Sir Wm. Winter, 12th of March, 1587, aboard the Arck, at Margat."

F. 312. 1587, Dec. —. (1.) "The Names of such Ships as were appointed to be under the charge of Sir Francis Drake, December 1587."

The Revenge, 250 men. The Nonpareil, 250. The Hope, 250. The Swifte, 180. The Ayde, 120. Th' Advice, 35. The Marchant Roial, 180. The Roebuck, 120. The Ed. Bonaventure, 120. The Hopewell, 100. The Goulden Noble, 100. The Griffin, 100. The Minion, 80. The Thomas, 80. The Talbott, 80. The Spart,† 80. The Hope Haukins, 70. The B[ark] Bond, 70. The B[ark] Bonner, 70. The B[ark] Hauckins, 70. The Eliz. Fones (*sic*), 60. The Unitie, 40. The Clizerate, 30. The Barque Yong, 60. The Barque Mannington, 55. The Buggins, 40. The Delighte, 35. The Chaunce, 30. The Diamond, 25. The Nightingale, 25. The Heartsease, 15. [Total,] 2,820.

* *Sic*, for 3¾*d*. † *Qu.* Spark.

(2.) "The Names of ships with the Lord Admiral at the Narrow Seas."

The Eliz. Jonas, 500 men. **The** Triumphe, **500. The** Beare, 500. The Victori, **400.** The Arck, 400. The Marirose, 250. The Goulden Lion, 250. The Eliz. Bonadventure, 250. The Dreadnought, 200. The Foresight, 160. The Swalloe, 160. The White Lion, 50. The Charles, 40. The Moone, 40. The Disdaine, 40. The Hay, **20.** The Marigold, 10. [Total,] 3,770.

F. 315. 1588, April 1, from the Court.—"M[inute] of the letter [from the Privy Council] unto the Ports, to furnish certain ships and pinnaces forth to the seas."

"Whereas her Majesty hath thought it very requisite to strengthen **and reinforce her Navies of** ships, which are set forth to the seas for the **defence of the realm, as by** daily advertisements she is given to understand that the **King of Spain** doth augment and increase his preparations : forasmuch as her Majesty hath perceived to her great comfort, the good disposition and forwardness that you, th'inhabitants of that town, have showed in former time in such public services as have been appointed unto you ; it is thought that in these times, ministering more occasions than any heretofore, you will make manifest your dutiful and zealous affections, both towards her Majesty, and the general defence of this your native country. Whereas heretofore (*sic*) her Highness doth understand that there are a good number of very apt and serviceable ships and vessels, appertaining to divers merchants and others inhabiting the said town, it is thought meet you should furnish some ships and vessels of service to the purpose aforesaid.

"These are therefore to require you, upon **the** receipt of these our letters, to make choice of one serviceable and good ship, **not to be** under the burden of 60 tons, and one handsome pinnace, and **to** cause the same presently to be put in a readiness, and furnished for two months with victuals, mariners, and munition, and other necessary provision and furniture, by the 25th of this present month of April, to join **with** her Majesty's Navy on the seas, or to be otherwise employed as you shall receive further direction from us, or from me, the Lord Admiral of England. And where some of the merchants of the said town have set forth certain ships in warlike sort by way of reprisal, whereby they have received no small gain and benefit, it is thought reason therefore that such of you should bear the greater part of this burden, which we **doubt** not but they will yield unto in respect of the benefit they have received of you. We pray you not to fail to advertise us of the names of the ships, and their burthen, you shall appoint for this service, and in what sort they are furnished."

[P.S.] "So soon as the **said** vessels shall be **in a readiness,** you shall forthwith repair to her Majesty's Navy under **the charge** of me, the Lord Admiral of England."

**F. 315b.** [1588.]—"The Names of the Places from whence is **[are]** to repair to Sir Francis Drake 20 Ships and 10 Pinnaces; **the Ships** containing 60 tons and upwards at the least."

(The first figure shows the number of ships ; the second, the number of pinnaces.)

Bristol, 3, 1. Bridgewater, 1, 1. Barstaple, 1, 1. Tarington, *1, 1. Foy [and] Lowe, 1, 1. Plymouthe, Ashe, [and] Tawstoke, 3, 1. Dartmouthe [and] Totnes, 2, 1. Exeter [and] Apson (*sic*),† 3, 1.

---

* Torrington.　　　　† Topsham.

Lime, Charde, [and] Exmister, 2, 1. Weymouthe [and] Melcombe, 2, 1. Pole, 1, 1.

(2.) "The Names of the Places from whence is [are] to repair to the Lord Admiral, where he shall appoint, 28 ships and 10 pinnaces."

The Isle of Wighte, 1, 1. Hampton, 2, 1. Chichester, 1, 0. Cinque Portes, 5, 1. Colchester, 1, 0. Ipswitche [and] Harwiche, 2, 2. Alboroughe, Oxforde, [and] Banwiche, [Orford, and Dunwich], 1, 0. Yearmouthe [and] Leystock (*sic*),* 1, 1. Linne [and] Blackney, 1, 1. Hull, 2, 1. Newcastle, 3, 1. London [and] Lee, 8,† 2.

"Over and above which 8 ships and 2 pinnaces the said City, of their own voluntary (*sic*), furnished 8 ships and 2 pinnaces more, besides 8 more set forth by the Merchants Adventurers, at such time as the Spanish navy appeared upon the coast."

F. 316. 1588, May 13.—The Queen to the Lord Admiral [Lord Howard of Effingham].

"Right trusty, &c. Whereas by our former instructions we did direct you to continue in the Narrow Seas, sometimes towards the north and sometimes towards the south, to prevent any attempt that might be made against this our realm or the realm of Scotland : we have now thought it convenient, for divers considerations, that you should repair into the west parts of our said realm, and so to dispose of our navy serving under you, in placing of the same between the coast of Spain and the said West parts, as may best serve to impeach the great navy now prepared in Spain for [from] attempting anything as well against our dominions of England and Ireland us also the realm of Scotland. And for that it is hard for us to give unto you any particular direction in this service, we hold it best for us to refer the matter to your own good consideration, to take that course for the furtherance of our said service, as to you in your own discretion shall be thought meet : of whose sufficiency and great care and love toward us we have heretofore had so long and approved experience, as we do most confidently assure our own selves that there shall be nothing left undone by you that may tend to our honour and surety in the present charge committed unto you."

F. 316. [1588, May.]—The Queen to Lord Henry Seimer [Seymour].

"Right trusty and well beloved, we greet you well. Whereas we have thought it convenient for sundry respects to have our right trusty and right well beloved Councillor, the Lord Hawarde of Effingham, our High Admiral of England, to repair with certain of our own ships, as also the ships prepared by Sir Francis Drake in the West parts of this our realm, and to lie upon the coast of Spain, leaving notwithstanding behind him certain of our ships here in the Narrow Seas, with other ships set out by certain of our subjects, as also such as are to be furnished by the States by virtue of the Contract, to make head and to prevent anything that may be attempted by sea by the Duke of Parma : we have thought good in the absence of our said High Admiral to commit the charge of the said ships that are to remain here on the Narrow Seas to your government, of whose sufficiency and zeal to further our service we have had so great proof as you may assure yourself we will always hold a most thankful memory thereof. And as touching the choice of such of our ships as shall be appointed to serve under your charge, we refer you to such order as we have taken therein with our said High Admiral, to whom you are greatly beholding for the

---

* Lowestoft.      † "23," written over.

good report that he hath made unto us of the care you have shewed to have of our Navy in the time of his absence, as also of your great sufficiency otherwise. And for the direction of your service on the Narrow Seas during his absence, we refer you to such direction as you shall receive from the Lord Admiral, at his coming down, and such further instructions as you may receive from our Privy Council upon such occasions as may from time to time occur."

F. 316*b*. 1588, May 26.—"A Note of the Names of the Ships appointed to keep in the Narrow Seas under the charge of the Lord Seymer.

"The Rainebowe, 500 tons. The Vauntgarde, 500. The Antelope, 300. The Tiger, 160. The Bull, 160. The Tremontane, 120. The Scowte, 120. The Achates, 100. The galley Bonavolua (*sic*), ——. The Brigandine, ——. The George, 10. The Spie, 35. The Marleon, 35. The Sonn, 40. The Signet, ——. The Fancie, ——.

" To be victualled by the Ports :

" Five ships and one pinnace from the V. (*sic*) Cinque Ports, and one ship from Colchester.

" Three great hoys from Ipswiche and Harwiche, one ship from Albroughe, Orford, and Donwiche.

" One ship and one pinnace from Yearmouthe and Lestock (*sic*).

" Two ships and one pinnace from Lin and Blackney.

" Three ships [and] one pinnace from Newcastle.

" Two ships and one pinnace from Hull.

" Thirty six from Holland and Zeland.

" The whole number of these ships and pinnaces appointed to serve on the Narrow Seas are 75."[*]

F. 317. [1588, May.]—" Instructions for the Lord Henry Seimer, Admiral of her Majesty's fleet to serve on the Narrow Seas, touching that service, given by me, Charles Lord Hawarde, Baron of Effingham, and Lord High Admiral of England.

" Your Lordship shall take under your charge all those ships whose names are set down in a schedule hereunto annexed.

" Forasmuch as the Duke of Parma hath prepared great forces as well in great number of ships as also of soldiers to be employed in them, and that it is greatly to be doubted, that if this treaty of peace do break off, that he will presently make some attempt either against some part of this realm or against Scotland ; and if against this realm, then it is most likely his enterprise will be against these parts : your Lordship, in your wisdom, must have a most especial care for the preventing and withstanding of them, as well for the defence of our own country, as also if they should go towards Scotland, for the impeaching of them in that their attempt.

" Your Lordship hath, by her Majesty's especial order, left with you Sir Wm. Winter, a man of most great experience, and also Sir Henry Palmer, whose counsel and advice I know your Lordship will most wisely follow ; and therefore, because the service may so fall out, that no man can well judge beforehand what is fittest to be done, I leave it unto your Lordship's good and wise judgment to direct and do as to you shall seem best, upon any occasion offered.

" And forasmuch as her Majesty hath had sundry private intelligences of some enterprise to be done against the City of London, she hath appointed Mr. Borroughes with the galley Bonavolia and the Brigandine

---

[*] *Cf. State Papers, Vol. 209, No. 114 (April 29) ; and Vol. 210, No. 10 (May 9).*

to lie at the mouth of the River of Thames, which notwithstanding if your Lordship shall hereafter see cause of great importance elsewhere to use, your Lordship may command. Provided always that your Lordship do foresee that no peril may grow to the said City by their absence.

" Whereas there are to come out of the Low Countries, by a Contract ' etween her Majesty and the States of those countries, certain ships, her Majesty hath understanding from the Lord Willoughbie and Mr. Killegrewe that they have provided 36 ships to come and serve under him that shall have the charge on the Narrow Seas. Wherefore when those said ships shall be come unto your Lordship your number will be great and your fleet strong, and the places whence th'enemy hath to offend, or to set out any forces unto the seas, are but two, viz., Sluce and Dunkirck; therefore it shall not be amiss that your Lordship do appoint certain ships to lie continually (as the weather will serve them) on that coast, and to give your Lordship intelligence thence, as much as in them shall lie.

" I think those ships of those parts of Holland and Zealand, which shall be under your Lordship's charge, being committed either to Sir William Winter or to Sir Henry Palmer, with two ships and a pinnace of her Majesty's, will be very fit for that purpose; yet that and all other services I leave to your Lordship's good discretion, as occasion shall happen.

" If her Majesty or my Lords of her Privy Council, in mine absence, give your Lordship any other order or instructions for her Majesty's service, you are to follow them.

" Your Lordship shall give notice unto Mr. Quarles 12 days before the time you will have your victuals brought down unto you; and if your Lordship shall see cause that it will be needful for you to have more than one month's victuals at one time, (which I, for my part, think fit you should never have less than 6 weeks' or a month's victuals), your Lordship shall do well to advertise the Lord Treasurer and Mr. Secretary your mind therein, that they may move her Majesty as a thing most convenient to be done.

" Your Lordship may do well to hearken after Count Maurice for intelligences, and to join with him to impeach anything that th'enemy shall attempt against her Majesty's cautionary town of Vlishinge, or other such like places of importance, for the said Count will assist you with all his marine forces to hinder and withstand th'enemy.

" All other things necessary for the furtherance of the service (by reason of the uncertainty of the same,) I refer to your Lordship's wisdom and discretion to consider and determine of as occasion shall serve."

F. 317b. 1588, Aug.—" The Lord Admiral's Commission for returning to the Seas."

" Elizabeth, Dei gratia, Anglie, Francie, et Hibernie Regina, Fidei Defensor, etc., Omnibus ad quos presentes litere pervenerint, salutem. Sciatis, quod nos, de fidelitate, prudentia, strenuitate, experientia, circumspectione, industria, integritate, et summa diligentia predilecti Consiliarii nostri Caroli, Domini Haward, Baronis de Effingham, preclari Ordinis Garterii nostri Militis, Magni Admiral[l]i nostri Anglie, Hibernie, et Wallie, et dominiorum et insularum earundem, ville Callecie et marchiarum eiusdem, Norman[nie], Gascon[ie], et Aquitan[ie], Classisque et Marine dictorum Regnorum nostrorum Anglie et Hibernie Prefecti Generalis, plurimum confidentes, eundem Carolum Locumtenentem nostrum Generalem, ducemque primarium et gubernatorem totius Classis et Exercitus nostri

super mare nunc versus partes ext[e]ras contra Hispanos eorumque adherentes et adiutores vel opem ferentes,* aliquid attentant[es] seu
molient[es] contra Regna, dominia, et subditos **nostros, atque** omnium
et singulorum Viceadmirallorum, Capitaneorum, Subcapitaneorum, et
Locatenencium, Baronum, Baronettorum, Dominorum, Militum, navium
ma[g]istorum, marinariorum, et hominum ad arma, armatorum, delec-
torum, sive destinatorum, sagittariorum, et aliorum in Classe **nostra**
Regia et Exercitu nostro predictis retentorum et retinendorum quorum-
cunque, assignamus, constituimus, ordinamus, preficimus, et deputamus
per presentes : Dantes eidem Carolo potestatem et plenam auctoritatem
nostras ad omnes et singulos ligeos et subditos nostros, cuiuscunque
status seu condicionis fuerint, in Classe et Exercitu nostris predictis
quovismodo retentos siue retinendos, ac in servicio nostro sibi quomodocunque in hac parte commissos, in resistenciam et debellacionem
Hispanorum ac aliorum eorum adherencium et adiutorum vel opem
ferencium, aliquid attentancium vel moliencium contra Regna, dominia,
et subditos nostros quoscunque, ducendi [vel] duci faciendi, necnon
Regna et dominia, terrasque et insulas, ac alia loca quecunque dictorum
Hispanorum, et aliorum eorum adherencium, adiutorum, vel opem
ferencium, aliquid attentancium seu moliencium contra Regna, dominia,
et subditos nostros, cum dictis Classe et Exercitu et subditis nostris
super mare in servicio nostro existentibus, ad bellum congregatis siue
araiatis, prout opus fuerit, ac quociens et quando ei magis videbitur
expedire, ad suum libitum et voluntatem, vbicunque et quandocunque
invadendi, intrandi, spoliandi, et gubernandi, atque Hispanos eorumque
adherentes et adiutores quoscunque vi armata molestandi, dampnificandi,
deprimendi, convincendi, et impugnandi, ac eos confligendi et debellandi,
ac Classem, Exercitum, ac dictos subditos nostros in invasione et conduc-
cione huiusmodi, et alijs premissis regendi, ordinandi, dirigendi, et
gubernandi, ac abinde, si opus fuerit, ad dictum Regnum nostrum
Hibernie vel alia loca quecunque ad voluntatem et libitum suos† cum
eisdem Classe, Exercitu, et subditis nostris predictis recedendi, itinerandi,
[et] velificandi‡ : Dantes insuper et concedentes eidem Carolo potestatem et auctoritatem nostras omnes et singulos Viceadmirallos, Capita-
neos, Subcapitaneos, Locumtenentes,§ Barones, Baronettos, Dominos,
Milites, navium magristros, marinarios, ac homines, sagittarios, et alios
quoscunque de Classe et Exercitu nostris predictis in servicio nostro ad
arma, armatos sive destinatos congregandi, ducendi, regendi, dirigendi, et
gubernandi ; acetiam lites, causas, querelas, et negotia quecunque omnium
et singulorum de hijs que ad officium Locumtenentis nostri Generalis
**huiusmodi super** mare de iure vel consuetudine qualitercunque pertinent‖
**audiendi, examinandi,** discuciendi, ordinandi, et determinandi ; necnon
ordinaciones **et** statuta pro sano et bono regimine Classis et Exercitus
nostri condendi, statuendi, et stabiliendi, et superinde proclamaciones
faciendi, eademque debite execucioni¶ demandandi ; **ac** quoscunque de
Classe et Exercitu nostris predictis quovismodo delinquentes castigandi,
puniendi, reformandi, et incarcerandi, atque, si sibi ita expediens visum
fuerit, incarceratos exonerandi, solvendi, dimittendi, et deliberandi ;
necnon quascunque causas capitales seu criminales tam vite quam
membrorum mutilacionis** ac de morte hominis in Classe et Exercitu
nostris predictis qualitercunque contingentes,†† cum suis incidentis (*sic*),
annexis, et connexis quibuscunque, cognoscendi, examinandi, audiendi,
et finaliter terminandi ; necnon sententias definitivas seu decreta

---

* *ferentem*, in MS.    † *sue*, **in MS.**    ‡ "et velificand'," on f. 305.
§ "Locatenencium" above.                      ‖ *pertinend*, in MS.
¶ *execõe*, in MS.    ** *mutelaco'es*, in MS.    †† *contingend'*, in MS.

quecunque in ea parte interponendi, ferendi, siue promulgandi, easque
siue ea execucioni plenarie et cum effectu demandandi et demandari
faciendi et mandandi; ceteraque omnia et singula alia que pro bono
regimine et gubernacione Classis et Exercitus nostri predicti fuerint
facienda, iuxta sanam discretionem suam, ac prout sibi magis expediens*
visum fuerit, de tempore in tempus ad suum libitum et voluntatem
libere faciendi, ordinandi, exercendi, expediendi, decernendi, et exe-
quendi, cum cuiuslibet coercionis potestate; atque etiam cum potestate
et auctoritate nostris alium vel alios sublocumtenentes siue sublocum-
tenentem ad premissa [omnia]† et singula vel eorum aliquod vice et
nomine nostris agenda, exercenda, expedienda, et exequenda, quociens
et quando sibi magis expediens vel necesse visum fuerit, nominandi,
ordinandi, faciendi, constituendi, deputandi, et proficiendi, ipsumque et
ipsos, si ita casus exigerit (sic), revocandi, ac alium vel alios eius seu
eorum loco ad effectum predictum vel eorum aliquod ordinandi et constituendi. Ac preterea damus eidem Carolo plenam potestatem et
auctoritatem per presentes quoscunque subditorum nostrorum in Classe
et Exercitu nostris predictis quovismodo retentorum siue retinendorum,
ac in servicio nostro sibi quomodocunque in hac parte commiss[orum],
iuxta sanam discretionem suam (exigentibus eorum meritis) ordine
militare, ac alijs titulis nobilitatis et dignitatis, honorandi et decorandi,
eisdemque arma et insignia armorum dandi, assignandi, et concedendi,
prout decet.‡ Damus autem vniversis et singulis Viceadmiral[1]is,
Capitaneis, Subcapitaneis, Locumtenentibus, Baronibus, Baronettis,
Dominis, Militibus, navium magistris, marinarijs, hominibus, sagittarijs,
et alijs quibuscunque in Classe et Exercitu nostris predictis qualitercunque conductis, retentis, et retinendis tenore presencium firmiter in
mandatis, quod eidem Carolo, Magno Admiral[l]o nostro et Locum-
tenenti Generali super mare predicto, in execucione premissorum et
eorum cuiuslibet de tempore in tempus, prout opus fuerit, intendentes,
auxiliantes, obedientes pariter et assistentes sint§ in omnibus, prout
decet, sub pena gravissima contemptus. In cuius rei testimonium, &c."

(*Not in the State Papers, Patent Rolls, Privy Seals, or Privy
Signet Bills.*)

F. 319. [1588, Aug.]—"The whole number of Ships and their men
and tonnage which were in the said Service, as well under the Lord
Admiral [Howard and] Sir Francis Drake, as others; and how they
were ordered."

*Cf. State Papers, Vol.* 213, *Nos.* 91, 92; *and Vol.* 215, *Nos.* 76,
82.

(The first number shows the tonnage, and the second shows the
number of men.)

The Arke Rawleigh, 800, 400. The Eliz[abeth] Bonaventure, 600,
250. The Rainbowe, 500, 250. The Golden Lyon, 500, 250. The
White Beare, 1,000, 500. The Vantgarde, 500, 250. The Revenge,
500, 250. The Eliz. Jonas, 900, 500. The Victory, 800, 400. The
Antelop, 400, 160. The Triumph, 1,100, 500. The Dreadnought, 400,
200. The Mary Rose, 600, 250. The Non Parly, 500, 250. The Hope
600, 250. The Galley Bonovolia (sic), ——, 250. The Swiftsure, 400,
180. The Swallowe, 300, 160. The Forsight, 300, 160. The Aide,
250, 120. The Bull, 200, 100. The Teiger, 200, 100. The Tremounte,

---

* *expeditus*, in MS.
† Omitted.
‡ This clause as to the creation of Knights was not contained in Lord Howard's
previous Commission of 16 Dec. 1587 (f. 305).
§ *siue*, in MS.

150, 70. The Scoute, 120, **70.** The Achates, **100**, 60. The Charles, 70, 40. The Moone, 60, 40. The Advice, 50, 35. **The Spie,** 50, 35. The Marlin, 50, **35.** The Soon, 40, 24. **The Signet,** 30, **20.** The Brigandin, ——, 36. The George, 120, 30, **The White** Lyon, 140, 50. The Disdaine, **80, 40.** The Larke, 50, 30. The **Edw.** of Muldon, 186, **40.** The Marigoulde, 30, 30. The Blacke Dogge, **20,** 20. The Katherin, 20, 20. The Fancy, 50, 50. The Pippinge, **20, 20. The** Nightingall, 160, 160.

"Ships with Sir Fra. Drake."

The Gallion Leycester, 400, **180.** The Marchant Ryall, 400, 160. **The Edw.** Bonaventur, 300, 120. The Roebucke, 300, 120. The Golden Noble, **250,** 120. The Griffin, 200, 100. The Myneon, 200, 80. The B[ark] Talbott, 200, **80. The** Thomas, 200, 80. The Sparke, 200, 80. The **H**opewell, 200, 80. **The Gallion** Dudley, 250, 120. The God Save, 200, 80. The Hope of Plimouth, **200, 80.** The B[ark] **Bonde,** 150, **70.** The B[ark] Bonner, 150, 70. **The Bark** Hawkins, 150, 70. The Unitie, 80, 40. The Eliz. Drake, 60, **30.** The B[ark]Buggins, 80, 40. The Friggott, **80,** 40. **The** B[ark] Sellinger, 160, 80. The B[ark] Manington, 160, 80. **The** Golden Hinde, 50, **30.** The **Make** Shifte, **60,** 30. The Diamonde **of Dartmouth,** 60, 30. **The Eliz. Jones, 100,** 60. The Spedwell, 60, 44. **The Beare,** 140, 60. **The Chaunce,** 60, 40. The Delight, **50, 30. The Nightingall, 40, 20.** The **small Carvill,** 30, 20.

"**Ships of** London, set forth by the same City."

**The** Hercules, 300, 130. The Toby, 250, 120 The **May** Flower, 200, **90.** The Mynion, 200, 90. The Riall Defence, **160, 70.** The Assention, 200, 90. The Guifte of God, **180, 80. The** Primrose, 200, 90. The Margrett and John, 200, 90. **The Golden Lyon, 140,** 70. The Diana, 80, 30. The B[ark] Burr, 160, 70. **The Teiger, 200, 80.** The Brave, 160, 70. The Red Lyon, 200, **80. The Senturian, 250,** 160. The Pasporte, 80, 30. The Moonshine, 60, 30. **The Tho.** Bonaventur, 140, 70. The Releefe, 60, 40. The Susan **Parnell, 220, 100. The** Violett, 220, 70. The Saloman, 170, 100. The **Ann Fraunces, 180,** 90. The Geo. Bonaventure, 200, 90. The **Jane** Bonaventur, **100, 50.** The **Vinyarde, 160,** 80. The Samuell, 140, 70. The Geo. Noble, 150, 80. **The Anthony,** 110, 60. The Toby Junior, 140, 70. The Sallomander, **120, 60. The Roase** Lyon, 110, 60. The Antelop, 120, 60. The **Jewell, 120, 60.** The Pannees (*sic*), 160, 80. **The** Providence, **130, 70. The Dolphin,** 160, 70.

"**Coasters with the Lord Admiral.**"

The **Barke Webb, 80, 40. The Jo.** Treloune, 150, 70. The Hart **of Dartm[outh],** 60, 30. **The B[ark]** Potts, 180, 80. The Little John, 40, 20. The **Barth** (*sic*) **of** Apsam,* 130, 70. **The Rose** of Apsam, 110, 60. **The Guifte** of Apsam, 25, 20. The **Jacob of Linne,** 90, 30. **The Revenge of Lynn,** 60, 30. The Wi[llia]m **of Bridgwater, 70,** 40. The Cressett **of** Dartm[outh], 140, 70. The Gallion **of Waym[outh],** 100, 50. **The Katherin** of Waym[outh], 60, 30. The John **of** Chichester, 70, 40. The **Harty Ann,** 60, 30. The Mineon, 230, **100. The H**andmayde, 80, **40. The Aide,** 60, 30. **The** Unicorne, 130, 70.

"Coasters with the Lord Henry Seimor."

"The Daniell, **160, 70. The Gallion** Hutchanis, **150, 70.** The Ba[rk] Lambe, 150, **70. The Fancie, 60, 30.** The Griffin, 70, 40.

---

* Topsham.

The Little Hare, 50, 30. The Handmayde, 75, 40. **The** Marigould, 150, 70. The Mathew, 35, 20. The Susan, 40, 20. The Wm. of Ipswich, 140, 70. The Katherin, 125, 60. The Primrose, 120, 60. The Ann Bonaventur, 60, 30. The Wi[llia]m of Ry, 80, 40. The Grace of God, 50, 20. The Elnathan of Dover, 120, 70. The Rubin, 110, 60. The Hazarde, 38, 20. The Grace of Yormouth (*sic*), 150, 70. The May Flower, 150, **70.** The **Wm. of** Brickleysey, 100, 50. The John Younge, 60, **30.**

"Voluntary Ships **with the** Lo[rd] Adm[iral]."

The Fraunces of Foy, **140,** 70. The Sampson, 300, 120. The Heathen of Waym[outh], 60, 30. The Golden Rial of Waym[outh], **120, 70.** The B[ark] Sutton of Weym[outh], 70, 30. The Carous, **50, 30.** The Samaritann, 250, 100. The Wm. of Plimouth, 120, 60. **The** Galego of Plimouth, 30, 20. The Ba[rk] Houlse, 60, 30. The Unicorne of Dartm[outh], 70, 30. The Grace of Apsam, 100, 50. The Tho. Bonaventure, 60, 30. The Ratt, 80, 40. The Margett, **60,** 30. The Elizabeth, 40, 20. The Raphell, 40, 20. The Fleaboat, 60, 40.

"Fifteen Ships that transported victuals Westwards."

The Eliz. Bonaventûr, 114, **30.** **The** Pellican, 112, 30. The Hope, 107, 30. **The** Unitie, 110, 30. The **Pearle,** 114, 30. The Eliz. of Lee, 115, **30.** **The** Jo. of London, 100, 25. The Bersabe, 110, 25. The Marigoulde, 88, 30. The White Hinde, 130, 30. The Guifte of God, 120, 30. The Jonas, 115, 30. The Saloman, 116, 40. The Rich. Duffeld, 120, 25. The Mary Rose, 180, 40.

"Abstract of this Book in total."

| | Ships. | Tonnage. | Men. | Captains. |
|---|---|---|---|---|
| Ships and **vessels of her** Majesty's. | 34 | 12,190 | 6,225 | **34** |
| Ships serving by tonnage with the Lord Admiral. | 10 | 756 | 243 | — |
| Ships **with** Sir Fra. Drake - | 33 | 5,220 | 2,334 | 33 |
| Ships **set out** by the City - | 34 | 6,130 | 3,020 | 33* |
| Coasters with the Lord Admiral. | 20 | 1,930 | 960 | — |
| Coasters with the Lord Henry Seimor. | 23 | 2,248 | 1,210 | 23 |
| Voluntary ships with the Lord Admiral. | 18 | 1,766 | 820 | — |
| Ships that transported victuals Westwards. | 15 | 1,795 | 455 | 15 |
| Sum - - | 181 | | 17,472 | |

* *Sic.*

The last leaf is numbered 322. At the end of the volume is a "Table of such Matters as are contained in this Book." There are two tables referring to pp. 294-324, but pp. 323 and **324 are now** wanting, having

been cut out. The first of **these tables, in a different** hand, describes
p. 323 as follows :
"The names **and order** of the principal Ships **attending the**
Lord Admiral - - - - - - 323
" The proceeding of the two Fleets after their meeting - **323.**"
The second table is headed, " The **Index** for the Sea **Causes,**" and
describes pp. 323-4 as follows :
" The names and order of the principal Ships, how they
marched under the Lord Admiral - - - **323**
" A Journal of the proceedings between our Navy and the
Spanish from the time they were discovered upon our
coast - - - - - - 324
" M[inute] **of her Majesty's letter to the** Lord Admiral for
his revocation - - - - - - 324."

---

L ETTERS OF J AMES D UKE OF Y ORK to the P RINCE OF O RANGE,
1678-1679 (bound in one volume).

### [1678] October **29, London.**

In my **last I gave you** an **account** of what had past then, since when
severall more have been accused by Oates, who I verily beleve to be very
innocent, and to have been falsly accused as well as the rest, for I looke
upon none but Colman to be faulty. Yesterday Madame de Mazarin was
accused, by the same man, and when he will make an end of accusing
people the Lord knows, but their chief malice is against me, for they
think they have no so sure way of ruining the King, as begining with
me. This day Lord Shafsbury and his gange shewd their malice to me,
and would have gott a thing done that might have proved very pre-
juditial to me, but they could not carry it, in our House. Tomorrow I
expect the same thing will be attempted in the House of Commons ; what
successe it will have there, the next post must tell you. I have not **tyme**
to say more, but that **you** shall always find me the same to you.

### [1678] **November 5, London.**

I received yesterday two of yours of **the** 8 and 11 of this month, by
the first of which I am sorry to find, you are like to have troublesome
**affairs** where you are. I am sure we have our belly full of them here, and
do not see how sone we are like to have an end of them, there being so
**many malitious** persons in the world. I have been fallen upon in both
Houses ; **in the Lords** the debate fell without a day (*sic*) ; in the Commons
it was adjourned till Friday, so that **I** have till then to provid for the
worke in that House. Tomorrow I expect to be fallen upon againe in
the Lords House, where I will defend myself as well **as I can.** I **have**
not tyme to say more, but to assure you that I shall always be very kind
to you.

### [1678] November 12, London.

I had not tyme to write to you by the last post, since when I received
yours of the 15, in which you told me of my daughter's being some what
indisposed, and was glad last night to have a letter from her, by which I
see she was better. As for affairs here, they do not mend, but every day
**grow** worse and worse, so that I am to prepare for a very great storme
to come upon me, and I do not see it **is** likly to stop at me, and that their
**chief** aime of removing of me, **is to** come the easier at the King. On

Thursday next the House of Commons is to take up againe the debate concerning me, and then I shall know what to trust to. If I should writ you all the newse and the malitious storys are told insteed of a letter you would have a volume from me, but realy I am so tired with having been almost all this day at the House, that I can say no more but I am yours.

[1678] November 15, London.

I have charged this **bearer** Sir G. Silvius to give you an account of all things here, and to speake to you about my owne concerns, which are now in a very ill postur, as well as the publike. I desire you will give him **full creadit**, to what he shall say **to** you from me, and so shall say no more **now but to assure** you I shall always be **as** kind **to you** as you can desire.

[1678] November 17, London.

I could not **refuse** this bearer, Captain Douglas, to recomend him to you, **that you** would be favorable to him, in letting him have some employment in your troups. He has served already under **you, and I** hope to your satisfaction. He is well esteemed of **here by those that** know him, and had been provided for here but for **his religeon. I shall** now say no more but that **you** shall always find me **very kind to you.**

[1678] November 19, London.

You will **before this have had a** large account of all things here by Sir G. Silvius, **since when I see little** hops of things mending here. As for what passes here, yesterday **Mr.** Secretary Williamson was sent to the Towre by the House of Commons for some warrants he had countersigned for the payment of some Catholike officers which had come out of France, but this morning his Majesty sent for the House of Commons and spake to them upon that subject, and releved him from his imprisonment, upon which they have made an adresse **to** his Majesty to continu him in the Towre; but he is out, and what answer will be given to it I do not know. I have not tyme to **say** more but that you shall **always** find me to be **very** kind **to** you.

[1678] November 22, London.

I had no **letters from you** by the last post, since when I have gott a **proviso** added **to** the **bill for** puting the Catholike Lords out of the **House,** and banishing **all those** of that perswation from the Court, **that** nothing in **that** act shall extend to me; so that in this, my enemys have mist of their aime, for their cheef designe by this bill, was to drive **me** from his Majesty's presence; and though I have carried this point, yett their malice to me continus as much and more then ever, and thay have [a] new designe on foott against me, and I am sure will leave no stone unturned to ruine me if they can, so that I am far from being secure, by having gaind that point yesterday. As for other newse, there is one Staily condemned for having spoken treasonable words against his Majesty, and will be hanged on Tusday next. Mr. Colman's tryal **is to** be on Wensday, and most thinke it will go hard with him; which **is all** I have now to say, but that you shall always find me very kind to **you.**

[1678] November 26, London.

The letters are not yett come, nor are they like to **be here** this day or two, by reason of the contrary winds, which have been **very** great. Our storms here on shoar continu still very violent, but I am more at ease then I was, since my proviso has past; but now there is another thing happned which I am sure will surprise you, which is that that great villan Oates did on Sonday last accuse the Queene of hir having designed to poison his Majesty, and that she knew of the whole designe against him, and yesterday had the impudence to say the same to his Majesty in full Councel. I have not tyme to tell you all the particulars, only that now Oates is so secured that he cannot gett away if he would, and I make no doubt but that all his vilines will be found out at last. Stayly was executed this day, and tomorrow Colman is to be tryed, and I beleve it will go hard with him. I have not tyme to say more but that you shall always find me the same to you.

[1678] December 3, London.

I have now two letters of yours to answer, the first of the 29 of last month, which I receved but on Friday night last, and that so late that it was to late to write by that post; since when I have receved also yours by Silvius, and assure you he has given me full satisfaction in what you charged him with, and that you did for the best. As for newse, affairs in generall go very ill, for you see the Commons will not so much as harken to the keeping up any longer the troups we have in Flanders and Brabant, so that they must of necessity be some sent for over, it being imposible to keep them there for want of mony, and a bill is now a passing in the House of Commons for their being disbanded out of hand, and to send for them presently over for that intent; and yesterday the ministers in generall were fallen upon, and all things look as they did in the begining of the late rebellion, and truly I beleve there will be great disorders here before it be long, if things continu at the rate they are at, and the Republican party is very busi at worke. As for what concerns my self, since my proviso has past I have been left alone, but how long that will continu I do not know, for some continu their good will to me still. Mr. Colman was executed this morning, and declared, as he was ready to be turned of, that he had been falsly accused by Oates and Bedlow, for that he had never seen them till they were brought as witnesses against him; that he knew nothing of a plot against his Majesty's life or governement, and never had gone about to endeaver the alteration of religeon by forse. It is late and I must end, and that with assuring you that I shall always be as kind to you as you can desire.

[1678] December 9, London.

I could not refuse this bearer, Machaut, to write to you by him, and this shall serve instead of a letter by the post, which is to go to morrow. As for affairs here, things go on very ill still, and I am affraide things will grow to a greater heat then ever, and that they will every day do some thing to lessen the King's authority; and I am told that they will againe falle upon the Queene and myself, and that to morrow will be the day. I beleve you have heard of some foolish discources have gone about towne concerning the Duke of Monmouth; they continu still, and some of his freinds talke as indiscretly on the same subject. The Republicans and others of the boldest phanatiks are they that spreed it most abroad, hoping to reape some advantage by it against our family, but if they can do us harme no other way I shall not much feare them. However, I shall be watchfull upon that matter, and not dispise it neither, and if I find it necessary shall take notice of it to his Majesty, who continu very kind to me. I have writen so freely, this going by a safe hand, and now shall say no more, but that I shall always be as kind to you as you can desire.

[1678] **December** 17, London.

I **have not** heard from you this good while, however that dos not hinder me from writing, though one has not great pleasur in giving any account of what passes here, things not going as they should. This day was once designed by some to have brought in an impechment against [the] Lord Tresorier,* but they have deferd it. Some thinke it is deferd only to see what successe the bill **for the** disbanding the army will have in our House, and, when that shall be past them, have at **us** all. Tomorrow we go upon **it in** a committy of the whole House, and we **shall,** I beleve, have a **warme debate** concerning some amendments which are of absolut **necessity to** be **made in it.** In the meane tyme his Majesty **is seing to draw over his troups as** sone **as he** can, and, the weather **being frosty as it is, has altred his, mind of having** those in Brabant **come downe the Scheld, from Antwerp, and** designs **now** to have them **march over land to Ostend to embarke there,** and is sending away orders **to** that purpose. I have not tyme to say more now but that you shall **always** find me very kind to you.

[1678] December 20, London.

Yours of **the 20** I receved but last night, **by the which I** see you thinke it very strange that people here do so presse for **the** disbanding of the army. I am of your opinion, but what will that signify, since it is so prest on by the Parliament. This day we made an end to **the** amendments of that bill, and to-morrow shall passe it and send it downe againe **to the** House of Commons. I beleve they will not aprove of our amendments, which will cause some debate bettween the Houses. I beleve **you** will be surprised to heare what Mr. Montegu has done, for being yesterday accused in Councell, of having had seecret conferences with the Pop's Nuntio at Paris, he, to reveng himself of that, produces letters writen to him by the Lord Tresorier, by his Majesty's command, when he was Embassador in France, and **shews them** to the **Commons,** who upon it ordred an impeachment to be drawne up against [the] **Lord** Tresorier, upon the matter contained in those letters, and other things they had against him. I am confident there was never so abominable action as this of Mr. Montegus, and so offensive to the King, in reveling what **he was trusted with** when he was employd by his Majesty All **honest men abhor him for** it, and to-morrow I beleve the impeachment **will be brought up to our** House, and then we shall see what the articles **will be. I make no doubt** but that [the] Lord Tresorier will defend himself very well; I am **sure** his Majesty is bound to stand by him. You see at what a rate things go here ; I see little hope of their mending. Next weeke is like to be a busy weeke with us, though it be the Christmas holydays, till when I shall say no more but that I shall always be very kind to you.

[1678] December 24, London.

I receved on Saturday last yours **of the 27,** by the which I see the French have taken their winter quarters in **the** Pais de Liège ; they are but troublesome neighbours. As for affairs here, there is no amendment, nor any liklyhood of it. Yesterday the impechment was brought up to **our** House by the Commons against the Lord Tresorier, upon which **we** had a long debate whether he should withdraw or no, and it was carried he should not ; and it being then very late the farther debate was put **of** till Thursday, and the House adjourned till then. This day

---

* The Earl of Danby.

his Majesty in Councell has **been very busy in examining** a new man that was taken two days ago, and now says he was one of **them** that was present when Sir Edmondbury Godfry was murthred. His story dos not att all agree with Bedlow's, so that both cannot speake truth. His name is Prance; he say[s] they were six that did it, and has named them all; three of them are secured, and were examined **before him** this **evening at** Councell. They all positivly deny it, though they **were promised pardon** if they would conffesse the truth. What Bedlow **will say to this I do not** yett know; some are not well pleased with **what this man** says, because it contradicts Bedlow. What all these **things will come to** the Lord knows, but this you may be assurd of that **I shall always be very** kind **to you.**

[1678-9] January 10, **London.**

I did not write to you the last post, having been **a** hunting, for the first tyme since the Parliament was prorogued, and was so weary I could not do it, and besids I had no thing considerable to say; since when I have receved yours of the 13, by the which I see you were a going in to Gelderland and the other neighboring provinces, and should be some tyme out of the Hage. As for newse, here is none considerable, but what I beleve pleases you no more then it dos me, which is that there are already three of the new raised regiments of horse disbanded, and the rest of the new raised troups will be so to, as fast **as** mony can be gott to pay them off. As for other things, the face **of** affairs looke[s] very ill still, and the ill affected people do keep up the feares and jealousis as much as ever, and men's minds are **as** unsettled as ever, and fitt **for** any disorder; and I very much feare **we** shall find the effect of it **so sone as the troups are** disbanded, **and then we shall not only be** lyable to **disorders at home, but be exposed to attemps from abroad.** This **is** all I shall say at present, but **to assure you of my being always very** kind to you.

[1678-9] January 17, London.

I did not write to you last post, having then but little to say, and now all that is, is that his Majesty declared in Councell this afternone, that he would put of the meetting of the Parliament till the 25 of next month, for that till that tyme, **he** beleved he should not be able to have dis**banded the new** raised troups, **or to have** found out the bottome of the plot, **both which he** would willingly **do** before they meett. As for the disbanding, as fast **as** they come out of Flanders, it will be done; and for **the** plot, a committy of Councell sitts every morning. I wish we may not repent, before few months passe, the parting with so many good troups, for I must confesse I do not like to heare the French are getting so considerable a fleett ready at Brest, espesialy when I consider the postur affairs are in at home; and I assure you, great arts are used by some to enflame men's minds, which is now easily **done, and** how all things will end the Lord only knows; and for my self, those **who apeared** against me when the Parliament satt, are as malitious against **me as** ever. This is all I shall now say to you, and you may be **sure I shall** always be very kind to you.

[1678-9] January 24, London.

I had not writen to you this post but to informe you of that which I beleve you did not expect, which is, that this day in Councell his Majesty declared his resolution, to disolve this present Parliment and to calle another, which is to meett the 6 of March. I hope it will have a good **effect,** for **in** all **liklyhood a new one will do better then** the old one would have done. Now that I am a writing I cannot help telling you, that when Irland and Grove were executed this day they both declared their innocency, and took God to witnesse as dying men, that they never knew anything of any designe against his Majesty's person or government, which confirms me in the opinion I had of their having been falsly accused. I would say more, but have not tyme, and so shall end with assuring you of my being always very kind to you.

### [1678-9] January 28, London.

It has been so very stormy weather the later end of the last weeke and the begining of this, that I do not wonder the letters are not yett come, and the frost has been sharper these three days last past then all the winter; and till now there has been very little ice in the river, and it is almost frosen up, but this day the weather is not so very bitter, though the frost continus. There happned on Sunday night last, a great fire in the Temple; it began about eleven and burnt furiously till eight next morning, about which tyme they masterd it. It has destroyd many houses, and poore my Lord Feversham is dangerously wounded in the head, by the blowing up of a house, neare which he stood. I saw him drest this morning; his scul is craked, and tomorrow he is to be trepand. The skilfull men beleve he will do well, and indeed I hope it; if he should miscarry, I should have a great losse of him. This is all I have to say but that I shall always be very kind to you.

[Postscript.] I had forgott to tell you that his Majesty was lett bloud, this afternone, having a witlow in his thumb, which put him to much paine, but since he was lett bloud he has found much ease by it.

### [1678-9] February 28, London.

I have only tyme to tell you, that the Dutchesse intends to make you another visite, and to sett out from hence on Monday next. I hope she will have as good a voyage as hir last, and desirs to be as much incognito as then. I have charge[d] Sir G. Silvius to write more at large, and should say some thing of consequence (espesialy for me), but realy have not tyme, it being so late, and not fitt to go out of cypher. I must end, and that I do with assuring you I shall always be as kind to you as you can desire.

### [1679] March 27, Brussels.

I came hether this morning, and would not faile to lay hold of the first oportunity of writing to you to thanke you for your kind usage whilst I was with you, of which I shall always be very sensible. I have found this place very empty of men, for the Duke de Villahermose is at Ghent, and will stay there all this weeke, and most of the people of quality are with him; the rest have been with me. The Count de Waldestin is here; he went back to London, when he hard I was come from thence, and came away againe the day after the meetting of the Parliament. He knows no more then what you heard, before [I] left you, but I have had letters this day of the 13/23 from London, that informe [me] that his Majesty had prorogued the Parliment for two days, in hops by that means, and some others, to accomodat the dispute about a Speaker, which till then had hindred all other businesse; but of this you will have an account by the English letters, which will be I beleve with you as sone as this letter, [so] that I need say no more on that subject; which is all I have tyme to say to you, but that I shall always be as kind to you as you can desire.

[1679] May 8, Brussels.

I see by yours of the 5, which I receved yesterday, that you had not then heard of the great newse of the making of a new Councelle, and the Earl of Shafsbury's being presedent of it, which did not only surprise me very much but all those of this country, and more espesialy those who governe here, they not understanding more then I do what could prevaile with his Majesty to lay aside so many of his truest servants, and put all his affairs into the hands of those who for so many years have oposed and obstructed all his affairs. For my part I dread the consequences of it, but shall be very glad to be mistaken, and wish with all my hart his Majesty may find ease in his affairs, by what he has done. A little tyme will lett us see much. I have been informed that all this great alteration was resolved on at Lord Sunderland's, none attending his Majesty there but [the] Duke of Monmouth and Lord Shafsbury. The Dutchesse is sayd to brage she helped to perswade his Majesty to do it. These people continu very civile to me. I am exceding glad to heare my daughter has mist hir ague; I hope she will have it no more now the warme weather is come. I should now make you a thousand complyments for your obliging letter, and the kind usage I had from you, but besids that I am very ill at making them, I have not tyme to do it, and I hope you will always beleve me as kind to you as you can desire.

[1679] May 11, Brussels.

I have just now receved yours of the 9, by the which I see you were surprised with what has happned in England as well as I was, and you are in the right to say one can yett make no judgment what effect it will have, tyme must shew it; and to returne your freedome, I feare it will not have a good effect, for by the last letters I had from thence I am informed that all those of the House of Commons who have now upon this new change had any preferment have already quite lost their creadit in that House, and that there are already new cabals and partys setting up there amongst those who have had no preferment, so that, to tell you freely my thoughts, in my mind all things tend to to a Republike. For you see all things tend towards the lessning of the King's authority, and the new moddell things are put into is the very same it was in the tyme of the Commonwealth, and I feare that hardly any that are new of the Councelle have courage enough to advise or stand by any vigorus resolution. I should be very glad to be deceved, and would say more but that the post is just ready to go. Lett what will happen, you shall always find me the same to you.

[Endorsed] For my sonne the Prince of Orange.

[1679] May 14, Brussels.

You have before this had an account of what was done by the House of Commons on this day sennight, that concerns me. You see how violently my enemys attaque me, and that Wensday last was the day that both Houses were to take into consideration my affairs. What the issue on't will be, I expect to here this night, or to morrow, and cannot now but looke on the monarky ist (sic) self in great danger as well as his Majesty's person, and that not from Papists, but from the Commonwelth party, and some of those who were latly brought into the Councell that gouverne the Duke of Monmouth, and who make a property of him to ruine our family; and things go on so fast and so violently, and there are so very few left about his Majesty that have either will or courage to give good advice to him, that I tremble to thinke what will happen, for if his Majesty and the House of Lords stick to me, then one may expect great desorders—nay, a rebellion. If his

Majesty **and** thay shall consent to what **the** Commons may do against me.
I shall then look on his Majesty as lesse then a Duke of Venice, and the
monarky and our family absolutly ruind and given up. But what to
do or what to advise as things now stand, is very hard to say. I
could wish you in England, though I dare not propose it to you to go,
not knowing how you might find things there, nor how it would consist
with your affairs in Holland, of which I can no way judge. Therefore
all I dare say to you is to desire you to consider well with your self
whether it be fitt for you to go or no. You see they would not fall
upon me till the Councell was new moddeled, and that they had turnd out
fower of the judges, all loyal men, and put in others in their places
that I feare will find what they please law. I could write a volume
upon this subject, but shall say no more till I have my next letters,
only assure you shall never find any alteration in my kindnesse to
you.

[1679] May 17, Brussels.

Since I wrot last to you, I have had the English letters of **Friday,**
and last night Churchill came hether, who left London on Sonday, **and**
brought me a very kind letter from his Majesty. You will by this have
seen his Majesty's and [the] Lord Chancelor's speech, which were spoken
**on** this day sennight to both Houses. They had this one effect, that it
put **of in** both places the debate that was to have been concerning mee,
but for all that I do not at all flatter my self that these speeches **will**
keep them from faling upon me, at least in the House of Commons; for
I do not find they are satisfyd with those to great condecensions of his
Majesty, and to tell you the truth, I am informed by my letters that
nothing will satisfy the Presbiterians, but the destroying of the
monarky, and the setting up of a Commonwelth, to which purpose
they flatter the Duke of Monmouth, as the only way to bring to passe
their ends, and to destroy our family ; and he is so indiscret as to give
into it, and to thinke he can find his account in it ; and as I told you in
my last I aprehend very much for his Majesty's persone, from those
kind of people, and I can hardly see how he can almost gett out of the
ill condition he is in. However, my freinds have some hopes, and
all advise me to leave this place and go into a Protestant country,
which they say may be of some advantage to me; therefore, if you
aprove of it, I would willingly go to Breda, as the properest place for
me to be in, to please them, and to be neare England, keeping still my
house here furnished, to come hether as occasion shall offer. Pray lett
**me** heare from you as sone as you can, that I may take my measurs
accordingly, for till I know whether you aprove of it, I do not intend
**to say** anything of it here. This is all I shall say now to you but **to**
**assure** you that nothing shall ever alter me from being as kind to you
as ever.

[1679] May 29, Brussels.

I intended to have answered yesterday yours of the 22 from the
Hage, but realy had not tyme, having had so much to write by an
expresse my freinds from England sent me, who I dispatched back last
night, [so] that I could not write to you by that post ; and this morning I
receved another from you of the 26, by the which I am very glad to
find that the journay to Dering has quite cured my daughter. You
know before this what past on Sonday was sennight in the House of
Commons upon my subject ;* it was the Presbiterians and the Duke of

---

* The Exclusion Bill.

Monmouth's freinds carried it, **and** were most violent against me, and now it is plaine that those first, I meane the Presbiterians, designe nothing lesse then the ruine of the monarky and our family; and truly I am of your mind, and thinke it is impossible for things there to last as they are not (*sic*) a weeke longer. For if his Majesty dos not intirly submitt to them and become lesse then a Duke of Venice, it is my opinion they will fly out into an open rebellion, and I hope in God his Majesty will never submitt as they would have him, and then the other must follow; and if his Majesty make but one step more, I meane make any farther concessions, he is gone, for if once they gett the navy, purge the gards and garrisions, and put new men in, they will be absolut masters. A very few days will lett us see what will become of it, and one shall know what to trust to, so that I shall stay here and not make use **of the** offer you make me of going to Breda, for now what my freinds in England designd by it is out of doors. But in all my misfortuns there is one thing which gives me a great deele of ease; it is that his Majesty apears very resolut for me, and exclams as I can desire at what has past in the House of Commons, and is very much unsatisfyd with the Duke of Monmouth, and uses all his endeavors to hinder the bill's passing in the House of Commons. I hope this vote of theirs will do there worke for them, for they that pretend to lay aside **one** for his religion, may as well lay aside another for some fancy or other, but I hope his Majesty will take courage and at last be a King. I shall say no more now but assure you that you shall always find me as kind to you as you can desire.

[1679] June 1, Brussels.

You will have seen by your last letters from England, how violently **they** procede **on** against me, and that the bill for depriving me of the succession **had** had **one** reading, and was to be read againe as **on** Monday last. So that except his Majesty begin to behave himself as **a** King aught to do, not only I, but himself and our whole family are gone; and things have been lett go to that passe, that the best I can expect is very great disorders, and unlesse some thing very vigorous be done within a very few days, the monarky is gone. For the Presbiterian party, which is the Republican, is growne so strong, that without they receve a sudden cheque, all is gone. A few days will now lett us see what we have to trust to; in the meane tyme be assured nothing shall alter **my kindnesse to you.**

[Endorsed] For my sonne the Prince of Orange.

[1679] June 8, Brussels.

**I** receved yours of the 31 of last month on Monday night last, just **after the** post was gone, so that I could not answer it soner. I know so **well the** concerne you have for me as easily to beleve the trouble all **these** extravagant procedings of the House of Commons against me has given you. I did not thinke they could have been so violent, and have so sone forgott the oath of allegiance that they had so latly taken, but when one considers how strong the Presbiterians are in that House, it is not so extraordinary a thing, for they will never faile to lay hold of any oportunity to downe with monarky; and Sir Thomas Clargis made a very good remarke in the speech he made against the bill, that most of those that were for it, I thinke he sayd all, were either Presbiterians or their sonns. But I hope this and some other procedings of the Commons will have so allarumd his Majesty and the Lords, that he will **at last** take some vigorus resolution, and they will stand by him; and I **have all** the assurences from my friends one can have, that if the bill some up to the House of Lords it will be rejected there, and his Majesty in his last letter to me of this day sennight assurd me the same thing. He continus very kind to me, and is unsatisfyd with the Duke of Monmouth's proceedings, but still continus kind in his mind to him, and endeavors and hops to make him behave himself as he aught to do. And now as to the affairs in England, one can do nothing but guesse at what may happen, for even there, I thinke, few can say what will be; what I conjectur is, that this Parliament must of necessity be either disolved or prorogued in a very few days, or the monarky is gone, and I hope now not only his Majesty's eis, but all the honest men's eis are opned, and see, that a Commonwealth is what is driven at, and that they will take their measur[s] accordingly; and I have some hope only, since his Majesty refused the adresse made him, for the drawing togather the militia of London and parts ajacent, during the tryal of the Lords, and I know he is very sensible that if he parts with any more of his power, that he is gone. He has yett the fleett, the garrisons, his gards, Irland and Scotland, firme to him, so that if he will yett stand by himself he may yett be a King. But for all that it cannot be without trouble and hazard, but firmnesse and good husbandry may carry him through all his dificultys; and I am very apt to beleve that when so ever he shewse he will be no longer used as he has been, and that they see he will be a King, that there will be a rebellion.

I have told you my mind freely; a few days will lett one know what to trust to. I am very sorry to find by your letter that my daughter had yett had a fitt after hir vomit. I hope though it will be the last, and shall be very impacient till I have the next letters, to know how she dos. It is now tyme for me to end my long letter, and be assured that you shall always find me very kind to you.

[1679] June 10, Brussels.

I beleve you will have been surprised to have heard of the prorogation of the Parliament till the middel of August. Till I heare from his Majesty I can make no judgment of it, which I expect to do tomorrow or next day; when I do I shall enforme you of it. Methinks it looks like a disolution and some vigorus resolutions taken, els why so long a prorogation? which is all I shall say to you till I heare againe from England, except it be to assure you that I am as kind to you as you can desire.

[Endorsed] For my sonne the Prince of Orange.

[1679] June 15, Brussels.

I receved yours of the 12 from Breda, by the which I see you were to go back the next morning to Dering. I am glad to heare my daughter had mist two fitts of her ague, and I hope to heare she will have had no more. You will before this have had your letters from England, and so be able to judge how things will go there. When Colonel Wesley went from hence I had some hops of being sone sent for by his Majesty, beleving by the prorogation vigorus councells would have been taken, but, by some things have been done since, I have reason to beleve such councelles will not be persued, and consequently I not sent for, but of this I shall not be able to make any certaine judgment till the end of next weeke. When I heare any thing I shall be sure to acquaint you with it, and in the meane tyme be assured that nobody has more kindnesse for you then I have.

[Endorsed] For my sonne the Prince of Orange.

[1679] June 22, Brussels.

I was in hops by this **tyme** to have had **a letter from his** Majesty by Grahame, who he **sayd** he would write by, before **he went to** Windsor, but he is not yett come, and I [am] still ignorent of the reasons that moved his Majesty to declare in Councell he would not lett me returne during the prorogation ; and though, by some things had been done, since that tyme, I did begin to beleve I should not be sent for so sone, yett I conffesse I **was** somewhat surprised at his Majesty declaring it so, and now do **not** expect to be sent for in hast, for I hardly beleve I shall be sent for when the Parliament meetts. I have been abroad all this day, and so have not tyme **to say more to you now** but **to** assure you, you shall always find me **very kind to you.**

[Endorsed] **For my sonne the Prince of Orange.**

[1679] June 26, Brussels.

I have just now **receved** yours of the 22, and have now lesse hops then ever of being **sent for, for** notwithstanding the rebellion in Scotland, which I thought **might have** served for an argument for my being called for home, by letters I have this day receved from his Majesty by Grahame I find he dos not yett thinke fitt to send for me, though he gives me all the assurences immaginable of his desiring it, but concluds for severall **reasons,** which would be to long now to write, the post being ready to go, **that it** would not be for his service, nor my good, to send for me yett, so **that,** to deele freely with you, I am affraide, so long as Lord Shaftsbury and some others who shall be namles, are at the head of affairs, I am not like to be called for home. As for the newse from Scotland, you know as much **of** it as we here, but did I (sic), I have not tyme to say any more to you **now** but that you **shall** always find **me** as kind to you as you can desire.

[Endorsed] For my sonne the Prince **of Orange.**

[1679] July 3, Brussels.

I had yours of **the 26 of** last month on Friday last, since when **I could** not write to you till now, and do easily beleve the trouble it is to you that **there** is so little **liklyhood** of my being **sent** for by his Majesty. I have againe venturd **to write to him upon** that subject, and have given him my reasons why I thinke it for **his** service to send for me to him, and that **presently.** What effect that will have I may know by the end of this **weeke** or the begining of the next, and then shall know what to trust **to ;** for if I be not sent for upon my last letters, I shall have little hops to **see** England **this** good while, and shall have reason to feare those measurs **will be** taken which **must ruine** our family, and with it the monarky, for **the** Republican **party** gett ground every day, being backed by the Presbiterians. **As** for the affairs in Scotland, that rebellious cru that is up in arms will, I believe, be sone dispersed, they having no considerable men amongst them, but I thinke what **may** follow upon **the** Duke of Monmouth's going downe thether may be of ill consequence. **When** I know any thing of importance I shall be sure **to** lett you **know it, and be** assured **I** shall always be as kind to you **as** ever.

[1679] July 6, Brussels.

I receved this morning yours of **the 4 from** Houndslardike, and **by** it see your newse from England concerning Scotland agrees with myne, and beleve the affairs in that country quiated by this ; but I am **not** all of your mind as to what concerns the meetting of the Parliament, for I can hope for no good from it, but on the contrary all the ill imaginable, and not only to me, but to his Majesty and our whole family, as may apeare by the bill that was read in the House of Commons against me, which was against law, and destroys the very being of the monarky, which, I thanke God, yett has had no dependancy on Parliments nor on nothing but God alone, nor never can, and be a monarky; and I hope his Majesty will be of this mind, and never lett this House of Commons sitt againe. If he dos, he is ruined for ever. I could say much more to you upon this subject, but have not tyme, and lett what will happen in England you shall always find me as kind to you as you can desire.

[Endorsed] For my **sonne the Prince of Orange.**

**[1679] July 9, Brussels.**

**I expect with great** impatience to **have an** answer to my last long letter to his Majesty, and though the wind has been contrary these two or three days last past, yett I hope by tomorrow night or Tusday to heare some thing, and if it be any thing to my satisfaction I shall be sure to lett you know it ; if it be only delays and putings of, I shall **stay** to lett you know it by the post. I beleve the next letters will bring us newse of the rebells in Scotland being defeated. I see by yours of the 7, which I receved this day, that the same report which was some tyme since at Nimeguen, of my being gone into France, is now come where you are. I cannot immagin how such a story should be made, since there was no ground for it, nor was it ever talked on here, but there are so many lys made in all places, and sworen to in England, that one aught not to wonder at any storys that are made ; and I beleve **you** will very sone see the Queene fallen upon with a designe of taking **away** hir life, or els I beleve those three great villans, Otes, Bedlow, and **Dugdal, would not** have behaved themselves so insolently as they did **the other day at** Councell, when they were sent for by his Majesty and asked there, what they had to say at Sir G. Wakeman's tryal against hir Majesty, and positively refused to do it ; which is all I have now tyme to say to you but that you shall always find me as kind to you as ever.

**[1679] July 16, Brussels.**

I receved yours of the 11, just after **the** post was gone, **so** that I could not answer it till now, and though I may have mistaken you, am still of opinion that this House of Commons, if ever they meett, will fall againe upon me, and never do any thing but harme to his Majesty's affaires ; and it would be a great blow to the monarky to let them sitt againe that did but offer to meddle with the succession, and had I any power with his Majesty they should not meett. I could say very much on the subject to lett you see I am in the right, but have not tyme, the post being ready to go, to say any more but that you shall always find me very kind to you.

[Endorsed] For my sonne the Prince of Orange.

**[1679] July 19, Brussels.**

In **my** last I told you I expected every houer an answer to my letters **I wrot by** Grahame. I have now had it, but no good one, for I must **still remaine a** banished man abroad, and have no other answer given me but that it is for his Majesty's service, and for my owne safty, so that my reasons have not prevailed at all, nor can I ever expect to be recalled so long as those who are now at the head of his Majesty's affairs continu to governe ; and I feare very much that the next sessions of

Parliament, lett it be when it will, will be a fatal one, not only for me, but for the very monarky its self. Lett his Majesty or any body els flatter them selvs as much as they please to the contrary. I could say much more, but will not, it being no very pleasing subject to discourse on. The Dutchesse of Modena came hether on Monday; and be assured I shall always be as kind to you as you can desire.

[Endorsed] For my sonne the Prince of Orange.

[1679] July 26, Brussels.

I receved so late yours of the 21, last post, that I could not answer it then; since when I beleve you have heard, as well as I, that his Majesty has disolved this Parliament, and called another to meette in October. I am very glad he has done it, and thinke he must have given up his crowne to them had he not done it, after the insolent behavior of the House of Commons to him. I hope it will teach the next better manners, but in case they should follow the foottsteps of that which is now broken, I hope they will be served after the same manner. Nobody desirs more then I that there may be a good unione bettwene the King and his Parliament, but I am not for their using him so insolently as this last did, nor for their meddling with the succession, nor making of King, with which they have nothing to do; and I am glad of this disolution, though it rather retards my being sent for, then **advances it, for** I always consider more what is more (sic) for his **Majesty's** service and the good of our family then any privat concerne **of my owne.** I find my enemys continu in favor as much as ever, and **are at** the head of affairs, and as long as that continus I have little hops **of** seing England; which is all I shall now say to you but to assure you, you shall always find me very kind to you.

[1679] July 30, Brussels.

I had yours of the 25 but yesterday, by **which** I find you had not then the newse of a new Parliament being to be in October. I supose you had it sone after, and you will have seen I am prepared for pacience, not expecting to be sent for home in haste; and truly I do not **see any** liklyhood when it can be, so long as I have such enemys about **his** Majesty, and therfor have need of a great stock of pacience, I acknowledg. I hope it will last, and you may be sure I shall do nothing hastily. I have not erred on that side yett. I wish in England some considerd the good of our family so much as I do, and then things would go better then they do; and to speake freely to you, I have but a very dismal prospect of our affairs in generall, and I do not see without a miracle how they can be mended, for his Majesty has so given up himself into the hands of his new councellors, that I can see nothing but the ruine of the monarky; and that which I thinke is a very bad signe is, that his Majesty is not so sensible as he should be at the ill condition he is in. You see I speake very freely to you of affairs as I thinke they now are, and shall always do so. My stag hounds are come, and I intend to begin **to** hunt this weeke, and shall do what I can to divert myself. I have **now** no more to say but that you shall always find me very kind to you.

[1679] August 10, Brussels.

It was so **late on** Monday **last** when I came from hunting that I could not then **lett** you know I had had yours of the 3, by the which I saw you were going for Gelderland, and my daughter for Aix, where I hope those waters will do hir good.

I had yesterday an expresse from England, who brought me a very kind letter from his Majesty, but tells me I must have pacience till the meeting of the Parliament and the tryal of the Lords in the Tower is over; that then he hops things may be in so good a temper as to make it fitt for him to send for me over; and till then I must have pacience, and will do what I can to divert myself in the meane tyme; which is all I have now to say, but that you shall find me as kind to you as you can desire.

[Endorsed] For my sonne the Prince of Orange.

[1679] August 17, Brussels.

Yours of the 1 of this month I receved but two days since, by the letters from England, whether it seems by mistake it was sent to the Dutch Embassador, who gave it to Colonel Villers at Windsor, to send it to me, and by it am very glad to find that now there is a good understanding bettwene you and M. Valkenire; I make no doubt you will find your account in't, and am very well pleased that you thinke the conversation I had with him did in any manner contribut to his behaving himself to you as he aught. Here is but very little newse sturing in these parts, but what I beleve I [you] may have already heard, which is, that the French have declared that Cheivre neare Ath, with 24 villages that depends upon it, belongs to them, and have warned them to pay no more obedience to this governement; which is all I have now to say, but that you may always be assured of the continuance of my kindnesse to you.

[Endorsed] For my sonne the Prince of Orange.

[1679] August 21, Brussels.

I have receved yours of the 15 from Derin, by the which I see my daughter was to go the next day for Aix, and that you intended to stay where you were, till the end of this month. The Dutchesse has taken the Spa waters some days, which agree very well with her. The weather begins not to be so very hott, which will make good hunting. I have had but little sport yett, my hounds being neither stanch nor in wind, and bad riding in the forrest, but I hope in one weeke more to bring them into good order. This place is as barren of newse as it is empty of company, so that I have no more to say but that you shall always find me very kind to you.

[Endorsed] For my sonne the Prince of Orange.

[1679] August 30, Brussels.

I did not answer yours of the 21 last post as I intended, having been a hunting that day, and having had a great chase, came home so late as I had not then tyme to write, and now for feare of such another accident write this day, though the post gos not till to morrow, intending then to hunt againe. Our English letters are come, which brings no newse but how the ellections go on, and who are chosen, but as yett there are so few chosen that one cannot ventur to make any certaine judgment what temper they will be of, though hetherto the most of those I have heard of are not such as one could wish. My daughters that are in England were to embarke either yesterday or this day at Greenwich, so that if the wind continus as it is they may very well be at Antwerp to morrow or next day, and the day after here; which is all the newse worth writing, so that I have no more to say but that you shall always find me as kind to you as you can desire.

[Endorsed] For my sonne the Prince of Orange.

[1679] September 7, Brussels.

I had so long a chase on Monday last, that it was ten a clock at night before I came home, so that I could not answer yours of the 28 of last month as I intended, but now I must write to you of another affaire. I had yesterday an expresse from Lord Sunderland to informe [me] of his Majesty being very much indisposd, having gott a great cold, which had put him into a feaver, but he then sayd, which was Sonday morning, that the feaver had left him, and that they hoped he should heare no more on't, and that it would not be so much as a tersian ague. But this day I receved another letter by expresse, that on Sonday night his Majesty had againe been indisposd, and had vomited, and been very sick in his stomake, so that they concluded his distemper would be an ague ; and seing his Majesty's illnesse continus, I have resolved to go and wayte on him, and intend to sett out from hence to morrow morning, and make what hast I can over, and that as privatly as I can, being very desirous to be with him before any body knows of it. I leave the Dutchesse and my two daughters here, till I know how my affairs are like to go in England, by which I must take my measurs. You may easily immagine I am now very busy ; you shall heare from me againe so sone as I can, and may depend on my being always very kind to you.

[1679] September 16/5 (sic), Windsor.

I had so much businesse upon my hands, and so many people to speake to, on Tusday last, which was the post day, and the day I arrived here, that I could not gett a moment's tyme to write to you, to lett you know of my being come safe hether. I found his Majesty upon the mending hand, who receved me very kindly, and now God be thanked he has gott so much strength that he walks into the parke. I cannot yett say what will become of me, having had no discourse with his Majesty, but, by what I have had with some others, beleve I may be sent back againe, because they thinke it best to have me away when the Parliament sitts. For my part I am content to do what his Majesty shall thinke best for his service. I am very glad to find I have so many freinds left, and that his Majesty has been undeceved in one thing had been told him, which was, that there would be a rebellion, and that the citty would rise in case I came back ; but neither of these have happned, and the citty is very quiat, and most of the riche men there are pleased with it. By the next post I shall be able to say more to you, and be always assurd of the continuance of my kindnesse to you.

[1679] September 9, Windsor.

I receved last night yours of the 12, and see by it you were surprisd at my coming hether. I have writen to you since my being here, and though his Majesty will have me returne back to Bruxcelles, which I shall obay, yett I am of opinion my journay hether will prove advantagious to me. By my next I shall be able to explaine it to you. His Majesty is God be praised very well, and has quite recovred his strength. There is yett no day sett for his going to Newmarkett, nor for my setting out for Bruxcelles. I beleve they will be both at the same tyme. His Majesty is just a going abroad, and I must wayte on him, so that I have not tyme to say more but that you shall always find me very kind to you.

[Endorsed] For my sonne the Prince of Orange.

[1679] September 12, Windsor.

I beleve you will be as much surprised with the newse you will have now as with that of my coming for England ; it is that the Duke of Monmouth is commanded to go out of England, and his command of Generall taken from him, which, though it may make him more popular amongst the ill men and seditious people, will quite dash his foolish hops that he so vainly persued. This his Majesty resolved on, upon it being represented to him that it was not reasonable to leave the Duke of Monmouth here, and send me back againe into Flanders, which he thought necessary for his service. The day for my going is not yett named, for he must go first, but I beleve it will be about the end of next weeke. He has of himself given up his command of the horse gards, desiring the Duke of Grafton may have that command; as for the Generalship, nobody will have it more. One of the Secretarys, which will be the Earl of Sunderland, is to manage that affaire as M. de Louvois dos in France. All things are very quiat in the citty and conntry, and will continu so if his Majesty dos but please. I have not tyme to say more **now, but** that you shall always find the continuance of my kindnesse to **you.**

I am told the Duke of Monmouth intends for Hamburg.

[1679] September **16**, Windsor.

Since my last to **you I have** receved yours of the 19 from Hounslardike, and by the last post gave you an account of what had past concerning the Duke of Monmouth, who, as I have been informed, has not behaved himself as became him, to his Majesty; for he has keep very ill company at London, and not followed his Majesty's orders in having no more to do with such kind of men. Mr. Mountegu is one of his greate councellors, and all the Presbiterians and discontented people flock to him, and endeavor to perswade him to disobay his Majesty's comands, and not to go; but his Majesty sent for him to come hether yesterday, intending, as I was told, to apoint a day for his going, and to give him good advice. I am informed the day is not sett, he saying he had a great deel of businesse to do. However, some say it will be Monday or Tusday next, and when he is gone I am to sett out a day or two after, his Majesty being still of opinion it is for his service I should go beyond sea againe, and though I am not of that mind, I must obay. Tomorrow we go to London, and by the next post I beleve I shall be able to say when I shall go; which is all I have to say now but that you shall always find me very kind to you.

[1679] September 23, London.

**I see by** yours **of the 26 from** Honslardike that you were very much surprised at the **newse I** wrot you concerning the Duke of Monmouth. I do not at all **wonder at** it, for most people here were so to. He has used with his Majesty all the perswasions he could to gett leave to stay but for some tyme longer, but could not obtaine it, and tomorrow he is to go. I am told he intends for Utrecht, and to stay there, having no mind to be far from hence. I am also to go away on Thursday for Bruxcelles, and on Friday their Majesties go for Newmarkett, where his stay will not be long, at least I hops so, for his presence here is very necessary in such troublesome tyms as these. So sone as I come to Bruxcelles, you shall heare from me, for now I have not tyme to say more but that I shall always be as kind to you as you can desire.

[Endorsed] For my sonne the Prince of Orange.

**[1679]** October 7, Bruxcelles.

**I am** just **now** come hether **by** the way of Ostend, and God be thanked had a very quicke passage thether, and at my arrival here, heard that my daughter* had designed to come hether to see us all, but

---

* Princess Mary

I have now writen to hir **not** to come, because I had taken my measurs for my daughters'* going into Holland and embarking there for England, and the yachts that are to carry them are, or will be, at the Brill, by to morrow. The Dutchesse and my self intend to go along with them to the Hage, and besids that, I would be glad to be with them as long as I could. It is necessary I should speake with **you** about our concerns in England, and I am sure, as things stand now bettwene you and the Spaniard, it is by no meaus fitt for you to come into their country; and besids I have directed an expresse, which I may expect from his Majesty by the end of next weeke, to come straight to the Hage, and it will be necessary for me to be with you when he arrivs, for **reasons which I** shall tell **you** when I see you. Therefore pray **send your yachts** to Willebrooke **so** sone as may be, that we may go **on board them there, and then make** what hast we can to you. When I see you I have a great deele to say to you, and now shall say no more but that you shall always find me very kind to you.

[Endorsed in an old handwriting, this letter probably being the outside one of a bundle.]

[1679] October 11, Bruxcelles.

I had yours by Mr. Eliott yesterday when I came from hunting, and though the yachts are already come to Willebrooke, cannot sett out from hence till Friday morning. I intend to go in my coaches to the yachts, **and if** the wind be never so little favorable, hope to be with you some **tyme on** Sonday, by Delfshaven, to avoyd the crowd of Rotterdam; **which is all I** shall say to you till I have the satisfaction of seing you, but to assure you that you shall always find me very **kind to you.**

[Endorsed] For my sonne the Prince of Orange.

[1679] October 14, London.

This was the first place I landed at, so that you could not heare from me soner. By that tyme I gott to the Brill the wind came contrary; however I turned it out (*sic*), but could not reach the Downes, being driven to leward, as far as Soutwold bay, on the cost of Suffolk. I fell in with the shoar before son sett, and that night sett Churchill on shoar at Alborough, who I sent to his Majesty to gett leave to go up to London, and so by land to Scotland, and gott to the buy (*sic*) of the Nore on Saturday night. On Sonday morning Churchill came back to me and found **me** there, and brought me word I might go to London, **orders having been** sent to the Downes by his Majesty to that purpose, **and so ou Sonday in** the afternone I arrived here, and their Majesties came **not hether till** Monday. I am now a preparing to go for Scotland by land as fast as **I** can; I cannot yett **say** what day I shall sett out. I have not tyme **to** say more, but that you shall always find me very kind to you.

[Endorsed] For my sonne the Prince of **Orange.**

• [1679] October 17, London.

In my last I gave you an account of my arrival here, since when his Majesty has put out Lord Shaftsbury from being Precedent of the Councell, and this day the Parliament was prorogued till the 26 of January, notwithstanding which my journay for Scotland continus, and I hope within a few days to begin my journay by land, though the ways are like to be very bad by reason of the great rains which have been

---

* **The other Princesses,** who were at Brussels; *see* before, September 7.

of late and still continu. I had not tyme in my last to lett you know a peece of intelligence I had, which it is fitt you should know. It is that there is a privat corrispondance bettwene Lord Shaftsbury and some Parliament men of his faction, and some of those [who] are called here the Louestin party, in Holland, which I am sure cannot be to your advantage, and had the Parliament satt now, they would have proceded in it. I hope the little man's being out of employment here may help to breake those measurs; however, you would do well to looke a little after it where you are, for beleve me the Presbiterians and other Republicans here have as little kindnesse for you as the rest of our family; which is all I have to say now, but that I shall ever be as kind to you as you can desire.

### [1679] October 27, Hatfeild.

You see I have began my journay and sett out from London this day about none. I shall be obliged to make but easy journays, by reason of the season of the yeare and the badnesse of the ways, so that I am like to be at least three weekes in my voyage. We have had no letters from any place on the other side of the water for these many days, but hope that the wind being now come esterly we may have them to-morrow. As for newse you will have what is from London. And now I shall say no more but that you shall always find me as kind to you as you can desire.

[Endorsed] For my sonne the Prince of Orange.

### [1679] November 3, Newarke.

I did not receve yours of the 31 of last month till since I left London. I see you were then at Soesdike, but by a letter from my daughter find you were a going to Deren, and if you have had as good weather there as we here, you will have past your tyme very well, for since I began my journay we have always had faire weather, but for all that the ways have been very bad, but now they tell me the worst are past. I have been very civily treated all the way I have come by every body, and at all the towns where I lay, all the persons of quality of both sexes came to see us. This night I am to ly at Welbeck, a house of the Duke of Newcastel's, and it will be Thursday before I can gett to York, which is but half way to Edenburg. I am just now a going to take coach, so that I can say no more but that you shall always find me as kind to you as you can desire.

[Endorsed] For my sonne the Prince of Orange.

### [1679] November 27, Edinburgh.

I receved yesterday yours of the 24, and arrived here on Monday, and was receved here as well as at the borders of this kingdome as well as I could expect, and truly I have great reason to be satisfyd with my reception in this country. As for what you say you heard at your arrival at the Hage, of a new league made bettwene England and France, the same newse is come here, a flying report, but not from good hands, and I do not beleve it; but before this Mr. Sidney is with you, and can informe you better then I can, who have been so long from London, and so little there, and so far from it. Of what passes there, this place affords no newse at all, but that the weather continus still very good, so that I have no more to say but that you shall find no alteration in my kindnesse to you.

[Endorsed] For my sonne the Prince of Orange.

Charles I. to his Sister [Elizabeth, Electress Palatine]. ]
1636, December 20, Hampton Court.

My onlie deare Sister
    **Your** servant Dinglie returning to you **I could not omitt** this occasion without remembring my love and service **to you**, though at **this** tyme I have nothing of business to wryte to you but **onlie** what **I** foregott in my last, to give you an account concerning the King of Poland ; in short he is unworthie of eather of our thoughts, except it bee to make him smart for his base dealing with us, for in a letter to mee he justifies his last Ambassador's proposition, concerning the change of my Neece's religion. Of this I desire you to take no notice, for it is fitt for us to misknow it, untill we fynd a time to make him repent it, at the rates of his harte [*sic*, roots of his heart ?]. In my next I hope to give you some account of **my** French Treatie, and so I rest
                Your loving brother **to serve you.**
*Copy.*

The Earl of Essex to Sir Thomas Trollope, William Ellis, Esquire, and the Deputy Lieutenants **with the** rest of the **well** affected Gentry in Lincolnshire.

1642, Nov 1.—Whereas through the great mercy of God we have lately obtained a victory over those who have engaged his Majesty in a bloody and unnatural war against his high court of Parliament, to the effusion of much innocent blood, and tending to the subversion of our religion, **laws, and** liberties, and the destruction both of his Majesty's sacred person and this his kingdom ; and whereas the body of that army is now removed from those parts towards Oxford, and **do not** only murder his Majesty's loyal subjects, and offer great violence **to the** persons of men, women, and children, but make free pillage on **the estates of all men,** taking away their horses, sheep, and **other cattle, not leaving them** bread to eat, or a bed to lie on ; the **which calamity is like to befall the** greatest part of the kingdom, if such their fury be **not speedily restrained,** whereof there is no probability, unless by the assistance of all **countries** of the kingdom, for we shall be unable to horse our foot forces, for more speedy pursuit of them, they having got the advantage of flying **far** before us, by horsing themselves with such horses as they take from countries where they come : These are therefore to request you to take such course (as shall be thought meet in your wisdoms) for calling together your neighbours, countrymen, and tenants, and making known unto them this our necessity, and to desire them, as they tender the enjoyment of their religion and estates (the which we only seek hereby to preserve), immediately **to** supply **us** with what men, horses, geldings, mares, saddles, bridles, cartgears, and other furniture they possibly **can,** not only for the setting on horseback our foot (which are much **wearied** with **hard** marching), but for drawing our artillery and other baggage ; all **which** men so **sent** unto us shall enter presently into pay, and every **such horse,** gelding, mare, or other furniture shall be appraised at such **rates** as they **are** worth, and secured by the public faith of both Houses of Parliament. Herein we entreat an account together with such assistance (as aforesaid) to be contributed by your country at Northampton on Saturday or Monday next, at the furthest. And also we desire your country (as they tender their safety) to rise in their own persons, with their tenants and servants, and come in to the assistance of the army, **wheresoever** it shall be, with such offensive weapons as they can procure.
*Copy.*

VISCOUNT IRWIN to FRANCIS 'FOULGHAM,' at his house near Rotherham.

1701, September 3, Temple Newsam.—Being prevailed upon by many gentlemen to stand for knight of the shire the next election, I therefore beg the favour of your interest for single votes.

SIR JOHN KAYE to FRANCIS FOLJAMBE, Aldwarke nigh Rotherham.

1701-2, March 24, London.—As this Parliament cannot sit more than six months after King William's death, it is generally thought it will be sooner dissolved. At a meeting here on Friday last several of the members of our county (without acquainting the rest, and other gentlemen of the county in town) agreed to make an interest for Lords Irwin and Fairfax, who are resolved to join against any opposer; notwithstanding which I am prevailed with to offer my service once more, requesting your interest and kind assistance in this great undertaking, and also that you will suspend your disposal of your other vote till further consideration.

SIR GEORGE SAVILE to ST. ANDREW THORNHAGH, at Osberton.

1703-4, February 24.—Gives reasons for having declined to stand for the county of Nottingham.
[A vacancy had just been caused there by the death of Gervase Eyre. John Thornhagh was elected member on the 29th March following.]

SIR HARDOLPH WASTENEYS, M.P. for Retford, to THE SAME.

1707, Nov. 15, Nov. 29, and Dec. 9.—Three letters concerning the presentation of a petition to Parliament from Nottinghamshire.

ISAAC KNIGHT to THE SAME, at Rolleston near Burton, Staff.

1707, December 10, Langold.—About obtaining signatures to the above petition, which appears to relate to devastations committed by the deer in Sherwood Forest, for the writer concludes—It might be convenient to have the case printed how that there is no harbour nor shelter left for the deer, and that they are so numerous that in hard weather they break into barns to get hay, and that they eat up and destroy all poor people's cabbages and carrots that live near the forest, and the farmers are afraid to sow any corn in the usual time for fear the deer should destroy it, and what they do sow they are forced to watch all night for some 6 months, and that they can scarce get any servants to live with and serve them because they will not watch their corn in the night time. All this you know to be true; there might a great deal more be said; this must be left to better judgments.

JOSEPH BANKS, M.P., to FRANCIS FOLJAMBE, at Aldwarke.

1719, April 18, Boswell Court.— . . .
This day the King came to the House and passed all the Bills, and prorogued us till 19th May; he made a long speech, which I keep this letter open to enclose it you if it come out this night. I like it very well, only am sorry he thereby intimates his design for Hanover this year, but that however shews no fear of Cardinal Alberoni.
Yesterday Mr. Secretary Craggs told me, we might depend the Spanish 'Armado' was either destroyed at sea or blown to the Canaries.

When I answered that it was well they were not gone to Jamaica or some of our plantations, he told me it was impossible, for they had good intelligence that they had but twenty-one days' provision on board. We wait (but not with patience) for greater certainties.

*Postscript.* As to the Peerage Bill, it was never sent us, so many of us joined with the Tories in crying out against it. In my opinion, and I have read all on both sides, it was a favour that we shall live to repent refusing. In short, as one gentleman wisely said, it was like offering a dog a whole shoulder of mutton, which instead of accepting make[s] him turn his head from it with bashful shame as a favour too great to be real, but in bits he would have taken it all. In short, though stopping the increase of peers makes every single peerage a more choice feather, yet no doubt, were there a third part more added out of the best estates in England, they would as a House have much greater interest by their increase of property, and would be able by their boroughs and interests to choose a good part of the Commons. And besides, all the opposers of the bill own it would prevent all designing Princes doing jobs with twelve at a time or more, &c.

OSWALD MOSLEY to his brother [in-law] ST. ANDREW THORNHAGH, at Mrs. Barker's in Coke's Court, near Lincoln's Inn.

1726-7, March 6, Derby.—I will not pretend to foresee the event of war, but there is something pleasing to me in the accounts which tell us that we are actually engaged in defence of what was confirmed to us by solemn treaties, because it will effectually silence some unreasonable clamours, and extinguish the vain hopes of a party that the nation would be weary with keeping up large fleets without entering upon action. The new schemes of the party have always produced new troubles to me from a vexatious neighbour, who upon any fresh hopes of a revolution has renewed his claims, and lately threatened me with a fresh cry of 'Rump and Roundhead,' which I told him I was not in the least apprehensive of now. It is said Mr. Cotton goes to London before May with some assurance of a place in the Stamp Office which Sir Richard Py had, and it is thought he gets it by Lord Ferrers's interest. If the Government could be fully informed of the secret transactions in a certain cabal not far from Stow, I believe that gentleman might as well stay in the country.

The Sheriff of Staffordshire, K[in]g St. George (?), is still named in the clubs of the Tories with the heaviest curses for his buying of their friends engaged at that time in the rebellious attempts, especially their leader.

Lord Chetwynd's interest is violently opposed in order to bring in some others that I believe are not well affected to this Government, and I believe you will be of my opinion when I have opportunity to tell you who they are. The Chetwynds have not been my friends; however, as they are I believe firm to our present establishment, I cannot think well of the opposition setting up against them.

THOMAS WHITE to ST. ANDREW THORNHAGH, at Osberton.

1727, [July ? *torn off*].— . . . Lord Chesterfield's brother and Mr. Warren are fixed for the town of Nottingham (a compromise they call it) ; Mr. Gregory and Mr. Plumptree desist. Mr. Gregory is fixed upon to try his ' fait ' with me at Retford, who I hope will be perfectly agreeable to you and my friends.

### GEORGE GREGORY to THE SAME.

1727, July 18. London.—Asking support in his candidature for Retford, his resolution to stand there being sudden from the usage he met with at Nottingham.

### SIR ROBERT SUTTON to ———.

1727, August 1.—Details certain arrangements with Mr. Levinz for the representation of Retford, Mr. Gregory having desisted from standing; and also regarding the candidature of Lord Howe and himself for Nottinghamshire, in opposition to Sir Robert Clifton.

### WILLIAM LEVINZ to ———.

1727, August 1, Grove.—On the same subject.

### SIR ROBERT SUTTON, THOMAS WHITE, and GEORGE GREGORY to ———.

1727, August 2.—State that they will punctually observe the agreement, both with regard to the borough of Retford and the county of Notts, as it is explained in letters previously written.

### RICHARD WARD to ——— NEWTON.

1751, November 23. At my lodgings at Mr. Shoeland's, Peruke maker, Temple Bar.—As to the progress through the House of Commons of a bill affecting Coroners, chiefly opposed in the previous session by Mr. Harding, who had since been brought over to the interest of the writer and his fellow coroners. Wants a remittance towards his expenses, to be collected from his brethren in the county.

### THE MARQUIS OF ROCKINGHAM to SIR GEORGE SAVILE.

1763, August 29, Birom [Byram, near Pontefract].

I have just received the letter of which I send you a copy, wrote by a faithful secretary. I imagine it will rather fluster you, as it has done me. I hope good will ensue. I must entreat of you to come here as soon as possible, that I may have your opinion in regard to the answer, and also your company if we determine upon a London journey.

I will only now say in general that it is my earnest and steady opinion that it is neither the conduct of an honest or of a wise man to abet the skinning over of the present confused system, but it is much the duty of both to give what help they can towards a perfect and probably permanent cure.

Whether the time is yet come, is a matter difficult to judge upon, but I hope and trust that nothing will be entered upon without the fullest and clearest prospect of stability.

### [Enclosure.]
#### W. PITT to THE MARQUIS OF ROCKINGHAM.

1763, August 28, Jermyn Street.—A matter has opened, which must make me very impatient to be able to learn your Lordship's sentiments, and to receive the advice of a person whose approbation and friendship I shall ever esteem the greatest honour, and without whose co-operation no system can, in my opinion, carry its due weight. I will, in this critical situation, venture to request of you to be so good to come **immediately to town.** May I add that I shall esteem it a great favour if **your Lordship could** engage Sir George Savile to take the same **journey, to whom I would** write if I knew that my letter would **be** sure **to find him. Be assured, I** shall think any plan highly defective **in** which a person of **such** honour **and ability does** not take **a** share. I saw the Duke of Newcastle at Claremont **this** morning, who joins in wishing extremely that your Lordship would **come** directly to town. As his Grace's desires on this subject will best stand **for my** apology for the liberty I am taking, I will add no more.

EDMUND BURKE to [SIR GEORGE SAVILE].

**[1766] June** 16.—Concerning the Collector of Hull, whose conduct **had been** enquired into by the Commissioners [of Customs?], who had sentenced him to a penalty. "You know my Lord Rockingham's " delicacy in a business circumstanced as this is. He is therefore of " opinion that **the whole proceeding** should be revised by the Treasury, " **in** a public **and solemn manner; and this, you** are sensible, must take " **up** a good **deal of time.** The papers are already **large** enough to " **make** a decent figure in a Chancery suit." . . .

GEORGE DONSTON to ———.

1768, March 2, Worksop.—As to the **candidature** of Sir **Cecil** Wray for Retford, and the attempts made to secure the votes of the tenants of the writer, who was giving whatever interest he might have in the borough to **his** neighbour Mr. White.

The MARQUIS OF ROCKINGHAM to SIR GEORGE SAVILE.

1768, March **24, Wentworth.**

I should **have** [been] much delighted **in having** had the pleasure of seeing you **at Y**ork, in order to have given **you the** detail of all the pleasing occurrencies there. I now imagine it will be some time before we meet, as I must return to London on Saturday or Sunday morning, and I scarce think it possible that you can be here before, as the county election comes on so soon.

Nothing ever was more fortunate than all the Yorkshire elections have turned out, where we were interested. Old Osbaldeston's carrying his election rejoices me much. The assistance we have been of in bringing Yorkshire men of large properties into Parliament, has given great satisfaction. **Weddel,** Beilby Thompson, Lord Downe, Charles Turner, &c. are **good instances on** that head.

**Charles** Turner was highly **pleased with** your letter to him, and means **to stay at York purposely to pay you his compliments at** the county **election.**

There **has** been a curious election at Pontefract. Sir Rowland Winn **is** chose there, but by what I hear, and by what I understand of the resolution of the House of Commons relative to the right of voting there, I should not think the House of Commons will sanctify the proceeding, as I hear the mob insisted that only *resident* burgages should vote. Lord Galway was chose, but would not be chaired or have anything to do in it. I hear Harvey and Sotheron were very active, and it was very lucky for lawyer Jos. Wilson that they were there, for otherwise the mob would absolutely have demolished him.

I have had an account from the south, that an *East Indian candidate* **(who,** by the bye, has got his money in fair trade and with a fair character, and is a very sensible and worthy man) has succeeded. A Lord, not actually a friend, pressed me to recommend a candidate to him to fight in support of his interest in a borough, which was attacked by Creolian powers. The service seemed dangerous, but hopeful, and my friend, the candidate, has had the support of the neighbouring gentlemen, and beat the Creole above a distance, reckoning 240 votes to a distance.

I had left off writing from the post having brought me my letters, among which there is one from Strachey, the candidate at Pontefract. He was secretary to Lord Clive in India. He is nephew to G. Quarme, and I believe I have shewn you very sensible accounts from him when in India. I now transmit to you his account of the transactions at Pontefract; they tally in part with what I had heard. You will not mention from whence your accounts of that affair come, but I think it is right you should know early how the matters stand, for probably you may find some eager spirits who don't distinguish at first sight between what may be the product of riot, and may rather give it the colour of commendable exertion of the desire of freedom. I own I am apt to think, in the light the transaction appears to me, I think (*sic*) it not creditable, and it has more the air of copying the violences which we suppose Nabob makers commit, than the transaction of a civilized country such as Yorkshire.

I have not suffered in health by the fatigues of body or of mind. I have had a good quantity of Madeira. On Monday last I was very tolerably drunk by 5 o'clock, and though I went through [a] variety of ceremonies, such as attending the assembly, supping and drinking with many companies, I walked home about 4 o'clock in the morning after having kept myself in fact continually drunk or elevated for eleven hours. I had a very good night's rest, and was not at all the worse for it next day.

I hope your fatigues have not affected you. Mr. Weddel is infinitely obliged to you, and so is Beilby Thompson, who is most exceedingly happy.

I propose paying a visit of cordial thanks to our friends at Hull, when I return into Yorkshire. Their conduct in regard to Weddel has been most honourable and obliging, and I am infinitely happy in it. Don't you admire the spirited proof of regard and friendship to Lord John Cavendish, which was shewn by the Lancastrian visitors at York, to attend his election? My correspondents in general imagine I never write; those to whom I do write, much wish that I would curtail my letters, and therefore, lest you should think this a long letter, I will conclude.

SIR GEORGE SAVILE to [his brother-in-law] JOHN HEWETT.

1769, September 2, Shireoaks.

The hurry which succeeded to the meeting at York on Wednesday, and at Doncaster races afterwards, together with the uncertainty how I was to direct to Buxton, hindered me from giving you an account of our proceedings till I got hither.

The number of persons at the meeting is differently guessed at, but I fancy 800 is as near the mark as any; and the property very considerable. Sir G. A[rmitage?] opened by requesting the two members would give an account of the transaction, their opinion upon it, and their notions of a remedy. After we had done, he moved a petition; was seconded by Sir C. W[ray?]; and here it had like to have ended unanimous, had not one person expressed a desire to be heard against it.

This gave Wed°* an opportunity of answering, which he did in a pretty long speech, and very well. Three hands were held up on the first question, but on the final one (for we were a little irregular in debating after the question) it was *nem. con.*

The proposed petition was then read, which is I think in every respect by a great deal the best of any yet produced in any county; indeed I think the only one that is correct and constitutionally to the point. A line being left out of the engrossment, it was all to copy again, so that many would not stay to sign, as it will be sent about; so I think only about 4 or 500 have signed. G. D. spoke for you to Mr. Lascelles and the High Sheriff; so much for news.

Now what I write about particularly is relating to the county of Nottingham. I have a letter for the Duke of Portland from Lord R[ockingham], the purport of which is to consult him on the subject of a Nottingham petition, and he says that if the Duke of Portland, Lord M., and some more of us are for it, it *ought* to be carried, and the rather as it will be a tacit yielding to another set, who had better be battled on such a popular point as this, than at an election. You know I enter very little into these kinds of schemes, but I think it is right you should be apprised of them. As to the business itself, and its merits (apart from county politics), I have not a doubt about it. The only question with me would be the probability of success. After Yorkshire has marched out, the war may be said to be begun in the North. The worst thing that can happen now is the non-compliance with the petitions, and the number of petitions may turn the scale. The work is half done, and to stop in the middle is just the worst possible.

The way I put it in with regard to myself in Yorkshire was thus. I would call no meeting nor be of any meeting, but I would *attend* the meeting to give an account to my constituents. Now in Nottingham-shire I am a freeholder, and no member, and I have no objection to taking an active part here, except it be the fear of success, or the being thought meddling beyond my pretensions, and that as I have made my option early for Yorkshire and have hardly ever resided in Nottingham-shire (I mean as might have been expected had I not given myself to Yorkshire), people might say "Isn't one county enough for the fellow, but he must be thrusting his finger everywhere?" &c., &c.

I cannot deliver the letter to the Duke of Portland till Tuesday (tomorrow) night, when he will, as I understand, be back from Wigan.

I wish I knew how the county is inclined, for, of the two, better not attempt than fail. Now I have no measure of the interests here. I thought all about Retford were Court, and I had heard were angry at Sir C. W[ray] and disappointed in the part he had taken. I now hear a quite different story, and that they are in general Liberty boys. Of Wbet^m (?) I understand the same, which I was not aware of. About Newark I know nothing, nor Nottingham, nor Mansfield. The idea I gave Lord Rockingham of this county was, four Dukes, two Lords, and three rabbit warrens, which I believe in fact takes in half the county in point of space. I have determined, while writing, to send this by express, for I could like to find a letter from you at Welbeck tomorrow night, or early on Wednesday morning.

There is I think a meeting on the 16th about the County Hall; this is I think the opportunity to apply for a meeting, if at all. If it should take place, and your health should not permit you to attend, you might perhaps do in writing what I did at York in person (on the supposition that you approve the line I took), and you may go as far as you think

---

* Qu. Alex. Wedderburn, afterwards Lord Loughborough.

right in the three articles, viz. 1. Evidence of the fact; 2. Opinion on it; and 3. The remedy. On the last indeed I thought it became me to be short. I think on the whole my conduct gave satisfaction.

D. HARTLEY to [JOHN HEWETT, M.P. for Notts, at Shireoaks].

1771, March 26, **Golden** Square.—Everything is here in confusion. I know but little of the particulars. Oliver was sent to the Tower this morning at 2 o'clock. The Mayor* had retired from illness, but I understand he is to go after the Alderman when he recovers. Sir George† made a **sort of** protest last night about 12 o'clock against the violence of the House, and retired. I imagine it was felt, but everything is bent for violence, and the whole House together go, I believe, against the sense of almost every individual (some excepted of the inner closet) in the House.

### THE SAME to THE SAME.

1771, March 30.—You hear that the Mansion House **was sent in** flannels to the Tower. They talk of violent measures. **There** is a secret Committee chosen by ballot, of 21, to sit during the holidays, and it is said that they intend to report very strong resolutions about privilege and the riots, &c., which are to make the ground **for** bills **of** pains and penalties upon the Lord Mayor, Oliver, and Wilkes.

### The REV. WM. MASON to F. F. FOLJAMBE.

1771, **December 4**, Cambridge.—I **did not call** at Aston in my way hither, but came immediately from York, **as** Dr. Brown wanted me on Mr. Gray's affairs. This place affords no news, and London almost as little. The Duke of Cumberland's curious marriage **is stale,** and the Princess Dowager's‡ death is not yet in the papers, though daily expected; an event which frightens Dr. Brown, because as Vice-Chancellor he must write **verses** about her. We have hitherto had the mildest and finest winter imaginable, &c.

### THE SAME to THE SAME.

1772, May 9, Aston.—You ask after Politics, but they are too wretched to waste paper about. A Marriage Act to increase the power of the Crown was what the Nation reaped by the Duke of Cumberland's sage match with the house of Lutterel. What further benefit we shall reap by her Majesty of D.'s divorce is yet unknown. Lord North keeps his post, and I believe would be a good minister if he were really *the* minister. The Rockingham party is more insignificant than ever. Lord H. is now at Hornby with his two ministers Jackson and Alderson; if the first was last and the last first I trust he would be better served.

### THE SAME to THE SAME.

1772, September 26, Aston.—The second packet of Mr. Gray's papers (for the first were lost) I lodged in Mr. Fraser's hands to forward to you at Venice. Gloucester has at last owned his marriage,

---

* Brass Crosby.     † Savile?     ‡ **Augusta; she died 8** Feb. 1772 (Burke).

and is put under the same lash with the Duke of Cumberland, and denied the royal presence; nothing in this age seems really opprobrious but matrimony, and that too under the most matrimonial sovereign in the universe.

DR. JOSEPH PRIESTLEY to SIR GEORGE SAVILE, Bart.

1775, October 28, Shelburne House.—I take the liberty to write to you, both because I may not find a good opportunity of speaking to you, and because I shall take up less of your time. It is, indeed, presumption in me to mention to you the subject of politics, and I should not do it if I did not think it would be agreeable, perhaps useful, to you, to be acquainted with Lord Shelburne's real wishes and views with respect to the present posture of affairs. I write without his knowledge, but he has so frequently expressed to me his great regard for you, and his desire that you might know his ideas, that I am confident I am not doing wrong. But if I should be doing wrong, I depend upon your prudence to prevent any inconvenience that might arise from it.

I think I may venture to say that I know Lord Shelburne very well, and I would be very far from leading Sir George Savile into a mistake with respect to him. He is by no means that artful ambitious politician that he has been represented, and he is far from wishing to draw you from any connection you may have with the Marquis of Rockingham and his friends; so far from it, that he would himself most cordially act with, and even *under*, the Marquis (for so I have heard him express himself many times), provided his measures were more distinct and decisive, going to the bottom of the present disorders of the State. And all he wishes with respect to you is, that, as he thinks you are naturally more disposed in favour of what is manly and decisive, you would use your influence with the Marquis of Rockingham and his connections, to induce them to adopt such measures.

Lord Shelburne is not without that prudence and circumspection that becomes his situation, but he has no deep political secrets. What he avowedly wishes is, when the times are a little more ripe to bear the proposal, that the power of the Crown should be abridged, especially with respect to the disposal of the Revenue, and that a thorough enquiry be made into the source of the present wretched Administration, and proper examples be made. I believe he will never be brought cordially to acquiesce in anything that he shall think to be less effectual remedies than these.

With respect to America, I cannot help thinking that the people of that country would have more confidence in Lord Shelburne, provided there should ever be an opening to treat with them (which, however, for my own part, I despair of), than in Lord Rockingham, whose *declaratory Act* will never go down with them.

I know Lord Shelburne wishes to explain himself to you upon these subjects, and would have no objection to do it in the presence of Lord Rockingham, or any of his friends. You will find him frank, plain, and open, like yourself; and I shall think myself happy if I should be the means of bringing about such an interview as would give an opportunity of a free and unreserved communication of your sentiments, and might lead men who equally wish well to the State to act in concert for its good. Be the issue what it may, I shall be easier for having written to you to this purpose. Your own discretion must do the rest.

### Sir GEORGE SAVILE to DR. JOSEPH PRIESTLEY.

(Endorsed : " Copy, nearly correct.")

1775, October 29, Leicester Fields.—I find myself now very unfit to write or almost to think upon any kind of business. What I cannot however omit, and indeed have unwillingly delayed so long, is to assure you how sensible I am of the confidence you place in me. For the very flattering partiality Lord Shelbourne has at any time expressed towards me I cannot with propriety commission you to say anything on my part to his Lordship, because you mention your writing to be without his knowledge, but I will beg you generally to embrace any opportunity of expressing my respect for his Lordship, and my sense of the honour he does me.

It has been for many years matter of great concern to me to observe that the even very moderate number of persons who seemed to me to entertain the most just and constitutional principles were rendered still less effective by being again subdivided amongst themselves, and so rendered less respectable than even a Minority need be, and it is now indeed a good while since I had given almost over all hopes of ever seeing it otherwise. Nothing could make me more happy than to find myself mistaken, and nothing so proud as being in any degree instrumental in bringing about so very desirable an event. I do assure you, were you a minister, you could offer me no contract, no job, that I should catch at so eagerly as that of which you give me the preference, but I do not feel that I have any powers to do it ; nay, I am free to confess to you that were the business in much more able hands than mine, I should have a great diffidence of the success. I have not yet thought myself authorized to show your letter to anyone, and before I do I could wish to communicate more freely and largely with you than can be upon paper, at least than I am able to express in writing, especially with an aching head, which you have made giddy too by putting me upon a high place.

Would you be so good as to call upon me ? Could you conveniently do it this evening, or would you rather I should come to you tomorrow morning, for I think I must not stir out today ?

### The MARQUIS OF ROCKINGHAM to SIR GEORGE SAVILE.

1778, August 12, Grosvenor Square.—Mr. Burke called upon me this morning and wished me to apply to you in behalf of his son, young Mr. Burke, who is now of Christ Church College, and of sufficient long standing to be a candidate for a Fellowship of Merton. I understand there are three vacancies, and possibly there may be four by August two years, which is the time of election. I remember having applied to you heretofore, and I think it secured the success of the candidate. . . . Who the voters are I don't know, nor do I find that Mr. Burke knows at present, but be they who they may, the opinion is that Sir George Savile has great weight with many of them.

Burke is as eager about it as if it was a much greater matter of emolument or honour for his son. In regard to the latter, I believe he thinks that your interesting yourself in his son's favour would secure that point, even though the attempt was unsuccessful.

### A[YSCOGHE] BOUCHERETT to JOHN HEWETT, Shireoaks, near Worksop.

1779, August 14, N[orth] Will[ingham], co. Lincoln].—Though I know John Turner wrote to you from the meeting at Lincoln, I thought it right for me to write too. Know then Mr. Monson was proposed by Sir Christopher Whichcote and seconded, when that hero Philip Glover in a long (they say) studied speech (though had you heard it you would not have thought so) objected to the proposed candidate in respect to his youth and being a soldier, and proposed Mr. Vinor, who thanked him and declined; then he proposed Glover. Mr. Wood proposed his brother in law Sir John Thorold, and was seconded, and seemed approved by the King's friends there present. Sir Cecil Wray was proposed by Mr. Monk, who I am credibly informed had wrote to Sir Cecil, who gave him for answer that if the county unanimously approved him, he should be ready to serve us faithfully and to the best of his abilities; there this ended, though the man not objected to. Thus far for candidates; but [I] must not forget my delivering your message to Lord Monson, and telling you I acquainted Mr. Pelham with your kind intentions towards him at the general election, for which he thanks you sincerely and desired me to say so. Now I am to inform you that our Archdeacon, Dr. Gordon (Scotch), moved a subscription to strengthen the hands of Government, which was hissed by many of the middling class, and very sensibly spoke to by Mr. Harrison (my neighbour), who condemned the measures pursued, and observed that it was extraordinary that private purses should be thus strongly called on when those who received the overgrown emoluments of Government had subscribed so triflingly, but whenever they subscribed proportionably to those emoluments and their fortunes, his share (in times of eminent danger like these, however brought on) should not be wanting, how much so ever it might reduce him in his manner of living. Thus we are left to choose Mr. Monson or Sir John Thorold; though I am told (but not from very respectable authority) that Sir John declared lately he would not engage in an opposition at any man's instigation. . . . .

P.S. Sir John stands, for I have this moment received a letter from him.

### CAPTAIN J. KIRKBY to [JOHN HEWETT?].

1779, August 20, Camp, Southsea Common.—I received your very friendly letter yesterday, and am extremely happy in having it in my power to assure you, how much my vote and interest are at your service. I fear the kingdom will soon be engaged in business of a more serious nature. By a letter received yesterday by a gentleman of the Cornwall regiment encamped here from his family at Plymouth, he is informed that the Ardent with two other ships of the line, after resolutely contending with 20 sail of the enemies', were taken in sight of that place; that they have 30 sail more cruising in the Channel, and that Sir Charles Hardy was not heard of. Plymouth was then in the greatest confusion, nothing heard but drums beating to arms; the writer concluded by saying he was called to the window to view the enemies' lines. It is supposed by this time the above place is reduced to ashes. No doubt Portsmouth will be their next resort. Expresses are daily going backwards and forwards. As newspapers are not to be depended upon, any news that may arrive here, properly authenticated, I will send you the earliest opportunity. My new occupation is extremely agreeable to me; it is a trade that, I fear, many will now be obliged to follow. Whatever may be the opinions of people in Nottinghamshire, all here think very seriously of this matter. Our fortifications have been for some time and are still repairing; it is thought we shall soon be thrown into them. I flatter myself, you will excuse so unconnected a scrawl, when I assure you I am in haste.

### R. MORRISON to [JOHN HEWETT ?].

1779, September 3.—I have been in town, am just returned, and cannot omit telling you the news of the day. It is up at Lodys* (as I
am told by a gentleman who says he saw it) that the French and
Spanish fleets are off Portsmouth, that Hardy is at St. Helen's, and
their being so near each other, an engagement is hourly expected, or
Hardy must retire to Portsmouth harbour and be blocked up; in that
case, the Sussex coast, or any other coast, will be open to them, or even
the river Thames; but as Hardy has had a reinforcement of 5 capital
ships, which makes his number 40, to 60 or 65, he may probably think
himself able to fight them; I know my friend and relation Sir Chaloner,
if he had been now living, would not once have hesitated to have
attacked them, nor would his cousin even now in his old age of 78, was
he but skilled in the art of war as much as Sir Chaloner was. God
send us a happy issue in these affairs. And my good wish to you in
your expedition to the Peak for good health, &c.

### SIR GEORGE SAVILE to his brother [in-law] JOHN HEWETT, at Shireoaks.

1779, October 17, Preston.—The enclosed, which has been I find by
the date running after me above a week, found me this morning at this
place, to which I came yesterday in the course of military duty, our
General (Faucitt) being here.

This Riot duty, from troublesome, grows somewhat tiresome; a
great deal of night work, and our enemy is a kind of invisible potentate
with whom we can neither fight nor treat. They assemble on the hills
(as the west country lads hunt) by shouting or drums, go and destroy
mills used in the cotton manufacture, &c., and disperse as easily as they
met, and as ready to meet again, observing always to go where there is
no military; only one battle having happened, when six dragoons
drove two or three hundred back, and some into the river, where one of
the dragoons alighting, and jumping in after and swearing he would cut
the man's head off, brought him out like a drowned rat. What could
the poor man do? if he ducked he was drowned, if he popped up his head
it was cut off; so the victory was complete. I am, from a poor private
Colonel of one regiment, become a General of five armies, for into so
many parts are my troops divided. . . .

### THE SAME to THE SAME.

1779, October 27, Liverpool.—I am at length returned from the
Riot duty, the disturbances being so far quieted that, though detachments
of the regiment are left at different places by way of precaution, yet it
seems probable that there will be little or no further disturbance.
Private affairs.

### THE MARQUIS OF ROCKINGHAM to SIR GEORGE SAVILE.

1779, November 8, Wentworth.—I hope you have it in your thoughts
to be in London some few days before the actual meeting of Parliament.
Most men now begin to feel the actual distresses which are brought
upon this country. The system and the measures of his Majesty and
his advisers have not now many advocates on their side, tho' I suppose

---

* Lloyd's.

in the House of Commons they may still be supported by numbers. Considerable alterations in the opinions of many of the members must nevertheless have been brought about by the events of this summer.

The inconveniences actually felt, and the alarm **and expectation** of the **certainty** of more and more increase of difficulties, **must** operate upon **the** generality of men's minds, and will produce some consequences. I rather think that the general inclination is to be angry at having **been** misled, and deceived into a scene of such woe and weakness as **now** appears.

The Irish Parliament have taken up their matters in a pretty high and decided tone. His Majesty's advisers have brought on this crisis by their conduct on the Irish affairs in the end of the last session. I believe it will be safest to expect that the counsels of his Majesty will try to ripen the disputes and **use** every art to create confusion. I see by the newspapers that the Alarum Bell is set a ringing in Lancashire. As yet I don't **hear** that our manufacturing parts have stirred at all; the tools of government have **not yet** got their lesson, and **the wiser** people seem inclined **to** weigh **and** consider before **they** decide.

I *must hope* that you will be in London *early*.

### Sir George Savile to John Hewett.

[1779, November.]—The nasty service we have been upon here **has** made me consider the Riot Act more a great deal than ever I did before. We have been in situations which would have been very puzzling and disagreeable if there had been resistance. I could be glad you would turn your thoughts to that subject a little. There are commonly received maxims regarding the military and civil powers, and the right of the former to act offensively and fire, &c., &c., which I do not very well understand, nor do I find anybody that does. It seems an unlucky Act; for it has always been looked upon as a stretch of power bearing hard on the people, and I am sure it puts the military to great difficulties too, and is much complained of by them.

### The Same to the Same.

1780, January 3, Sandbeck.—Describes his late illness, &c.

### The Same to the Same.

**1780,** May **9,** London.

Against Triennial [Parliaments], 182 to 90.

Mr Fox for—Mr. Burke against.

T. Townshend and the Cavendishes voted for the bringing in, out of **respect** to the people, but against the measure.

### The Same to the Same.

1780, May **28, London.— . . . .**

The march of my regiment (which I think you know is for Newcastle, Morpeth, Alnwick, &c.) is **put** off till **the** middle of June.

Mr. Powis moved the other night **that the** House of Commons had done nothing essential to relieve the grievances of the people, but they were ashamed to say so. Is it not a singular thing for a Committee to come to a resolution, and then divide on the question of reporting it to the House? The House might as well, I think, pass a bill, and then **vote** it **should** not be carried to the Lords. I should have thought it (although in form a question to be sure) yet a matter of course that a Committee should report what they have resolved, and not *unresolve* it again in effect by resolving never to say a word about it.

### THE SAME to THE SAME.

1780, July 3, **Grosvenor** Street.—Here am **I** still possessing your castle, which I have found **tenable** against all foes. I fancy today will be the last of **any business in the** House of Commons, and the subject will be the order given to "**the** military to act without waiting for the " directions of the civil magistrates, and to use force for dispersing the " illegal **and** tumultuous assemblies of the people." This connected with Lord Amherst's letters to Col. Twisleden seem to me to form a **body** of *red Law* which, however excusable from the haste or justifiable **in reason** from the emergency, yet was unlawful, and, if not to be **censured**, ought to be regularly indemnified, (&c. &c.)

### WILL. (?) BAYNES to JOHN HEWETT, Shireoaks.

1780, August 12.—I was all yesterday on **the most cheerful water** party up **the river, as** high as Sunbury. **At Richmond we were ex-** tremely fortunate in overtaking Mr. Sharp's **barge (or his** country house, which has every accommodation of beds, &c.), w^{th} **a good** band of vocal **and instrumental music, and also the** Navigation barge, w^{th} my Lord **and** Lady Mayoress **and a number** gutling common councilmen, wives, **&c.**, going the boundaries of the river, and w^{th} them also a band of music, w^{ch}, together with all the colours of **my** Lord Mayor's barge flying, drew people of all ranks down to the water-side, and exhibited most truly as cheerful and lively a scene **as** you can imagine. The banks of the river are [so] exceedingly delightful that you have no sooner passed one villa but another is in view, and as I believe they call it the Swan- hopping season, all the gardens next the river are lined w^{th} ladies and gentlemen to see the show and hear the music; and as the barges stop at many and fixed places purposely, which bring down all the belles to show off, and to this is added many carriages, ladies, &c. **on horseback** riding opposite **the** barges—in short I never passed a day **more agree- ably.** In **the evening we** returned to Westminster bridge, where our **carriages waited for** us, [so] that we did not get here till about one **this morning.**

### SIR GEORGE SAVILE to JOHN HEWETT.

1780, August 20, Newcastle.—Since the receipt of your two letters I **have been** in general **a good deal on** the ramble, the regiment having been dispersed on account of the assizes, during which I passed some of the time at Sunderland and Morpeth, and the rest in performing the constitutional duties of eating and drinking with mayors &c. (not to omit the Prince Bishop at the neighbouring assizes), and likewise attending, abetting, and comforting those who danced **at the assemblies** here, although I **was** not a principal myself. **All** these important duties have jumbled several other businesses on **one** side, and made me postpone answers in **all** cases but where **the** business required an immediate **one.**

### The MARQUIS of ROCKINGHAM to SIR GEORGE SAVILE.

1780, September 17, Sunday night, Wentworth.—The events have come on so quick, that in truth I have had as little time to communicate my thoughts to you, as you could have to communicate yours to me.

I saw your letter to the freeholders of the county. I liked it very much, though there may be parts on which I may have doubts. I find Lord John Cavendish did not show you the copy of Mr. Henry Duncombe's letter to me, and the copy of my answer to him. I gave it him to show you, if you was at the meeting, but he forgot it. I therefore now enclose you the two copies.

I had wrote thus far on Friday night, but being weary with writing many letters, I desisted, and intended to have gone on with this letter yesterday morning, and sent it along with other letters to York. A bad night with much pain of my old complaint in my stomach, prevented my getting up yesterday till between one or two, and I was not in good order for writing or for any business, till late last night, when Mr. Ste. Croft's express came with the account of Mr. Lascelles having declined, and the account of the sort of meeting &c. which had been held yesterday at York.

I do rejoice exceedingly, and I heartily congratulate you. The whole proceeding has been well and honourably and pleasingly conducted.

I believe you can scarce be more glad, in your private feelings respecting yourself, that you are rid of one colleague,* than that you are glad (sic) that you have got so agreeable a one as Mr. Henry Duncombe.

Lord John Cavendish tells me he had some conversation with Mr. Wyvill and you and Lord Mahon and Mr. Hartley. He showed me a sort of minute of a proposition, of postponing the consideration of any attempt about shortening the duration of Parliament, but rather to bring up again the *consideration about the* 100 *additional county members*.

I see in the paper in Mr. Wyvill's handwriting, that his idea as first stated in it, was to *state the firm resolution to persevere in the propositions for an economical reform, and amelioration of Parliamentary reformation* (probably the word is *representation*). These words are afterwards inserted, viz.: *by the addition of at least one hundred county members*. I think it stood better as first expressed in general words, but I could wish to suggest that nothing should be precipitated. I must observe, that the lines and the objects, as adopted and expressed in the original petition in December, undoubtedly met with great and almost general approbation. Very many counties followed the example of Yorkshire, and I believe many more would. The specific points in the Association and the terms &c. have assuredly not met with that concurrence of opinion, throughout the various counties.

Upwards of 60,000 signed to the petitions from the various counties, &c. More freeholders, as I understand, signed the petition in Yorkshire, than have signed the Association, and in regard to other counties, I do not know that there is one, where an association on the points and terms similar to the Yorkshire one, has been entered into and signed.

You will have heard that some doubts and difficulties were attempted to be set up, in the city of York, not very friendly indeed, to Lord John Cavendish, &c. You will also have heard that the good citizens of York roused themselves upon the occasion, and the trouble intended was frustrated. Some apologies and some assurances that nothing ill was intended, afterwards ensued. Indeed, the good citizens of York did act most kindly and most honourably.

Mr. Henry Duncombe's letter to me stating the grounds on which he was induced to offer himself, the appointing Mr. Smith of Heath, a warm and zealous petitioner, though not an Associator, to be chairman of the meeting, and other circumstances, to make the support of you

* Sir George Savile was M.P. for Yorkshire.

and **Mr.** Henry Duncombe to extend most generally **to every** well wisher of the liberties and welfare and happiness of this country, were all points well judged   You must have seen by the complexion **of** the meeting on Thursday, that everything answered well.

I must again say, that I wish that nothing may may be precipitately proceeded on.   I have not as yet seen one advertisement, either from a county or from any candidate, which points at, or still less, specifically names, the two objects in **the** Association, as terms to be made or offered. It strikes me, that great attention and discretion will be necessary in the selecting the objects for the first step to proceed upon when the new Parliament **meets.**   Large numbers of the former Parliament will probably be in this new one, and I should think, some tried proposition whereon great numbers have voted in the former Parliament, might be **the** best on **which to** try the **new** Parliament.   Every one may have a crotchet; **I will hazard** mine, which would be, to take early the sense of Parliament on Dunning's motion, viz., the increase and increasing **influence** of the Crown, and *that it ought to be diminished.*   Depend upon **it,** the generality of the old stagers will vote it, and the new **comers** who have either been chose on popular ground, or who indeed are **not** the abject tools brought in by Government, will cheerfully **concur.** Surely it would be good management, if it can be obtained, that very large numbers of a new Parliament should, in the very early infancy of the Parliament, plump themselves into a declaration in favour of the most essential principle, on which any good for this country can be built.   Perhaps it will be thought that it is trying Parliament in a high form.   You know I thought better of the persons who composed the large number who did vote it, in the former Parliament, than others **have** or did so.

**Good** men may have different opinions on the modes and measures to be adopted, in order to diminish the influence of the Crown on the *elector* and on the *elected.*   But the principle of its being necessary, I trust, exists in all good men's minds, and surely the first object is, to obtain a great union on principle.

Some of our friends have been unsuccessful in their elections, others have been rather unexpectedly successful.   How the balance will stand, **cannot as** yet be ascertained.   I had no expectation that Mr. Hartley **would succeed** at Hull; some of our friends there had long said so, and those of them who[m] I saw at York races, seemed to have no hopes, though they said they would support him, which I dare say they did. Mr. Burke at Bristol also failed of success.   The American war and its **concomitant** calamities had too deeply affected the wealth of the **merchants, who so** honourably and at such a large expense had supported **and carried** his former election.

The post has come in.   I have a letter **from Mr.** Hammond wrote yesterday at Doncaster, by which I find **that** you was gone to Leeds and was making some canvassing visits.   I **think** you judged very right in going yourself into that neighbourhood.   The nonsense about the danger of Popery, and the politics **of** Mr. Wesley, were likely enough to be played off against you.   I assure you, in this neighbourhood, I had **par-**ticularly desired that there should be much alertness in securing **all** freeholders, and especially those who were supposed to be Methodists. I had great satisfaction in finding that in general the whole southern part of the West Riding would have turned out exceeding well.   I had very good answers from almost all the members of the corporation of Doncaster; some very few hesitated.   Indeed the generality of the free-holders round here were extraordinarily well inclined.

I imagine, as Mr. Lascelles has declined, you will probably return to York, and I have therefore directed this letter to you at York. If you are not there, the letter will be forwarded to you. Perhaps if you continue a canvassing tour, we may have a chance of seeing you, and of which I shall be **very** glad. I don't suppose **you** will return to your regiment before **your** election is over.

Doncaster **races, I** don't doubt, **will be a full** and a **cheerful meeting.** One of the stewards will look a little awkward and blank.

Sawbridge lost his election for the City of London on the mere nonsense **of** the cry about Popery. I am sure he has paid sufficient court to what are called popular opinions, but it did not avail. I am very sorry for his defeat, as I am sure he has always acted fairly and honourably, and a very steady part. I have hopes that Charles Fox will succeed, but as **I** never could learn the exact numbers of the voters for Westminster, I **cannot** be certain whether he is safe, though he is now, after so many days' poll, upwards of 700 ahead of Lord Lincoln.

I received by tonight's flyer answers to my letters to the Duke of Bolton and Lord Egremont. **They** have sent me letters to forward to their principal agents; everything as well as can be. I expect answers tomorrow from Lord Thanet, Lord Downe, and Lord Carmarthen. **I** have no doubt but that their answers will be as favourable. I have an answer too from Lord Aylesbury; it is not quite decisive, but much expression of great regard towards you and towards Mr. **Henry** Duncombe.

I wrote **to** the Duke of Rutland, and indeed many other letters; some I omitted, in great measure from being fairly worn down. I had not wrote to Major Lister, which I am sorry for, but I do not conceive that he would have been otherwise than right. Lord Surrey had given me full powers on credit, so that as soon as Mr. Henry Duncombe had offered himself and that I got home from Tolsted (?) Lodge, I made the best use I could of the authority and sent for Mr. Parker of Woodthorp near Sheffield, according to Lord Surrey's directions, and desired him to be active about Sheffield. I dare say there has been great alertness shewn in every part of the county by your friends and by Mr. Henry Duncombe's friends, so that I trust nothing could have endangered **the** success. I am nevertheless glad that we are not kept on in all the hurry, bustle, expense, and squabbles of a contested election.

THE BAILIFFS, CORONERS, &c., OF SCARBOROUGH to SIR GEORGE SAVILE, Bart.

**1781,** November 23, Scarborough.— We, the Bailiffs, Coroners, Chamberlains, and capital or select Burgesses of this Borough, having taken into consideration the Bill " more effectually to supply with seamen his Majesty's ships of war, when occasion shall require, and to encourage men, under certain regulations and bounties, voluntarily to engage themselves **for** that service, whenever they shall be duly called for," **do** hereby request that you will join your colleague and the members **for** this Borough (to whom we have also wrote) in opposing the same, and prevent if possible such Bill passing into a law, as we consider it subversive of the freedom of this nation, destructive of its trade and navigation, and tending to destroy the end it is pretended to answer, namely, the increase of seamen.

We are, (&c.)

Jo. Huntriss

Thos. Hinderwell, Junr. } Bailiffs.

James **Tindall** } Coroners.

Tho. **Haggett** }

John Robinson, **Jno.** Halley, Thos. Hinderwell, **Richd.** Sollitt, Wm.
Duesbery, John Harrison, Jerh. Wilkinson, Jerh. Wilkinson, Junr.,
Vn. Dickinson, Jonas Sutton, James Goland, Benjn. Fowler, Francis
Coulson, Jonan. Thornton, Ralph Parkin, Richd. Fox, John Garnett,
Thos. Maling, Leod. Abbott, Jno. Maling, William Hall, Anthy
Beswick, Willm. Clarkson

### Sir George Savile to [F. F. Foljambe].

1782, March **31**, Lincoln.—I am here on my way to London, as
you will learn I intended to be by a letter from Hull, if you have not
already received it.

I want your help on the subject of the vote on Conway's motion con-
demning the American war; which I think you told me you had
examined. It strikes me that if there was a *weighty* majority of county
members divided with us on that question, and county members are the
purest part of the representation, and Lord Rockingham wishes to
have a pure representation in order that the King may be truly informed
of the sense of the people in questions of peace and war, which are in
his prerogative, then I say Lord Rockingham may have a guess, by the
sample of county members on that question, what the sense of a pure
House of Commons would have been; and if he persists in the American
war, I think he should be told this, or let the question be tried
again, and see if he'll promise to take the county members for his
guide.

Let me hear soon, and likewise how the *others* voted, for I should
like to know how corruption as well as incorruption voted on that
question, that I may judge how it will be altered when corruption has
put on incorruption.

### Charles Pelham to F. F. Foljambe.

1789, January 5, Arlington Street.—Our weather still continues as
severe as ever, and so it may say I, for God only knows when we may
have it in our power to leave this place. It is not news to inform you
our Speaker is dead, nor indeed can one write any nowadays, as everything is to be found in the papers. His enemies say he killed himself
with drinking porter — I rather think that is saying too much;
certain it is he drank somewhat more than either of us generally do.
But does not all this prove Charles Fox's ideas (indeed as they at all
times are) perfectly just and constitutional, however impudent they might
be just at the time? William Grenville, the joint Paymaster, is to be the
Speaker proposed by Administration, and Sir Gilbert Elliot by our friends.
I hardly believe we stand any chance against one of *that family*, but it
is done in order to lay claim, perhaps in a new Parliament. The Prince
will accept of the Regency, though used like a *dog* by Prince Pitt.
Should this be the case, I rather think we shall have a vacancy for
Westminster. I don't think it likely Fox will have much opposition, as
all the last expenses are discharged within 1,500*l*. All our friends feel
anxious that that sum should be paid, and then, say they, there can be
no doubt of success. I wish you would send us up an hundred towards
it; you would have a thousand thanks for it; in a word, I have been
desired by Lord Robert* to mention this circumstance to you, and I trust
your friendship will pardon the liberty I have taken. If possible it
froze harder last night than ever, and I think bids fair to continue as
ever.

* Spencer?

## CHARLES PELHAM to F. F. FOLJAMBE.

1789, January 13th, House of Commons.—In the name of many of your friends I am sat down to return you many thanks for the note you have favoured me with, and which I have given to Lord Robert. We have been waiting here for two days for the physician's report. My country[man?] Willis is now under examination; if I can contrive to procure another report besides my own I will send it down [to] Aldwark. We are to go into the State of the Nation on Thursday —nevertheless I can hardly believe we shall. Pitt promised this, and from his usual conduct I am concerned to say I cannot give great credit to his words. Pray is not Dr. Wood some relation of Mr. Glover's? Though I do not believe the Halifax address carries much weight with it, yet I am sorry there should be any from Yorkshire at all. They say too that Leeds is to send a violent one. Many handbills, &c. have been sent into Yorkshire—do you believe they do any good? While I am writing this, they tell me the frost is going; if it is, I don't believe there can be any hunting these ten days; at all events I don't think it possible I shall have it in my power to set my face northward this fortnight or three weeks. They tell us here that Lord Lonsdale is dying—if he leaves his estate to Sir William Lowther, I fear his parliamentary interest will not go with us.

## EARL FITZWILLIAM to F. F. FOLJAMBE.

1789, January 15, Milton.—It is a satisfaction to think that all the manufacturing parts of Yorkshire are not of one mind upon the present critical business. The corporation of Leeds are to meet for the purpose of addressing Pitt the very day our friends are to meet at Halifax for the purpose of disavowing Dr. Wood's notable address. Though I have had no intelligence directly from Leeds, I think we have such a strength there, that no address will pass with anything like unanimity, but if it should, I hope Halifax will set all straight the very same day. General opinion has been exceedingly biassed by the reports so assiduously and successfully propagated of the King's amendment and of the probability of his recovery. The present examination before the Committee of the House of Commons will produce its effect at the very right moment for the Yorkshire meetings, and I think will come so very opportunely that Pitt's friends will not have time to remove the effect, either as to [the] point of the King's recovery, or as to the suspicion of *foul play* upon the subject. Truth will come out, and the public will see through the juggle between Pitt and the Queen. The bargain is just this—her Majesty is to have the fingering [of] the private savings, and in return [Pitt] is to hold all the patronage and power that can be filched from the Regent for his (Pitt's) use. Thus the darling passion of each will be gratified—his ambition, her rapacity.

Since you are decided not to look at the county, what should you say to Hull? The interest which Sir George and my uncle kept up there, is still alive; I am almost sanguine enough to think it would be found as strong as ever; its defeat was owing to its unfortunate champion: of all men David Hartley was the worst for that purpose, and indeed he knew it himself, and fairly told me so, but had not resolution enough to give up what he knew he could not carry, though another person might have carried it. You know Thornton and Stanhope are the present members— the first being extremely strong, being in fact the representative of Wilberforce's interest: the latter exceedingly weak, and a good coun tenance would make him fly. He has lately been reconnoitring, has

spent about 300*l.* among the lowest class, which **will not do** him 300
pennyworth of service when the day of trial comes. In my opinion,
whoever tries Hull will find Stanhope their best friend : being already in
possession and extremely desirous of being in Parliament, a third person
immediately creates a contest, which will satisfy the mob, but as soon
**as** ever Stanhope sees the face of an enemy he will be off. I have
great reason to think the old interest will **be** collected together again
very easily, and nobody will be better received **by** them than yourself ;
indeed they would look upon the support of **you, as** resorting again to
the standard of Sir George. Will you turn **this in your** thoughts ?

## Sir George Savile.

Two small bundles of papers relate respectively to the Yorkshire
election in 1780 and to Sir George Savile's resignation of his seat in
1783. They contain little of public interest. There are also some
papers and correspondence relating to the erection of a monument **in**
York Minster to Sir George Savile in 1789. The total cost of it was
1,026*l.* 13*s.*, of which only 617*l.* 15*s.* had been collected from, or promised by, different subscribers, the deficiency being apparently afterwards
made good by Mr R. Lumley Savile and Mr. F. F. Foljambe.

# INDEX.

L

# E.

# F.

## CIRCULAR OF THE COMMISSION.

Public Record Office, Chancery Lane,
London, W.C.

HER MAJESTY has been pleased to appoint under Her Sign Manual certain Commissioners to ascertain what unpublished MSS. are extant in the collections of private persons and in institutions which are calculated to throw light upon subjects connected with the civil, ecclesiastical, literary, or scientific history of this country. The present Commissioners are :—

Lord Esher, Master of the Rolls, the Marquess of Salisbury, K.G., the Marquess of Lothian, K.T., the Earl of Rosebery, K.G., Lord Edmond Fitzmaurice, the Bishop of Oxford, the Bishop of Limerick, Lord Acton, Lord Carlingford, K.P., and Sir H. C. Maxwell-Lyte, K.C.B.

The Commissioners think it probable that you may feel an interest in this object and be willing to assist in the attainment of it; and with that view they desire to lay before you an outline of the course which they usually follow.

If any nobleman or gentleman express his willingness to submit any unprinted book, or collection of documents in his possession or custody to the examination of the Commissioners, they will cause an inspection to be made by some competent person, and should the MSS. appear to come within the scope of their enquiry, a report containing copies or abstracts of them will be drawn up, printed, and submitted to the owner, with a view to obtaining his consent to the publication of the whole, or of such part of it as he may think fit, among the proceedings of the Commission, which are presented to Parliament every Session.

To avoid any possible apprehension that the examination of papers by the Commissioners may extend to title-deeds or documents of present legal value, positive instructions are given to every person who inspects MSS. on their behalf that nothing relating to the titles of existing owners is to be divulged, and that if in the course of his work any modern title-deeds or papers of a private character chance to come before him, they are to be instantly put aside, and are not to be examined or calendared under any pretence whatever.

The object of the Commission is solely the discovery of unknown historical and literary materials, and in all their proceedings the Commissioners will direct their attention to that object exclusively.

In practice it has been found more satisfactory, when the collection of manuscripts is a large one, for the inspector to make a selection therefrom at the place of deposit and to obtain the owner's consent to remove the selected papers to the Public Record Office in London, where they can be more fully dealt with, and where they are preserved with the same care as if they formed part of the muniments of the realm, during the term of their examinaton. Among the numerous owners of MSS. who have allowed their family papers of historical interest to be temporarily removed from their muniment rooms and lent to the Commissioners to facilitate the preparation of a report may be named: The Duke of Rutland, the Duke of Portland, the Marquess of Salisbury, the Marquess Townshend, the Earl of Dartmouth, the Earl of Ancaster, Lord Braye, Lord Hothfield, Mrs. Stopford Sackville, Mr. le Fleming, of Rydal, and Mr. Fortescue, of Dropmore.

The costs of inspections, reports and calendars, and the conveyance of documents, will be defrayed at the public expense, without any charge to owners.

The Commissioners will also, if so requested, give their advice as to the best means of repairing and preserving any papers or MSS. which may be in a state of decay, and are of historical or literary value.

The Commissioners will feel much obliged if you will communicate to them the names of any gentlemen who may be able and willing to assist in obtaining the objects for which this Commission has been issued.

J. J. CARTWRIGHT,
Secretary.

# HISTORICAL MANUSCRIPTS COMMISSION.

| Date. | — | Size. | Sessional Paper. | Price. |
|---|---|---|---|---|
| | | | | s. d. |
| 1870 (Reprinted 1874.) | FIRST REPORT, WITH APPENDIX - - . Contents :— ENGLAND. House of Lords; Cambridge Colleges; Abingdon, and other Corporations, &c. SCOTLAND. Advocates' Library, Glasgow Corporation, &c. IRELAND. Dublin, Cork, and other Corporations, &c. | f'cap. | [C. 55] | 1 6 |
| 1871 | SECOND REPORT, WITH APPENDIX, AND INDEX TO THE FIRST AND SECOND REPORTS - - - - - Contents :— ENGLAND. House of Lords; Cambridge Colleges; Oxford Colleges; Monastery of Dominican Friars at Woodchester, Duke of Bedford, Earl Spencer, &c. SCOTLAND. Aberdeen and St. Andrew's Universities, &c. IRELAND. Marquis of Ormonde; Dr. Lyons, &c. | „ | [C. 441] | 3 10 |
| 1872 (Reprinted 1895.) | THIRD REPORT, WITH APPENDIX AND INDEX - - - - - Contents :— ENGLAND. House of Lords; Cambridge Colleges; Stonyhurst College; Bridgewater and other Corporations; Duke of Northumberland, Marquis of Lansdowne, Marquis of Bath, &c. SCOTLAND. University of Glasgow; Duke of Montrose, &c. IRELAND. Marquis of Ormonde; Black Book of Limerick, &c. | „ | [C. 673] | 6 0 |
| 1873 | FOURTH REPORT, WITH APPENDIX. PART I. - - - - - Contents :— ENGLAND. House of Lords; Westminster Abbey; Cambridge and Oxford Colleges; Cinque Ports, Hythe, and other Corporations, Marquis of Bath, Earl of Denbigh, &c. SCOTLAND. Duke of Argyll, &c. IRELAND. Trinity College, Dublin; Marquis of Ormonde. | „ | [C. 857] | 6 8 |
| 1873 | DITTO. PART II. INDEX - - - | „ | [C.857i.] | 2 6 |

| Date. | — | Size. | Sessional Paper. | Price. |
|---|---|---|---|---|
| | | | | *s. d.* |
| 1876 | FIFTH REPORT, WITH APPENDIX. PART I. - Contents :— ENGLAND. House of Lords; Oxford and Cambridge Colleges; Dean and Chapter of Canterbury; Rye, Lydd, and other Corporations, Duke of Sutherland, Marquis of Lansdowne, Reginald Cholmondeley, Esq., &c. SCOTLAND. Earl of Aberdeen, &c. | f'cap. | [C.1432] | 7 0 |
| ,, | DITTO. PART II. INDEX - - - | ,, | [C.1432 i.] | 3 6 |
| 1877 | SIXTH REPORT, WITH APPENDIX. PART I. - Contents :— ENGLAND. House of Lords; Oxford and Cambridge Colleges; Lambeth Palace; Black Book of the Archdeacon of Canterbury; Bridport, Wallingford, and other Corporations; Lord Leconfield, Sir Reginald Graham, Sir Henry Ingilby, &c. SCOTLAND. Duke of Argyll, Earl of Moray, &c. IRELAND. Marquis of Ormonde. | ,, | [C.1745] | 8 6 |
| (Reprinted 1893.) | DITTO. PART II. INDEX - - - | ,, | [C.2102] | 1 10 |
| 1879 (Reprinted 1895.) | SEVENTH REPORT, WITH APPENDIX. PART I. - - - - - - Contents :— House of Lords; County of Somerset; Earl of Egmont, Sir Frederick Graham, Sir Harry Verney, &c. | ,, | [C.2340] | 7 6 |
| (Reprinted 1895.) | DITTO. PART II. APPENDIX AND INDEX - Contents :— Duke of Athole, Marquis of Ormonde, S. F. Livingstone, Esq., &c. | ,, | [C.2340 i.] | 3 6 |
| 1881 | EIGHTH REPORT, WITH APPENDIX AND INDEX. PART I. - - - Contents :— List of collections examined, 1869–1880. ENGLAND. House of Lords; Duke of Marlborough; Magdalen College, Oxford; Royal College of Physicians; Queen Anne's Bounty Office; Corporations of Chester, Leicester, &c. IRELAND. Marquis of Ormonde, Lord Emly, The O'Conor Don, Trinity College, Dublin, &c. | ,, | [C.3040] | 8 6 |
| 1881 | DITTO. PART II. APPENDIX AND INDEX - Contents :— Duke of Manchester | ,, | [C.3040 i.] | 1 9 |

| Date. | — | Size. | Sessional Paper. | Price. |
|---|---|---|---|---|
| | | | | *s. d.* |
| 1881 | DITTO. PART III. APPENDIX AND INDEX<br>Contents :—<br>Earl of Ashburnham. | f'cap. | [C. 3040 ii.] | 1 4 |
| 1883<br>(Re-printed 1895.) | NINTH REPORT, WITH APPENDIX AND INDEX. PART I. - - -<br>Contents :—<br>St. Paul's and Canterbury Cathedrals; Eton College ; Carlisle, Yarmouth, Canterbury, and Barnstaple Corporations, &c. | „ | [C.3773] | 5 2 |
| 1884<br>(Re-printed 1895.) | DITTO. PART II. APPENDIX AND INDEX -<br>Contents :—<br>ENGLAND. House of Lords, Earl of Leicester ; C. Pole Gell, Alfred Morrison, Esqs., &c.<br>SCOTLAND. Lord Elphinstone, H. C. Maxwell Stuart, Esq., &c.<br>IRELAND. Duke of Leinster, Marquis of Drogheda, &c. | „ | [C.3773 i.] | 6 3 |
| 1884 | NINTH REPORT. PART III. APPENDIX AND INDEX - - - -<br>Contents :—<br>Mrs. Stopford Sackville. | „ | [C.3773 ii.] | 1 7 |
| 1883<br>(Re-printed 1895.) | CALENDAR OF THE MANUSCRIPTS OF THE MARQUIS OF SALISBURY, K.G. (or CECIL MSS.). PART I. - - - | 8vo. | [C.3777] | 3 5 |
| 1888 | DITTO. PART II. - - - | „ | [C.5463] | 3 5 |
| 1889 | DITTO. PART III. - - - | „ | [C. 5889 v.] | 2 1 |
| 1892 | DITTO. PART IV. - - - | „ | [C.6823] | 2 11 |
| 1894 | DITTO. PART V. - - - | „ | [C.7574] | 2 6 |
| 1895 | DITTO. PART VI. - - - | „ | [C.7884] | 2 8 |
| 1885 | TENTH REPORT - - - -<br>This is introductory to the following :— | „ | [C.4548] | 0 3½ |
| 1885<br>(Re-printed 1895.) | (1.) APPENDIX AND INDEX - - -<br>Earl of Eglinton, Sir J. S. Maxwell, Bart., and C. S. H. Drummond Moray, C. F. Weston Underwood, G. W. Digby, Esqs. | „ | [C.4575] | 3 7 |
| 1885 | (2.) APPENDIX AND INDEX - -<br>The Family of Gawdy. | „ | [C. 4576 iii.] | 1 4 |
| 1885 | (3.) APPENDIX AND INDEX - •<br>Wells Cathedral. | „ | [C. 4576 ii.] | 2 0 |

| Date. | — | Size. | Sessional Paper. | Price. |
|---|---|---|---|---|
| | | | | s. d. |
| 1885 | (4.) APPENDIX AND INDEX - - Earl of Westmorland; Capt. Stewart; Lord Stafford; Sir N. W. Throckmorton, Sir P. T. Mainwaring, Lord Muncaster, Capt. J. F. Bagot, Earl of Kilmorey, Earl of Powis, and others, the Corporations of Kendal, Wenlock, Bridgnorth, Eye, Plymouth, and the County of Essex; and Stonyhurst College. | 8vo. | [C.4576] | 3 6 |
| 1885 (Reprinted 1895.) | (5.) APPENDIX AND INDEX - - - The Marquis of Ormonde, Earl of Fingall, Corporations of Galway, Waterford, the Sees of Dublin and Ossory, the Jesuits in Ireland. | „ | [C. 4576 i.] | 2 10 |
| 1887 | (6.) APPENDIX AND INDEX - - - Marquis of Abergavenny, Lord Braye, G. F. Luttrell, P. P. Bouverie, W. Bromley Davenport, R. T. Balfour, Esquires. | „ | [C.5242] | 1 7 |
| 1887 | ELEVENTH REPORT - - - - This is introductory to the following :— | „ | [C. 5060 vi.] | 0 3 |
| 1887 | (1.) APPENDIX AND INDEX - - - H. D. Skrine, Esq., Salvetti Correspondence. | „ | [C.5060] | 1 1 |
| 1887 | (2.) APPENDIX AND INDEX - - - House of Lords. 1678-1688. | „ | [C. 5060 i.] | 2 0 |
| 1887 | (3.) APPENDIX AND INDEX - - - Corporations of Southampton and Lynn. | „ | [C. 5060 ii.] | 1 8 |
| 1887 | (4.) APPENDIX AND INDEX - - - Marquis Townshend. | „ | [C. 5060 iii.] | 2 6 |
| 1887 | (5.) APPENDIX AND INDEX - - - Earl of Dartmouth. | „ | [C. 5060 iv.] | 2 8 |
| 1887 | (6.) APPENDIX AND INDEX - - - Duke of Hamilton. | „ | [C. 5060 v.] | 1 6 |
| 1888 | (7.) APPENDIX AND INDEX - - - Duke of Leeds, Marchioness of Waterford, Lord Hothfield, &c.; Bridgwater Trust Office, Reading Corporation, Inner Temple Library. | „ | [C.5612] | 2 0 |
| 1890 | TWELFTH REPORT - - - - This is introductory to the following :— | „ | [C.5889] | 0 3 |
| 1888 | (1.) APPENDIX - - - - Earl Cowper, K.G. (Coke MSS., at Melbourne Hall, Derby). Vol. I. | „ | [C.5472] | 2 7 |
| 1888 | (2.) APPENDIX - - - - Ditto. Vol. II. | „ | [C.5613] | 2 5 |

| Date. | — | Size. | Sessional Paper. | Price. |
|---|---|---|---|---|
| | | | | *s. d.* |
| 1889 | (3.) APPENDIX AND INDEX - - - Ditto. Vol. III. | 8vo. | [C. 5889 i.] | 1 4 |
| 1888 | (4.) APPENDIX - - - - The Duke of Rutland, G.C.B. Vol. I. | „ | [C.5614] | 3 2 |
| 1891 | (5.) APPENDIX AND INDEX - - - Ditto. Vol. II. | „ | [C. 5889 ii.] | 2 0 |
| 1889 | (6.) APPENDIX AND INDEX - - - House of Lords, 1689–1690. | „ | [C. 5889 iii.] | 2 1 |
| 1890 | (7.) APPENDIX AND INDEX - - - S. H. le Fleming, Esq., of Rydal. | „ | [C. 5889 iv.] | 1 11 |
| 1891 | (8.) APPENDIX AND INDEX - - - The Duke of Athole, K.T., and the Earl of Home. | „ | [C.6338] | 1 0 |
| 1891 | (9.) APPENDIX AND INDEX - - - The Duke of Beaufort, K.G., the Earl of Donoughmore, J. H. Gurney, W. W. B. Hulton, R. W. Ketton, G. A. Aitken, P. V. Smith, Esqs.; Bishop of Ely; Cathedrals of Ely, Glouces- ter, Lincoln, and Peterborough; Corporations of Gloucester, Higham Ferrers, and Newark; Southwell Minster; Lincoln District Registry. | „ | [C. 6338 i.] | 2 6 |
| 1891 | (10.) APPENDIX - - - The First Earl of Charlemont. Vol. I. 1745–1783. | „ | [C. 6338 ii.] | 1 11 |
| 1892 | THIRTEENTH REPORT - - - This is introductory to the following :— | „ | [C.6827] | 0 3 |
| 1891 | (1.) APPENDIX - - - The Duke of Portland. Vol. I. | „ | [C.6474] | 3 0 |
| | (2.) APPENDIX AND INDEX - - - Ditto. Vol. II. | „ | [C. 6827 i.] | 2 0 |
| 1892 | (3.) APPENDIX - - - - - J. B. Fortescue, Esq., of Dropmore, Vol. I. | „ | [C.6660] | 2 7 |
| 1892 | (4.) APPENDIX AND INDEX - - - Corporations of Rye, Hastings, and Hereford. Capt. F. C. Loder- Symonds, E. R. Wodehouse, M.P., J. Dovaston, Esqs., Sir T. B. Lennard, Bart., Rev. W. D. Macray, and Earl of Dartmouth (Supple- mentary Report). | „ | [C.6810] | 2 4 |
| 1892 | (5.) APPENDIX AND INDEX - - - House of Lords, 1690–1691. | „ | [C.6822] | 2 4 |
| 1893 | (6.) APPENDIX AND INDEX - - - Sir W. FitzHerbert, Bart. The De- laval Family, of Seaton Delaval; The Earl of Ancaster and General Lyttelton-Annesley. | „ | [C.7166] | 1 4 |

| Date. | — | Size. | Sessional Paper. | Price. |
|---|---|---|---|---|
| | | | | *s. d,* |
| 1893 | (7.) APPENDIX AND INDEX - The Earl of Lonsdale. | 8vo. | [C.7241] | 1 3 |
| 1893 | (8.) APPENDIX AND INDEX The First Earl of Charlemont. Vol. II. 1784–1799. | ,, | [C.7424] | 1 11 |
| 1896 | FOURTEENTH REPORT This is introductory to the following :— | ,, | [C.7983] | 0 3 |
| 1894 | (1.) APPENDIX AND INDEX The Duke of Rutland, G.C.B. Vol. III. | ,, | [C.7476] | 1 11 |
| 1894 | (2.) APPENDIX The Duke of Portland. Vol. III. | ,, | [C.7569] | 2 |
| 1894 | (3.) APPENDIX AND INDEX The Duke of Roxburghe ; Sir H. H. Campbell, Bart. ; the Earl of Strathmore ; and the Countess Dowager of Seafield. | ,, | [C.7570] | 1 2 |
| 1894 | (4.) APPENDIX AND INDEX Lord Kenyon. | ,, | [C.7571] | 2 10 |
| 1896 | (5.) APPENDIX J. B. Fortescue, Esq., of Dropmore. Vol. II. | ,, | [C.7572] | 2 8 |
| 1895 | (6.) APPENDIX AND INDEX House of Lords, 1692–1693. | ,, | [C.7573] | 1 11 |
| 1895 | (7.) APPENDIX The Marquess of Ormonde. | ,, | [C.7678] | 1 10 |
| 1895 | (8.) APPENDIX AND INDEX Lincoln, Bury St. Edmunds, Hertford, and Great Grimsby Corporations; The Dean and Chapter of Worcester, and of Lichfield ; The Bishop's Registry of Worcester. | ,, | [C.7881] | 1 5 |
| 1895 | (9.) APPENDIX AND INDEX The Earl of Buckinghamshire, the Earl of Lindsey, the Earl of Onslow, Lord Emly, Theodore J. Hare, Esq., and James Round, Esq., M.P. | ,, | [C.7882] | 2 6 |
| 1895 | (10.) APPENDIX AND INDEX The Earl of Dartmouth. Vol. II. American Papers. | ,, | [C.7883] | 2 9 |
| | FIFTEENTH REPORT. This is introductory to the following :— | | | |
| 1896 | (1.) APPENDIX AND INDEX The Earl of Dartmouth. Vol. III. | ,, | [C.8156] | 1 5 |
| 1897 | (2.) APPENDIX AND INDEX J. Eliot Hodgkin, Esq., of Richmond, Surrey. | ,, | [C.8327] | 1 8 |
| 1897 | (3.) APPENDIX AND INDEX Charles Haliday, Esq., of Dublin. | ,, | [C.8364] | 1 4 |

| Date. | — | Size. | Sessional Paper. | Price. |
|-------|---|-------|------------------|--------|
| | | | | *s. d.* |
| 1897 | (4.) APPENDIX - - - - The Duke of Portland. Vol. IV. | 8vo. | [C.8497] | 2 11 |
| 1897 | (5.) APPENDIX AND INDEX - - - The Right Hon. F. J. Savile Foljambe of Osberton. | ,, | [C.8550] | 0 10 |
| 1897 | (6.) APPENDIX AND INDEX - - - The Earl of Carlisle. | ,, | (*In the Press.*) | |
| 1897 | (7.) APPENDIX AND INDEX - - - The Duke of Somerset, the Marquis of Ailesbury, and Sir T. G. Puleston, Bart. | ,, | (*Ditto.*) | |
| 1897 | (8.) APPENDIX AND INDEX - - - The Duke of Buccleuch and Queensberry, K.G., K.T., at Drumlanrig. | ,, | (*Ditto.*) | |
| 1897 | (9.) APPENDIX AND INDEX - - - J. J. Hope Johnstone, Esq., of Annandale. | ,, | (*Ditto.*) | |

www.ingramcontent.com/pod-product-compliance
Lightning Source LLC
Chambersburg PA
CBHW020623030726
47497CB00007B/2386